The Hand of Fate

Contemporary Fiction/Western Romance/Adult Content

Gloria Antypowich

The Hand of Fate

Book Three
of the
Belanger Creek Ranch Series

Gloria Antypowich

Gloria Antypowich

Copyright@ 2014 by Gloria Antypowich
Canadian Copyright Number:
Library and Archives Canada Cataloguing

ISBN
ISBN-13: 978-1511598873
ISBN-10: 1511598875

Published by Gloria Antypowich

5 stars! Reviewed by Rabia Tanveer for Readers' Favorite

In The Hand of Fate by Gloria Antypowich, will Tim be able to tell Christina that having MRHK syndrome does not mean she is not cut out for the intimacies of love? Christina appears to be a healthy, happy woman. Since she took her job as an office manager at Swift Current Accounting and Bookkeeping Services, she kept her past to herself. After a heartbreaking divorce from her ex-husband because she had the MRHK genetics disorder, she has shunned love and intimacy from her life. She does not allow anyone to get too close and in return saves herself from future heartbreak.

Tim Bates did not have it any better. He was rejected and dismissed by his step-family. He came to Swift Current four years ago when he was reeling from a divorce from a woman who never truly loved him. When he was given the opportunity, he took it. When he met Christina for the first time, he did not like her. But time made them good friends. He comes across a mystery that could mean everything he knew about his birth could be wrong. He asks Christina to help him discover the truth. However, he starts developing feelings for her that he cannot ignore. Will she accept him or reject him like everyone else in his life?

The Hand of Fate by Gloria Antypowich was a wonderful read and I literally breezed through it. The mystery of Tim's past and Christina's battle with herself was very intriguing. In fact, this is probably the first novel that I have read in a long time that does not irk me in some way. Everything was perfect! I really enjoyed this book. The author has a nice flair with words.

Gloria Antypowich

4 stars! Reviewed by Mamta Madhavan for Readers' Favorite

In The Hand of Fate (The Belanger Creek Ranch Series Book 3) by Gloria Antypowich, readers see the marriage of Christina Holmes crumbling due to her rare congenital condition, MRHK syndrome. She has managed to keep it a secret at her current workplace, the Swift Current Accounting and Bookkeeping Services. Her condition makes her ashamed and also makes her wary of getting into intimate relationships. Tim Bates knows Christina from the time he joined Swift Current and he had no high opinion of her. But over the course of four years, they have come to know each other better and have started enjoying each other's company. The twist in the story happens when Tim discovers a picture at Belanger Creek Ranch. Will something unexpected happen in the lives of Tim and Christina?

The plot has many dimensions to capture the attention of readers and keep them guessing and glued to the book. The story is all about family bonding, friendship, unconditional love, loyalty, mystery and how dreams can come true. The author manages to weave a lot of things together with expertise, without losing the fluidity and pace of the plot and happenings in the story. All the characters are well sketched and they give good support to the main characters of Tim Bates and Christina Holmes. The narration is descriptive and the imagery is wonderful. Third in the Belanger Creek Ranch Series, this romantic fiction can stand on its own and readers will be able to connect with the plot easily, even without reading the first two books.

4 stars! Reviewed by Janelle Alex, Ph.D. for Readers' Favorite

Gloria Antypowich's The Hand of Fate: Book Three of the Belanger Creek Ranch Series kicks off with the main characters from the series all gathered to share Easter dinner.

They were truly a "family" by heart, not by blood. Yet, Tim Bates discovered something that threw him into a tizzy that evening. Christina, having feelings for him she had not yet explored, wanted to understand and be there for him. He wasn't ready to share his discovery though. The passion between them was something they both kept denying until Christina admitted she had feelings. But, Tim still needed to deal with his secrets and open his heart to allow Christina in. Somehow Ollie Crampton was connected to Tim's deceased mother, and he needed to find out how. Of course, Christina had her own secret and needed to share it with Tim if they ever hoped to have a relationship. Antypowich advances the story fairly quickly and continues it even after Tim and Christina get married. She puts Shauna Lee, a mutual friend, in a position that has a great impact on the Bates' lives. Even more, Antypowich brings a private investigator mildly into the mix to reveal the truth about Tim and Ollie.

You will discover a unique take on a modern romance in The Hand of Fate. If you have not read the first two books in the series, it is highly advised that you read them first. Otherwise, you may very well be confused by the numerous characters. Antypowich doesn't really give you much back story on the other characters or how they are connected to each other. This made the story hard to follow initially. Also, the author jumps between in depth events with Tim and Christina to Ollie and Ellie to others. Often the details go above and beyond what a typical romance novel might include. Yet, there are a number of beautiful and intriguing pieces within the storyline. From Ollie and Tim to how Tim and Christina might be able to have their own biological children; this is one to stick with because you will discover a heart-warming tale.

The Hand of Fate has some spots I found to be a bit choppy in the writing, but Gloria Antypowich has a woven a story of sweet love and perseverance into this contemporary romance novel. The Belanger Creek Series is different, and helps The Hand of Fate stand out in the romance genre. Where will Antypowich take you in the fourth book in the Belanger Creek Ranch Series?

CONTENTS

Gloria Antypowich

DEDICATION

This book is dedicated to couples who are dealing with the issue of infertility. Infertility and miscarriages are more common than many are aware of. It isn't talked about because it is a painful subject and for those affected, there are often feelings of inferiority, shame, and sadness attached to their struggle. As one person told me, *it's a pain that cuts to the bone.*

This book is also dedicated to **Dr. Sheila Boehm from Williams Lake, British Columbia, Canada**. She acted as a surrogate for a family member. Her wonderful, selfless act was the seed of thought for this book. I had heard about surrogacy before but had never known anyone who actually participated in the program.

OTHER BOOKS

by Gloria Antypowich:

The Second Time Around, Book One of the Belanger Creek Ranch Series

Full Circle, Book Two of the Belanger Creek Ranch Series

Second Chances, Book Four of the Belanger Creek Ranch Series

ACKNOWLEDGEMENTS

I want to express heartfelt appreciation to the following people who read and reread this manuscript, edited it and seeing it through fresh eyes, have made unbiased suggestions: Monicka Gregory, Sharron Hynes, Darlene Bell, Diane Maureen Pleasance, Cathy Hoy, and Donna Wassenaar Rezansoff. There were times when I struggled; this project would have been much more difficult without your support. You are all very special to me.

Monicka Gregory is a Social Media maven. She is the owner Bizz~Linkzz Social Media Services. She also has a successful web page of her own; Kids Goals at **http://kidsgoals.com/** When my original editor became ill, I contracted Monicka to edit this book. She is honest, diligent and insightful and I am very pleased with the work she did.

Sharron Hynes is a long-time friend, who is very creative in her own right. She designs and sells beautiful all-occasion cards and business cards. She is a musician and singer. She and her husband, Mel, sing and play with their band the Kootenay Legends. Their CD's are enjoyed by many people around the world.

I also want to say a big Thank You to Steve Caresser and the team at ePrintedBooks- (http://eprintedbooks.com/) *Steve Caresser* and I have worked together before, and I appreciate the quality of work that he produces. It is a pleasure to work with him again. ePintedBbooks offers a wide range of author services, as well as a virtual bookstore. Steve is also the author of five books. I have read *the Sacred Crow, What Every Married Woman Needs, and Five Gallon Bucket.* He has produced several audible poems and he is in the process creating "The Whole World News" Reality is what you make it. Steve and Jason Skinner are the newscasters for this production.

Laura Wright LaRoche, at LLPix Designs, (http://llpix.com/) designed the covers for the Belanger Creek Ranch Series. She was a pleasure to work with. I'm convinced she can do anything—that she has magic in her fingers! I also discovered that Laura is an author and her creative imagination shines in that field too. I have read both *Black Woods* and *Black Woods Revealed.* They have a touch of paranormal, along with mystery and horror. I thoroughly enjoyed them and the image of the "beast" lingered with me for days! *Broken Soul* is on my Kindle, waiting to be read. Her books are available on Amazon.com.

I also want to thank *Jen Bloo*d for evaluating the four book series in the first draft. She gave me terrific input, suggestions, and encouragement. Since then, she has established a successful editing service (http://jenblood.net/adian-enterprises/) and has become a bestselling author. It was a once in a lifetime opportunity for me and I would never be so fortunate now. (I cannot claim that she is a close friend) I am a big fan of her writing, and I have read all of the books in the *Erin Solomon Pentalogy.* Look for them on Amazon!

And last, but not least, my husband Lloyd Antypowich, a prolific author who has published six books at this time: *A Hunting We Did Go, From Moccasins to Cowboy Boots, Horns and Hair of the High Country, A Chip off the Old Block, Louisiana Man and Grasshopper McLain and Gotleep the Frog*); also my children and their spouses, my grandchildren and the great-grandchildren that I'm blessed to have—I love you all. I appreciate the times you have encouraged me, ragged on me for spending too many hours sitting at the computer and asked when the books were going to be published –after two years, you must have wondered if it would ever happen!

CHAPTER ONE

Christina Holmes gathered eighteen-month-old Leanne Johnson in her arms and sat in the rocking chair by the window. Her heart filled with warmth as she snuggled her best friend's daughter against her breast. Christina had learned to accept most of life's trials, but knowing that she could never give birth to a child of her own child, was the one disappointment that left a raw spot in her soul.

Leanne's blue eyes brimmed with tears as she pushed away and sat up. She was sucking her thumb as she looked up into Christina's face.

"What's the matter, baby?" Christina asked.

"The poor little tyke is probably tired," Ellie Crampton commented as she emptied a bottle of 7Up into the juice in a punch bowl. "It's a long drive out to the ranch from Swift Current. Add the excitement of playing with Selena and Sam all afternoon, and you know she's got to be exhausted."

Shauna Lee glanced at the clock on the wall, then, looked lovingly at her small daughter. "You're right Ellie; it's been a long day for her."

Colt Thompson turned to Brad Johnson, who was mashing a pot of potatoes by the stove. "I swear she was conceived through

Immaculate Conception. I don't see any trace of you in her."

Frank Thompson reached across the island where they were all preparing Easter dinner and smacked her husband with a spatula. "Colt!"

"Hey, that stung!" He gave his wife a look of exaggerated pain, and then defended his words. "It's the truth. Look at her; she's a carbon copy of Shauna Lee!" Leanne's tiny bone structure, her wispy blonde hair and her big blue eyes fringed by dark eyelashes supported his words.

Shauna Lee looked at Brad and smiled. "Oh, she definitely has his genes! Haven't you noticed how she works her way around, schmoozing to get what she wants? She's just like him; she simply doesn't take 'No' for an answer." Everyone laughed, knowing how tenaciously Brad had pursued Shauna Lee until he'd worn down her every resistance and convinced her that she loved him. She looked at Frank. "Dinner's almost ready, isn't it?"

Tim Bates spoke up as he put bottles of wine on the big country-style table that Christina had just set. "It looks like the boss just needs to finish carving the ham."

Colt nodded. "Call Grayson, Ollie and the twins. By the time you get the food on the table, I'll be done."

Tim walked over to the rocking chair and knelt down by Christina. He reached out to brush a finger along Leanne's cheek. "Are you hungry little one?" he asked. The tearful blue eyes brightened as she broke into a big smile and a spate of baby babble. He smiled as he extended his hands and Leanne said "Me up," and leaned forward to fall into them. His eyes met Christina's as he took the child. There was a current of understanding between them. He talked to the baby as he stood up and then extended a hand to help Christina out of the chair.

While everyone else put the food on the table, Ellie went to the family room. Grayson McNaughton was watching hockey on TV and Ollie, her sixty-four-year-old husband, was on the floor with the Thompson twins playing *ranch*. He had built them a barn for Christmas and now they were 'chasing' cows and moving them into the realistic-looking corrals that he'd made to go with it. She smiled.

Selena and Sam had become the grandchildren he would never have—unless by some miracle they found his unknown son. Possibly, he had grandchildren but they wouldn't know him the way the twins did. After four years of searching, it seemed unlikely that his son would be found. That was a fact that grated on his mind continuously.

"Dinner is ready." Ellie reached down and ruffled Ollie's graying hair. He looked up at her with smiling eyes. They'd been married for two years, but they had 'lived in sin' as her indignant children had called it, for almost two years before they had made it legal. Ollie had never had a wife before and he would have married her right away. However, while the chemistry and companionship were perfect between them, Ellie had been wed before and was in no hurry to rush into a permanent relationship at her age. Now she wondered why she'd hesitated because she couldn't imagine her life without him.

The twins jumped up and held out their hands to grasp his. It had become a ritual, a game they always played and he grunted and groaned while they pulled him to his feet, winking at his wife when the children couldn't see him.

When everyone was seated, Colt honored the occasion by saying grace, giving thanks for this 'family' that had come together to share the Easter bounty.

Christina looked around the table, marveling at how they had truly become a family in every way, except for the ties of blood. Four years earlier they had all been mere acquaintances connected by one common thread; *Thompson Holdings, Belanger Creek Ranch, and Cantaur Farms*

Colt, Frank, and the twins had been the nucleus of it. Shauna Lee and Brad had met through Colt. Ellie had joined the group as a babysitter for the twins and when they met at the ranch, she and Ollie had connected immediately. Colt had hired Tim to manage *Cantaur Farms*, and Grayson had joined the crew at *Belanger Creek Ranch* after Patch Bergeron had died. Christina had worked as Shauna Lee's receptionist and office manager at *Swift Current Accounting and Bookkeeping Services* for years, but they'd never had anything more than a business relationship before Shauna Lee and Brad had gotten together. Now all those 'strangers' had become a family.

During the past four years common threads of joy and grief, celebration and tragedy, work and pleasure had bound their lives together. The ranch had become the place to meet and share the good times and the sad.

After the dishes had been done, everyone sat around and enjoyed an evening of conversation. Grayson went back to the bunkhouse and Tim offered to go down to the old ranch house, where Ollie and Ellie lived, to get Ollie's prescription pills for acid reflux. He was gone for quite a while and when he got back to the house, he was very distant and unsettled. Christina tried to catch his eye, but he refused to look at her. Finally, she waylaid him in the hallway.

"What's up with you, Tim?"

"Nothing," he said brusquely. "I'm going home."

"Tonight?"

"Yes."

"Why?"

He ignored her question. "You can catch a ride back with Brad and Shauna Lee."

"They don't have room for me. They've got the car seats and all the kids' stuff, as well as the kennel and Karma."

"They'll make room. I'm getting out of here."

"Tim, what's going on? You've been different ever since you came back from Ollie's."

"Damn it, Christina. Just leave it alone."

"But…"

"I said *leave it alone*. I'm going now. You'll get a ride."

His attitude chilled Christina. Suddenly he had morphed back into the old Tim, the cold, distant man who had arrived in Swift Current four years earlier. She wanted to shake him, but her instincts told her that something very profound had happened…and he wasn't about to tell her what it was. She couldn't let him leave in this frame of mind. "Tim, I'm coming with you. I…"

He glared at her. "I need some time alone."

"Well, now isn't the time. I'm going with you."

"I don't need anyone prying right now."

She glared at him. "Prying?"

"Yes, prying. You can never leave things alone."

"Fine. I won't ask any questions, but you're not going home alone in this frame of mind."

He swore as he turned away. He said an abrupt goodbye to Colt and headed out to his truck.

Shauna Lee looked puzzled. "What's up with him?"

Christina shrugged. "God only knows. It's like something

flipped a switch; he's gone right back to being the cold, miserable jerk, that he was when he first came here."

"Maybe you should just let him go by himself."

Christina shook her head. "He wants me to catch a ride back with you, but something's really wrong. Even Tim wouldn't regress that far in an hour...I'm worried about him."

Christina said a hurried goodbye and went out to the truck that was idling while Tim waited for her. She got in and closed the door.

He scowled at her. "You're so damn stubborn. You should have stayed."

"Just shut up and get on the road. We've got a long drive ahead of us."

He tightened his jaw and glared at her while he put the truck into gear and sped out of the yard. They drove in silence. When they were halfway to Maple Creek, it started to snow heavily. Then the wind picked up, whipping it into a blinding blizzard. "What the hell," Tim snarled. "It's almost the end of April. Where does this crap come from?"

Christina said nothing. The visibility became very poor, and he slowed to a crawl as he strained to look into the storm. At one point, he almost missed a curve in the road, his front wheel catching the shoulder. He swore again. Blinded by the blowing snow, all of Tim's senses were on alert as he inched the truck forward. When they finally reached Maple Creek, they couldn't see the lights of the town.

"Shit!" Tim exclaimed. "Why the hell didn't you stay at the ranch?"

"And what difference would that have made? It's insane to try to drive in this, whether I'm here or not."

"I'd go on home if you weren't here."

"Then go."

"I don't want to be responsible for something happening to you." His frustration was evident. "I didn't ask you to come along."

"Hey, buddy, you could have left, but you waited for me. On some level, you wanted my company. And, I sure didn't come because you're so charming. The fact is, you're acting like a miserable jerk. I came because I felt like I needed to be here for you. So get over it. You're stuck with me."

He snorted. "Why would you feel you needed to be here for me? You don't have any responsibility for what happens to me."

"Well, excuse me--I consider you to be a friend. Friends are there for each other."

"I have no friends."

Christina exploded. "You stupid bastard—who do you think all those….."

He slammed on the brakes, then reached over and grabbed the front her coat. "Don't ever call me a *bastard* again!"

She pushed at his hands, but he had a firm grip. His blue eyes were blazing.

"Let go of me," Christina yelled. He released his hold on her coat and she frantically unhooked her seat belt, opened the truck door and hurled herself out into the storm.

"What are you doing?" he yelled. "You can't go out there." He bailed out after her, running to catch her as she floundered through the snow. He grabbed her by the arm. "Are you trying to commit suicide? You'll get lost and freeze to death."

"Right now that might be a better option than being beaten up by an ungrateful, hotheaded maniac."

"I'd never beat you."

"You lost your cool, mister, and I don't take kindly to being pushed around."

"I…I wouldn't hurt you," he stammered. He kept a firm grip on her arm while he led the way back to the truck. When they reached it, he opened the passenger door to help her get in. He looked into her face in the glow of the interior light. Suddenly he pulled her against him and kissed her angrily.

"Are you crazy?" she gasped, pushing him away. She clamored inside and he slammed the door. She rubbed away the feel of his kiss with her coat sleeve, as she glared at him plodding through the snow in the front of the truck.

His mind was in turmoil. *What the hell was wrong with him? Why had he kissed her?* He stood, staring into the storm for a few seconds before he got in. Then he started the truck and edged onto the highway, squinting against the blinding whiteness as he turned toward Swift Current.

Suddenly, emergency lights were flashing across the road in front of him. "A god damned roadblock?" Tim swore again, as he rolled down his window. Christina noted that she had heard him curse more in the last two hours than she remembered him doing in the past three years. He didn't normally swear, although he had when he'd first arrived at the farm at Cantaur. He'd been cold, angry and bristling with defensiveness and, he'd cursed a lot.

Two policemen approached the truck, bracing themselves against the fury of the storm. "The highway is closed in both directions." The RCMP officer rested his hand against the truck door and peered inside to look at them. "You'll be up against it to find a place to stay for the night. The hotels and motels are full. The restaurants and bars have stayed open, but there's not much room left. There is a small bed and breakfast just up that road behind you and to your right. We've sent two parties there already, but they might be able to make more room."

Frustration oozed out of Tim. "We came from Belanger Creek and it wasn't snowing when we left."

"This storm moved in from Swift Current. There hasn't been any traffic for about an hour and a half. Last reports estimated up to three-foot drifts in places. I'd advise you to try the B&B. It's the best chance you'll get tonight."

Tim rolled up the window and stared ahead. "Could things get any worse?" He looked across at Christina. "Now what do we do?"

She shook her head. "Well, we can't drive any further, so we'd better try the B&B."

He shifted the truck into reverse and eased backward, then turned onto the adjacent road. The drifts were already hardening and the truck had to fight through the snow in four-wheel drive. They reached the B&B sign and turned into the yard. The lights were a dim haze in the snow. There were three snow-covered vehicles in the yard.

Tim looked at Christina. "He said they'd sent two parties here; there are three cars."

Christina shrugged. "Maybe they have a couch, or if nothing else the floor will do. We don't have many choices." She unclasped her seatbelt and opened the door. "Let's go see what they have."

When they stepped onto the porch, the door opened and a tall, slender man stepped into the light to greet them. Tim shuffled uneasily. "The police said you might have a vacancy."

"We're fully booked."

Christina bit her lip. "You know, a blanket on the floor will do. We just need a place to stay warm and safe."

"Well...come in and I'll talk to my wife. We have a bed in the attic. We don't use it for the business because it's only a double so it's smaller than most people expect, but seeing this is an emergency…"

"Actually we need two," Tim growled.

Christina glared at him. "No! If that's what is available, we'll take it."

Tim scowled.

Christina sighed wearily. "For cripes sake, Tim, it's better than sitting in the truck, freezing. We can't piss each other off any more than we already have tonight. We might as well make up our minds to get a decent rest." She opened her purse. "How much is the room?" She paid, saying, "I'm Christina Holmes, and Smiley here, is Tim Bates."

The man nodded. "This is my wife, Lily and I'm Alvin Bronson. This is a rare storm for this time of the year, but it's not unheard of. It caught a lot of people off guard. We've had a couple of other groups come in tonight. Do you have any luggage?"

"No. I have a small bag in the truck, but I'll sleep in my clothes and get it in the morning," Christina replied.

Lily stepped forward. "That room is pretty chilly at this time of the year. We only use it for the grandkids in the summer. I have a king-sized down filled comforter that'll provide more warmth." When she came back, she handed Tim an extra pillow and the comforter. She handed Christina a pair of long, thermal underwear. "These are mine. We're about the same size so I think they'll fit you and they'll be more comfortable than trying to sleep in your clothes. I'm sorry, but there are no services up there so you'll have to use the washroom down here."

She looked at Tim. "Our son is about your size. He has a fleece jogging suit here. I'll get it. I'm sure you'll be a lot more comfortable in it than in your jeans and shirt."

Tim started to protest, but Lily cut him off. "I don't want to hear another word. I think you're going to have enough trouble getting comfortable."

Lily came back with a blue jogging suit and handed it to Tim. Alvin led them up the narrow stairs to the room in the attic. After Alvin had left, they looked around the small room. Frost was forming on the single window, and they could see wisps of their breath floating in the chilly air.

Tim glared at Christina. "I guess I get the floor."

"Quit being an ass and get a grip on yourself. There is no need for anyone to sleep on the floor. I'm sure we are mature enough to make the best out of this rotten situation. I'm not going to freak out if your leg touches mine. It's not as if either of us is interested in anything other than sleep and keeping warm."

He stared at her. "Are you suggesting we share the bed?"

"Cripes! Pretend I'm your brother."

"My brother? Then I definitely wouldn't be getting into bed with you. I like him even less than you."

Christina shook her head. "Pretend I'm someone you don't dislike then. What would you do if I were Colt or Brad? You'd damn well get in bed and sleep. I'm going downstairs to change into these long johns and I'll leave my socks on too so you won't be able to accidently touch my skin. I suggest you get into that fleecy thing she gave you and hustle into bed." She went towards the door, paused and looked back at him. "Turn off the light so you can't see me when I get back. That way you can pretend it's someone else on the other side of the bed."

When Christina returned, the light was off. She leaned over to touch the end of the bed in the darkness and felt her way along to the far side. She was edging her way to the head of the bed when her foot hit something, and she lost her balance. She gave a muffled gasp as she fell over Tim's body.

Fury, hot and raw, exploded in her chest. "What are you doing down there on the floor?"

"I'm not sleeping in that bed with you. I laid down here so you could just walk in and get into bed when you came back."

"I always sleep on this side of the bed," she hissed.

"How was I to know that?" he huffed as he tried to push her away so he could get out from under her.

She tried to get her balance as she struggled amid the twists of his legs, knees and hips under the quilt.

Finally, he got up on all fours in the tangle of the quilt and pushed her up. The room was pitch-black, but she felt her way to the foot of the bed, reaching out for the wall. She slid her hand along until she felt the light switch, and she flipped it on, bathing the room in shocking light.

Their stare locked. Her fury was tangible, radiating off her with a heat he could feel. Tim looked away first. She walked over and stripped the quilt off him and threw it on the bed, then turned to him, sparks snapping in her eyes.

" You're not sleeping on the floor in this cold room. Stop acting like an adolescent and get in the bed. I don't know what happened to you today, but the man I've come to know as a friend, has regressed into an idiot. Grow up, Tim!"

She switched the light off and felt her way up to the head of the bed and crawled in. She pulled the sheets and the quilt up around her neck, turned on her right side with her back to him and lay still, waiting to feel his weight settle on the mattress. It seemed like an eternity before it did.

Tim lay on his left side, with his back to her, crowded as close to the edge of the bed as he could get. He was tense as a board, his senses alert. He listened for every breath, every stirring she made and was shocked, almost angered, when a few minutes later he heard her breathing become a whisper, slow and relaxed, and he realized that she was sleeping. *How could she be asleep already?* He shifted gingerly, desperate not to wake her. He was uncomfortable. He usually slept on his back, sprawled across the whole bed. He hadn't shared a bed with anyone since his wife had left him.

His mind was in turmoil. Not only was he in a damnable situation there in the bed, but so many unanswered questions raced through his thoughts. What had he really stumbled upon when he'd gone to Ollie and Ellie's house? Why was that picture laying on the desk in Ollie's office? Seeing it there had shocked him. At first, he'd thought he had to be mistaken, but when he picked it up and looked closely, he knew he'd seen it before. It was his mother.

Then Christina had insisted on coming home with him, and she'd called him a *Bastard!* The word swirled in his mind. Why couldn't he push it away? He tossed and turned, then finally found refuge in sleep. The warmth of the bed lured him.

Hours later, Christina surfaced slowly, instinctively relaxing into the warmth against her back and the weight encircling her waist. The comfort of it lulled her back into the depths of slumber.

CHAPTER TWO

About twenty minutes after Tim and Christina left that evening, snow started to fall heavily at *Belanger Creek Ranch*. Shortly after, the relentless winds came, driving in a blinding blizzard. Colt and Brad drove down to the barn to check on the two hundred head of cows with late calves housed in the corrals. The high board shelters on the windward side of the corrals protected them from the brunt of the storm, and most of the calves were huddled in the calf shelters.

Ollie and Grayson were already there. They had moved a couple dozen smaller calves inside a covered area because they were newborns and the heavy wet snow would weaken them, promoting scours or pneumonia in the herd.

Ollie voiced Colt's main concern. "This doesn't bode well for the cows and calves that we turned out into the feeding area down by the river."

Colt nodded. "I know. They won't fight against the storm. They'll put their backs into the wind and drift with it. That'll take them down off the hilltops where we've been feeding them, into the shelter of the ravines or clumps of willow."

Ollie's look was sober. "I've seen it happen. If it's bad enough, they'll get down in those narrow sheltered spots and crowd in like sardines in a can. The calves can get trampled pretty easily."

Colt looked into the storm. "The calves in that group are older and stronger, but when three-hundred cows start to crowd, even the bigger, healthy animals can lose footing and go down."

Ollie nodded. "It depends on how long this lasts. I've seen these storms last for a couple of days. The cattle can get hung up in the willows and suffocate under the drifts that blow over them. I haven't been checking the weather forecast the past couple of days, so have no idea what they are predicting for this one. I didn't even realize it was coming."

Colt looked at Brad. "I didn't either. We were playing cards when it started to snow, but I didn't pay much attention until the wind came up. I just figured it was a quick spring flurry. I should've been more aware."

Ollie brushed the snow off his jacket. "I should have, too. The Cypress Hills can drop some unpredictable surprises on this country."

Colt slapped his gloves against his jeans. "I think this storm actually came in from Swift Current way. There isn't much we can do right now. Even if we were able to ride out there, the cattle would fight us at every turn. Hopefully, this will have blown itself out by dawn, and then we'll ride out with the horses. Right now, we're better off to get some sleep and conserve the horses. Can you stick around and give us a hand in the morning, Brad?"

"We won't leave until you get everything straightened out here. Tomorrow is a holiday anyway, and if I need to, I can get one of the installers to go to the shop for me on Tuesday. Christina will be home, so she'll open the office for Shauna Lee."

Colt looked at Grayson. "Will you help Ollie attach the blade to the tractor in the morning before we go? Fran will ride out with Brad, you and me. Ollie can follow us with the tractor and plow the snow off the road so we can drive the truck in if we have any animals that need to be hauled home."

Ollie & Grayson nodded in agreement and everyone went their separate ways. At five o'clock, they were up again. Frank and Shauna Lee had breakfast ready and after they'd eaten, Frank left with the men to saddle up.

Shauna Lee could barely see them ride out in the early dawn light and a few minutes later she watched Ollie leave with the tractor, plowing their tracks in the snow off the road. She watched until he was out of sight, and then started to clean up the kitchen.

Thirty minutes later, Colt sighed with relief as they rode into the pasture. "It looks like we lucked out this time. This could have been a disaster. Fortunately, it stayed mild and we've only had a foot of snow here. It's so wet and heavy that it won't have piled up in the coulees and ravines the way a dry, cold snow would have with those strong winds."

Brad nodded in agreement. "It's fortunate that the wind only lasted a couple of hours."

Colt and Frank rode through the upper end, checking the ravines and willow bluffs as they went. Brad and Grayson rode the lower end of the field, along the river fence and up the east side. Fortunately, no calves had been trampled, and no cows were down. They drove the animals back to the feeding areas.

By then Ollie was plowing snow in different sections of the pasture so it would be easier to feed. Colt and Brad went to the feed yard. Colt started the big tractor with the bale buster hooked on behind it. Brad waited at the gate, and watched as he backed up to the stack and loaded one of the sixteen-hundred-pound bales into the tub and then picked up a second bale with the machine and headed out into the field.

Brad open and closed the gate so no hungry cows could get into the stack yard. He watched with fascination, as the bale buster shredded the bale and augered it out into a long windrow on the ground. When the first bale had been fed, he dropped the second one into the tub and shredded it as well. The cows lined up along the windrows to eat. Colt made three more trips to different areas of the pasture before he was done with the feeding.

Frank and Grayson rode their horses among the cows as they ate, watching for any signs of a problem; an injured foot or leg, a bruised rib causing breathing problems, early stages of pneumonia or scours. Frank's veterinary training alerted her to conditions that might have been missed, but during the past four years she'd learned to count on Grayson's quick eye for problems in the herd, and they conferred regularly.

After the feeding was finished and the tractor parked back in the feed yard, the four of them mounted their horses to ride home. Ollie had plowed the drifts out and riding was easier for man and beast. The sun was shining and it was clear that, except where it had drifted in the shaded areas, the snow wouldn't last very long.

Ollie had gone back to the ranch as soon as he'd finished plowing and when they arrived, he was finishing up the chores. They tied their horses to the hitching rail by the barn. Colt and Brad went to help Ollie, while Frank and Grayson took a quick walk through the calves. They found no obvious problems, so they led the horses into the barn, unsaddled them and brushed them down. They had turned them into stalls and were giving them each a portion of grain when they heard the quad coming down the hill.

Seconds later, Sam came dashing in the barn door. "Hey, Mom! Ellie and Auntie Shauna Lee are making something to eat at our place. Everyone is supposed to come up there.

"That sounds great. I'll catch a ride back on the quad with you. Dad and the other guys can come in the truck."

"Okay, Mom." They went out and got on the quad. Sam started it, revved it up, and sped up the hill, sending a plume of wet snow and water spraying away from the wheels.

"Sam! You're going to get me soaking wet! Slow down."

"You're wet already, Mom. Didn't you look at your pants and boots?"

She looked down at her clothes. "I am, and I'm cold too."

"How can you be cold? It's nice out and the snow is melting like crazy. Look at the way it's running down the tracks on the road. "

"Well, buddy...you haven't been out riding since dawn. We've been wading through snow banks and walking around, looking at the cows and calves. Your turn will come one day and then you'll know what it's like. You'll be chilled to the bone just like we are!"

The quad rolled to a stop at the door and Frank tweaked her son's ear as she got off. "Thanks for the ride, big guy; even if you did soak me again."

The pickup pulled into the yard right behind them and Colt and Brad got out.

"What happened to Grayson and Ollie?" Frank asked. "They're supposed to come too."

"They're changing into some dry clothes. Then they'll come up."

The smells from the kitchen greeted them when they opened the door. "All of a sudden I'm famished." Colt looked at his watch. "It's no wonder. It's after two o'clock. We were out there for more than eight hours."

Frank and Colt went to their bedroom and took a quick shower to warm up. When they joined the others in the kitchen, Brad was already there and Shauna Lee was handing him a hot cup of coffee spiked with a shot of Baileys.

"I've got one here for you, too, Frank," she said handing her a hot cup.

"Mm... this is wonderful," she cradled it in her hands, savoring the warmth.

"And me?" Colt asked with a hopeful grin.

"Coming right up," Shauna Lee answered. "It sounds like Ollie and Grayson are here now, too," she said hearing the porch door open. "Do you guys want coffee with Baileys in it?"

Grayson said yes, but before Ollie answered, Ellie was pouring a shot of Jack Daniels into a glass for him. Ollie smiled as she handed it to him. "Thanks, love," he said and raised the glass to the others. "This is my poison—it warms you right to the core!"

Everyone sat down at the table and enjoyed a flavourful meal of hot stew and baking powder biscuits. They ate until they were content, and then sat and talked about the storm, and how fortunate things had turned out.

"I wonder if Tim and Christina got caught in it," Colt said thoughtfully.

"That was strange," Frank commented. "You know, the way he decided to leave so abruptly."

Brad nodded. "Yeah, what the heck happened there, anyway? He was happy and relaxed all day, and then all of a sudden he just did a complete turn around."

Shauna Lee shook her head. "I have no idea. Christina didn't know what was going on either. She was so concerned that she decided to go home with him, even though he didn't want her to."

"Is there something going on between those two?" Colt asked.

Shauna Lee shook her head. "No. They're just friends."

"I've wondered about that," Brad commented. "Lately they're pretty comfortable with each other."

"I've noticed it, too" Frank commented.

Shauna Lee nodded. "Well, I think they've worked out most of their angst by now. He was so bitter when he first came and she really took a dislike to him. Christina always referred to him as the *cold fish*. But they're civil now."

"I'm really impressed with how he's managing the farm," Colt added.

Brad nodded. "He was a great guy when I knew him in the Peace River country. He loved being a farmer and he was a smart businessman. When he got married, everyone who knew them wondered how it had happened. They were like water and oil from the very beginning. I think she thought there were diamonds sparkling in the grain bins and had big ideas about being a rich land owner's wife. The marriage sort of hung together for about eight years, but it was over long before they split.

"When Tim's mother died, it was a big blow to him. His siblings are nothing like him. They're a lot younger and spoiled rotten. He has one brother and he was a cocky, egotistical brat that never did a day of hard work in his life. He gave Tim a bad time when he got old enough to think he could flex his muscles as far as the business went. When his dad died, the farm was worth millions, but they just tore it apart trying to get their hands on all the money. They killed the goose that laid the golden egg, and Tim got 'plucked' in the process."

CHAPTER THREE

Tim awakened slowly, savoring the warmth. A fragrant cloud lay against his cheek, tickling his nose. It smelled like lilacs. He softly blew a tendril from across the tip of his nose. Hair!

He became aware of the softness resting against his chest, molding to his hips, his thighs and the leg that intertwined with his. He felt the hip bone beneath his arm as it lay over a curvy waist. He stiffened. *What the hell is she doing?*

Realization flooded through him. No! What the hell was he doing? She was curled up on her side of the bed. He was the one who was cuddling her, snuggled up as close as he could get. Panicked, he listened to the rhythm of her breathing. If he was careful, possibly he could ease his body over onto his own side without waking her up. He inched away carefully.

She stirred and murmured something, stretching her legs gently. Her hand groped, searching for the warmth that had moved away, but she stayed asleep. He eased over slowly and turned onto his left side again, clinging to the edge of the bed. He exhaled slowly. He'd made it!

His breathing was rapid, and he tried to calm it. He couldn't keep his thoughts in line. It felt good to wake up to a warm, soft, fragrant body next to him. He thought he put that behind him, but that primal instinct was still there. Damned women, they were always a temptation to a stupid, vulnerable man. He lay quietly, thinking about life; his life.

His mother had been the one constant in his life and he'd worshiped her. He thought he knew everything about her, but he didn't know how she figured into Ollie Crampton's life. She'd always said she didn't have any family, so why was her picture on his desk? He had turned it over and looked at the back of it. It was date-stamped four years earlier, just a few months after he'd come to the farm, and it bore the name of a legal firm in Vancouver, British Columbia. She had died over eight years before.

He rolled onto his back with a sigh and flung his arm across his eyes. *Could Ollie be checking me out? But why? I could understand if Colt had done that before I started working for him, but I was already at the farm when that picture was dated. Ollie and I have talked lots of times over the past four years; we've had some serious conversations about life. Why didn't he say anything about having Mom's picture?*

And why would anyone send a picture of Mom to him? It would have come to Shauna Lee's office, not to Ollie. So what is going on here? Don't they trust me? After Bob Thompson died last year, Colt sold me his shares in Cantaur Farms. We're partners now, and we haven't had any problems. None of this makes any sense. I've considered those guys to be my friends. I hope I'm not going to get screwed over again.

"You survived the night!" Christina said softly, breaking into his thoughts.

He lowered his arm and looked across at her. His eyes strayed to the curtain of dark hair that spilled onto her pillow and the intoxicating scent of it came back to him. He smiled crookedly. "I see you did, too."

"I was so tired, I just died! And the bed was so warm and comfy." Her fingers plucked at the comforter. "It must have been this feather quilt. I'm going to have to get one for home. It was heavenly. Were you warm enough?"

"It was more comfortable than I'd expected it to be. I needed a good sleep."

"So are you in a better frame of mind this morning?"

"A good sleep can't fix everything, Christina, but I'm okay."

"Am I still the enemy, or do you see me as a friend now?" She giggled. "After all, we've slept together; that's closer than most friends ever get." Her look turned serious. "I'm a good listener, Tim. I don't break confidences either. I've got my own ugly secrets. Honestly, it probably would help to discuss whatever happened yesterday and get it off your chest. It had to be big to make you do such a complete turn around."

"I don't want to talk about it. I have to figure out what actually happened by myself, what it means to me. I'm going to get up and check the road report." He threw back the blankets and stood up. He looked out the small window, but all he could see was frosted edges and a sea of white. "That doesn't look very promising," he grumbled. He grabbed his jeans and his shirt. "Look away; I'm going to put on my clothes."

She buried her head under the quilt and waited until he said, "Alright, I'm out of here. I'm warning you, it is damned cold in here. You'd better dress downstairs in the bathroom."

She looked up as he opened the door. He hesitated, and then said, "Christina... I'm sorry."

"Sorry for what?" She grinned. "Oh, you mean for keeping me warm? To be honest, I'd forgotten how good it felt to cuddle with someone."

His jaw slackened, and then his face flushed red.

"Yes, Tim, I know. I woke up earlier; there's no harm done. Warmth and sleep are basic essentials."

"You are a bitch."

"I know...and you're still a bastard, too. A good sleep can't fix everything."

He slammed the door and went down the stairs. She got up and got dressed. She shivered. The room *was* cold.

"Good morning." Lily greeted her when she entered the kitchen. "Did you sleep well?"

"I was so tired, I just passed out. The bed was warm and toasty. It had to be that marvelous quilt."

"I'm glad the bed worked out alright. Tim said he had a good sleep too, and he seemed a lot more relaxed this morning. Would you like a cup of coffee? Tim went out to get his razor and he's bringing your overnight bag in. He'll have a cup when he comes back."

Christina turned to look when the entry door opened and Tim stepped inside. Their eyes met as he handed her bag to her. Her amber eyes were twinkling when she took it. "Thank you, Tim."

He tried to scowl but didn't quite succeed. "I knew you'd need your hairbrush and I've heard you complain about your morning breath and needing your toothbrush."

"I'm shocked you remembered all that. Obviously a good sleep does improve some things." She winked at him as she turned away and went to the washroom.

When she returned, Tim was sitting at one of the tables in the dining room, drinking coffee. A glance told her that a full cup was waiting for her too, so she joined him. He looked at her with a twinkle in his eye and grinned. "Hey, you look pretty good now."

She sat down and took a drink of her coffee. *Is he flirting? No, that couldn't be happening.* "Hmm…I've never seen you with a five o'clock shadow before. It's looks kind of rakish on you." She rubbed her hand down her cheek and along her chin.

He looked at her for a long moment. *Is she flirting with me? Get a grip man. That is not happening.*

"So, what do you want for breakfast? The B&B package comes with cold cereal and toast or hot baking powder biscuits and jam or a croissant and a bowl of fresh fruit; your choice."

"I'll have a hot biscuit and jam. I love biscuits." She looked at him curiously. "What are you having? Let me guess; cold cereal and toast."

"How did you know?"

She smiled and gave a shrug. "You're pretty predictable."

He snorted in reply and went to get their breakfasts while she smirked as she finished drinking her coffee.

The highway was open by ten-thirty that morning and Tim and Christina were on the road as soon as they got word that they could travel. Most of the trip was made in silence, but it wasn't the hostile silence of the previous night's journey from Belanger Creek. It was a companionable silence, two friends traveling together.

About two-thirds of the way home, Tim sighed deeply and looked at her. "About yesterday…when I went down to Ollie's house to get his pills, they weren't in the medicine chest in the bathroom, or on the windowsill by the kitchen sink. They were on the desk in his office."

Christina waited for him to continue, but when he didn't, she said, "Okay. What was so significant about that, Tim?"

He drummed his fingers on the steering wheel, staring ahead, down the road. "I saw my Mom's picture."

"What?"

"It was there on his desk. Just lying there, as if he'd been sitting there looking at it before he'd left the house."

"But why? I mean… are you certain it was her?"

"At first, I thought I was imagining things, but I picked it up and studied it. It was a picture taken when she was young, probably in her twenties. There's no doubt that it's her. I've seen it before among her things."

"It doesn't make sense, Tim. How would Ollie get a picture of your mom? And why?"

"I've been asking myself the same thing, and I have no idea why. There was a date on the back. It was four years ago, in late May, and the name of a legal firm in Vancouver B.C. was stamped underneath it. I was already at the farm then. I'd been there a few months by that time."

Christina frowned thoughtfully. "And neither Colt nor Ollie has ever mentioned it to you in all this time?"

"No. To be honest, that's what really bothers me about this whole thing. What the hell is going on? Why has no one mentioned that they knew her or had a picture of her? God, I've come to feel like I was part of the family; like they are all my close friends. Honestly, Christina, why would the people I consider friends keep something like that from me? It wasn't shoved away and forgotten in a corner. It was right there on the desk, in front of his chair. Ellie has to know. How would you feel?"

"Why didn't you ask Ollie? You could have done it when you came back up to the house."

"When I first saw the picture, I was shocked and I just sat there for a long time, feeling confused. To be honest, I felt betrayed. Then I got mad and I didn't know who I could believe or trust. I just wanted to get out of there."

"Tim, I haven't really known everyone much longer than you have. I've worked for Shauna Lee for years, but until she met Brad, she was nothing more than an employer. I knew she had gone out with Colt before he married Frank, and I'd seen Colt and Bob come into the office, but I didn't really know them on a personal basis. I saw Ollie off and on over the years, but just in passing.

"But now, I believe in all of them; they are true friends. I...you...we've seen it over and over again. They...we... support each other through thick and thin. We're there for each other when things go wrong, we celebrate together when things go well. Everyone works hard, they play together...they're awesome people. There's something that we're missing."

"But what can it be?" He sighed and looked out the side window. "I'm so tired of having life go sideways on me. I was beginning to settle in, feel a part of things." He thumped the steering wheel with his hand. "And then this happens and now I'm questioning everything again. I can't deal with another betrayal."

"Okay, let's try using some logic, instead of emotion. Was your mom still alive when you came here? Somehow I thought your dad died last."

"He did. That's the thing. Mom was gone for six years before Dad died. So, why would anyone be sending out her picture four years later?"

"Don't assume the worst, Tim. You should talk to Ollie and Colt. You need to go back to the ranch as soon as you can and get it all out in the open. If you can wait until next weekend, I'll go with you, for support."

His eyes met hers. "You mean you'd do that for me after I've been such a miserable..."

"Bastard?" Her expression became thoughtful. "What is it about that word that really gets to you?"

"I am one."

CHAPTER FOUR

At Belanger Creek Ranch, the weather stayed mild and by the end of the week, most of the snow had melted. Colt and Frank took a leisurely ride out to the pasture to check the cattle. In truth, it was more for pleasure than work. In a month, the cattle would be moved out onto the range and leisurely rides would be few and far between.

They leaned against the gate at the feed yard and silently gazed out over the hills and ravines. Colt straightened and looked at Frank. "You know, that blizzard was probably the best thing that could have happened. It dumped a lot of moisture on the fields just when we needed it. The growth will be unbelievable in the next few weeks."

Frank pushed her hat back. "That's true. Our weather patterns seem to be changing. We didn't get very much snow during the winter. Coming at this time of the year as it did, the moisture will help a lot." She glanced at her watch. "It's getting close to two-thirty already. We probably should head for home. Ellie will be finishing up with class. She's been feeling tired all week, so I don't want to make her wait."

"Maybe she's getting a cold or something. We'll start back now and we'll be there by three o'clock. I'll unsaddle and take care of the horses and you can take the truck up to the house. If she's really tired give her a ride down to their place."

"She'll never let me do that. She'll tell me that it's good exercise."

When they reached the barn, Frank handed her reins to Colt and took the truck up to the house. Ellie was enjoying a cup of tea while Sam and Selena were sitting at the kitchen table drinking hot chocolate.

Sam was excited. "Mom! Miss Ellie says we're ahead with our lessons. And because we've worked real hard, we'll have finished all of this year's school work by next week. Then we can do fun things. We'll read stories and we can watch some movies."

Selena vied for attention. "Miss Ellie said we could even go for a ride with you and Dad sometimes."

"And she's going to plant a garden again this year!" Sam exclaimed. "And she says since we'll be done with our classes, we can help her work in it." Sam liked to work with plants.

"Wow, that's exciting guys." Frank looked at Ellie. "So, my babies will be going into grade three next year! I can hardly believe it! Ellie, I can't tell you how much we appreciate the job that you do home schooling them. From what we've observed, Sam and Selena are far more advanced with their schooling, in comparison to what we see with other kids."

"They are a pleasure to teach, Frank. They learn quickly and they enjoy the lessons. I love teaching them and this Home School program is excellent."

"How are you feeling, Ellie. Are you still feeling tired? I'll give you a ride home."

Ellie hesitated. "I'd appreciate that. Maybe I'm getting the flu. I've had indigestion this afternoon. I think I'll just heat up leftovers tonight and go to bed early. I'll take it easy this weekend and get some rest. I'm sure I'll be alright by Monday."

"Okay, I'll take you down in the truck. Ollie is out fencing with Grayson. I'll tell Colt to go out and send him to the house."

"No," Ellie protested. "I'll be alright. I'm not sick, I'm just tired. If Colt sends Ollie home early, he'll start to think there's something wrong and he'll worry about me."

"Okay, but you make sure you get some rest. Let's go."

After Frank had dropped Ellie off, she stopped at the barn to see Colt. He looked up with surprise when she walked in. "Was everything okay up there?" he asked with concern.

"The kids are doing great. They are ahead of schedule and Ellie says they'll be finished their lessons for the year by next week. They're excited about that because the next six weeks will be all fun stuff for them. They'll be able to go riding with us, and Ellie told Sam he could help her plant the garden."

"How was Ellie?"

"I'm a bit concerned. She actually let me drive her home and that is definitely not like Ellie. She thinks she might be getting the flu. I told her I'd have you send Ollie home, but she doesn't want you to do that. She said he'd just worry. Still, maybe you could let the guys come in early. I don't know why, but I'm worried about her. This isn't the first time she's complained about feeling really tired in the past month or so."

"It's probably nothing serious. She's not a spring chicken anymore either, so it stands to reason that she might get tired when she's teaching all week and keeping up with things at home."

"But, she didn't get tired like that a year ago. She was unstoppable."

"Yeah, she was, but things can change in a year. Look at my dad."

Frank looked at him and nodded. "That's just it, Colt."

Colt stopped short. "I don't think…"

"No one ever does."

"You're right. Okay, I'll take a run out to where Ollie and Grayson are working and tell them to knock off early. It's been a long week. They've earned some down time."

"I'll have supper ready when you get back."

That evening, Frank and Colt put the twins to bed and watched a movie before they retired to the bedroom at eleven o'clock. Frank was slumbering lightly when the phone rang. She yawned as she reached out and fumbled on her night table in the darkness. Finally, her fingers found it and she automatically pressed the talk button.

"Is that you Colt?" Ollie's voice sounded panicked. "God damn it, answer! Colt..."

"Ollie…what's wrong."

"It's Ellie. Something's wrong. We've got to get her to the hospital."

Frank shook Colt awake, as she tried to make sense of what she was hearing. "Ollie, just calm down and tell me what's happening."

"She's having trouble breathing and her chest is hurting."

"Hold on, Ollie. We'll be right there."

Colt and Frank threw on the clothes they'd taken off just hours earlier, and rushed out to the truck. Frank sucked in a breath. "I'm scared, Colt."

"Let's wait and see what's happening before we jump to any conclusions."

"I know, but my gut has been gnawing at me all week. "

Ollie met them at the door, fear in his eyes. "We've got to get her to the hospital."

Colt was calm and reassuring. "Let's see her, Ollie."

"She's in the there."

Frank slipped into the bedroom ahead of them. "Ellie, what is happening?"

"Oh…Ollie's just being a worry-wart," Ellie said with a strained smile. "I'm just really tired."

"Ollie said your chest was hurting and you're having trouble breathing."

Ellie shook her head. "It was burning up here," she touched just below the hollow of her throat. "I just have indigestion. That's been happening lately, and you know it's not unusual to feel short of breath when you have really bad heartburn."

"Ellie, I think you should go to the hospital in Maple Creek." She rested a hand on the older woman's shoulder and looked into her eyes. "Just go to be on the safe side, and it'll ease Ollie's mind too."

"Well, there's no point in rushing in there now. I'll go when the stores are open, and then I can pick up a few things."

Ollie opened his mouth to protest, but Colt put out a hand to restrain him. "Ellie, it would be better if we went now. That way we'll make it home in time to do chores, and the emergency room probably won't be so busy this early in the morning. You never know what it will be like later."

Frank touched Ellie's hand. "Colt is right. I'll help you get dressed."

Ellie sighed and stood up. Frank noticed her waver. "Are you dizzy Ellie?"

"I just stood up too fast…it happens sometimes. It's nothing to worry about."

Colt and Ollie took Ellie to the hospital and Frank went to the house to check on the twins. She waited impatiently for Colt to call.

Different scenarios skittered through her mind. What if Ellie had a really bad heart attack and they are fighting to save her life? What if something else happened...what if they had an accident and they didn't get there? What if...?

"I can't stand this any longer." She grabbed the phone and started dialing the number for the hospital. *Colt, you're in big trouble if you took them for breakfast and didn't let me know Ellie was alright. I've been sitting here...* An emergency room nurse answered.

"Hi. This is Frank Thompson. My husband left here about two hours ago with Ellie Crampton and her husband. He hasn't called to let me know that they've arrived and to be honest I'm worried sick. We thought Ellie might have been having a heart attack."

"Mrs. Crampton is in emergency. We are doing some tests now."

"Is Colt Thompson there? "

"I believe he's with Mr. Crampton. Would you like me to call him to the phone?"

"Would you ask him to call home instead? He can use his cell."

The nurse said she would. Five minutes later Frank snatched up the phone when it rang.

"Colt! What's happening?"

"They haven't told us anything conclusive yet, but thcy've done a lot of tests. She did pretty well until we were here for about half an hour and then she had one of those burning chest pains, and she started getting pain in her jaw and both shoulders. It hurt enough that she began to cry. She said it hadn't been that bad before. I guess those are symptoms of heart attack, too. It isn't always a crushing chest pain that radiates down your left arm that most of us think."

"I'm so glad you took her in. I've had an uneasy feeling about this for a few days."

"I know you have. It never occurred to me. I'll phone you as soon as we know more."

"Please do. I was ready to do you serious damage, thinking you may have taken them out for breakfast while you waited for the pharmacy to open and didn't let me know what was going on. I've been going crazy waiting!"

Frank's heart was heavy as she checked on Selena and Sam, who were still sleeping in their rooms. Anxiety and fear of the unknown drove her as she wandered through the house. Ellie was part of their family… they'd be lost without her. She sat down at the table, propped her elbows on the top and cradled her head her hands. Tears rolled down her cheeks. "Nothing can happen to her. Poor Ollie…he'd be devastated. She has to be alright."

She brushed away her tears and stood up. After pouring another cup of coffee, she walked to the big window and looked down onto the heart of the ranch that spread out below. It was a view that she loved: the barn and the cattle shelters, the cows and calves moving around in the corral pens, the blades of the wind generator revolving in a steady rhythm, as it produced power for the barnyard.

She moved to the far side and looked down toward the old ranch house where Ollie and Ellie lived. She could only get a glimpse of the place that she had shared with Ollie when she'd come here to work as a ranch-hand nine years earlier. Now the naked caragana hedge filtered the view. The hedge would be covered with leaves in six weeks, and obscure the house from this vantage point.

She sighed. "We take so much for granted all the time. I know I do; Ollie and Ellie, Colt, Selena and Sam and this ranch. I love this way of life, the animals, the open spaces on the range, riding the horses, being out in the fresh air, close to nature. Yet in truth, our comfortable world can change in the blink of an eye. Health, injury, nature's whims…so many things we never imagine can happen."

She walked back to the kitchen island and sat her half-empty coffee cup on the counter. *It's a good thing we don't know what can or will happen. We'd be so afraid, we'd never truly live,* she thought.

"I have to do something. Just sitting around like this is driving me nuts. I'll go out and do chores. Grayson will be up pretty soon." Frank dressed in her chore coat and boots. *I don't want to miss Colt's call,* she thought as she grabbed the phone and took it with her.

She strode down the driveway to the barnyard, enjoying the athletic movement of her body, releasing her stress. She fed the horses first, throwing a few flakes of hay into the feeder, talking to them and petting them as she moved among them. After she poured grain into the trough, she walked out of the pen and started toward the corrals where the cows and the calves were. As she headed past the barn, she heard movement inside. "Grayson?" she called.

Grayson came to the door, two five-gallon pails in hand. "Frank? What are you doing out here? Where is Colt? I don't see any sign of Ollie yet and there are no lights on at his place."

"Colt and Ollie took Ellie to the hospital in Maple Creek. She's been feeling really tired and just a bit off-kilter lately. She had pains in her chest in the night, so Ollie called us. She thought it was indigestion, and didn't want to go in, but Colt pretty much insisted.

"It was a good thing because after they got there she had a stronger pain. Now they're running tests for a heart attack. I waited to hear from Colt for a couple of hours." She grimaced. "You know what that's like...every minute seems like an hour! Finally, I couldn't stand it anymore so I called him. He told me what he knew and he's going to call as soon as they know more." She reached into her pocket and pulled out the phone. "I don't want to miss his call, but I was going stir crazy, just sitting there waiting, so I came out here to do something to occupy my mind."

Grayson rubbed his chin as he looked down at the ground. Finally, he spoke. "Ellie is such a go-getter, it's hard to imagine her having heart trouble."

"No kidding. She was in denial about what was happening, but I guess in honesty that's something we all do about a lot of things."

Grayson nodded. "Isn't that the truth?"

Frank nodded at the pails. "I'll feed the grain if you'll put round bales into the feeders. Hopefully, we'll hear from Colt by the time we're finished here. Then you can come up to the house for a cup of coffee and I'll make breakfast. The twins should be awake by then."

Grayson grinned. "That sounds good to me, especially if I don't have to cook my own breakfast!"

An hour later, the chores were finished and there had been no call from Colt. They went to the main house and had a cup of coffee. Frank was feeling anxious and it showed. The phone finally rang while she was making pancakes. She grabbed it and gasped, "Colt?"

"No. It's Tim. What's up? Isn't Colt home?"

"No. I was hoping your call was from him. Ollie and Colt took Ellie to hospital in Maple Creek this morning. They went about four hours ago. She hasn't been feeling very good. She thought she had indigestion and didn't think she needed help, but Ollie was really worried and Colt more or less insisted she go. She had another episode in the hospital...it was worse. I talked to Colt a couple of hours ago. They were running tests and waiting for a diagnosis, but they thought she'd had a heart attack. He said he'd call as soon as they knew anything, but I haven't heard from him."

"That's scary. Let me know what happens eh?"

"We will. Why did you call, Tim?"

"Oh, it's not important; nothing that can't wait. I just wanted to talk to Colt and Ollie about something, but this obviously isn't the time for it."

"Can I help you, Tim? I can deliver a message to Colt."

"No, I was thinking about coming out to the ranch. We'll do it after everything settles down."

"Okay, Tim. I'll let you know what happens with Ellie."

Frank had just ended the call when Colt called.

"Colt...what's happening?"

"They're sending her to Regina. There isn't a specialist here to verify a diagnosis. They are bringing in the STARS air ambulance. She's having more pain. She's feeling nauseous when it hits. It's a good thing we brought her in when we did."

"Colt...that is so freaky. You just never know. Is Ollie going with her?"

"I don't think they'll let him ride in the chopper."

"Colt, do what you can to make it happen. It would be best for both if he could go. You can drive his truck to Regina, and the twins and I can follow in ours. Grayson can manage here. "

"I'll see what I can do about Ollie. He's pretty upset."

CHAPTER FIVE

Tuesday morning Christina fumbled through the files on her desk. Her fingers were moving, but her mind wasn't focused on what she was doing. She couldn't stop thinking about Tim's response when she'd ask him what it was about being called a bastard that really got to him. She hadn't expected the answer he gave her. *I am one.*

Then he'd clammed up and wouldn't say anything else. As they'd gotten closer to Cantaur, the snow had diminished, and by the time they'd arrived at the farm, the weather was mild and there was only a couple of inches on the ground.

Tim had gotten out, started her car and cleaned off the snow. He'd opened the driver's door for her and waited for her to get in, then closed it. He had also politely and courteously closed the door on any opportunity for her to ask any more questions, and he'd waved as she'd driven away.

But... he hadn't stopped her mind from racing, chasing his answer around and around. *"I am one."*

She'd bet he hadn't slept any better than she had last night as he lay wondering about the picture that he'd found on Ollie's desk.

She sighed and adjusted herself in her seat. *Buck up Christina.*

Carl, John, and Marinda worked on the weekend to get everything done up for the last minute rush. We've got three days until the April-thirtieth deadline. I've got to get these phone calls made so the guys can talk to their accountants and answer any concerns. As she made each call, she laid the forms aside on the edge of her desk. Then she picked up the one for *Thompson Holdings, Cantuar Division.*

Suddenly she was awake and alert. She dialed Tim's cell phone and waited. She exhaled as he answered.

"Tim Bates here."

"Hi, Tim. It's Christina Holmes."

He chuckled dryly. "I recognized your voice, Christina."

"Carl worked on your tax returns over the weekend, and he left a note for me to have you call him. He has a couple of questions. I could put you through to him now unless you plan to be in town in the next day or so. It's only three days before the deadline, so you can't put it off for too long."

"I'm coming into Swift Current this afternoon. I'll stop in then."

"Good enough. I'll make note of it and we'll see you when you get here."

"See you then," he replied and hung up.

She smiled as she made a note on the file and then took it into Carl Skinners office. "Tim will be in this afternoon," she said as she handed him the file before she turned and went back to her desk. Suddenly she was no longer tired and she tackled the work in front of her eagerly. A shimmer of excitement coursed through her body. She didn't question why, she just went with the flow. Her eyes lit up when Tim came through the door at three-thirty.

"Hi," she greeted him a sparkle in her eye. "Carl is waiting for you. I'll take you right in." He watched her walk ahead of him, noticing with pleasure the soft roundness of her figure and the enticing sway of her hips when she moved. They were in Carl's office before he became aware of his thoughts and reactions. The meeting lasted over an hour. When he came out, Christina was tidying her desk, getting ready to leave.

"Are you finished for the day?"

"Yes." She looked at the clock. "It's four-thirty and it's been a long day. It's time to relax a bit, have supper and get a good sleep."

"Would you like to go out for supper? I need to eat too."

She hesitated, smiled. "I'd love to. Thanks for the invite, Tim.

Sometimes it gets lonely, eating by myself night after night."

"I can relate to that."

"Where do you want to go? I'll follow in my car."

"Do you like The Steakhouse?"

"It's fine with me." She shut off the lights in the front of the building and called to Carl and John to let them know she was locking up and leaving. Tim opened the door and they stepped outside. He waited while she locked the doors, then walked with her to her car and waited until she got in before he went across the street to his pickup. He started it and led the way to The Steakhouse.

After they were settled at their table, Christina looked across at Tim. "So, did you have a good sleep last night?"

He looked at her for a long moment. "Well, the bed was big and empty and lacking in warmth."

She blushed, then reached out and swatted him with the supper menu.

He grinned. "You asked me if I slept. I assumed you were wondering if I'd missed you, so I told you what I noticed."

"What I meant was, were you able to settle down and go to sleep, after what happened on the way home?" She looked at him solemnly, "Because I couldn't. Your last remark left me in a tailspin."

"What do you mean my last remark? I said goodbye to you."

"Don't play dumb. You know what I mean, Tim. How could you say something like that and just leave it hanging out there with no explanation?"

Tim frowned. "Christina…you're my friend, not my keeper. Let's order supper and forget the twenty questions, alright? I don't want to get into this."

"Can we talk about it after supper then?"

Tim glared at her. "You are one pushy…"

"Bitch? I've already told you that calling me that means nothing to me. You've got no leverage there."

The waitress came and took their orders, and they looked at each other in silence until she brought them each a drink. They took a few sips and then Tim looked at her thoughtfully. "I didn't know you were married."

"I'm not."

"All right, I didn't know that you used to be. That night you said your ex called you the "B" word."

"Not *the* B word, *a* B word, and we're talking about you, Tim."

"Actually, we both said things in the heat of the moment that night. I said what I did, but you ...you really caught me off guard."

"Caught you off guard? Who are you kidding? You're so involved in your own drama; I'm amazed you even heard what I said."

"Oh, I heard alright. I was just too ...."

The waitress brought their meals at that moment, interrupting the conversation. When she left, Tim looked at Christina and shook his head, signaling that the conversation was over. He picked up his knife and fork and began to eat."

Frustrated, she followed suit. They ate in silence, unspoken thoughts whirling in their minds.

Tim glanced at her surreptitiously. *Damn her, she's not going to let this go.* He looked around the room as he finished eating. Then he looked at her again. *Why am I letting her get away with this? I'd have shut anyone else down long ago.* His blue eyes studied her face. *To be honest, two years ago, I'd have kicked her to the curb for sticking her nose into my business.*

"So, will you recognize me the next time you see me?"

He frowned. "What...?"

"You've been staring at me. "

He shifted uneasily. "Sorry. I was just thinking."

"About?"

"Wondering why I'm letting you pry into my life."

"And...?

He looked into her eyes. "I...I don't really know. I guess I've gotten soft. You...no one... would have gotten away with that when I came here."

"You were so damn cold and rigid when you arrived, it was amazing you didn't crack and break in two."

"Give me a break, Christina. I'd just been through hell. For the past eight years, I'd been fighting a losing battle. Little by little, I watched my whole world fall apart and I couldn't do anything to stop it."

Christina reached out and touched his hand. "When you came here, you pushed everyone away. Every signal you gave out said, *I don't trust anyone, and I hate women.*"

"It was the truth. I didn't trust anyone and I certainly didn't have any use for women. Even now, I don't have any interest in them."

"So…what am I?"

He looked away for a moment. "You're too damned nosey."

"I asked you a simple question."

His eyes came back to search her face. "I have no simple answer to it."

"Not even a thought?"

He sighed. "What am I to you?"

She toyed with her fork. "Can you handle the truth?"

He stared into her hazel eyes, noting the glint of gold in them.

"I'm your friend." She laid down the fork and lowered her eyes, nervously pushing at the cuticle of her thumbnail. "If I'm honest, I have other feelings for you, too. I…I care for you…a lot. Now that I've spilled the beans, are you going to run?"

The silence was deafening. She looked away as tears started to fill her eyes. "Damn-- I shouldn't have said anything. Can I take it back, please?" She heard his chair scrape the floor, and she knew he'd stood up. *I am such an idiot. He's going to walk away.*

Suddenly, she felt his hand on her arm. "Wipe your tears," he said softly, handing her a napkin. She looked up at him. She couldn't read his expression. "Let's go," he whispered. She dabbed at her cheeks as he helped her stand up, then gathered her purse and jacket and handed them to her. "I'll go pay the bill."

She cursed herself for being a fool. Now she was embarrassed and just wanted to get out of there. She slipped out while Tim was at the till and ran to her car. She was speeding out of the parking lot when he hurried outside.

"Christina!" The words died on his lips. He stood there dazed, watching her car disappear. After a few dozen heartbeats, he walked to his truck and unlocked it. He got in and sat behind the wheel. Her words echoed in his mind. *If I'm honest, I have other feelings for you….*

"Christina," he said softly. He closed his eyes and concentrated on how he felt. He was shocked that she had said it, but surprisingly he wasn't upset. In fact… it actually felt good; like it did when he woke up cuddled against her in bed.

He opened his eyes and stared out the window. Things had changed between them over the past couple of years. He was comfortable with her. He trusted her and if he was honest, he liked knowing she was there for him, just as she had been the other night at the Thompsons. She had picked up on how he was feeling right away. She was right; he could have left without her, but he waited because… he didn't really want to be alone.

His hands gripped the steering wheel. "You're an ass, Tim Bates." He started the truck and eased out of the parking lot.

Christina sat in the living room with the lights turned off. "Big Mouth," she berated herself. "How could you be so stupid? Now you've probably even wrecked the friendship we had."

She buried her face in her palms. *And it means a lot to me. I haven't let any guy get as close to me as he has since my divorce, but why him? He doesn't need anybody."*

She heard a vehicle pull up in her driveway. Who could that be? The lights were all off in the house. If she just sat still they wouldn't know she was home. She held her breath as the doorbell rang several times. Then everything was silent, but the vehicle didn't leave. Suddenly, there was a loud rap at the back door. She ignored it again. There was silence for a few moments. Then, she heard the sound of the back door opening.

She jumped to her feet, her heart pounding. Grabbing the phone, she ran to the back porch. "Who's there?" she yelled. "You'd better leave now. I'm calling the cops."

"Christina! Don't do that…it's me; Tim."

"How…where did you get the key? How dare you just let yourself in?"

"I've been with you when you came in this door before and I knew where the key was hidden. Your car is in the carport, so I knew you were here. When you didn't answer, I knew you were sitting here feeling miserable. I have to talk to you."

"Well, you came; you saw. Now please leave!"

Tim reached out and pulled her against his chest. His hand cupped the back of her head, and his fingers threaded into the cloud of dark hair. As he tucked her head under his chin, he inhaled the scent of lilacs. "We need to talk Christina. We need to clear the air and figure out where we stand with each other."

She pushed against him. "Because I didn't keep my big mouth shut and you want to let me down easy? Don't worry my feet are planted solidly on the ground. Thank goodness I wasn't deranged enough to imagine I love you. I said I have feelings for you. Well, I *do* have feelings for you… and right now I can't stand the sight of you."

He pulled her to him again and took her face in his hands. He stared into her red-rimmed, furious eyes, and then kissed her soundly. The kiss was demanding at first, and then gradually became gentle and tender. "I have feelings for you, too, Christina."

The fight went out of her and she laid her head against his chest, tears flooding her eyes. Tim's arms encircled her gently. "I haven't dared to examine my feelings until now. I've just enjoyed being with you. I've appreciated how attuned you are to my needs, and that you care about me. It's been comforting, after the years I've lived with conflict. You've become my friend...and so much more than I even acknowledged until tonight."

"Please don't patronize me, Tim."

He tipped her chin up so he could look in her face. "Christina, look at me. I'm not patronizing you."

"I feel like such a fool," Christina murmured.

"No, I'm glad you were honest. I'd have played dumb as long as I could have, because I'm afraid of feelings. Now, I've had to look at mine and I'm glad." He slid his arm around her waist. "Can we sit down and talk?"

Christina sniffled and wiped her tears away with her shirt sleeve, as she led the way to the living room. She sat on the loveseat. Tim chose not to sit next to her and sat in the recliner. He leaned forward, his elbows on his knees. "Christina...I'm going to be honest with you. I'd like to take this slow. I don't want to rush things...do you understand?"

She nodded. "Are you saying you don't want any declarations of love and no sex before we get used to the idea of being more than friends?"

Tim grinned sheepishly. "Well...I did like waking up to your warm body in my bed." He looked down. "But seriously, I have a lot of baggage. You know I've been married, and that didn't turn out so well. I need to figure out what I did to contribute to its failure. If I'm honest, I've avoided that. It's been easier to blame Marsha. There's a lot of other stuff in the background, too."

"Like the 'Bastard' business?"

He nodded.

"Well Tim, I'm not as pure as the driven snow either. I have a past, too."

"You've been married, right?"

"Yes, and it ended badly...and I know the role I played in its demise."

Tim looked at her intently. "Were you unfaithful?"

She looked shocked. "No, I wasn't. Were you?"

"Not in the usual sense of the word, but I guess my work was like a mistress. I wasn't socially inclined and I was a workaholic. Marsha was very social and she resented my love for the farm."

"Was she unfaithful?"

"Yes. Was your husband unfaithful?"

"Let's just say I couldn't give him what he wanted, so he went somewhere else to get it."

"Couldn't or wouldn't? Tim asked.

"Couldn't."

"Christina. I'm out of my comfort zone here. It's been so long since I've even thought about having a relationship..."

She smiled. "I haven't dated for almost nineteen years, Tim. I came to Swift Current right after my divorce. I hid away for a couple of years and licked my wounds. Then I went to work for Shauna Lee and my social circle has been the people I work with and their families. We've become good friends and we do a lot of things together, but none of us know the intimacies of each other's lives. I've never told anyone I was married. Shauna Lee doesn't even know. Truthfully, I haven't considered being in a relationship again. The reasons for the last one failing have not changed and I can't face that kind of degradation again."

"So, why me, Christina?"

"Why me, Tim?"

He looked thoughtful. "To be honest, I couldn't stand you when I first got here."

Christina laughed. "And, you were so cold and defensive, you really pissed me off." She giggled. "I thought you were such a cold fish!"

"Thanks. That's really good for my ego. So if I was so miserable and pissed you off so much, how did we get to here?"

She shrugged. "Well, after Brad and Shauna Lee's wedding, our whole group became closer and gradually you started to get over yourself and relax."

He nodded. "You and I didn't have partners, so I guess we were thrown together more."

"I started to see another side of you. You were gentle with the kids, and your thoughtful, compassionate side started to come through. You were fun to be around and gradually I looked forward to being with you."

"Yeah, I didn't realize how much I'd come to count on you. I didn't take my blinders off until tonight."

"When I opened my big mouth and shoved my foot in it," Christina said soberly.

Tim shook his head. "Don't say that." He stood up and walked over to stand in front of her. "I'm glad you dropped the bomb." He sat down beside her and took her hand in his. "Some of us need a jolt to make us aware." His thumb rubbed the back of hers. "But, where do we go from here?"

"I don't know. We're friends and that seems like a good place to start."

"I don't feel this way about Colt or Brad. We're just guys who hang out."

"Well, we used to just hang out."

"Is that what you meant when you told me you had 'feelings' for me?"

She pulled her hand away "No, we already did that. I'd like...more."

"Christina, I want to be sure where we're headed with this. Are you looking for love and commitment?"

She was afraid to look at him. "What about you? You just told me you had feelings for me, too. What are you looking for?"

"I...I asked you first."

"You chicken-shit! You want me to make the first move again, don't you?"

He touched her chin and lifted her face to his. "If I'm going to do this again, I want to be sure that we are both on the same page."

"Why do you have to make this so complicated?"

"There's a lot we don't know about each other, Chris. We have to be sure that this is real, not the result of being thrown together socially and getting comfortable with each other. If I do this again, I want what Frank and Colt have, and I want what Brad and Shauna Lee have. I want honesty, loyalty, passion and a commitment."

Her eyes implored him. "Tim, do you doubt that I'd want anything less?"

He sighed. "No. This isn't the first time for either of us. I trust that you wouldn't have opened that door if you weren't sincere." He looked around. He'd sat in this room many times before and they'd laughed and talked as good friends. "Let's have a drink, okay?"

Christina stood up. "Come, and I'll show you the Happy Cupboard."

"I already know where it is."

Christina felt stupid; of course, he did. They'd sat here and yakked up a storm over a drink many times.

He opened the pantry door.

She pointed to a shelf. "There it is; rye, rum, wine, vodka, mix and there's Beer in the fridge. I like a drink of wine, but I'll sip a rum and coke and I'll guzzle a beer occasionally, too…but then you know that already."

"I guess I do.

"And I know you'll have rye and seven."

She got two glasses and set them on the counter. She and Tim reached for the bottle of rye at the same time, and their hands touched. She pulled away like she'd been burnt.

He started to pour the rye in a glass and she stood watching him. He looked at her questioning. She flushed.

"Why is this so bloody awkward?" she stammered.

"I don't know, but it is, isn't it?"

"I hate it! I think we should forget this *feeling* business."

"We can't turn back time, Chris."

"It was so much easier when we were comfortable as friends."

"You started this."

"I know, but…"

He leaned against the counter and looked at her. "It's impossible to take back our words and thoughts now: the door has been opened."

"Damn it," Christina groaned. "This isn't working."

"We are not being ourselves anymore. We're second guessing everything we do."

"I'm so self-conscious now. I don't know how to act around you. It's crazy."

Tim set the bottle of rye on the counter. "Maybe we should explore our feelings and let the rest fall into place."

"You said you wanted to go slow," she whispered as he pulled her into his arms and settled his lips on hers. She moaned as the kiss stole her breath away. Her arms lifted and wound around his neck and she pushed her fingers into his short sandy-coloured hair. Her heart accelerated while heat ran through her veins. *Oh my god*, she thought as she felt the tightness in her core. *I almost forgot how this feels. Oh ...Oh my god...I can still feel this way!*

Tim leaned her back against the counter and ground his hips against hers. A hunger he didn't know he still possessed roared through him, overwhelming his rigid self-control. It had been so long since he'd explored these feelings; so long since this heat had been released. Suddenly it was an unquenchable need.

His mouth ravaged hers, moving down her throat as his hand slipped under her shirt and moved up to cup her breast. They both moaned with pleasure. Christina worked her hands under his pullover and splayed them across his chest, then strayed down to the waistband of his jeans. Her hand brushed against the hardness behind his zipper. He gasped as his hand flew down to push hers against it. Then he cupped her buttocks and rocked her against him.

She started to move, taking him with her, around the counter, past the dining room, along the hall to her bedroom.

"Are you sure?" he whispered, nipping at the corner of her lip.

"Oh, yes," she murmured.

"Is this too soon?"

"We are both consenting adults. I didn't know I could feel this way. I don't want to miss it."

She pulled his top over his head, as he started to remove her shirt. Hungry hands stripped away their clothing, and they fell on the bed.

Later, they lay entwined under the sheets, sated and bathing in the afterglow of the most sexually potent lovemaking they ever experienced.

Tim inhaled the scent of her hair. "Lilacs," he said softly.

"Uhh...?"

"Your hair. I noticed it that night at the B&B."

She turned to give him a flirty smile. "Is that all you noticed?"

He squeezed her gently. "I was so damn freaked when I realized that I was almost on top of you, I didn't think about anything other than how I could move to my own side of the bed without waking you up."

Christina giggled. "And I already knew! Feeling your warmth and your strong body was so comforting, I just settled against you and fell back to sleep." She laid her head on his shoulder and traced her finger down his chest. "I didn't notice how buff you are. I've never imagined you working out...do you?"

"No, I've never needed too, probably because I've always been so active."

"Tell me about yourself. What were you like as a young boy?"

"I don't know. I was just like any other kid, I imagine. Mom had me when she lived in Vancouver. She was the one constant in my life. It was just the two of us for seven years and she meant everything to me."

"What happened to your daddy?"

"I never knew him. I'm not sure he even knew I existed."

She pushed up on her elbow. "Is that what lies behind the 'Bastard' thing?"

He studied her face and then nodded.

"Good grief, Tim. That is so trite. No one uses that term that way anymore. There are so many children just like you these days, no one thinks about it."

"They don't come from my family."

She frowned. "What do you mean?"

"It's a long story."

"I promise I won't turn into a pumpkin. We have all night and I want to hear this."

"Mom met Harry Bates when we moved to Dawson Creek. When they got married, he adopted me. He said I was part of the package. He loved me and I idolized him. We lived on the original farm and I spent every moment I could with him. He loved being a farmer and I'm sure he passed his love for the land on to me.

"When I went to school, I was so proud to have a daddy like all the other kids. I was the center of Mom and Dad's world for three years and then Janelle arrived. I was ten years old and I didn't feel insecure or left out. Mom was busy, but Dad and I were still best buddies and it was exciting to have a new sister. Over the next ten years, they had five more kids, pretty much two years apart. The second was another girl, Sylvia, the third was my brother, Gerard and then there were three more girls; Suzanna, Jolene, and Dot."

Christina shook her head in wonder. "Your mom was one busy woman."

"She was a hard worker and a wonderful mother to all of us. Dad and I continued to do everything together. Dad kept adding to the farm, buying a section here, and a half section there as it became available. When I was eleven, I was running the tractor and hauling grain with him, and I loved every moment. Occasionally I was allowed to skip school and help him, which was really cool for me. As I got older, he would talk things over with me if he was going to get a new piece of equipment or buy more land. Even then, we were like partners.

"After I graduated, I went to university and got my Masters in Ag Economics. I went back to the farm to work with Dad. I was twenty-four by the time I finished university. We were fortunate to have had some prosperous times. We had good crops and good prices and we were able to expand quickly. In ten years we were farming eight thousand acres; fifteen-hundred were leased from other farmers, but we were buying the rest."

"No wonder you are a workaholic. Your dad was one and you idolized him. Work is all you learned to do. I have to wonder though, now that you have shares in Cantaur Farms, do you have visions of expanding like that again?"

Tim lay looking at the ceiling for a moment. "No, I don't think I'd do it again. You know, I still love the farm, but I… in some ways, I'm still reeling from everything that happened after Dad died. What do I need all that for? I'm not married. I have no kids to share it with, and I'm not getting any younger. I'm forty-eight now…"

"Are you really?"

"Yeah…what did you think?"

"I guess I didn't actually consider your age. You are just you."

He faked a groan. "Don't go thinking I'm too old now." He grinned. "I'm pretty sure I'm still as good as I ever was…"

She rubbed her cheek against his shoulder. "Well, from what I know, you definitely are…even better than some."

"Some?"

"Stuff it, Bates. I didn't want to admit that my one and only wasn't nearly as good as you."

"One and only? Come on, Christina. You've got to be kidding."

"I'm not kidding. I married young and he was the only guy I've ever had sex with until now. By the time that the relationship had run its course, I wasn't up for another one."

He shook his head. "That's unbelievable! You are warm, generous, funny, and loyal: any man would be lucky to have you for his wife. You're also a natural mother. I see it when you're with Leanne. That was one of the things that hurt me most about Marsha. She didn't want kids, but she didn't tell me that until after we were married."

Tears filled Christina's eyes. "Tim, I can't have kids. If that's a major thing for you, we might as well get out of this bed right now and call this *feeling* thing quits."

"I feel for you, sweetheart," he said softly. "Truthfully, I gave up on having a family long ago, and it isn't important to me now. In two years, I'll be fifty years old. That's a little late to worry about getting started, but I can see it hurts you. Is that why your marriage failed; you couldn't have children?"

She nodded, brushing away a tear that spilled over. "I always wanted kids. I still would, but I'm resigned to the fact I can't, now." She reached behind her to the night table and plucked a tissue from the box. "Enough of what might have been. Finish telling me about your family. I'm trying to understand the *Bastard* thing."

Tim shifted slightly to lay flat on his back and looked at the ceiling. "The other kids grew up in a different world. Things on the farm were going good, money came easily for them and they didn't have to work for it like I did. I was so much older than they were. I was more like an uncle than a brother. They were spoilt. I saw what was happening, but it didn't really bother me. I was doing what I loved and I thrived on the challenge.

"After Gerard graduated he went to Australia and New Zealand for a year. I think Dad and Mom hoped he'd get the wildness out of his system and be ready to settle down, but when he came back, he still wasn't interested in the farm. He worked on the rigs for a while and made good money, but he spent it faster than he made it. He had a fancy truck, a jet boat, a big quad, and the fastest snow machine. He had to have the newest, biggest, and fastest of everything and if it didn't come that way, he'd modify it until it was.

"His credit was maxed to the limit, but everyone knew he was Harry Bates' son. If he got in over his head, they knew Dad would bail him out to protect the family name. Mom died when he was twenty-four." Tim's eyes shimmered with tears. Christina reached out and caressed his hand.

"What happened?"

"Cancer. She took care of all of us, but she neglected herself. She'd had migraines all her life, so we all thought that was why she was having so many headaches. Finally, the girls talked to Dad and insisted she go in for a checkup. The doctor just attributed the dizziness to the migraines like we did, until she began losing her balance and seemed confused at times. She just wasn't herself.

"By the time they figured out what was wrong, she had a stage four tumor about the size of an orange on her brain. They did surgery, but they couldn't get it all. They kept her in an induced coma until the swelling of the brain went down. Then they brought her out of it and sent her home."

Tears filled his eyes. "The one blessing was, when they reduced the size of the tumor, it took the pressure off her brain and the headaches disappeared, along with the pain." He covered his face with his hands. "It was hard to watch her deteriorate. It didn't really take long, but it felt like years. One part of me was grateful when it was over, the other part was devastated."

Christina shifted against him and laid her arm across his chest, caressing his arm gently. "You must have felt so helpless." She touched his chest briefly with her lips. "I can't really fathom how much that hurt, I can only try to imagine."

Tim was silent for a few moments and then sighed. "Things really changed after Mom went. She had been the glue that kept our family together. Dad never really got over losing her. He just lost interest in everything, even the farm. I think he was burdened with guilt. He said many times that he had been so wrapped up in everything else that he hadn't paid enough attention to what was happening to her.

"After that, Gerard decided he wanted to be part of the operation. He told everyone he was coming home to claim his heritage. He said he was through working in the dirt and cold in the oil field. He boasted that he was going to take over the farm. He'd always mocked me about my cushy white collar job. He never could see past what he thought was my easy life, running all the big, fancy equipment with GPS and air conditioned cabs, with a stereo system installed."

"He'd never driven a tractor or any other piece of equipment for more than half a day, so he had no real hands-on experience. He had no knowledge of the technicalities of farming; fertilizer, weed control, the *pH* balance of the soil, cultivation practices or any of the basic things.

"He simply had no idea what it took to run such a big operation. He didn't have a clue about the people we dealt with, contracts and futures, any of the marketing aspects. All he knew was that we had lots of land and money had always come easy and went easy for him. He wouldn't take any advice, especially from me. Worst of all, I had no idea how much he resented me and my relationship with Dad.

"One day he blindsided me when he started mouthing off, telling me I wasn't a Bates. He said I was just a bastard; a mistake our mother had brought with her. He said Dad had taken pity on me and adopted me and now I thought I ran the whole show, when rightfully none of the business belonged to me. I was nothing more than a hired hand.

"Those were fighting words and we had a rumble. I bested him in the fight, but it only fuelled his anger. He taunted me every chance he got. He was careful not to do it around Dad, but he got bolder. He started telling the guys around town that I wasn't really a Bates, just a bastard interloper. Most people in town knew him better than me. I'd never hung out around town. The businessmen, who knew me, thought he was an ass. The old-timers in the community knew how close Dad and I were, but the guys Gerard hung out with didn't.

"Sadly, he eventually poisoned my sisters against me, and they began to see me in the same light. In a way, I'd always been an outsider. That was partly because of the age difference, but also because I always worked and didn't hang out with them."

Christina felt sick for him. "What spoiled brats. Did they ever realize how wrong they were?"

Tim shook his head. "No. Three years after Mom died, Dad was killed in a car accident. I think Gerard believed he would simply push me out. None of us knew what Dad had stipulated in his will until it was read. He made it clear that the decision-making for the working operation and the financial end of the business was to be left to me. Every year, we would each get an equal amount, according to what would be determined to be in the best interests of the business, by the legal entity he had appointed as his executor."

"I'm sure that was like throwing gasoline on hot coals," Christina murmured.

"More like nuclear war. The farm and the equipment, and the solid reputation of Bates Seed and Grain Farms Ltd. were worth several million and would have provided a nice profit for all of us for years. The girls didn't want anything to do with the farm; they just wanted their share of the money as soon as they could get their hands on it. Gerard didn't want to run the farm either. He just wanted the money and the recognition and prestige of being a Bates. Above all, he wanted to get rid of me. They were six against one and they went to court to overthrow the will. They won and the farm was sold to a big syndicate

"The Bates family played the *Bastard* card to the hilt and no one can convince me that people don't still see an illegitimate kid in that way. They threw it in my face all the time. The trial was big news in the area because Dad and the business were respected and well-known. The media interviewed Gerard. He played the big shot and told everyone that I wasn't a Bates, just a bastard child who Mom and Dad had adopted. For a week or so, the family feud was hot news. The ugliness of it was on TV, radio and even in the paper."

Christina gasped. "Tim! How could they do that? You could've sued them all for defamation of character."

"It literally made me ill. I was so angry, so embarrassed, so humiliated and empty: I sunk into depression. In fact, I pretty much lost it. There were times when I seriously thought it would be best to end it all. At times, I could even imagine killing Gerard.

"The lawyer for the company was a good friend of mine. He made me realize what was happening to me and convinced me to go for help. I owe him big time, because the way I was feeling, I can't be sure what I might have done. The biggest thing in my favor was that I wasn't violent by nature, but my whole world was falling apart. I'd lost both my parents, and now everyone I'd considered family had turned on me and wanted to strip me of my identity, my life work, my greatest passion.

"I thought it couldn't get worse, but I was wrong. My wife filed for divorce. The marriage had never been great, but all of the gossip and media coverage didn't help. I know living with my depression had to have been a nightmare for her. Up until the farm sold, I had no liquid assets because Dad had created a limited company and she couldn't touch it. Suddenly the door was open for her to grab a piece of the action, and God help me, she did. When I came here, she was still putting the squeeze on me, trying to wring out the last drop of blood.

"After working almost nonstop for seventeen years, putting everything I had into a business that I'd loved with all my soul and growing it into a multi-million dollar company, the amount I came away with was barely enough to cover my deal with Colt when I bought Bob's shares in the farm. I admit it left me feeling bitter."

Christina was silent. She thought back on her initial reaction to Tim when he'd come to town; how she had judged him to be a cold and distant person, how he'd seemed so flat to her, how defensive he'd been. She had wholeheartedly disliked him, even called him a *cold fish*. Hearing his story now, she felt guilty. She knew better than to judge people, but she'd judged him.

She pushed herself up on her elbow and leaned over him so she could look into his eyes. "I'm sorry, Tim, and I am so humbled. I admit, I did judge you by what I saw when you came to town." She closed her eyes and shook her head. "Why don't we ever learn that there are usually reasons for people to react the way they do? We should never jump to conclusions because we haven't walked in their shoes." She leaned in and kissed him gently. "You are an amazing man, Tim Bates, and you have support from your friends here. None of us would turn our backs on you like that."

She laid her head on his chest, her hair spreading out across it. Gradually he relaxed and inhaled the scent of lilacs, and then wrapped his arms around her and pulled her close. They fell asleep.

CHAPTER SIX

At the Maple Creek Hospital, Colt watched the STARS air ambulance crew secure Ellie on the gurney and put her into the helicopter.

The gravity of her situation had hit home for her now, and she was frightened. She'd plead for Ollie to go with her, and the staff agreed, knowing it would be best for both. The hospital staff at Maple Creek had stabilized her condition, and the STARS attendants were trained to hospital standards and had the best cardiac monitoring equipment on board.

Ollie sat down beside her and held her hand. The attendants had hooked her up to an oxygen supply and she had an intravenous tube running into a vein. He had listened, but had not retained the knowledge of the litany of drugs they administered. There was something to break down blood clots, and they'd given her nitroglycerin and he heard something about beta blockers to slow the heartbeat and something to take away the pain. He was certain of nothing now. All he knew for sure was that the only woman he'd ever loved was in a desperate state and he couldn't bear to lose her. They'd only had four wonderful years together, and he wanted to spend at least another couple of decades with her.

Ellie squeezed his hand. "I love you," she whispered. "I'll be alright, thanks to you, Colt, and Frank for insisting that we go to the hospital when we did; things might not have gone so well if we'd waited like I wanted to."

He gave her a strained smile. "You've been stubborn as long as I've known you. I'm counting on you putting that stubbornness to good use now. You just direct all that energy into getting well. I'm going to take good care of you when we get back home. No more fats, bacon, milk, and sugar. We are going to walk every day and we'll get an exercise bike. It's a good thing the kids are done their lessons for this school term because you need time to rest. And I'm going to tell Colt I need to retire now."

She smiled and tapped his hand gently. "Ollie! We have to *live*. I'll go crazy if you hover over me all the time. We'll do what needs to be done, but we can't live in fear that something will go wrong all the time."

Ollie's eyes filled with tears. "This business scared the *bejeezus* out of me. I don't want to do it again, Ellie." He bent down and kissed her hand. "I love you, girl."

"I know that, hon."

When they landed at the Regina General Hospital an hour and fifteen minutes later, Ellie's pain had subsided completely and she was embarrassed, thinking to herself that they had all made a big fuss about nothing. When she voiced her thoughts, the emergency team assured her that she needed to be there, and then they wheeled her into the emergency department and processed her into the system.

She changed into an RGH hospital gown and housecoat. The hospital clothes she'd worn from Maple Creek were put in a plastic bag and given to Ollie. There was a quick consultation with the STARS team when they gave the emergency staff the paperwork. Grumbling, Ellie signed a consent form for the doctors to do whatever procedures necessary, and they whisked her off to cardio-sciences.

Ollie was directed to the reception area in the Cardio-Sciences Department. He went to the desk and asked if he could go in with his wife. He was told him that he would have to take a seat and wait. Someone would let him know what was happening as soon as possible.

The receptionist watched his eyes get watery as he turned away and walked dejectedly to a chair against the wall. She witnessed this daily and recognized his anxiety. Her heart always went out to the people who waited there. She was certain that in many ways, it was harder for the one who sat helplessly waiting and drowning in the fear of the unknown, than it was for the one caught in the throes of the drama. No matter how bad the patient's situation, they were in the moment. If they were conscious, they knew what was happening, and action was more comforting than helplessly waiting, filled with dread.

Ellie's world became a flurry of activity. As soon as she reached the Cardio Department, they moved her to a narrow examination table near an ECG machine. They had hooked her up to one at the hospital in Maple Creek and it had spewed out a chart that she didn't understand, but the squiggly lines on it had caused enough concern that they had decided to fly her to Regina.

As the technician placed the adhesive electrodes on her chest and arms and legs, Ellie spoke softly. "They already did this in Maple Creek."

The woman smiled. "We have their report, but we're going to do it again and see if there has been any change since then."

Ellie frowned. "It's only been a couple of hours. What could change?"

"Your doctor will explain all this to you. I'm only the technician who runs the machine."

In spite of her brave assurances to Ollie, Ellie was nervous. Uncertainty and fear had begun to creep in when the doctor on call had decided to fly her to Regina. She had protested, saying that she and Ollie could drive there and she needed to go home first and get some of her personal effects before they left. He had assured her that Ollie could go with her in the helicopter and he could buy whatever she needed in Regina. He'd looked into her eyes and told her that her situation was serious and she needed to get to Regina as soon as possible to prevent more damage to her heart. At that moment, she'd faced reality; something was very wrong. She didn't want to worry Ollie more, but she knew she had to do what she was told.

They sent her to another department after the ECG was complete She looked at the sign. It read Cardiac Catheterization Laboratory. *Catheterization, what the heck?* All she could think of was urinary catheterization, which was what they had done to her first husband before he died. A chill ran through her.

Gloria Antypowich

When the surgeon came to see her, she asked him the questions swirling in her mind. Why had she needed the second ECG? And why were they going to put a catheter in her?"

Reassuringly, he laid a hand on her shoulder. "The ECG taken in Maple Creek only revealed the heart rate and rhythm at the time that it was taken. If intermittent abnormalities are present, the ECG was likely to miss them, so we wanted to check again."

"And?" Ellie asked.

"The results of the blood tests and the ECG indicate that you've had a myocardial infarction."

"Can you tell me what that means in layman's terms?"

He smiled. "Mrs. Crampton, you've had a heart attack, so now we're going to take measures to reduce the risk of another one."

Ellie's eyes shimmered with tears. "I…I'm not in pain now. Are you sure there isn't some mistake?"

"There is no mistake. The fact that you are not in pain right now is not uncommon. It can come back anytime, and without taking action it can be worse than you ever imagined."

"I never dreamt…" She swallowed hard.

"Few people do unless they've had some experience with this kind of situation, but you'll be fine. We're going to do a relatively simple procedure known as an angioplasty to remove the blockage." He put a piece of paper with a simple diagram of a human body in front of her. "This should help explain what we're going to do." He touched his pen to a point near the groin and traced a line from there to the heart, as he proceeded to tell her in simple terms what they were going to do.

Ellie swallowed hard. "It sounds pretty complicated to me."

He squeezed her shoulder gently. "Cardiac catheterization is very specialized and my team is second to none. I assure you that you are in good hands, Mrs. Crampton. You'll be awake during the procedure, but we'll give you a mild sedative to ensure that you are relaxed and comfortable. We do this all the time, so you have nothing to worry about."

Ellie nervously licked her lips. "How long will it take?"

"Anywhere from thirty minutes to an hour, depending on what we find. Now, do you have any other concerns?"

Ellie shook her head.

"Alright, let's get at it."

Forty-five minutes later, Ellie was taken to ICU. She was awake, but so relaxed from the mild sedation, that she felt very tired. Ollie was at her side as soon as the ICU nurse allowed him in. Ellie smiled at him with love in her eyes. "Have you talked to the doctor?" she asked.

He shook his head. "The nurse said you have to lay flat on your back and move as little as possible until tomorrow. They don't want the artery to start bleeding."

Ellie frowned. "What artery? Why would the artery bleed? How would they know? He said it was a simple, risk-free procedure." There was panic in her voice.

"Ellie, I don't think it's anything to do with the heart. She told me they'd made a small cut in your groin to put in a catheter or something and it has to seal itself. You are not supposed to lift anything heavier than five pounds for the next week."

"Oh...yes. That makes sense. I remember now, they went into the artery in the groin." She sighed. "For a moment, that scared me." She yawned. "I'm tired Ollie. I think I need a nap."

"It's been a long day for you," Ollie replied. "I'll sit here and watch over you."

Later the nurse noticed they were both asleep, holding hands.

At five o'clock that evening, the CIU nurse stepped in and gently touched Ollie's shoulder. He was startled and looked around groggily. "I fell asleep!" he exclaimed with disbelief. "What's wrong?" He sat up and looked at the bed, panic in his eyes. "Ellie? Is she alright?"

The nursed touched his shoulder reassuringly. "She is doing fine and you both needed some rest. I just came to tell you that there is someone at reception, looking for you."

"For me? Who would that be?" He frowned.

The nurse smiled kindly. "A tall man, with incredibly green eyes, and pretty auburn-haired woman and a boy and a girl."

Ollie relaxed and smiled. "That is Colt and Frank! They must have left as soon as he got home from Maple Creek. Man, a guy can't ask for better friends than that." He stood up and looked at Ellie lovingly, bent to drop a light kiss on her hair, then turned to go out to see them.

When he walked into the waiting room, Selena and Sam rushed forward and reached up to hug him. "Is she okay?" they asked in loud whispers.

Ollie hugged them close. "She's sleeping right now," he whispered back. "But I'm sure they took good care of her and she'll be okay." He stood up, taking each of their hands as he walked the few steps to Colt and Frank.

Colt reached out, patting his back as he embraced him. Ollie hugged him back, grateful for the comforting touch. His eyes filled with tears as he turned to Frank, who dropped a quick kiss on his cheek while she wrapped her arms around his slender form. She felt the wetness of them as they coursed down his weathered skin. "Everything will be okay, Ollie," she whispered softly. "She's in good hands here and we'll make sure she follows doctor's orders when she gets home."

Emotion overwhelmed Ollie and he couldn't smother the sob that escaped. "You don't know how much I appreciate you coming here so soon. This has been the worst day of my life. I couldn't go with her, so I had to sit in the waiting room while they took her away. I suddenly realized how alone I am and I was a scared old man. I felt like a lost kid in a strange country." He wiped his eyes with his shirt sleeve. "I love that ranch; it's truly my home. And except for Ellie, you guys are my only family."

He looked at Colt, his heart in his eyes. "You're like a son to me. I apparently have another one out there somewhere, but you are truly my *son*; the one I share my thoughts with, work with and love like my own. Frank, I couldn't be prouder if you were my flesh and blood, and I couldn't love you more. And those two kids are my grandchildren in my heart."

Frank reached out and squeezed his hand. "Ollie, you mean just as much to us. You are an unequivocal part of our family. I'll tell you honestly, Sam and Selena see you and Ellie more as grandparents than they do their other ones. Family knows no boundaries, Ollie. It's based on sharing and caring and trust and togetherness."

Ollie's open display of emotion was uncharacteristic. He wasn't one to voice his feelings, even though they all knew he cared. Colt and Frank looked at each other, knowing that the events of the day had shaken him to the core.

"Have you had anything to eat, Ollie," Frank asked.

Ollie looked at her blankly at first, and then shook his head. "I wanted to be here when Ellie came out of surgery, so I didn't go anywhere."

"Can I go in to see her?"

"Sure, go ahead. She was still sleeping when I came out here."

When Frank stepped into the ICU, she could see Ellie talking to a nurse in one of the rooms. Ellie's eyes brightened when she recognized Frank and she was smiling as she said something to the nurse, who turned to look. She stepped out of the room and greeted Frank. "Mrs. Crampton would like to see you. She had a procedure about two and a half hours ago, and she's not allowed to move around or sit up for a few hours yet. You can stay for a couple of minutes."

Frank thanked the nurse and smiled at Ellie when she stepped into her room. "How are you doing?" she asked as she went to the bed and kissed her cheek. "You're looking good; better than you did when I last saw you this morning. You were in so much pain."

"I have to thank you and Colt. Ollie tried to persuade me to go, but I was sure it was just indigestion. I thought you had a heavy, squeezing pain in your chest if you were having a heart attack. I expected a pain running down my left arm into my fingers. It turns out that those are only a couple of the symptoms that may show up. There are a lot of others that are easy to miss unless you are very aware. I got a real education about the old ticker today!"

"What did they do, Ellie?"

"They did blood tests, an ECG and then they did an angioplasty and put in a stent. I was awake, but they gave me a light sedative to relax and I honestly, don't remember too much. You might know more about that than I do. Colt's dad had a heart attack, didn't he?"

"Yes, he had three. The third one was massive and he didn't live, but they did do an angioplasty after the second one."

Ellie frowned. "He had one after the angioplasty? So it isn't necessarily a cure?"

"Ellie, I'm not an expert on heart disease, but I know Colt's dad had a lot of other problems too and he wasn't very good at following doctor's orders."

She could read Ellie's concern and regretted that her response had created unease. *She doesn't need that right now,* she thought with anxiety. She tried to change the subject. "It's a beautiful day, Ellie. It's sunny and warm. The leaves will be popping out everywhere pretty soon. We were noticing how the grass is coming up now. We left shortly after Colt got home this morning. He brought Ollie's truck, so he has a way to get around town and I followed with ours. The kids are with us. They were hoping they'd get to say hi to you, but I did warn them that they might not be allowed to."

Ellie's smile brightened. "I'd love to see them. Let me ask the nurse if they can come in, just for a minute."

The nurse was hesitant, but did agree to let the twins slip in and say a quick hello, reminding them that Ellie wasn't allowed to sit up or move around in the bed. The twins were very careful not to make her move, but they each squeezed her hand and told her to get better soon. They all left when the nurse came to take Ellie's vital signs and check the pressure pad on her groin.

Colt and Ollie had decided they would both say a quick hi to Ellie and then everyone would go out for supper. Ollie was feeling less forlorn and emotional, and suddenly he realized that he was hungry.

After supper, they got a motel rooms for Ollie and one for the Thompsons. Ollie bought a bouquet of flowers for Ellie, and he and Colt went up to the hospital to check on her. They found her sound asleep, so Ollie left the flowers and gave the nurse the phone number at the hotel and his room number. It had been a long day for all of them and they went to bed early.

Colt and Frank stayed with Ollie until they felt certain that Ellie was safe. At the end of the second day, everyone was ready to go back home, so they left the next morning. On the way, they stopped at the farm to see Tim. They found him at the shop, fine tuning a few small problems on the seeder.

Frank offered to go into the house to make coffee while Colt and Tim talked farming. While Colt's first love was ranching, he'd grown up on this farm, and worked there with his dad and then operated it himself for several years after his dad's heart attack. He knew the land and the equipment intimately and he and Tim could almost read each other's thoughts.

Frank put the coffee pot on and went out to the truck to get some squares and cookies that she had bought when she'd shopped for groceries in Regina. She put them on a plate and placed three cups and glasses for the twins on the table. She wandered around the kitchen and living room remembering the years she and Colt had lived there. Colt had grown up in this house, and they had started their marriage here with the twins. The place held many wonderful memories.

She stepped into the office and looked around the familiar room. Tim had some magazines on the desk, and his laptop was sitting there. There were a few open envelopes piled next to it along with other things anyone would expect in an office, but two did catch her eye. A picture of a young boy who looked like Tim with a man and a woman, set on one corner of the desk. She picked it up and studied it. Tim was about the age that the twins were now. They made a nice family. Something about the woman caught her attention. She almost seemed familiar, but Frank couldn't place her so she put the picture back in place.

She leaned across and reached for a picture that lay on the desk at the corner of his laptop. She smiled as she picked it up. It was a picture of Christina taken at a wiener roast at the ranch the previous fall. She chuckled and put it back where it had been.

She could hear the twins playing on the deck and she saw Colt and Tim coming up the sidewalk, deep in conversation. She poured a glass of milk for each of the twins and put the coffee pot on the table.

When they came in everyone sat around the table and started to talk. Then Sam piped up and said, "Ellie had a heart attack."

Tim looked embarrassed. "I should have remembered." He looked at Frank. "You said Colt and Ollie had taken her to Maple Creek when I called Saturday morning. Was it serious?"

"Bad enough," Colt answered. "They brought in the STARS helicopter and flew her to Regina. Her left aorta was totally blocked. They did an angioplasty and put in a stent. There were two other lesser blockages, but I think they decided to treat them with medication rather than angioplasty."

Tim was thoughtful. "She's not really the type you would think of having a heart attack."

Frank sighed. "She'd been complaining about feeling tired for the past month, and last week she just wasn't herself. I was concerned about her, but I couldn't pinpoint what was happening, and of course she was in total denial."

"Poor Ollie" Colt added. "He really took it hard. He waited all these years to fall in love and seeing her like that scared him half to death. I really felt sorry for him."

"You know my dad never got over losing Mom. He was a workaholic and he loved the farm, but when Mom died, he lost interest in everything. He was killed in a car accident three years later, and to be honest I always felt it shouldn't have happened. I think he just wasn't paying attention."

"After seeing Ollie this weekend, I think he'd be the same way. He has no other family. Well, he supposedly has a son, but he has no idea where he is or who he is. That's been tough on him too. I think he was pretty wild and footloose when he was young.

"He only talked about his childhood once and it sounded pretty tragic. His dad left and his mother pawned Ollie off on her brother, who treated him like shit and used him for child labor. He's been on his own since he was fifteen. He's been with us for fifteen years. That's probably longer than he's been anywhere. We are his family now."

CHAPTER SEVEN

Tim felt restless after Colt and Frank left. The picture he had seen on Ollie's desk haunted him He needed answers for his own peace of mind, but he understood the position Ollie was in. He couldn't demand answers while the older man was dealing with his wife's health problems. Not now...not until Ellie had time to get back on her feet.

He went into his office and sat behind his desk. He picked up the picture that sat on the corner and studied it. For the life of him, he couldn't find any answers. The fact that he'd found her picture on Ollie's desk made no sense.

He put it back in its place, before picking up the picture he had taken of Christina last fall. He'd always liked this picture of her. It was taken at night, with the light of the fire dancing on her hair, and revealing her laughing eyes and her infectious smile. She was holding a can of Canadian beer in one hand and a loaded hot dog in the other. He had printed it, and intended to frame it, but had never gotten around to it.

This was the Christina he knew, the one who had become his friend. The woman who was gutsy enough to admit she had feelings for him and lured him out of his self-imposed exile. She had reawakened a fire in him that he'd thought he'd smudged out several years ago. She was the woman he'd told his deepest, most painful secrets to while she lay naked against him. At this moment, she was the woman that he wanted to hold again, and the friend he needed to talk to. He picked up the phone and dialed *Swift Current Accounting and Bookkeeping Services*.

"Good afternoon." She spoke in her professional voice. "Is this Mr. Timothy Bates?"

He chuckled. "Sorry, you can't trust call display."

"Oh," she said softly. "So is this Tim or Loverboy?"

"Well, Tim wants to take you out for supper."

"And...?"

"And Loverboy would like to spend the night."

"I like the way they both think. What's the occasion?"

"Tim wants to talk to his friend; Loverboy wants to see if lightning strikes in the same place twice."

Christina giggled. "I already feel the sizzle. What time shall we meet?"

"Why don't you go home after work? If I get there before you do, I know how to get in, unless you moved the key."

"I kind of enjoyed having my house invaded the other night." She chuckled.

"See you later, my beautiful lilac."

Tim was waiting for her when she got home. To her surprise, the aroma of coffee greeted her as he opened the door to let her in. He wrapped his arms around her and inhaled the smell of her hair, enjoying the feel of her body against his. Then he kissed her.

When they came up for air, she leaned back and looked at him. One word fell from her lips. "Coffee?"

"Yes, Tim made it. He wants to talk to you before we go out to supper. He thought that wine might make him lose concentration, and Loverboy's sure there won't be any time for friend talk when we get back here. So take off your jacket and Tim will pour you a cup of coffee."

She shook her head and smiled. "Okay, Tim, what's the occasion?"

"I missed my friend. Also, Colt and Frank and the twins stopped by today."

"And?" She looked at him curiously.

"They were on their way home from Regina. Last Saturday,

Ellie had a heart attack. Colt and Ollie took her to the hospital in Maple Creek early that morning. They brought in the air ambulance and flew her to Regina and Ollie went with her. Colt drove his truck to Regina and Frank followed in theirs. They spent Sunday and Monday there with Ollie."

Christina looked stunned. "I'd never have expected that to happen to her. She watches what she eats, she's active and she's slim."

"Heart disease seems to be no respecter of persons."

"That's true." She looked at Tim. "I imagine they're all pretty shook up."

"Yeah. They said Ollie took it hard. It really scared him."

Christina looked thoughtful. "It'll probably be a while before you can talk to him about the picture,"

"I know. I'm not insensitive to their feelings, but I can't just drop it, either."

"I understand. Is there another way of approaching it?"

"Since I have no idea what it's about, I don't see how else I can do that."

"What if we posted the picture on the internet? Or, we could do a search for your mother's maiden name? We might come up with some information."

"I don't want to put her picture out there, but we could do a search. I hadn't thought of that."

Christina finished her coffee and smiled at him. "OK, Loverboy. Where are you taking me for supper...or was that Tim's idea?"

He picked up her cup and rinsed it off in the sink, along with his own. He grinned as he turned to look at her. "It was Tim's idea."

"Uhmm...I'm looking forward to that. Where are we going?"

He was at her side in an instant, pulling her into his arms. "Loverboy thinks we should have an appetizer first," he whispered as he nuzzled her hair.

"An appetizer?"

"I know the perfect place..." His meaning was clear, and she felt his arousal straining against his jeans as he held her against him.

She blushed. "Down the hall?"

His hungry mouth ravaged hers as he swept her into his arms and carried her to the bedroom. He uttered a throaty moan, as he stood her on the floor, then cradled her face in his hands and looked deep into her hazel eyes.

"How could I have been so blind, for so long?" He kissed her feverishly again. "I've been such an idiot."

He pressed her head against his chest as he held her close. She could feel the pounding of his heart as she kissed his chest again and again, then slipped her arms around him and ran her hands over his back, kneading gently.

He undid the buttons on her blouse one by one, his fingers caressing her softly with each touch. He kissed her throat, as he slipped the blouse off her shoulders, and down her arms.

Christina marveled at his gentleness. Suddenly everything seemed to be in slow motion. He undid her bra and slid it away, then stood back and looked at her. His eyes explored her voluptuous breasts, examining them as he might have a fine painting. "You're beautiful, Chris." He said softly. "I love your curves. You are so soft and feminine."

Christina swallowed hard and she fought a flood of tears. At five-foot-eight-inches, she was not a small woman and she was not slender like Frank. She weighed one-hundred-sixty pounds, but she was firm and athletic. She knew she looked good, but she'd never thought of herself as being feminine, the way she saw Shauna Lee to be. She searched Tim's face and saw his sincerity.

She smiled and reached out to him. "Thank you," she whispered. "No one has ever told me that before."

"Then they were blind," he said softly

Later, they lay tangled on the bedcover, slick with perspiration and pleasantly exhausted. Tim ran his fingers through her shoulder-length hair. Christina lay with her cheek on his chest. "Is this too good to be true?" she asked.

"No. This is destiny, my love.

She rose up on her elbow and looked at him. "You have changed overnight, Tim." She reached out and touched his face. "Your expression is different now. You have an inner glow."

"Give me a break," he laughed. "Pregnant women have that."

She sat up and slapped him playfully. "No, seriously. There's happiness in your eyes. You look relaxed and…how do I explain it? You're just different."

He grabbed her hand and pulled her down across his chest. "I *am* different. I'm in love."

"A few days ago you were shocked and wanted to take it slow."

He grinned. "Look gorgeous, I was in denial. I swore I'd never go this route again. I was shocked, but now I realize that I've loved you for months. I can't tell you exactly when it happened, but even last fall, I think I knew on some level. I took a picture of you at the wiener roast at the ranch. I uploaded it to my computer and printed it off. I was always going to frame it, but I never got it done. I had it with my things in the office and I looked at it once in a while. I had thought of you as a friend, but Brad and Colt are my friends, and I don't have any pictures of them lying around."

"Isn't it amazing, how a different perspective can make you see things in a totally different light. For years, I've been paralyzed by the fact that I can't have a child. After the way my marriage ended, I couldn't see anyone loving me for me…"

"Chris, that is so crazy. Did your ex leave you because you couldn't have children?

"It was his excuse, but I was up front about it when we were married. I found out when I was sixteen I couldn't have kids."

"What happened when you were sixteen?" When she hesitated to answer, he cupped her face. "This is me, Chris. I don't care if you can't have a baby. And if we really wanted one, we could adopt."

"I have MRKH syndrome."

"What does MRKH stand for?"

"Mayer-Rokitansky-Küster-Hauser syndrome."

"That's a mouthful. Is it very common?"

"Not really, but it's not as unusual as you might think. About one in five thousand women are born with it; some statistics say one in seven-thousand. Typically, you are born without a fully developed uterus and vagina, but can still have fallopian tubes and functioning ovaries, which is what happened to me. It can cause abnormalities in the urinary tract and kidneys, and sometimes it causes spinal problems too. Thank god, I was spared those problems."

"Chris, I had no idea."

"We didn't either, but I wasn't having my period by the time I was sixteen. All the other girls my age were and everyone else was talking about what a pain it was, when I hadn't even started. I felt weird. Mom took me to see her doctor and they discovered that I didn't have a normal vagina. It was only about an inch deep.

"He sent me to a gynecologist who ordered a sonogram. It showed that my uterus was about the size of a walnut and it wasn't connected to my deformed vagina. There was no cervix either. However, I had ovaries, as well as fallopian tubes that just sort of went nowhere. They did a bunch of tests and determined that although my ovaries were working, I would never be able to have a baby. At that time, I didn't care too much about it; I just knew I wasn't normal and I felt like some kind of a freak.

"I didn't tell anybody; my sister didn't even know. I pretended I was just like the rest of my friends. Only Mom, Dad, and the doctors knew what the real deal was. When I was seventeen, the Gyno sent me to a specialist who did the surgery to lengthen my vagina so I could have normal sex."

"How did they do that?"

She wrinkled her nose. "I'm not sure. I had a small incision near my belly button and a couple more in my belly. That happened more than twenty years ago and at the time, the whole idea of even needing it just sort of grossed me out. All I remember is that it took a couple of hours, and it didn't take very long to heal. I was back to school in a week. I never dated. Guys at school asked me out, but I was so freaked about the vagina thing, I always said no. Eventually, I got a reputation for being weird; which I guess I kind of was."

"So, when did you meet the guy you married?"

"After I graduated, I worked as a waitress for the summer. I'd seen Dave Isanov around town before, and he started coming into the restaurant every day. It wasn't long before he began hitting on me and then he asked me out. He worked at one of the mills in Swan River. He was good looking and he treated me nice.

"Anyway, the doctors had assured me that I'd be like anyone else as far as sex went, so I finally went out with him. Not that I intended to go to bed with him right away, but from what the girls at school said, all the guys expected you to put out. We dated for a couple of months before we got to that. I got an apartment of my own when I started college. It wasn't long after that when we had sex. The first time I was scared shitless. I had no idea what to expect. I didn't know if I'd be different than other girls, but it turned out okay, and he didn't drop me like a hot potato.

"We'd gone together four months when I told him I couldn't have kids. He was twenty-three then, and he wasn't thinking about a family. He insisted it didn't matter, and, to be honest, I don't think it did matter to him, then. He gave me a ring for Christmas and asked me to marry him. We were married by a marriage commissioner on the fourteenth of January. I was nineteen and he was twenty-three.

"A few months later, his best friend told him that his girlfriend was pregnant. Dave laughed and told me he felt sorry for John. He was convinced Karry had gotten pregnant on purpose, so she could trap him into marriage. Things seemed to be going well for us. I was going to college and he was still working at the mill.

"When Karry began getting thick in the waist he'd make remarks about how I'd never have to worry about losing my girlish figure; stuff like that. When she really started to show, he constantly threw digs at her about how big she was getting. It made me feel uncomfortable. One time John told him to put his hand on her belly and feel the baby kick. When he felt the movement, it really turned Dave on. Then his conversations started to be about how we'd never know what it was like. Eventually, they got more edgy, about how *I* couldn't have a baby."

Tim squeezed her close. "What an insensitive jerk."

"The baby was a boy. When it was born, John was as proud as punch. Dave was fascinated with the child. He held him every chance he could, and I began to realize that he was almost jealous of John and Karry. I became insecure and I started gaining weight. He started making nasty remarks about it, and a few times, he reminded me that I had no reason to gain weight because I couldn't get pregnant. The more anxiety I felt, the more weight I gained. Then he'd make snide remarks, began calling me 'the barren'; it hurt and my self-confidence took a nosedive.

"Gradually, more of his friends started having families and his resentment grew. I heard him tell one of them that I was a non-breeder and another time he called me a barren cow. I was so humiliated; I couldn't face them anymore."

"Christina, what kind of so-called friends would let him talk that way about you. They were as sick as he was. Someone should have cold cocked him."

She nodded. "The guys were his friends before I came along and he worked with them, too."

"But the women? What was wrong with them?"

"I guess they didn't want to rock the boat. I began to say I was busy and couldn't go when we were invited out. Pretty soon he was going out on his own all the time, and I had no idea where he went or what he did. Our relationship was so strained by then, I was happier if he wasn't around.

"I'd finished college two years after we were married and I'd been working at a local business for almost two years when suddenly, his attitude got cockier. There was a spring in his step and he was happy with the world.

"They say the wife is always the last one to know and in my case that was true. I suspected he was having an affair, and I pretty much expected him to leave me. What I hadn't expected, was to learn his girlfriend was four months pregnant when he left.

"He couldn't just go and leave me with some shred of dignity. He bragged about his new woman and the baby. That hurt, but his final insult before he walked out the door, was to tell me that nature had a way of taking care of itself and the big guy upstairs had known how useless I was, so he'd neutered me so there wouldn't be any more bitches like me."

Tim cursed. "That lowdown fucker. Someone should have castrated him."

"I was devastated. I couldn't face anyone. I handed in my resignation. When I gave it to my supervisor, she asked me why I was leaving. I tried to make some excuse, but she was truly concerned about me. She had watched me deteriorate during the past months, and she'd heard gossip around town.

"I fell apart when she reached out to me, and I needed someone so badly. She asked me if I was going home to my parents. I told her I couldn't bear to do that. Our relationship had become strained over Dave. Mom and Dad didn't like him from the beginning. They felt he'd tried to isolate me from them; I realized later he had done just that. In the beginning, I'd been so awed a good looking man like him would want someone as defective as me, I'd have done anything for him so I turned my back on my family."

"That son of a bitch. Is he still alive? I'd like to get my hands on him." He pulled her against him.

"No, Tim. I've worked hard to forget that part of my life. You can't get involved and bring it all up again. Besides, Dave's fourteen-year-old son doesn't deserve to have his life turned upside down by something that happened before he was born. The whole thing is behind me now."

"That's not quite true; it isn't all behind you."

"Tim. I don't want to stir up the past. Nothing would be gained, except more pain."

He nodded.

She looked into his eyes and smiled. "Okay, Loverboy. Let's change this line of thought. Now that we've enjoyed the appetizer, don't we have reservations for supper?"

Tim grinned. "Yes, we do. I found this quaint place called Crawford House on the outskirts of town. It's classic and romantic and the food is reported to be fabulous."

"Crawford House. I've never heard of it, which is surprising, after all the years I've lived in Swift Current."

"It's out of the way, but I did some checking and I heard nothing but great things about it."

Crawford House was a beautiful old manor-style house surrounded by a veranda and a large lawn. The lights were dim, the setting romantic and comfortable. The food and service were great and they served specialty wines and draft beers. Soft music played in the background. When Christina finished her supper, she leaned forward and lifted her wine glass in a toast to Tim. "To my friend and lover. You have impressed my romantic soul tonight."

He touched his glass to hers. "To a night that's just begun," he promised.

Tim helped her get into his truck on the driver's side. He slid in right after her and snuggled her close to him, leaning over to kiss her on the lips. The kiss was tender and it stirred her emotions.

When Tim pulled away, she looked into his eyes and smiled. "Supper was wonderful, and so were you. I want to be with you this way, but doesn't this feel kind of weird out here in public? Not bad, just kind of strange. We've been friends so long; you sitting here, me over there. No tender touches, no sexy kisses, no snuggles: we've had two years of practicing friendship. It's going to take a while to feel *right* sitting here in the middle and showing my feelings! It's kind of like *Cripes, what will people think.*"

Tim laughed. "Chris, you might be amazed at how many people have wondered why we haven't gotten together before now. We've been good friends and we get along well. I'm sure no one else will be as shocked as we were. I doubt if anyone will be critical and most of them will be really happy for us."

Christina reached up and touched his cheek. "You've come a long way since last week."

He nodded. "I'd just never considered getting into a romantic relationship again. Now that it's on my radar, I'm like a heat-seeking missile, locked in and determined to hit the target. I can't get you off my mind, and the more I think, the stronger my feelings are and the more I want you with me. Like today after Frank and Colt left, I wanted to be with *you* and talk about what was happening with Ellie and Ollie. And, damn it, now I know that the bed is lonely and cold at night."

Christina giggled. "As I said before, you were the one who wanted to go slow."

He started the truck and eased out of the parking lot. "That was before I'd felt the heat."

CHAPTER EIGHT

The phone rang at Belanger Creek Ranch. Frank answered it and broke into a smile. When she disconnected the call, she turned to the twins. "Miss Ellie and Ollie are on their way home, kids."

"Goodie!" Sam exclaimed. "It seems like they've been gone forever! I can't wait to help her get started with the garden."

"Hold on cowboy. It's too early to plant seeds yet and besides that, Ellie just got out of the hospital. She's been really sick."

"Yes," Selena piped up. "Don't you remember how sick she was in the hospital?"

Sam scowled at his sister. "Yes, I know Ellie was sick."

Frank smiled. "I'm going to call Dad and tell him that they are coming home today." She dialed his cell and waited for him to answer.

"What's up?" he asked.

"Ollie and Ellie are coming home today. I thought I'd give you a heads-up. I'll make supper for them too, so she can just come home and rest."

"I'm headed over to pick up Grayson in the north pasture. We'll be home by mid-afternoon. See you then."

"Love you." She said softly.

"Back to you," he replied, a smile in his voice.

Ollie and Ellie arrived at the ranch at four-thirty that afternoon. Colt and Grayson drove in shortly after. Sam and Selena were running down the hill to see them before Frank got out the door. She could hear them screaming with excitement when she started down the hill. She met Colt and Grayson and they walked to the house together.

Ollie sat Ellie in a big chair, and the twins were on each side of her, vying for her attention. She was smiling happily, holding their hands as they each tried to talk louder than the other. Ollie shook his head when the adults arrived.

Frank gave him a hug. "How is she?" she asked.

Ollie smiled wearily. "The drive home tired us both out, but she's doing fine. The doctors are satisfied. She just needs to take it easy for a while."

Frank nodded, then walked over and hugged Ellie. Then she turned to the twins. "Okay guys, Ellie needs some quiet time now. She's had a long ride home and she needs to rest." The twins stepped back reluctantly, looking at Ellie uncertainly. Frank noted that she didn't protest and knew that she was more tired than she was willing to admit. "I've made supper for you and Ollie, too. You can come up or I'll have Colt bring it down here if that would be easier."

Ellie looked at Ollie. A look passed between them and Ollie asked Colt if he would bring the meal down to them.

"Sure thing, old timer. It's no trouble at all. I want you to take time to rest up, too. No work around the ranch for you for a while."

Ollie nodded in gratitude. "I want to be close to home this next while."

"Ollie, you are worrying too much," Ellie protested.

Colt smiled. "He's entitled, Ellie. You gave all of us a scare."

Colt noticed that Frank was quiet and thoughtful that evening. After they tucked the twins into bed, he pulled her into his arms and began nuzzling her ear and dropping kisses down her neck. When she didn't collapse into him, soaking up his caresses, he looked down at her questioningly. "You've been pretty quiet tonight. What's up?"

She shrugged "I'm just...I'm not into sex right now." She laid her head on his chest. "I just want to cuddle and feel you close. We have so much to be thankful for; each other, the twins, our life together." She shook her head and looked up at him. "Seeing Ollie and Ellie tonight really hit home. This took a lot out of both of them. I think Ollie has aged ten years. Did you notice?"

Colt answered soberly. "I noticed that both of them are showing the stress of what happened. She's his whole world. He'll do anything to protect her and he's going to be watching for the slightest hiccup with her for a long time now, afraid of the worst."

"We are going to have to watch out for him too. I'm shocked at how tired he looks. He almost seems fragile now."

"That's why I told him not to come to work for a while. Later, I'll find enough for him to do around the ranch to make him feel useful, but as far as I'm concerned Ollie is pretty much retired now. It took him so long to find someone he loves, I want him to make the most of his time with her, and I hope they have many years together."

"Ellie has had a setback, too. She's trying to act like she's fine and she was in denial about this whole thing when it first started, but she isn't now."

Colt took her by the hand and led her to the bedroom. They undressed and slid into bed, lying spooned together. "I love you," she whispered as she stroked his arm. "I want to always appreciate what we have. I think of what happened to your dad. When did you last go to the doctor for a physical? Not since we've been married. That's eight years, and way too long."

"I'm healthy as a horse, hon."

"No one ever thinks it will happen to them until something starts to show up. Then it may be hard to correct. I want you to go in. I'll make an appointment tomorrow."

He pulled her closer. "Now you're being a worry-wart, but I know you'll never give me any peace until I do it, so make the appointment."

She nodded. "I think we should phone Brad, Shauna Lee, and Tim and let them know that Ellie and Ollie are home. I think that we could invite everyone out to the ranch for the May long weekend. That's about three weeks away, so that'll give Ellie & Ollie time to recoup before everyone arrives. Everyone will want to see them."

"That sounds like a good idea. Maybe we could move the cattle out to the lease that weekend. Brad would enjoy the ride."

"So would Shauna Lee, but we need to find a babysitter for that weekend. Ellie shouldn't take on that much for a while, no matter

Gloria Antypowich

how much she insists she can. Patch and Leanne are way too active to saddle her with for the whole day, and I'm thinking that Selena and Sam will enjoy riding with us, so they won't be here to help out."

"I've been thinking, hon. Maybe we should look for someone else to help out around the house and yard for the summer. The twins are old enough to ride the range with us this summer and it's impractical for you to cook and clean when you work outside with me all the time. I think it's too much to ask of Ellie too. If she wants too and feels she still can teach the twins next fall, we'll stay with that program. But I think we should look for someone to help around the house and cook and clean for the crew."

Frank thought for a moment. "My first instinct is to say 'No' the way I did when you first wanted to hire Ellie. But, you were right about that and I have to agree, having someone else around would take the pressure off of me and Ellie. The new person could live in the suite we made for Ellie behind the house. That will give everyone privacy and yet be efficient for us all."

"It's been on my mind since Ellie went to Regina. I'll get on it tomorrow."

"We could ask around again. Brad suggested asking Tim. Your mom put us in touch with someone who knew Ellie. Maybe Shauna Lee or Christina would have some ideas for this."

"Good thinking. We'll check with them, too."

Frank chuckled as she turned toward Colt. "Did I tell you what I saw in Tim's office when we stopped there on our way back from Regina?"

Colt grinned, noting the sparkle in her eyes. "Oh, oh...what did you see?"

"He's got a picture of Christina on his desk. I think it was taken here at the ranch last fall."

"So...?"

Frank gave him a gentle push. "So...why would he have a picture of her on his desk?"

"They're friends."

"Duuh! He doesn't have a picture of you or Brad."

"So, do you think something is going on between them?"

"Well, they're pretty comfortable together."

"That sneaky old dog. It's interesting though. They are both so casual, they never really show anything."

"Maybe they don't really admit it themselves, yet. They've been friends for so long, it would be a huge turnabout. I just found it kind of interesting. It looked like he'd printed it off. It was lying on the desk by his laptop." Frank's expression became thoughtful. "He had another framed photo on the corner of the desk. I think he was about eight or nine years old, and he was with his mom and dad. She was a pretty woman. It's crazy, but she seemed familiar to me. Have you ever seen his picture of her?"

"No. But you know, they say we all have a double somewhere."

The next morning Colt checked with employment services. Then he called Christina at *Swift Current Accounting and Bookkeeping Services.* "Is Shauna Lee in, Christina?"

"No. I think she's at home, Colt. Can I help you?"

Colt groaned. "Sorry, Christina. I'm sure you can; you know old habits die hard. You'd think after this long I'd remember you're the one to call. We've decided to hire someone to cook and do laundry and clean house and work around the yard here at the ranch. Ellie and Frank did that together before, but now I think it's too much to ask of Ellie, and Ollie needs time off to be with her.

"Frank's going to fill in for him, so she'll be outside most of the time. We need someone around the house to keep everything running smoothly. I phoned Employment Services, but nothing sounded promising. Can you do some checking for me? Maybe you'll hear about somebody locally. I'd like to fill the spot before the May long weekend."

Christina smiled, thinking about when they had checked out Tim. "Sure Colt. I'll put out the word and see what we can come up with. I think you're doing the right thing. How is Ellie, anyway?"

"They're both worn out by this whole thing. Ellie is putting on a good front, but she got a big wake-up call. It's hit them both hard. Ollie looks like he's aged ten years. He's worried about her and she's concerned about him. Frank suggested we might have a get-together on the long weekend in May and have all you guys come out. We'll wait and see how everything works out between now and then. We'll get back to you and the rest of the gang in ten days or so."

CHAPTER NINE

Christina dialed Tim's number as soon as Colt hung up.

"Hello there, beautiful."

She giggled. "Hi there, Loverboy. I just talked to Colt. Ellie and Ollie came home today."

"That's good to hear. How are they?"

"Colt said they're both exhausted. He says Ollie looks like he's aged ten years, but the doctors must have felt it was safe to send Ellie home."

"Yeah, but I can see how something like that would be emotionally exhausting for them."

"Colt and Frank are looking for someone to work around the house; cooking, cleaning, laundry, and some yard work He said both Ollie and Ellie need some time off, so Frank is going to work outside to take up the slack. If you hear of anyone, let me know."

"I'm glad to hear he's doing that. I'll keep an eye open. I should say I'll keep an ear open. I don't see many people out here on the farm. I'm in the shop most of the time now. I'll be starting to seed grain pretty soon."

"Aha, and the workaholic will re-emerge."

"For a few weeks, until I'm done; then things will be slower until it's time to spray the weeds. After that, it'll be time to hay and then it'll be harvest time. I'll still eat and sleep, but … I'd do everything better if you spent a few days a week out here."

"Oh…seducing me, are you? I just might get sucked in by your line."

"Can I come into town and take you out for supper tonight? I can work at perfecting my lines, maybe snuggle with you and uhh….well, who knows where things may lead." His voice was seductive and low.

"Right to my bed." she said with a giggle.

"I can hope."

"So what time are you coming in?"

"I'll meet you at the house when you get off work. We'll see what we can do about appetizers before we go out."

"Naughty, naughty!" she whispered and hung up the phone.

She was still smiling when she dialed Shauna Lee's number. When Shauna Lee answered, Christina knew she was having a hectic day. Christina chuckled. "What's going on, Mummy?"

Shauna Lee sighed. "Please drop the *mummy* bit! I've heard that all day. Patch is driving me nuts. Every five minutes it's 'Mummy I want this', or 'Mummy, Leanne has my truck' or 'Mummy, Leanne is doing this'. I totally love them both, but right now, I'm ready to pull my hair out. I need to hear someone call me girlfriend or sweetheart or something other than *mummy*."

"Well girlfriend, do you want me to come over. The rush for the tax deadline is over, and things are slower right now. It's eleven o'clock, so I could take off early for lunch and give you a break. We can just talk or even better, you can get out for an hour or so and I'll watch the kids. Get Brad to take you out for lunch."

"Don't tempt me!"

"I'm serious, Shauna. You know I love looking after them. They are the closest thing I'll ever have as children of my own."

"You've still got time Christina." Shauna Lee chuckled. "I think Tim is still available. He actually is a nice guy, and now that you two aren't hissing and scratching at each other all the time, you should consider it."

Christina bit her lip as she smiled to herself. *Oh yes, girlfriend. I have already considered it! I know how nice he is!* "Alright, you've done your thing as a matchmaker; now shall we deal with your problem? Why don't you make a lunch date with your husband, and

I'll let Carl know that I'm checking out early and head over to your place. "

"You twisted my arm. I must be PMS-ing today! Whatever: I'd appreciate getting out for a while. I'll see you in a few minutes."

When Christina rang the doorbell twenty minutes later, Patch and Leanne came running. She could hear Patch grumbling as he tried to open it, but before he succeeded, Leanne was there, too. "Mummy," Patch screamed. "Leanne won't let me open the door. She's in my way."

Christina could hear Shauna Lee's footsteps. "Okay guys, stop fighting. I'll open it."

Christina laughed as she reached to hug her friend. "I see what you mean! Take a break and I'll see if I can reprogram them." Patch was clinging to Christina's legs and pushing at Leanne to keep her away.

Shauna Lee rolled her eyes. "This has been going on since they got up this morning. I gave him a short time out in his room, but as soon as I let him out, it started all over again."

"I'll give them lunch and then see what I can do to change the tone of the day."

"I feel guilty leaving you with them like this. I just can't seem to get a grip on it this morning."

"It's got to be PMS. Go! You'll all feel better after having a break from each other."

Christina took Patch and Leanne by the hand and led them into the kitchen while Shauna Lee went into the bedroom to touch up her makeup and grab her purse. When she came back to the kitchen, Christina had put Leanne in her highchair and Patch was sitting on a stool by the island counter. She was telling them a story about a dog named Karma, who happened to be running around her feet.

"Christina is making us macaroni and cheese, Mummy," Patch said happily.

Shauna Lee shook her head. "I feel like a real loser. You've got everything under control already."

"You know better than that. You're a great mom. It's an age-old fact; kids always pull this crap on their mom because she's with them twenty-four hours a day and they've got her number. Mom walks out the door and the kids become angels because they aren't sure how far they can push the new person, even when they know them well."

"You know exactly what to say! Thanks, Christina."

"Oh! I forgot to tell you that Ellie and Ollie came home last night. Colt said she's doing okay, but they've both been hit hard by what happened. He said he's sure Ollie's aged ten years."

"I'm glad to hear they're home. We'll have to take a drive out to see them soon."

"Colt mentioned having us all come out to the ranch on the May long weekend. That'll give Ellie & Ollie time to rest up a bit. He'll give you a call later."

"That would be great. I'm on my way now and thanks, girlfriend."

"I almost forgot something else, too. Colt and Frank are looking for someone to take over in the house. Colt told Ollie to take some time off, so Frank will be working on the ranch with him and Grayson. If you hear about someone looking for work, let him know."

Shauna Lee nodded as she went out the door.

Christina entertained the kids with a story while she made lunch. After they finished eating, she decided to take them outside. They went to look at the horses and then played in the yard for a while before they went back into the house. She smiled as she watched Patch reach down to help his sister up the steps. The change in environment had derailed the irritation that had built during the morning, and Patch and Leanne were relaxed and companionable now.

Christina glanced at her watch. It was one-ten. She decided it was time to put Patch and Leanne down for a nap. If they were asleep, Shauna Lee would have a chance to relax before they got up.

The house felt like a quiet oasis when Shauna Lee got home. Christina had done the dishes and was watching TV. Shauna Lee smiled with appreciation. "I'm late, but you're covered. I stopped by the office and said hi to everyone. I told them you were being an angel and giving me a break. Carl said he'd cover the front desk until you got back."

"So did you enjoy your lunch with Brad?"

"Yes. We seldom get to do that...just the two of us. In fact, it probably hasn't happened since you last took pity on me. I'm fussy about who I leave them with. Leanne is still a baby and even Patch...I can't imagine leaving them with a twelve-year-old babysitter or some teenager who has her mind somewhere else. They are only this small for a short time. When I look ahead and realize that Patch will be in school in two years, it kind of freaks me out. I want to spend as much time as possible with them." She looked guilty. "But, there are days like today…you can't know how much I appreciated your intervention!"

"My pleasure. Like I told you, I love those kids like they are my own."

Shauna Lee laughed. "And like I told you, it's not too late for you. Look outside the box, Christina. Tim and you could be a great fit. You are so comfortable with each other and you are friends already."

Christina looked away. "Even if I did find a man, I'll never have children."

"Don't be silly. You were born to be a mother, Christina." Shauna Lee stopped short when she saw the shimmer of tears in her friend's eyes. "You…" Her words faded away.

Christina shook her head. "Shauna Lee, I…I can't have kids."

Shauna Lee sucked in her breath. "Oh. Oh Jeeze, Christina. I'm so sorry. Me and my big mouth. I had no idea."

"Other than you, very few people know. I've only told one other person in Swift Current. I was born with a deformed uterus. I can never carry a child." Tears spilled over onto her cheeks.

Shauna Lee reached out and enfolded her in her arms. "Oh Christina! Is there nothing…"

"No. I do have ovaries, but without a womb, I can't carry a baby." She smothered a sob. "I don't know why I'm crying now. I came to terms with it years ago. I seldom go there anymore."

"I'm so sorry I said anything…"

Christina shook her head, wiping her tears away. "You had no way of knowing. Thank you for letting me get my *Mummy fix* with your kids. You have no idea how much it means to me."

"Jeeze, Christina. I'm happy that they help you. I can't even imagine…"

Christina shook her head. "Let's drop this conversation. It changes nothing. I have to get back to work." She looked at Shauna Lee, appeal in her eyes. "Please don't tell anyone else. It's been my secret for so long. I fought with feelings of being a freak and less of a woman for so many years. I think I'm passed that now, but I still don't want everyone to know."

"I won't breathe a word. It's no one else's business. If it helps, you can talk to me, but I will never bring it up again. It'll be your call." She pulled her close and hugged her. "Oh, and for the record, you never were a freak and you are one of the most wonderful women I have ever met."

Christina was still feeling sober when she got to the office. Carl greeted her with a smile. "Hey, did the rug-rats get you down too? It sounded like Shauna Lee really appreciated the break."

"I guess Patch got out on the wrong side of the bed this morning. I gave them lunch and then we went for a walk. By the time we got back inside, he'd gotten his mind off the morning's tiff and everything was okay." She grinned. "They're just like us, you know. Good days and bad days."

"You're right. Oh… Tim Bates called for you. He didn't leave a message. He said he'd call back."

"Okay, maybe I'll call him and see what he wanted."

The call to Tim went to his answering service, so she just left a message saying she was returning his call and hung up. After some hesitation, she called her sister, Julie. She tapped on her tooth with the end of her pen while the phone rang a few times, and finally went to the answering machine. "Hi Julie, it's Christina here. Just wondering how you guys are doing. I'll give you a call later."

As she hung up the phone, her thoughts stayed with her sister. She had helped Julie plan her wedding eight years earlier. It had been a brief interlude in time when they had shared a measure of closeness as adults. She'd been five years old when Julie was born and she'd worshiped her baby sister. They'd been best buddies, but things had begun a natural change once she started school. Her world had expanded to include new friends and she spent less time with Julie. Julie had missed her immensely, but once she had started school, her world had expanded to include new people too.

Julie had matured quickly and she'd begun to menstruate at eleven years old. It had been like a knife in Christina's back. At sixteen, she was desperately anticipating the event and she had been sick with envy, unable to commiserate with her sister about 'the curse', which would have been a blessing to her.

After her mother had taken her to the doctor, and she'd faced the reality that she would never be like everyone else, she couldn't stifle the resentment that smoldered in her. From early adolescence, she had loved babies and dreamed of being a mother one day.

During the first year and a half, she'd felt that nature had cheated her. Nothing about her worked; she didn't have a normal vagina and her uterus was deformed and useless. At that time, she didn't realize how blessed she had been; some girls with reproductive issues never did develop breasts or hair in private places. It wasn't until she'd had her vaginal surgery that she realized that she had been fortunate in many ways. To all outward appearances, she had developed and matured nicely.

Her mother and father had respected her privacy and Julie had never known about her condition. Christina had held her sister at arm's length until just months before Dave Isanov humiliated her and shattered her world. Things weren't going right in her marriage and she had confided in Julie. However, the confidence didn't erase the years of hurt and anger that had accumulated in Julie's heart because of Christina's earlier rejection. Julie hadn't been able to see past her own feelings, to understand Christina's pain, and she'd offered no comfort.

By then, her relationship with her family was strained to the breaking point. Her parents had not approved of the marriage and they were convinced that Dave was keeping her away from them. Her own pride and lack of self-confidence kept her from admitting that her husband's attitude toward her was controlling and demeaning.

Later she'd realized that they were right, but her emotional vulnerability kept her from reaching out to them. When Christina left Swan River, she had shut her family out of her life. She'd come to Swift Current because her supervisor's parents had a house there, and their previous renters had left the month before. She was able to move in immediately and it had been a welcome refuge during that difficult time of her life. She rented the place for five years and then she'd bought it. That house was still her home.

Julie had married Jack Regeer when she was twenty-five. She had matured, and while she was looking forward to her own family, she had suddenly realized how devastating Christina's reality was. She had reached out to her then, asking her to be part of the bridal party, and to help plan the wedding. It had been bittersweet for Christina. There was comfort in reconnecting with her family, but painful to know that her own marriage had been a failure. Julie would undoubtedly have a family and live the life she had always dreamed of having.

It had been twice as difficult to return to Swan River for the weekend of the wedding. She had stayed close to her parents' home most of the time, hoping to avoid running into Dave and his family. As it turned out, she managed to do that. She'd run into a couple of his friends and their wives, but she'd been elusive, only having time to give them a quick waggle of her fingers as she passed by.

Her confidence had been boosted by the fact that she had lost forty pounds since she'd moved to Swift Current and she knew she looked stunning in her dress. She'd had her hair colored and streaked and cut and styled. She'd completed the polished look with a set of gel nails and a great pedicure. She was the only one who knew how hard she'd had to fight to keep a happy smile in place, or how she struggled to force the sparkle into her eyes.

Christina had survived the wedding, and when she left for home, Julie and her mother had pledged to keep in touch. But gradually, the everyday patterns slipped back into place and weeks and then months passed between phone calls. Christina knew communication was a two-way street, but she held back. She still felt like she was *less than* and found comfort in her isolation.

Two years later, Julie had phoned to tell her she was pregnant. Julie reached out to her with sincerity, and Christina felt it. Outwardly, Christina was appropriately happy and excited for Julie and Jack, but she struggled with the hollowness she felt in the secret depths of her soul. However, on the surface, she refused to let it show.

During the pregnancy, she listened to her mother's excited anticipation of her first grandchild. She bought baby clothes and attended the baby shower, and was in the delivery room when Joylin Emily was born. Tears rolled down her cheeks as she held her niece. Her heart warmed as she looked at the beauty in her arms, but a tiny piece of her died knowing she would never have her own.

Joylin Emily became the center of her grandparent's world. The happiness she brought them, compounded by the proximity of Julie and her husband, left Christina on the outer edges of everyone's consciousness. She could have become a part of the family if she had been proactive about it, but the remnants of her depression made it easier for her to curl inward.

The phone startled her from her reverie. She glanced at the call display as she picked up the phone. "Hi, Tim. Carl said you'd called."

"Yeah. I'm leaving for Swift Current in half an hour. Where shall we go for supper?"

"Let's meet at the house. Maybe we can have an appetizer."

"Top of the list--I'm expecting something hot and spicy."

"I'm drooling with anticipation. Hot and juicy..."

Tim groaned. "You're killing me. I'm on my way."

"Let me know when you're at the railroad tracks. I'll head home to meet you."

Christina's mind was not on her work. Talking with Shauna Lee and sharing the secret that had paralyzed her life in so many ways, was almost a relief. Knowing that she no longer carried it alone seemed to lighten the burden. Tim knew and now her best friend knew. They hadn't shrunk away or looked at her like she was defective. She wasn't going to go shouting it to the world, but she wasn't hiding in fear. Reaching out to Julie and rethinking their past, had given her fresh perspective.

She stood up and walked into Carl's office. "Things are quiet, Carl. I'm going to take the rest of the day off. In fact, I'll just book the whole day off as a holiday. I haven't been here in mind all day."

"You put in more than your share of extra hours during tax time. Take the rest of the day with a clear conscience. I'll lock up and we'll see you tomorrow or the next day. Give your brain a rest."

She smiled and thanked him. She stopped at Safeway and bought a package of pork chops, a bundle of asparagus, a can of mushroom soup and ingredients for a salad. She hurried home and quickly braised the pork chops. She put them in a glass cooking dish, then opened the can of mushroom soup and emptied it over the meat and popped the dish into the preheated oven. She quickly measured rice and water into the rice cooker and plugged it in.

She had cleaned up the counter before the phone rang. She knew it would be Tim, telling her he was at the railroad track. She smiled as she answered. "Hi. Are you at the railroad tracks already?" When he said he was, she told him to go to the house and let himself in.

She dashed to the bathroom, quickly stripped off her clothing and showered. She smiled as she blew her hair dry, knowing how he loved the smell of her shampoo. She appraised herself, as she stood naked in front of the mirror. Her hips were softly rounded, but her tummy was flat. She ran her fingers up from the curve of her hips to her breasts. Was there a bit of sag there? She detected a tiny bit, but not much. She had good legs and nice feet. She ran her hands to the patch of down that guarded the entrance to her femininity. She shivered as she let her finger slip gently through it to the welcoming moistness that waited there. She felt herself contract involuntarily.

"Hurry up, Loverboy. The appetizer is ready," she whispered, tossing her hair so it floated around her head.

She was turning back the sheets on the bed when she heard the crunch of tires on the driveway. She quickly lit candles and as she heard the back door open, she tiptoed into the hall. He was taking off his boots when she stepped into the room; positioning her nude body in a sexy pose.

"Holy hell!" He whistled softly. "Hot and spicy!" he murmured as he stepped forward. He reached out and gently touched her breasts. "So damned beautiful," he whispered hoarsely.

She took his hand and guided it down to the junction of her legs, watching him as she guided his fingers to the welcoming entrance. He closed his eyes as he felt her slippery heat. She leaned in and kissed him, running her fingers over the swelling behind his zipper. He groaned as he pulled her to him, his mouth hungrily devouring hers.

They made guttural sounds as their hands worked frenziedly to rid him of his clothes. She hooked a leg up onto his hip and he bucked against her nakedness as it clung to him, the hardness of his erection probing for the hot moistness that beckoned it. He pulled her up, and she folded her legs around his waist, then relaxed and wiggled down until she settled over him and drew him inside her. His response was a feral growl as he moved her toward the bedroom. She protested as he pulled out momentarily while he lowered her onto the bed.

"Don't make me wait," she pleaded as she pulled his head down and covered his mouth desperately. "I need you *now.*"

"Chris," he breathed, his voice ragged as he positioned himself between her thighs and filled her. Their coupling was quick and breathtaking. When they were finished, he collapsed beside her, his hand on her belly. He could feel her still convulsing with pleasure as she squeezed her legs tight to savor the feel.

He kissed her shoulder. "Chris, whatever you ate or drank or did this afternoon—just make it a regular occurrence. You were so damned hot."

She giggled. "I left work early. I couldn't wait to get home and shower. I wanted to surprise you."

He chuckled. "Well, you succeeded. When you met me at the door in your *best dress*, you blew my mind."

She rubbed her cheek against his chest. "Your best dress is pretty hot too." Her fingers walked down his abs to the juncture of his legs.

He groaned and grabbed her hand. "Are you trying to kill me? I'm wiped out—burnt up. As I told you before, I'm as good as I ever was, but ...."

She laughed as she laid a finger over his lips, then she lay down beside him. "I know what you need...nourishment! I put pork chops in the oven before you got here. The rice should be cooked. I just have to steam the asparagus and you can help me make a salad."

"I didn't plan on you cooking after having spent the day at work," he protested.

"I wanted to prove to you that I'm more than just a pretty face."

"As if I didn't already know that," he said softly. He turned, aligning her body with his, and pulled her close. "Let's just lay here for a few minutes. I worked today, and I'm tired. Besides that, I want to soak up the feel of having you here beside me; your softness, the smell of your hair, everything about you. You're constantly on my mind."

"I think about you all the time too." Christina rose up on her elbow so she could look into his eyes. She was grinning. "It was funny today. Shauna Lee told me that I needed to think outside the box. She informed me that you really are a nice guy and pointed out how comfortable we are together and that we are good friends."

"Did you tell her we're way ahead of her?"

Christina shook her head. "Are we ready to go public?"

"Are we? I am, how about you? Are you ready? Are you sure, Christina?"

"I know I'm happier than I've ever been in my entire life. I guess my only hesitation is the fact that I can't have a baby. Are you sure that you don't care? That you won't come to regret it? Other than that, I have no doubts. But I just can't ever face that again..."

"I told you, I have no expectations of having children, and if we really wanted kids we could adopt."

"Tim, the only reason I'd want a child now, would be to have your baby, and I'm not willing to share you with someone else, so that's a moot point."

"Well, I'm not interested in going there, so don't worry."

"Being with you has already changed my life, Tim. I'm beginning to understand that I've been my own worst enemy." Tears misted her eyes as she looked at him. "I've felt inferior because I can't have kids, and I've assumed everyone else would see me that way too."

She touched his cheek gently. "If I'd been open about it, instead of acting like it was something to be ashamed of, I wouldn't have crippled my relationships with my sister and my friends at school. Dave's friends probably wouldn't have accepted the way he treated me if they'd known we couldn't have children from the start.

"Today I told Shauna Lee that I can't have kids. A month ago, I'd never have done that, but you didn't turn tail and run and somehow that has given me strength. To be honest, with you beside me, I feel like I can do anything."

"That's how I feel too. I know I can trust you and I know you'll stand by me. You've proven that already. I want to spend the rest of my life in a loving, peaceful and comfortable relationship. I've lived through enough drama and betrayal. I want what Brad and Shauna Lee and Colt and Frank have."

"And Ollie and Ellie," Christina added. "It's so cool to see people their age, so happy and obviously in love."

Tim pulled her down against him again. "Well, we definitely have the sex part right. On top of that, our relationship has grown slowly and it has a solid base. We'll be fine."

"We will," she whispered. "So when do we tell everyone?"

"We aren't tied to a timetable. It'll come out gradually. We're still getting used to the idea. Now, did you say you have supper in the oven?" He kissed her soundly and slapped her hip playfully. "You worked me hard, my beautiful woman. I'm hungry now."

CHAPTER TEN

Life was busy at Belanger Creek Ranch. Frank put a pot roast in the slow cooker and turned it on low. Supper would be ready when they came in, ravenous and tired, after spending the day in the saddle. She sighed, wondering how long it would be until they found someone to help around the house. The idea appealed to her more as each day went by. Trying to keep up with the cooking, laundry and housework was a continuous struggle, now that she was working full time outside with Colt and Grayson.

The twins were going riding with them for the day, so she checked each of the four insulated lunch boxes sitting on the counter, making sure that they each contained water and juice, as well as food. As she was putting on her cowboy boots and denim jacket, she heard Colt and the twins come into the porch.

"Hey Mom, is my lunch made?" Sam called as he charged into the kitchen with his muddy boots on.

"Sam! You just tracked mud on the floor."

Sam looked contrite, as he stared at the floor. "I'm sorry Mom. I didn't think. Is that my lunch?" he asked pointing to the green lunch box.

"That's your lunch and it's ready, but you have to get the mop from the laundry room and clean up your mess."

He screwed up his face in frustration and headed for the laundry room.

"Sam!" Frank yelled with exasperation. "Go to the porch and take off your boots, then come back and get the mop and wipe up your tracks. You have to start thinking about what you do. I'm too busy to run around cleaning up after you."

Colt and Selena followed Sam back into the kitchen. Selena looked at the floor and looked at Sam as he went to the laundry room. "Dummy! What a mess…"

"Selena! Don't call Sam names. I've told you before, it's not acceptable."

"Okay! But look at the mess he made."

"I've already reprimanded him for that, and he's going to clean it up. Your lunch box is there on the counter. Colt will you grab yours and mine, and the two thermoses beside them? I have to put a load of laundry in the dryer. I just about forgot." She disappeared into the laundry room.

Colt could hear her scolding Sam for not rinsing the mop properly before he put it back in the empty bucket. He shook his head as picked up the lunch bags and thermoses and carried them to the door. "The horses are saddled and ready to go, hon," he called.

Sam came out of the laundry room, followed by Frank. She frowned as she looked around the room one last time. "Okay, I guess I'm ready. Supper is in the slow cooker, so it'll be ready when we get back. Let's get going."

When they stepped out the door, Frank smiled when she saw the four horses tied at the hitching rail. Colt had insisted on putting it there, declaring that every ranch house needed one. And while it was seldom used, it was today.

Colt put a lunch box in the saddle bag on each horse, and then he helped the twins onto their horses while Frank mounted hers. He swung up into the saddle and the four of them rode to where Grayson was waiting for them. They rode down the driveway, over the bridge at Belanger Creek, to the highway. They crossed the road and Grayson got off to open and close a gate. They rode into a field, that ran down the valley and up into the coulees and ravines on either side.

"Whoopee!" Sam hollered as he took off his cowboy hat, waving it over his head as he spurred his horse into a run.

Selena hesitated a moment, then took off after him. Colt and Frank looked at each other and shook their heads, smiling as they watched them ride away.

Grayson laughed. "What a picture they make. One day they'll realize how lucky they were to grow up here."

"Where did you grow up Grayson?" Frank asked. "It's crazy, but you've been here for four years and I don't ever remember you talking about your family or where you grew up."

Grayson looked out across the field. "That's probably because I haven't said much. I'm pretty private."

"So, where did you grow up, Grayson?" Colt asked.

Grayson looked out to the hills. "I grew up in Elliot Lake."

"Ontario?"

"Yeah." He grinned and pointed ahead. "Here the twins come. They are having a blast out here."

Selena's horse surged ahead. "That was fun!" she yelled as Sam came charging in.

"Okay, it's time to get to work now. Frank, you and Grayson can ride around the pasture to the left. The kids and I will ride the other way. We're going to check for broken or loose wires on the fence and open gates. We'll see how the grass is growing, too. I plan to move the cattle out here later this week. We'll leave them here until we haul them out to the lease."

They rode back to the barn six hours later. Sam and Selena were bubbling with the excitement of having spent the entire day riding with their parents and could hardly wait to tell Ellie about it.

Everyone dismounted and Colt and Frank unsaddled the horses and brushed them down before giving them hay and grain. Sam and Selena ran to see Ollie and Ellie. Grayson went to do the evening chores. When they finished the work, the five of them walked up the hill to the house.

The welcome aroma of pot roast wafted from the kitchen when they opened the door. Suddenly, their mouths filled with saliva and their stomachs gurgled. They shrugged out of their coats and pulled off their boots. Colt and Frank washed their hands at the kitchen sink, leaving the washroom near the entry for Grayson to use.

Colt set the table while Frank cut the roast and transferred the vegetables and gravy into a serving dish. Grayson made coffee and the twins went to their rooms, changed into their pajamas and washed their face and hands. When they came back, everyone sat down and silence settled over the group, as they ate hungrily. Selena was beginning to yawn and Sam actually nodded off at one point. Neither one of them protested when Colt told them to go to bed.

Colt, Frank and Grayson sat around the table, savouring a cup of coffee, and decided they would ride out to the pasture by the river in the morning and move all the cows and calves back to the corals.

Finally, Frank yawned and looked at the clock on the wall. "I don't know about you guys, but I'm bushed. It might be only eight-thirty, but I'm going to bed."

At eight o'clock the next morning, Frank and Colt and the twins met Grayson at the barn. While they were saddling their horses, a shadow fell on the alley in the barn. Frank looked out to see who was there. "Ollie!" she exclaimed. "What are you doing here?"

"I'm coming with you guys today."

"But, you're not supposed to come to work for a while."

"Look. I'm not the one who had a heart attack. That was Ellie. She's doing okay, and I'm going stir-crazy. You'll have to hogtie me to make me stay at home."

Colt sauntered over. "What's up, old timer?"

"I'm riding with you today."

"You sure you're up to it?"

"Absolutely, and I'm going."

Colt nodded. "Go get your horse and saddle up, then we'll hit the trail."

"Ollie," Selena yelled. "Are you going riding with us?"

"Darn right. You guys had so much fun yesterday; I decided I'm not getting left behind again."

After Ollie had saddled his favorite Appaloosa horse, they all mounted up and rode down the road, enjoying the sunshine and the beauty of the spring day. When they reached the pasture Colt, Frank, and the twins rode up through the coulees to the plateau at the top. Grayson and Ollie rode along the river and up the other side. They met at the top and started working their way down through the draws and the aspen and willow patches, gathering the cattle as they rode and moving them down into the feeding area at the bottom. When they had collected them all, the six riders fanned out and started moving the herd toward the gate and onto the road home.

The bellows of the cattle filled the air, as they forged forward. The road was familiar to them, and they knew they were headed for the ranch. Once on the way they moved easily, a ribbon of brown and black, moving en masse. When they arrived at the ranch, Grayson pushed ahead to make sure that the herd went through the open gates, into the corral.

As soon as the riders dismounted, Sam ran to the old house to see Ellie. The smell of fresh baking greeted him. "Oh yummy." His eyes sparkled. He walked to the counter. "You made cookies! Can I have one?" he asked as he reached out his hand to take one.

Ellie nodded. "Yes, and go tell everyone that I've got coffee on and lunch is ready."

Sam grinned as he threw his arms around her. "I'm glad you're feeling better, Miss Ellie." He chomped on the cookie as he stepped outside and closed the door.

Frank turned and watched her son as he came running toward her, waving his hand with the cookie in it. "What have you got?" she asked. Her eyes widened. "Where did you get that cookie? Has Ellie been cooking?"

He nodded. "She said lunch is ready for everyone."

That woman, Frank thought, shaking her head. Then she yelled "Hey guys. Ellie has lunch ready for us."

Colt looked surprised, but Ollie just laughed. "You can't keep a good woman down. She loves cooking and it makes her feel like she's part of everything again. There's nothing worse than feeling useless. I'll make sure she doesn't overwork, but we can't smother her either."

"Did you know she was going to do this?" Colt asked.

Ollie nodded. "I know you mean well, but we want to get back to living. We both needed a rest after Ellie was in the hospital, but now we're bored. I helped her cut up vegetables last night and she's made soup for lunch. She probably made biscuits or something to go with it, and I see she made cookies. She loves doing it and it's good for her."

Colt looked at the ground. "We just want to protect her, Ollie."

"She needs something to do. She's looking forward to teaching next fall. You'll have a real problem on your hands if you try to stop her from doing that. She loves working with those kids."

Frank looked at Colt and then smiled at Ollie. "We've already discussed that and as long as she is able to teach that's not going to change."

"Come on, you guys," Sam said impatiently. "Miss Ellie is

waiting for us."

After lunch, the adults went out to sort twenty-five cows and their calves from the main herd and put them in the pen closest to the calf table. They lit the propane torch, and the branding irons were placed in a metal trough where the flame would heat them. Frank went to the tack room and got ear tags, dehorning paste, a couple of bottles of vaccine, needles, and the record book.

By five o'clock, they were finished.

When they went to the house, Frank found a note from Ellie on the table. She had put a casserole in the oven before lunch, and left instructions for her to heat the oven to four hundred degrees and put the dish in for half an hour. Frank's heart filled with warmth but at the same time, she was concerned. After she had put the casserole in the oven, she called Ellie and thanked her. Ellie assured her that she had driven Ollie's truck up to the house instead of carrying the casserole there, so she had not stressed herself.

It would take the rest of the week to work through all the calves. The job entailed a lot of physical work, so they needed to pace themselves, so they didn't become so exhausted that they couldn't recuperate after a good night's rest.

The last evening, Grayson sighed as he stretched his sore muscles. "Thank god you have the calf table. Can you imagine how sore and beat up we'd all be if we branded the way they did in the old days?"

"It's so much easier on the calves, too. Once they're on the table, it gives you easy access to work without having to wrestle and fight with the animal. It's much less stressful for everyone involved and you don't get the shit kicked out of you."

Grayson laughed. "Well, speak for yourself. I got thumped quite a few times when I was pushing them up the alley and I've got the bruises to prove it." He looked down at his clothes. "I've got plenty of shit on me, too!"

CHAPTER ELEVEN

Tim and his crew had started seeding wheat the day before. The three men worked rotating shifts. Tim always worked the night shift on the tractor, and he made sure that the next operator had grain and fertilizer and fuel to keep him going until the following shift came on, so it was often noon before he fell asleep.

At three o'clock, Tim threw back the sheets and crawled out of his lonely bed. He padded across the floor and opened the curtain, looking out the window, squinting against the glare of the afternoon sun. The sky was crystalline blue and green leaves were showing up in the trees. He stretched. "I didn't get enough sleep," he thought. "I have a feeling the only thing that will make it better, is having Christina here with me every day."

He took a shower, then came back and sat on the side of the bed. He leaned over and opened the drawer in his night table. He smiled as he reached in and took out a small gray box. His thumb caressed the satin surface as he flicked it open. He took the ring out and held it up, gazing at the brilliance of the stone. He hoped she liked the platinum setting.

As soon as he'd seen the ring, he'd known it was the one he wanted to give her. It had been expensive, but he hadn't hesitated.

He gazed at it for a few seconds and then tucked it back into the box. He was too busy right now, but they'd be done seeding in about a month, and then he'd plan a romantic getaway. He wanted the location to be as perfect as the ring when he gave it to her.

He took a clean pair of socks and shorts from the chest of drawers. As he sat down to pull them on, he was overwhelmed by loneliness. He needed to see her, to be with her. Even though he knew he had to go to work at midnight he decided to take Christina out for supper.

It was Friday so he hoped she would come to the farm and spend the weekend with him. He would be working long hours, but he wanted to hold her close and smell her hair as it spread on his pillow. He wanted to have coffee on the veranda with her in the morning and enjoy supper with her before he went to work. He wanted her with him, sharing his life.

Christina smiled when she put down the phone. Tim had just called to ask her out for supper. They'd arranged to meet at the house when she got home from work.

I'll surprise him again. That sheer negligee that I bought the other day will definitely set the stage for our ritual appetizer. She felt heat rise in her sweet spot. *God, I never dreamed I could be so horny.* She thought for a moment, then picked up the phone and dialed Tim's cell number.

"Chris? Is that you?"

"Yes, Loverboy. My work day is almost finished; I could cut out an hour early. Obviously, you're awake. Is there any chance you could come in now? We could have an appetizer before supper?"

Tim grinned as he shifted his jeans to accommodate the throbbing tightness behind his fly. He was so hard it was almost painful. "I've just finished getting dressed. I'm on my way."

"Drive careful luv. I'll be waiting."

Christina phoned Carls desk. "I'm going to take the rest of the day off; personal reasons. I'll be back after the weekend."

Carl chuckled. "No problem, Chris. Hope it's nothing serious."

Christina giggled. "Oh, it's very serious."

"It sounds like love to me," he teased.

"Carl! Don't you dare suggest that to anyone else."

He laughed. "I must have hit pretty close to home. Enjoy your weekend."

Christina hurried home and showered. Then she grabbed her overnight bag and filled it with the things she'd need. She tucked in the sheer negligee too. She wanted to seduce him and excite him with it. Her 'best dress' was perfect for now: there would be less to take off when he got there. He knew she was waiting for him now and his need would be as urgent as hers.

She was startled when she heard a vehicle pull up in front of the house. She glanced at her watch. *Cripes! Who can that be? Tim can't be here yet.* She groaned and bit her lip. *What friggin' lousy timing! I can't have company now.*

She sighed with relief when she heard his footsteps pounding on the sidewalk along the house to the back door. She heard him turn the door knob and come in. As she stepped forward to meet him, he reached out and swept her up into his arms.

Minutes later, they lay entangled on her bed, basking in the afterglow of sexual release. He tangled his finger through her soft hair and gently tugged her head back so he could look into her eyes. "We have to do something about this, you know. You can't keep taking time off from work, and I need to get more than three hours sleep."

He pulled her close and began running his hand up and down her back, enjoying the feel of her skin. "This feels so good," he murmured drowsily. "Let's just relax and enjoy this for a few more minutes and then we'll go."

Five hours later, Christina slowly surfaced. Her cheek was still on his chest and she could hear the steady beat of his heart and the relaxed sound of his breathing. She shifted her body and felt him come awake.

"Tim," she said softly. "We'd better get up."

He grinned sleepily. "Yeah, I know. I'm feeling lazy now."

"It's almost ten o'clock. Should I make coffee, or maybe a quick supper? If I make something simple, we can eat and when we get to the farm, you can go right to work. I won't distract you anymore."

"Hmmm…but, I like it when you distract me."

"But I don't want to be responsible for disrupting your schedule."

"I think you've already done that."

Christina gave him a playful shove. "It's too late to groan after you've moaned with pleasure. And besides that, now you've actually gotten a decent sleep."

He pulled her into his arms again. "You're right on that score. That's the best sleep I've had since the last time we slept together. I think you need to move out to my place."

They went to The Steakhouse and chatted easily while they ate. It was eleven-thirty when they arrived at the farm. Tim came in and changed into his work clothes, then left for his shift on the tractor.

Christina wasn't tired. After Tim left, she wandered through the house. She was comfortable there. In the past, she had spent many nights in the spare bedroom as Tim's friend. More recently, she had spent them in his bed, as his lover.

He doesn't do too badly, for a busy bachelor, she thought as she looked around. The house was fairly neat and clean. A jacket had been tossed on a chair near the door, and a shirt was draped over the back of a kitchen chair, but there were no papers or junk lying around.

"He's been putting in such long hours that he can't be spending much time here," she murmured. She sat her bag at the bottom of the stairs and then walked over to the sink. There were dishes from the day before piled in it. She turned over the dirty pot. "Macaroni and cheese and wieners." She wrinkled her nose. "I hope that's not your diet staple, Loverboy."

A cereal bowl that he'd used when he'd came in off his shift and a glass with a half an inch of milk sat on the counter. Christina turned on the satellite radio on the counter and then rinsed off the dishes and put them in the dishwasher.

She picked up the coat and hung it on the rack by the door. Then she took the shirt off the back of the chair and held it to her face. It smelled of diesel fuel and dust, with undertones of Tim's body. She carried it into the laundry room. There were a couple of changes of clothes in the laundry basket. She opened the washing machine, picked out the shirts, colored socks and shorts and threw them in. She was ready to push the button when she hesitated. "I'd better check the bedroom first; there may be more up there."

She picked up her bag and walked up the stairs. She smiled as her hand brushed along the banister railing. "I love this old house. It has so much character." When she reached the top, she could see through the open bedroom door. The bed was rumpled and unmade. There was a pair of dirty socks tossed on it. A shirt lay on the chair in the corner and a pair of jeans pooled on the floor.

She washed Tim's clothes and the sheets off the bed. She

vacuumed floors, cleaned counters, and dusted and polished furniture throughout the house. Every room sparkled, and pleasure filled her when she looked around. *This feels like home,* she thought. *It feels so right.* "Okay, Tim," she said softly. "How long are we going to wait?"

It was five o'clock in the morning, she made herself a cup of coffee and turned on the TV to watch the local news. In moments, she had drifted off to sleep. That's where Tim found her when he slipped into the house three hours later.

He stooped to lift her in his arms and carried her up the stairs to the bedroom. She woke up when he tried to pull back the sheets so he could lay her between them. She gasped. "Oh...you're home. I must have crashed. I was going to wait up and go to bed with you."

"I came in early. It's only eight o'clock. When Norman came to take over at six, I cheated a bit. I knew that he had enough grain and fertilizer to cover until Ben comes on at ten, so I just took him fuel and came home. I told him I have company for the weekend. Norman will have to top up the grain and fertilizer, but it will work out alright."

"I wanted to make you a good breakfast," she protested.

"You can do that tomorrow. It looks like you worked around the house all night, so let's go to bed and get a good sleep." He slipped in beside her and snuggled her back against his chest. In moments, they were both sound asleep, seduced by the pleasure of being together and the comfort of each other's body warmth.

Christina woke up at three o'clock. Tim was still asleep, so she eased herself away from him slowly, afraid she'd wake him. He mumbled a couple of times as he felt for her in the bed, then turned over and lost himself to sleep again.

Christina grabbed her clothes and slipped downstairs to use the bathroom. She put on a pot of coffee, raided his freezer and found a package of pork chops. She chuckled. She'd cooked pork chops for him the last time she'd made supper for him. She defrosted them in the microwave and then braised them in a frying pan. She made a bread dressing with apricots and cranberries and layered it over the chops in a glass dish. After covering it with tinfoil, she put it in the oven on a low heat. She cooked a pot of rice and prepared carrots to steam. She used apples she found in the fridge to make apple crumble for dessert.

While the food was cooking, she went outside to explore the

back yard. Neglected beds were overrun with grass and weeds. She explored each one, her mind humming with possibilities. She found a couple of clumps of daffodils and tulips persistently fighting for space. She cut their blooms, took them inside and put them on the table in a jar of water.

Tim came downstairs at around five o'clock. He found Christina outside, pulling grass out of the beds. She looked up when she heard the screen door close. Her smile was bright when she stood up and walked to him. "Did you have a good sleep?"

He nodded as he wrapped his arms around her. "This feels good," he whispered. "Waking up to my best friend and my love." He kissed her hungrily. "When did you get up?"

"At about three o'clock, but I'd slept for three hours or more before you got home. I started supper. I just have to cook the vegetables. What do you want to do? Have supper now or just before you go to work?"

"I'll have a coffee now. When the veggies are cooked, we can eat."

"What do you usually do when you are working these shifts?"

He grinned and shrugged. "I just eat when I feel like it. Usually something simple, like eggs and bacon, or macaroni and cheese."

Christina grimaced. "I saw the mac and cheese and wiener pot in the sink."

"When you're a bachelor, it works."

"We're going to have to do something about that. It's not a very healthy way of eating."

He grinned. "Maybe we'll have to put our heads together and come up with a solution."

Christina chuckled and turned toward the house. "I'll put the vegetables on. While I'm doing that, do you have any idea where there might be some garden tools?"

"I'll check the shed out back. The Thompsons may have stored their garden tools in there. I have to confess, I haven't looked in it. I'm not a gardener. My attention was fixed on the machine shed and the shop."

Tim laid a couple of garden trowels on the back porch when he came inside. "I found them in that shed. There are other tools, too. I left the door unlocked for you." He sniffed appreciably. "It smells wonderful in here. I could get used to this," he said as he slid an arm around her waist. "Where did you get the flowers?"

"They're blooming in one of the old flower beds in the backyard. Tomorrow afternoon, I'm going to work on them. I want to pull out the grass and whatever weeds I can find."

They enjoyed their meal, chatting comfortably about many things, the way they'd done when they'd sat there as friends. Tim looked at her and smiled. "I didn't realize how much I missed having someone to talk to."

"What do you do now, Tim? You've been up for two hours, it's five more hours until you go to work and then you have a twelve-hour shift ahead of you. It'll be twenty-one hours before you sleep again. Do you keep doing that day after day until seeding is done?"

"Not really. Some days I sleep longer, some days I sleep less. It just depends. I admit things are kind of wacky when you first start. I've always worked the midnight shift because the other guys have families and it gives them a better schedule. Until now, it's never mattered to me. I didn't have anyone else to consider."

She looked at him. "So...should you try to catch a nap for a while before you leave for work?"

He lifted his eyebrow. "Hmmm. Well, I'd be all for going to bed."

She laughed. "Look, Loverboy, I'm trying to keep you healthy. I don't want to wear you out."

He stood up and collected the plates and cutlery. "I'll give you a hand. It won't take long and then we can go up together."

She smiled as she rinsed off the pots and put them in the dishwasher. Working together, they had everything finished in five minutes. Tim shut off the lights and they walked up the stairs together. He chuckled when they entered the bedroom. "By the way, I meant to mention how great the house looks. It needs a woman's touch. I try, but when I'm busy like this, it's my last priority. Sorry, I didn't mean for you to spend all your time cleaning."

"I enjoyed it." She stood in front of him and threaded her arms around his neck, weaving her fingers together at the back of his head. "Tim, do you know where you want to go with this relationship?"

He looked into her eyes. "I know what I want."

"What do you want?" she asked softly.

He sat on the edge of the bed and pulled her down beside him, then reached back and opened the night table drawer. "This isn't how I planned to do this."

He watched her face as he brought out the small gray box. Christina swallowed hard and her eyes misted over as she looked into his. She held her breath as he flipped up the lid and showed her its contents.

"I want to marry you, Christina."

She sucked in her breath, and a tear slipped down her cheek.

"Is it too soon to give this to you?" he asked.

"No. No… it's not too soon. We've been working at this for four years; we just didn't realize what we were doing." She held out her hand. "Please…put it on and let me see it," she whispered.

Tim slipped the ring onto her finger.

Her eyes widened as she looked at it. He had chosen a beautiful solitaire, set on a wide platinum band, with a slender ribbon of gold twisting over the base of the setting to the shoulder of the ring on each side. "Tim, it's gorgeous." Her eyes danced with happiness when she looked up at him through tears. "It even fits perfectly!" she giggled.

"I know the feel of your fingers in my hands. I knew it would fit when I picked it up."

She laid her cheek against his chest. "I feel like I'm living in a dream. Suddenly my world has gone from just everyday humdrum to heart pounding, tingling excitement. Love makes everything feel different. I want to pinch myself. Is this real?"

"It's real hon. I can't promise you a lot of exciting, fun filled days. I'm a hard working farmer and the next few months will be busy for me. We'll catch a breather after the seeding is done, but then it'll be time to spray. After that, we'll jump into haying and then it will be harvest time."

"I have a pretty good picture of a farmer's life, Tim. We deal with them all the time at the office and you can't live in Saskatchewan and not be aware of how busy the spring, summer, and fall is. But we'll be *together*."

"There won't be time for a big wedding or a honeymoon until after the fall work is done."

She nodded. "I know that."

He wrapped his arms around her and lay back on the bed, pulling her with him. "That sounds good: having my love and my best friend with me every morning and every night." He kissed her deeply.

She lifted herself up on her elbow and looked into his eyes.

"Tim, let's not waste any more time. Can we just go to the marriage commissioner and get married right away? We've both been married before and we both know big fancy weddings don't matter a whole lot. I just want to be with you."

"Are you sure about that? Don't you want the fancy dress and the bridesmaids and all that?"

"I sort of did that once already and it didn't guarantee happiness. We're not kids. We could live together, but I want to be your *wife*. I never thought I'd want that again, but I do."

"What about your family, Chris?"

"I'd be just as happy if we went to see them after the fact, and I could introduce you as my husband."

"Our friends?"

"We could have a barbecue after seeding is done and celebrate with them. They'll whine and moan, and tell us how disappointed they are, but they'll get over it."

"So, what do we need to do to get a marriage license?"

"I'll check it out online tomorrow."

"If you are sure you won't regret it later, I'm happy about getting married as soon as possible. I'll even take a day off!"

She wiggled against him. "I'll make a few calls on Monday and get the ball rolling." She kissed his cheek. "I am so happy, I could burst. I love you so much!"

He leaned away and looked at her. "Will you move in with me this weekend? I want to have breakfast with you every morning and supper with you every evening and feel you beside me in bed all night long."

She nodded and kissed him quickly. "I'll drive into town and get some of my things tomorrow while you're sleeping. I can bring a few more things every day during the week." She smiled and ran her hand along his cheek. "You need to catch a nap, love. You have to go to work in three hours."

"I'm more interested in this," he whispered, pushing her down on the mattress and capturing her lips. Moments later, they helped each other undress and made slow, sensuous love. Then Tim set his alarm for eleven-thirty and they fell asleep.

Tim shut the alarm off on the second ring. Christina woke up, too, but he insisted she stay in bed. He dressed quickly and kissed her, promising he would try to be in by eight o'clock again the next morning. He hurried down the stairs and out into the night.

Christina lay in the darkness, listening to the truck drive away. Finally, she turned on the light and stretched out her hand, looking at the ring that sparkled on her finger. It was beautiful; she felt the urge to pinch herself and make sure she wasn't dreaming.

The next morning Christina was up by six-thirty. She slipped downstairs to make coffee and then began to survey the meager contents of the fridge. Tim didn't stock a very big variety of food. She found a block of cheddar cheese that had dried and cracked around the edges, part of a package of Bavarian smokies, eggs, bacon, a jar of peanut butter and one of jam and a container of mayonnaise.

She searched through the cupboards and found a few cans of peaches and three tins of pork and beans. Another cupboard revealed a box of Oreo cookies, a bag of peanut butter cookies and a couple of boxes of energy bars. She shook her head. "Tim, Tim. You definitely need someone to look after you!"

She took a notepad out of her purse and began to make a list of basics for the kitchen: flour, sugar, salt and pepper, canned goods, spices, fresh vegetables, fresh meat, cleaning supplies. The list grew to cover several pages.

She considered what she needed to bring from her house. Tim had no culinary extras, but she could afford to buy them and she had the latest of everything that interested her. She would bring her slow cooker, her specialty coffee maker, the electric grill, the rice cooker, and the Kitchen Aid mixer and anything else she could cram into her car after she got groceries.

Tim came home a few minutes after eight o'clock. She met him at the door with a kiss and a warm smile. Then she stood back and looked at him.

"What?"

"I was just thinking about how different farming is now than it was when my grandpa farmed. He always came in covered with grease and dust. Look at you—you are as clean as you were when you left the house last night. It's hard to imagine you've been working in the field for nine hours."

He chuckled. "That part is true. The cab on the tractor is as clean and comfortable as a pickup. I have air-conditioning, a stereo, and GPS. Everything is computerized. But, god help you if something goes wrong and all the fancy equipment can't communicate. Nothing will work. You can't just crawl under it and tear it apart to fix it. Sometimes dirt on your clothes and grease on your hands would be preferable to the frustration and anxiety of waiting for hours or days for a technician to arrive.

Christina smiled. "Grandpa wouldn't believe his eyes if he saw your equipment. Now everything is so technical and *huge,* compared to what he used. And it looks so different! I remember him cultivating, harrowing, then seeding and fertilizing in separate operations; four separate passes over the same ground. Now you don't even cultivate and harrow the soil. He would never believe that zero tillage could work, and he'd wonder what the heck an air seeder was. It's amazing how the industry changes."

Tim smiled. "GPS is a whole new ball game on its own. It's unbelievable what can be done with it. I haven't gotten into the really advanced stuff yet, but some of it is almost scary."

She ran her hand down his sleeve. "I have pancakes and bacon in the oven. I'll cook the eggs while you wash up."

She was pouring him a cup of coffee when he came up behind her. "This is heaven," he said softly and kissed the nape of her neck.

"What?" she asked with a smile.

"Having you here in the kitchen in the morning. Sharing a cup of coffee with you, looking into your eyes, seeing your smile." He kissed her. "Knowing you are mine."

They sat down at the big oak table and ate together, enjoying each other's company. Finally, Christina stood up. "You have to go to sleep, Tim."

"Come lay with me for a while?" he asked softly as he pulled her close, claiming her lips with passion. She felt his hardness grow between them and nodded."

"Just for a little while. Then I have things to do; I'm going to run into town to buy some food."

He grinned. "There's food in the house."

"Yeah you have smokies and mac n' cheese."

"And there's cheese, pork and beans, and peanut butter and jam."

"Yes, a full lineup of bachelor food! You really do need someone to look after you, man."

He rubbed himself against her, pushing his hardness into her. "Well, I have several needs and I know you can look after all of them."

She followed him upstairs and they satisfied their most

demanding need. She drifted languidly in his arms as he fell into a deep sleep. Then she eased herself out of the bed and left the room.

She trailed her hand lovingly down the oak banister as she moved down the steps. Warmth flooded through her when she looked around. *This place holds so many wonderful memories,* she thought. *Bob and Serena Thompson, Colt and Frank and the twins, and now it will be our home.* She stopped on the bottom step and looked at her ring. "Christina Bates," she said softly, experimentally. "Mrs. Tim Bates."

She giggled. "Who would have imagined this could happen? I'm thirty-eight years old, and I'm as besotted as a teenager. I can't believe I was so wrong about Tim when he first came to town. He is not even close to being the *cold fish* I thought he was." She squeezed her eyes shut. "He's passionate and sexy and considerate, everything I didn't expect him to be." She hugged herself. "And he truly doesn't care that I can't have babies. He loves me just the way I am."

She sat down on the step. The present drifted away as her mind slipped into the past. She was eighteen again. She and Dave were engaged and she was giddy with excitement. It amazed her that someone like him would even look at her. The best part was that he didn't think she was a freak; he swore it didn't matter that she couldn't have children. They were young, and nothing but the feelings of the moment had mattered.

But, it didn't take very long for him to change his mind, she thought. She brushed away the tears that brimmed in her eyes. "Tim and I are in a different place," she whispered, reassuring herself. "We're old enough to understand the reality of it. As he said, he's going to be fifty. He said that's too old to worry about bringing a baby into the world, but I know he'd make a wonderful dad." She buried her face in her hands. "I'd make a wonderful mother too, but it's not going to happen."

She spread out her hand and admired her ring. Then curled her fingers under, so the ring stood up above her knuckles. *I can't get over how beautiful it is,* she thought as she touched her lips to the ring.

CHAPTER TWELVE

Spring was evident everywhere at the ranch. The aspen and bamagilian trees were leafing out, the hills were becoming green, and Belanger Creek was running full. Frank stood on the deck and looked down over the barnyard. She smiled as she watched Colt and the twins join Ollie and walk away from the corner of the barn toward the old house. Ellie must have called them for cookies and coffee.

She stretched, inhaled the fresh air, then turned and went inside. "Laundry, vacuuming, and lunch and supper. It never seems to end," she groaned. "God, I never really realized how much Ellie helped around here. Of course, I wasn't working outside all the time then either, so we did a lot of the work together."

She went into the laundry room and took out the load of clothes she'd put in the dryer earlier. She put them on the folding table and transferred the wet laundry from the washer to the dryer. She pushed a button and started it, then put another load in the washer. Then, she began folding the load on the table; a pile for Selena and a pile for Sam; jeans, shirts, and socks. When she was done, she took each pile to their respective rooms and put them in drawers.

She sighed. "Tomorrow I'll change the sheets and wash them.

It's past time for that to be done. The days just fly by so fast right now." She quickly cleaned the bathrooms and collected the used towels and facecloths from each room. She took the armload to the laundry room and left it in a basket, then went to the closet in the hall and uncoiled the long hose for the central vacuum system. She inserted it in the fixture and started to clean, moving from room to room. When she was finished, the laundry was ready to be dealt with. She glanced at the clock on the wall and groaned. "Damn! It's lunch time already." She thought for a moment. "I'd better take the clothes out of the dryer and put the other load in. I can fold them after lunch. Thank goodness, there is some casserole left from last night. We'll have that for lunch."

Colt and the twins came in as she was setting the table. The twins were talking over each other to get her attention, and the noise irritated her. "Calm down guys, I can only listen to one of you at a time."

"Me, first. I'm oldest, Mom," Selena chimed.

"You are not. We're twins."

Selena pushed Sam aside. "I came first, so I'm oldest."

Colt looked at Frank, reading her frustration. "Come on guys. Give your mom a break." He slid his arm around her waist. "I can tell you've had a busy morning. Are you ready to take a break and go riding after lunch?"

Frank sighed. "Not really. I've still got clothes to fold and I have to get something ready for supper."

Colt frowned. "I'll call Christina and see if she has found anyone yet. You're doing double duty, and this is too much for you to handle by yourself." He looked at the twins. "Okay, guys, after lunch you're going to clean up and put the dishes in the dishwasher while I fold the laundry. Mom can make something really simple for supper." He looked at Frank. "Macaroni and cheese and wieners will do. Heat a can of pork and beans when we get in. You don't have to slave over a big meal. Come, riding with us and have some fun."

Frank was ready to protest, but then thought better. *I'm losing sight of the important things. I can finish the laundry tomorrow...or the next day. And Colt's right, we don't need a big supper. We all enjoy mac n' cheese and wieners once in a while. In the long run, the things we'll all remember won't be big suppers and clean laundry. It'll be the times we spent together, working and playing.*

"You're right, Colt. I'll put macaroni and onions and cheese in the slow cooker and I'll cut up some wieners and add them. If I put it on low, it'll be done when we come in. We'll warm up some pork and beans then and make toast and that will be supper."

"Yippee...Mac n' Cheese!" the twins yelled. "That's great, Mom."

That evening after supper, Colt tried to call Christina at home. *No answer,* he thought. *I'll call early tomorrow morning. I want to find someone soon.*

The next morning he called again and still got no answer. He called Brad and Shauna Lee's place. Shauna Lee answered the phone. "Hi, Colt. What's up?"

"I'm looking for Christina. I asked her to look for someone to help around here. I was wondering if she's come up with any ideas. I called her place last night, but I didn't get an answer and there isn't one this morning. Do you have any idea where she is?"

"I thought she was at home. I saw her at the grocery store yesterday afternoon." Shauna Lee frowned. "When I think about it, it was kind of odd. She was really happy..."

"So, what was odd about that? She's usually pretty happy."

"No, that isn't what was odd, but come to think of it, she was radiant. No, what seemed unusual was that her cart was piled full of stuff. I mean, what would she do with so many groceries?"

"Maybe she was having a party."

"No, I was second in line behind her. She had staples like flour and sugar and all kinds of basic things. You'd have thought she was stocking someone's kitchen from scratch."

"But you have no idea where she is?"

"No, but you could try Tim's place. She might have gone there for the night."

"I'm sure he's busy putting in the crop. I'll try her there, but I can't see her being at the farm."

"Stranger things have happened." Shauna Lee chuckled. "I told her she should go after him. He's a nice guy. Maybe she thought about it and took my advice."

Colt laughed. "Now that would be a stretch! But, they *are* really comfortable together. I guess it's not impossible. I'll call Tim's place."

Monday morning Christina had to leave for work before Tim came home. When she got home that evening, Tim was getting up. She quickly seasoned chicken breasts and placed them in a casserole dish, topping them with a package stove top stuffing mix. She put some broccoli on to steam and made a salad.

When Tim walked past his office, he noticed the flashing light that indicated there was a message on his phone. He stopped to check it, then came out and handed the phone to Christina. "Colt called yesterday. He left a message for you."

When she listened to Colt's message, she winced. "I forgot all about that. I've been so involved with us, that I forgot about Colt asking me to look for someone to help Frank. I can't do much about it now, but I'll call first thing tomorrow morning."

It weighed on her mind while she ate, and she decided to call Julie after they were finished supper. She'd left a message when she'd called before, but neither she nor Julie had followed up on the call. She didn't know why she felt so compelled to ask Julie, but she did.

When she called, her sister answered on the third ring. "Hi, Julie. It's Christina. I called a couple of weeks ago and you weren't in."

"Oh," she gasped. "I didn't get back to you, did I? I'm sorry. Life's just been so busy here. How about you?"

"Everything's great. I'm still working. Spring has arrived. You know how it goes. I was just wondering how everyone is; you guys, mom, and dad."

"We're all fine. Can you believe it? Joylin's in grade one already and Robert is four. My babies are growing up. Jack's busy at the store and he's gotten into photography big time. Mom and Dad keep busy. They went to Arizona for the winter. They came home on the first of April. They loved it, so I'm sure they'll be going back next winter."

"I'm glad to hear that you're all doing well. Julie, I'm looking for a woman to cook and do housework for one of our clients. He and his wife are friends of mine too. They live on a ranch near the Cypress Hills and she works outside with him all the time. Their housekeeper/babysitter had a heart attack a few weeks ago, so they are looking for someone to take over the housework and cooking. They'll pay a fair wage and they have a suite that she would live in. Any ideas?"

"I know a young woman who's been working at a restaurant here in town. Her name is Sarah Brite. She's really a nice person and a good worker, but things are pretty slow here right now and she needs more than the few hours she gets working at the restaurant. She has a son, but he's well-mannered and quiet. We've gotten friendly and they've been here several times. She could be a good fit for your friends."

"Ask her if she is interested, and give her my number. I'd appreciate it if she called me as soon as possible. Colt called me again today, asking if I'd found anyone."

"Will you be in tonight?"

"This is my cell number. Call me on it. I'll make sure I have it with me. That way I'll be certain to get the call."

"She's coming over later this evening. I'll talk to her and if she's interested I'll have her call you. I'd think she'd jump at the opportunity, but you never know."

Christina smiled as she hung up, thinking how interesting it was that she'd felt compelled to call Julie, as if it was meant to be. She joined Tim. "Hopefully something will come out of my conversation with Julie." She was thoughtful. "It's weird that we only live a day's drive apart and yet we have no contact. I didn't even know that mom and Dad had gone to Arizona." She sighed ruefully. "I guess it goes both ways. I didn't call them either."

She and Tim sat down at Tim's laptop and checked how long it would take to get a marriage license. They needed to have their birth certificates and a photo ID and they both would have to sign the license. They could be married the next day. She wrinkled her nose. "We both need our divorce certificates, too. I have my birth certificate, and I know my divorce papers are somewhere, I just don't know where. I'll have to go back to the house and look through my papers."

Her cell phone rang, and she scooped it up, quickly checking the call display before she answered. She smiled, recognizing her sister's number. "Christina speaking," she answered.

"Hi. I told Sarah about the job and she wants to talk to you. I'll give her the phone now."

When their conversation concluded, Christina was impressed with Sarah. She sounded like she would be a good fit for the Thompsons. "Sarah, I'll phone Colt immediately and if he's in, I'll have him call Julie's place right away. If I can't reach him, I'll phone back and let you know, so you don't hang around waiting. But I'll make sure you guys connect one way or another soon."

Colt answered the phone and Christina told him about Sarah and gave him Julie's number.

She turned to Tim. "There! I think that problem is solved."

"So I take it she's interested in the job?"

"Yeah, and she sounds like she could be a good fit. She has a ten-year-old kid, but Colt didn't seem alarmed by that." She turned back to the computer. "So where were we? Oh…your birth certificate. Have you got it?"

"It's in the safe."

"And your divorce papers? Actually it says divorce certificate."

He looked thoughtful and frowned. "They have to be somewhere in my office. I was so pissed off about everything then, I'm not sure what I did with them. I'll have to look."

"Have you any idea where they might be. Maybe we can look for them tomorrow night, after supper."

The next morning Christina got up early and sat on the wicker lounge on the veranda, enjoying a fresh cup of coffee. She savored the crisp early morning air, enjoying the silence, which was interrupted only by the chirp of a few spring birds. She decided what she would make for supper that evening, then went inside to shower and get ready for work.

The sparkle of the ring caught her eye as she used a blow dryer and brush to style her hair. *I'm surprised nobody noticed yesterday*, she thought with a chuckle.

As usual, on work days she had to leave before Tim got home in the morning. The rest of the staff was already at the office when she arrived. *I spent too long on the veranda. I'm going to have to leave the farm earlier*, she thought.

Everyone was in their office or at their desk, and once they got to work, there was little personal interaction. Anything they needed was dealt with by a phone call or texting and Christina slipped out at lunch time to go to her house without talking to them personally.

In one way this is killing me, she thought. *I want to run through the office and flash my ring in their faces. I know they'll be thrilled for me. But, if we can get married within the next week, it'll be so much fun to sign my name as Christina Bates, and see their reaction.* She giggled. "I am acting like a juvenile, but it's so cool to feel this way, even if it's silly. I never imagined it could happen. I wasn't this happy when I got married the first time," she said softly.

She glanced at herself in the rear-view mirror and chuckled. "And who could have guessed that Tim would be the one to me so happy! Shauna Lee and Brad will be shocked." She sighed, as she pulled up in front of her house. "No, that's not true. Shauna Lee told me I should see him differently. She'll think she played matchmaker."

She was smiling from ear to ear when she got out of the car, looking at the place that had been home for fourteen years. She still loved it, but she had no regrets about moving to the farm. When she unlocked the door and stepped inside, she realized that even after just three days, it didn't really feel like home anymore. It was just a familiar house.

"They say home is where the heart is and my heart is with Tim," she murmured softly. She wandered through the rooms, trying to decide what she should pack first. She had taken a lot of the kitchen appliances to the farm on Sunday, so she considered what she should take next: dishes, pots, and pans; sheets, towels, clothes?

She stopped at the door to her office. "Divorce papers," she said softly. "I have to find my divorce papers." She walked in and looked at the filing cabinet that stood by her desk. She had collected huge amounts of paperwork throughout the past fourteen years. She'd saved the receipts and manuals for everything she bought, from big ticket items like her washer and dryer, to flash drives for her computer. She opened the top drawer: insurance papers, medical papers, life insurance, bank statements, and investment records. Everything was in well-marked file folders, but there were no divorce papers.

She opened the second drawer. She shook her head. "Manuals, manuals, manuals" she mumbled. She leafed through the folders. "I don't even own some of this stuff anymore. I need to weed them out. Anyway, there are no divorce papers here."

She opened the third drawer. The file folders weren't as full. She squatted down and ran her fingers along the tabs. "Report cards, college degree, wedding pictures…cripes! Why on earth did I keep those?" She pulled the folder out and stood up. She laid it on the desk and opened it, thinking that maybe she had put her divorce papers in with them. A small bundle of pictures, held together by a green elastic band, lay there. She picked it up, stripped off the band, and started thumbing through them.

There were only seven pictures. She remembered asking Dave's friend to take them with her small camera. She had worn a simple short white dress and carried a small bouquet of flowers. She caressed the pictures with her thumb while looked at them. *We were happy then*, she acknowledged. *It wasn't the kind of happiness Tim and I have though. I was happy someone would love me and... I think deep down Dave wanted to belong somewhere...to someone. Getting married gave him the closest thing he'd had to a family. But after the newness wore off...I wasn't enough. He wanted more...he wanted a complete family.* She brushed a tear from her cheek. *The longer we were together, the more cheated he must have felt and he took it out on me.* She chewed her lip. *He could have just asked for a divorce. He didn't have to be so demeaning,* she thought as she folded the pictures together and put the elastic back around them. She closed the folder and bent down put it back in the drawer.

Suddenly she felt tired. She was tempted to close the drawer and leave the search for another time. As she started to stand up, she noticed a file a third of the way from the end. She had labeled it *FREEDOM*. She reached for it, pulled it out and soon discovered she'd found what she was looking for. She stood up again and put it on the desk.

She sat down in her office chair and thumbed through the file. The divorce papers were there. She had walked away, taking nothing from her marriage except freedom: no alimony and no joint property division. She'd just signed the papers and left town. Her old supervisor had forwarded her mail for the first few months and she had mailed the divorce decree when it had come.

She glanced at her watch and realized that she was five minutes late for work. She closed the drawer of the filing cabinet, picked up the folder and hurried out of the house, locking it behind her. Nobody said anything when she slipped into the building and hurried to her desk. She quickly answered the phone that was ringing, and the afternoon at work started again.

Carl stopped at her desk and handed her a file he'd been working on. "Give him a call will you, Christina. Look at the notes I made inside before you do it and fill him in. I'd do it myself, but I have another appointment right away. I'm going over to meet with *Shuster Engineering* and see what their book-keeping system is like. He dropped by on Friday and asked me stop in." As he turned to leave, he stopped to look at her again. "So, how was your weekend?"

She blushed. "Fabulous!"

"That good, eh? So, is it love?"

"Time will tell." She laid her hand on the file, the diamond ring in plain sight. Carl didn't even notice it before he turned to walk to his office. *How could he not notice! It's so gorgeous. He must be blind!!* She was still fuming when the phone rang.

She smiled when she heard Shauna Lee's voice. "Where were you on the weekend?"

Christina chuckled. "I was around. I saw you at Safeway."

"You didn't stop to talk. You had enough groceries for an army. What were you doing?"

Christina was grinning like a Cheshire cat. "I went out to the farm. Tim is seeding, and that man does not look after himself. He needs a keeper."

"Did you say he is a keeper?" Shauna Lee teased.

Christina ignored the question. "He had nothing but junk food in the house, so I came back to town and bought groceries. He needed something besides macaroni and cheese, smokies, a loaf of bread and peanut butter."

"So what did he think of you taking over in his kitchen?"

"I got nothing but thanks. Did you ever meet a man who didn't enjoy a good meal?"

"Were you out there all weekend?"

"Basically. The three of them do overlapping twelve-hour shifts, and Tim works from midnight until ten in the morning, so I puttered around in the flower beds and worked in the yard a bit. I enjoyed myself."

"Careful. It could become a habit."

"Worse things could happen," Christina said with a smile in her voice.

"Colt was looking for you. Did he catch up with you?"

"I missed him, but he left a message on my cell phone. He's looking for someone to help around the house. I put him in touch with someone. I haven't heard how it worked out, though."

"Would you like to come for lunch tomorrow? Actually, what I'm asking is would you like to spend a couple of hours with my kids while I go to the dentist. Brad's out of town tomorrow so he can't look after them, and I know how much you enjoy being with them."

Christina hesitated for just a second. She needed to pack some more things to take to the farm, but she couldn't let Shauna Lee down and she would love to spend time with the kids. "I'd love to! I'm due for a kid fix again. What time should I come over?"

"My appointment is at one o'clock. If you come at noon, we can have lunch before I go."

"Alright. I'll tell Carl that I'll be at your place for a couple of hours. He's pretty good about keeping an eye on the front end."

"I appreciate you bailing me out... again."

"It's my pleasure. Besides, you own the business, so how could I say 'no' to the boss?"

"That's something else I've been thinking about. If I were to sell the business, would you be interested in buying it?"

"Uhhh...I don't know. I'd have to think about it." After Christina hung up the phone, she thought about Shauna Lee's question. *Would I want to own this business? A month ago, I'd have jumped at it. But now... I honestly don't know.* She leaned forward and rested her elbows on the desk in front of her, cradling her chin in her hands. She was lost in thought when Carl came out of his office.

"I'd say the woman is in love," he said with a laugh. "What's going on Christina? I've never seen you so distracted before. Who is the lucky guy?"

She jumped, and color suffused her face. "You startled me!"

"You were daydreaming, and that's the second time you've blushed today."

She turned her chair to face him, her hand resting on the top of the desk with the ring in plain sight. "I was just talking to Shauna Lee. She asked me to look after the kids tomorrow while she goes to the dentist, so I'll be out for a couple of hours after lunch. Will you handle the front end?"

"No problem." He handed her another file. "I've got some more work for you here. I made my notes inside. Will you give Tim Bates a call and bring him up to speed?"

She nodded as she took the file. Color rose in her cheeks again and she looked away from him.

Carl looked at her quizzically. "Okay, Christina. Is it Bates that's got you all dreamy eyed and flustered?"

Her color deepened. "Carl, get out of here."

"Good for you guys. I like him."

She smiled. "So do I, but right now everything is so new, I don't want it to be public knowledge or the latest office gossip, so please don't tell anyone. You're the only one who knows, besides Tim and me."

"You two have been friends for a long time."

She nodded. "We have. It's strange to suddenly realize that we love each other. It's like…like being in a whole new dimension."

He leaned against her desk. "I can't tell you how happy I am for you. You are such a nice person. My wife and I have both wondered why someone hadn't snapped you up before now."

Christina smiled. "We all have our stories, Carl. Let's just say, I never intended to get married *again,* so this whole thing; these feelings, have caught both of us off guard. It's crazy, but he's on my mind all the time now, and he feels the same way. It's like being a teenager again."

Carl laughed out loud. "So, I guess you'll be planning a big wedding soon."

She shook her head. "No, we're not going to have a big wedding. We've both been married before, so we'll probably just get married quietly and present it *fait accompli.* Everyone will whine about it, but we don't want wedding presents and all that stuff. We just want to be together and crazily, we want to get married. Tim's really busy on the farm right now, so we'll have a barbecue later on to celebrate with our friends." She stopped. "I've told you way too much. Don't you dare tell *anyone.*"

He shook his head. "I won't. I understand where you're coming from. So when are you planning to get married?"

She giggled. "ASAP! I'm slowly moving my things out to the farm." She held out her hand. "And this weekend he gave me this."

Carl's eyes widened. "I must be blind! I didn't notice."

"I noticed…that you didn't notice." She admired the ring. "He picked it out himself and he surprised me with it. I love it."

"That's terrific! And my lips are sealed. Does Shauna Lee know?"

Christina shook her head. "If she notices my ring and asks I'll tell her, but Tim and I have agreed we'll just get married and then tell everyone, or things will get too complicated."

"You know she'll be hurt if you don't tell her?"

Christina looked down at her desk. "I know." She sighed. "I'll discuss it with Tim tonight. We just don't want a full-blown circus."

Carl went back to his desk and Christina went into Shauna Lee's old office to do some filing. Ten minutes later, she heard the door open and went out to greet the newcomer.

"Hi, Christina."

Her jaw dropped. "Julie! What are you doing here?"

"We're on our way to *Belanger Creek Ranch* to meet with Colt

Thompson. This is Sarah Brite and her son, Taylor. She talked to Colt last night and the job sounds promising, so I offered to drive her there. We're going to stay overnight and head back to Swan River in the morning, but I wanted to stop in and see you on the way."

Christina reached out and grasped the back of her chair. She was reeling with surprise. This was awkward. Should she hug her? They hadn't been huggers. She didn't know how to act, but she knew she couldn't just stand there like a dummy.

Julie took a step forward, breaking the ice. "Give me a hug, sis. It's been far too long since we've seen each other."

Christina inhaled and met her halfway. "I'm just so surprised!" she said as they met.

After they embraced, Julie stepped back. "You're looking terrific, Christina." She chuckled. "Except for the fact that you are shocked speechless by my appearance, you have a happy glow about you."

Christina flushed with embarrassment. Her hand flew to her cheek. "I'm sorry Julie. I admit I was stunned when you walked in. This is the first time in fourteen years that you've stopped to see me. I just didn't expect to see you."

Julie reached out and took her hand. "I'll have to remedy that. None of us are very good at being family, are we?"

Christina nodded in agreement. "I'm as guilty of that as anybody."

Julie's fingers caressed hers as she let her hand go. "Well, I'm glad I saw you. Mom and Dad said to say hello." She glanced at her watch. "We'd better get going. According to my GPS, we've still got a three and a half hour drive."

Christina nodded. "Thanks for stopping by."

Julie waved and turned to the door. She started to push it open, then turned and looked at Christina quizzically. "Christina?" she asked as she reached for her hand and lifted it up to look at her ring. "I thought I felt this! It's beautiful. Are you engaged?"

Christina swallowed hard. "Y…yes. Just a few days ago. We haven't told anyone yet."

Julie's face beamed. "Who is the lucky guy?"

"Tim Bates. He's a local farmer. We've been friends for a long time." She blushed. "It just took a small nudge to make us realize that we love each other."

Julie's eyes sparkled with happiness. "I'm so happy for you, sis.

Everything is…you're sure it's okay isn't it?"

Christina smiled softly. "Yes, Julie. Tim loves me exactly the way I am. We are mature adults; it's different this time."

Julie looked away. "I…I just don't want you to get hurt again."

"I won't. Tim is a wonderful man. He's been married before too, and we both know what we *don't* want. We are happy to simply love each other and be together." She chuckled. "That says a lot, since we both swore we'd never get married again and now we can't wait to do it."

"So, when is the big day?"

"We're not planning to have a big wedding. We're just going to go to the marriage commissioner as soon as we can and have a civil ceremony. We hadn't planned to tell anyone until after it was done. But, one of the guys here at worked noticed my ring." She stretched out her hand and looked at it sparkling in the sunlight. "I couldn't lie." She grinned. "It's been hard not to yell at the top of my voice and tell everyone that we're getting married. I want to run around showing my ring to everyone who will look. I love it and I'm so happy!"

"Why aren't you telling?"

"We don't want a big deal. We've decided we'll have a barbecue and invite our friends over after Tim is done seeding, but we don't want to wait to get married. We want to do it now. If everyone knows, we'll get caught up in all the well-meaning things our friends will want to do: planning the wedding, bridal showers, stag party. We really don't have the time or the inclination for all that."

"So, do the Thompsons know?"

"Not yet, and don't tell them. Let us do it our way. Please?"

Julie hugged her again. "I won't say anything on one condition; you make certain we are invited to the barbecue."

"Would you really come?"

"Christina, you couldn't keep us away. And you'll have to invite Mom and Dad too."

"Don't tell them before I do, please! You can count on an invitation for all of you."

Christina was making supper when Tim got up and came downstairs. "Hi handsome," she said softly over her shoulder.

He placed his hands on the back of his hips and arched

backward, stretching his back.

"You're a welcome sight," he said with a smile in his voice. He took six long strides and put his hands around her waist, lifting her up and pulling her against him. "I don't know what kept me going before you came out here."

"Sheer willpower," she said softly.

He nodded. "These night shifts add up after a while and I am getting tired. But just knowing you're here changes everything." He nuzzled his face in her hair and kissed the top of her head. "I'm starved. What is for supper?"

While they ate, they discussed their day. Thankfully, Tim had slept well and everything had gone smoothly the night before.

"That sounds wonderful! Now, I have to tell you about my day. It was anything but uneventful!"

Tim hesitated, with his fork halfway to his mouth. "What happened?"

"First of all, I was almost late for work. I can't dawdle so much in the morning before I leave here. Everyone was in before I got there." She grinned. "And once again no one noticed my ring. It almost killed me! It took all my willpower to not run through the office and show it to everyone." She shook her head. "Carl was so close to my hand, the ring would have bit him if it had been a snake."

Tim's lips twitched with amusement.

"I know I said I didn't want to tell anyone until after we are married, but it's so hard."

Tim grinned openly as he watched her take a sip from her cup.

"At lunch, I went to the house and tried to decide what to pack. When I went to my office, I started looking for my divorce papers. I knew I had them somewhere because I wouldn't have thrown them out, but I didn't find them until just before I had to go back to the office. I was a couple minutes late again."

"You're setting a bad example as an office manager," Tim said with a twinkle in his eye.

"I got to my desk and Shauna Lee called. She wants me to come for lunch and stay to look after the kids for a couple of hours tomorrow. She has a dental appointment." She frowned at Tim. "How do I keep our engagement a secret? She's bound to notice my ring."

Tim put his knife and fork on his empty plate and pushed it

aside. "I think you'd better tell her, Chris."

Christina nodded. "I know. Besides, I'm not sure I could stand not telling her. Not only would she be hurt, she'd be ready to kill me if she missed noticing the ring and found out later that I was there and didn't show her."

Tim picked up his cup and took a drink. "We're going to need witnesses when we go to the marriage commissioner. Shauna Lee and Brad are the logical ones to ask."

"But you know what's going to happen when she finds out. Before we know it, we'll get sucked into a big wedding. All the people I work with will want to come and the guys from the ranch. It isn't that I don't want to share it with them. I just don't want to be bothered with all the rigmarole."

"Hon, I think if you explain it to Shauna Lee, she'll understand."

"This afternoon, Carl guessed something was going on." She looked guilty. "I finally showed him my ring and told him it was from you. He was really happy for us and asked when the big day was. I told him what we were going to do and asked him not to tell everyone now. He was alright with that, but he told me I should tell Shauna Lee or she'll be hurt."

Tim nodded. "He's probably right."

Christina sighed. "And then...Tim, you'll never guess what else happened."

CHAPTER THIRTEEN

Tim put down his cup and looked at her expectantly. "What?"

"I almost keeled over. Julie stopped by the office."

"Julie? As in your sister, Julie?"

"Yes. She was on her way to the ranch with the woman who is interested in working for Colt and Frank. Her name is Sarah Brite. I told you that I talked to her the other night and made arrangements for Colt to call her. She had her son with her too."

"So what did you think of her?"

"To be honest, I was so stunned I barely noticed. She's about my height, slender with dark hair that she wore pulled back in a low ponytail. The boy is a nice looking kid. I think Julie said the other night he was ten years old."

"So, he's about the same age as the twins; a year older I guess."

Christina nodded. "The kicker is, Julie noticed my ring. I couldn't lie to her when she asked me, so now she knows we're engaged. She asked if the Thompsons knew, because I told her the other day that we're friends with them. I asked her not to say anything. I had to promise that we'd invite my family to the barbecue if she kept quiet." Christina was thoughtful. "It was kind of nice, Tim. She was happy for me and concerned after what happened last time. She asked me if I was sure *everything* would be alright. It didn't even tick me off that she asked. I was just happy to tell her how wonderful you are."

"It would be nice if your family would reconnect. At least we'd have one set of parents and siblings to share our happiness with."

Christina stood up and collected the dishes. "I haven't worried about that for a long time. We've always been like ships passing in the night. And who really knows if anything will really change now."

"We can reach out to them. Actually, I'd like to go back to Swan River and show the jerk you were married to how proud I am to be your husband. In fact, I wouldn't mind feeding him a knuckle sandwich and a bit of gravel. He was a disgusting specimen of a man."

She giggled. "My bodyguard! But it isn't worth a knuckle sandwich now. That's all water under the bridge." She reached out and took his hand. "Let's go to bed and cuddle for a while before you go to work. I've missed you."

The next day when Shauna Lee opened the door, Patch and Leanne rushed forward to meet Christina. She stooped down and hugged them both. "Hi, guys. How are you?"

"They've been running wild all morning, waiting for you to come. They love you as much as you love them." She ruffled Patch's hair. "They're pretty lucky kids to have a godmother like you."

Christina took both their hands and they pulled her inside, jabbering a mile a minute. "Okay, guys; your Mom and I are going to chat for a few minutes. We'll play while she's gone."

Shauna Lee sat them at the table and gave them their lunch. She pointed Christina to the island. "Grab a stool and I'll put our lunch on the counter."

"What are we having?"

"Crab salad and I'll make green tea."

"Yummy."

Shauna Lee gave her a teasing look as she slid onto a stool. "So what have you been up to, Christina? Have you become Tim's keeper?"

Christina colored. "Umm...I guess you could say that." She cleared her throat. "I'm living at the farm now."

Shauna Lee shot her a sharp glance. "Why? I mean..."

Christina laughed and extended her hand, showing off her ring.

Shauna Lee almost tipped her cup over as she set it down. "Jeeze Louise! Is that what I think it is? You're engaged? To Tim? When did this all happen?"

"Actually, we've been headed that way for a while. When we came back from the ranch at Easter, I was really mad at him for leaving the way we did. We yelled at each other. We ended up having to stay at a B&B because of the storm, and we had to share the same bed because they didn't have any more room."

Christina laughed at the look on Shauna Lees face. "Get real, girl. We didn't jump each other's bones or anything like that. He was so damned freaked about being in the same bed with me, he was going to sleep on the floor until I read him the riot act and told him to grow up."

"That is so damned funny," Shauna Lee howled. "I'm trying to imagine it!"

Christina shook her head. "It wasn't very pretty. I was really ticked off and I didn't hold back when I laid into him. I wasn't sure he'd get into the bed, but I turned off the light and got in on my side. Finally, he did, but he stayed so close to the edge of the bed, I thought he might fall out."

Shauna Lee continued to laugh. "I'd love to have been a fly on the wall."

"No, you wouldn't. It was so cold in that room, you wouldn't have been able to function."

"So then what happened?"

"In the morning he was fine. He went and got my bag before I got downstairs and...I don't know. The rest of the day was pretty comfortable, we talked a lot and somewhere along the way I began to realize how much he meant to me. Crazy....but I got up enough nerve to tell him how I felt a couple of days later and...well... he didn't exactly jump up and down and tell me he felt the same way. I thought I'd really screwed up our friendship. I was just sick. After he got over the shock of hearing me say I had feelings for him, he came back to the house and we worked things out."

"I told you to think outside the box."

"We were already together by then."

"And you didn't even give me a hint!"

"It felt kind of weird 'coming out' and doing lover-like things in public, when we'd been just friends for so long. Tim was better at it than I was. He didn't think anyone would really be shocked."

"I'm not. I'm just happy for you." She leaned close and inspected the ring. "That is absolutely gorgeous."

"It is, isn't it? He has great taste. He surprised me with it on the weekend."

Shauna Lee slid off her stool. "I have to phone Brad and tell him!"

Christina reached out and grabbed her arm. "We're sort of trying to keep it down to a dull roar, Shauna Lee. We're not going to have a big wedding."

"Why on earth not?"

Christina frowned and looked defensive. "We've both been married before. We're going to the marriage commissioner and keeping it simple."

Shauna Lees eyes got big, "Jeeze, Christina! Are you pregna…, Ooh crap… I'm sorry I asked that…but what's the big rush to get married?"

"Because we don't want to wait. After Tim is done in the field, we'll have a barbecue to celebrate with our friends."

Shauna Lee couldn't hide her amusement. "I've got news for you, my friend. You're not going to get away with sneaking off and shutting the rest of us out. This is a big deal, and we're all going to celebrate."

Christina rolled her eyes. "I knew you'd do this." She glared at Shauna Lee. "We don't want to wait six months, so we can plan a big wedding."

"Who said anything about six months? Look how quickly you helped us put ours together."

"We don't want to wait three months either. We're getting married as soon as we get our marriage license; like the end of this week or early next week."

"Then I guess we'd better get to work!"

"Shauna Lee," Christina protested with exasperation.

"We'll plan this later. I have to go now." Shauna Lee turned to Patch and Leanne. "Have fun with Christina, guys. I'll see you all later." She wiggled her fingers at Christina when she dashed out the door.

CHAPTER FOURTEEN

Frank checked the call display when she answered the phone. Shauna Lee's voice was filled with excitement. "Where are you?"

Frank frowned. "In the kitchen. I'm putting spareribs in the oven before I go out to help the guys. Why?"

"Have I got exciting news!"

"What is it?"

"This weekend we're going to have a wedding at the ranch!"

"But, that's May long weekend and we're moving cattle out to the lease."

"You're going to have to postpone moving the cattle until Sunday."

Frank laughed. "You're going to have to convince Colt. Who's getting married anyway?"

"Tim and Christina!"

"Come on, Shauna Lee... where did you come up with that idea?"

"Christina's at my house right now. She's watching the kids for me while I go to the dentist. You should see the ring Tim gave her! It's absolutely gorgeous. But, they plan to sneak off to the marriage commissioner's office and I told her there was no way they're getting away with that!"

"But this weekend? Colt has already arranged for the cattle liners to come out. That's a big job and Colt was expecting to get help from the guys."

"Look, we'll all be there anyway. We've got three days; we can put together a small wedding and a barbecue on Saturday. Then everyone will help Colt on Sunday and Monday. Brad plans to stay until the job is done anyway."

Frank sighed with frustration. "Why does it have to be right away? Why can't it be in two or three weeks?"

"Because they don't want to wait. They just want to get married, but Frank, this should be a special occasion. I want her to have a real wedding to remember."

"I know...." Frank pinched the bridge of her nose and sighed. "And, I agree with you. I'll have to talk to Colt and see if we can work around the trucks. I'll get back to you this evening."

Half an hour later Colt and the twins rode up to the house. When they came in Frank told him about Shauna Lee's call. He leaned against the doorframe and looked at the floor. A grin spread over his face. "That's great news. I wondered if they'd ever get it together."

"They're planning to go to the marriage commissioner and get married this weekend, but Shauna Lee wants them to have a wedding here...but you've already arranged for the trucks to come."

"It's pretty short notice to plan a wedding. I'll see what I can do about the trucks; I may be able to shift them by a day or two. If not, we can do it next weekend. The truckers would probably like to have the long weekend off and we'll manage without the guys helping. It'll just take longer, but we've done it before. Ollie is out working with Grayson all the time now."

"Call the truckers first and see if you can change the schedule. Then I'll call Shauna Lee and let her know how things stand."

The May long weekend was warm and sunny: perfect for an outdoor wedding. Christina's day was full of surprises. Her father was there to walk her down the aisle between the rows of chairs that had been set up. There were tears in his eyes, as he gave her to Tim. He and her mother had come, along with Julie and her family. All the staff members from *Swift Current Accounting and Bookkeeping* were there too.

Shauna Lee and Frank had paid attention to the smallest details.

Shauna Lee had bought potted plants and flowers and she and Frank used balloons and streamers to decorate the wedding setting. A sound system was set up, so the bride and groom's vows could be heard clearly. By noon, they had set up a potent punch bowl, as well as non-alcoholic drinks and they had piled tables with snacks for the guests who were arriving.

Julie's husband had a tripod set up to video the event. He also had a fancy digital camera and happily became the self-appointed photographer.

Music played while Brad joined Tim in front of the decorated garden archway. They both beamed as they watched Shauna Lee come down the aisle, followed by Selena, who sprinkled artificial rose petals along the way. Sam grinned broadly, as he walked with his hands shoved in his back pant pockets.

Finally, Christina and her father came down the aisle. Christina wore a simple, elegant, full-skirted white ballet-length dress, strappy white shoes with wedged heels and a smile that wouldn't quit. She wore a short, net headpiece and carried two dark pink calla lilies.

Tim swallowed hard when he saw the moisture in her father's eyes and he had to fight his own emotions when his eyes locked with hers. She took his breath away. *My god, she is beautiful,* he thought as he reached for her hand. *And, she loves me. How did I get so lucky?*

The ceremony was brief, but all the guests were touched when they watched Christina and Tim make their commitment to each other. After the marriage commissioner pronounced them man and wife, and all the papers signed, Tim took his bride's hand and pulled her close to him. He whistled shrilly to get everyone's attention.

"Christina and I want to thank you all for making this day so special...I know I'm supposed to do this later, but I'm so happy, I want to say it right now. Brad and Shauna Lee and Colt and Frank-- thank you for being such terrific friends." He shifted on his feet, struggling with the words he wanted to say. His gaze focused on Brad and then moved to Colt.

He cleared his throat. "When I came here four years ago, I thought you were all fools." His voice became hoarse; he slipped his arm around Christina's waist and pulled her against him. "But you have shown me that things can be different. Marriage doesn't have to be filled with drama and betrayal and anger."

He blinked hard, forcing back his emotions. "Christina and I want to have the kind of marriage that you have. Without having witnessed your relationships and commitment, I might never have admitted my feelings for Christina." He leaned over and kissed away the tear that slipped down her cheek. "That scares the hell out of me!"

Tim guided his bride down the aisle, past the last rows of chairs, to where they were met by Bert and Hazel Holmes. Bert reached out, took Tim's hand, and looked him directly in the eye. Then he turned to Christina and pulled her against him. "Christina, after all these years, all the hurt you've known, you've finally met the right man for you." He smiled at Tim. "I know in my heart, you will never hurt my daughter. I am proud to call you my son-in-law."

Christina wiped away her tears as she hugged her father, before turning to her mother. "I am so happy you both came. I truly never expected you or all the rest of these people to be here."

"You have wonderful friends, Christina. The Johnson, the Thompsons, and the Cramptons; they all love you both. It's like you're one big family."

Christina nodded. "That's true. We are."

Before, supper Christina cornered Shauna Lee and Frank in the kitchen. "I feel like such a real jerk. I haven't been as appreciative as I should have been, and I'm here to admit I was *wrong*. Tim and I would have missed so much if we'd just gone to the marriage commissioner's office. You worked a miracle here. I can't believe you put this together in such a short time." She brushed away the moisture in her eyes. "The whole idea doing all of that just overwhelmed me. Now I feel terrible about not pitching in and helping you."

Shauna Lee laughed. "You'd have been in the way. Frank and Ellie and I work together like a well-oiled machine."

Frank grinned. "Don't forget Brad and Ollie and Colt."

Shauna Lee touched her shoulder. "You did what you really needed to do; you must have found Tim's divorce decree and got him into town to get the license."

"It was touch and go for a while. I didn't find it in all the logical places and I was getting frantic. Eventually, I found it stuffed in an old suitcase in the basement."

"Well, the important thing is that you found it." Shauna Lee fingered the sheer overlay of her dress. "And you bought this fabulous dress and those cool shoes. You look absolutely beautiful."

"Thanks, Shauna Lee. I have to admit, I love the dress and I sort of feel like a princess in it."

Frank chuckled. "Everyone else thinks so, too. They were all thrilled to be invited. They wouldn't have missed your wedding for anything, especially your family. Your mom and dad insisted on bringing the Baron of Beef and a huge ham for tonight. And Julie brought a couple dozen bottles of wine and some goodies. Jack insisted on being the photographer."

"I'm humbled. I didn't think they cared about me that much. We haven't been close for years."

Frank's look was solemn. "Sometimes that happens when families don't live close to each other, but you'd be surprised to know how much they do care."

Christina blinked away tears. "I kind of get that idea now. Dad was emotional. I've never experienced that side of him." She bit her lip. "The other night Tim said we should reach out to them, and try to make things better between us. I was wrong again, because I couldn't imagine that happening." She steepled her fingers together in front of her and rocked forward on her toes. "Dad was so nice to Tim."

Tim slipped up behind her and slid his arms around her waist, pulling her back against his chest as he kissed her neck lightly. "Did I hear my name, *Mrs. Bates*?"

She grinned and tilted her head back to look up at him. "You did Mr. Bates." She turned in his arms and kissed him on the lips. "*Mr. and Mrs. Bates*...now that's music to my ears."

"Alright, you two," Shauna Lee chided. "You have to cool it for a few more hours. You still have to get through supper before you make the rest of us wish you'd get a room."

Tim chuckled and gave his wife another leisurely kiss. Then, he winked at Shauna Lee, as he turned Christina toward the door. "We need to go out and circulate among our guests. All those people made a lot of effort to get here on such short notice so they could celebrate with us."

They mingled with the crowd and accepted their congratulations. When Patch rushed up and crushed her crinoline and floating skirts around her legs, Christina knelt down and hugged him. "Hi, sweetie. You look very handsome!"

"You look like Cinderella."

Christina chuckled as she kissed him. "And you look like my

prince charming!"

He planted a juicy kiss on her cheek. "I love you."

She stood up and lifted him into her arms, swinging him around. Laughter peeled from him and people turned to watch.

Hazel Holmes watched them with a soft expression on her face. "She would have made such a wonderful mother," she said softly as she turned to Ellie.

";She still can be. They just can't waste any time getting pregnant," Ellie said with a twinkle in her eye.

Hazel expression was sad. "No, that isn't possible. Christina can't have children."

"She's not too old yet," Ellie protested.

Hazel shook her head. "It's not that, Ellie. Christina was born without a womb." She wiped her eyes. "It's one of those strange quirks of nature and it's affected her whole life. It's been very hard for her to accept."

Ellie was stunned, and her expression showed it. "I didn't know...that is so unfair...."

"I probably shouldn't have said anything. It just hurts to see her with children like that and know she'll never have any."

Ellie watched Christina put Patch down and scoop up Leanne. She pushed her face into the child's tummy, tickling her. Leanne giggled and squealed and everyone could see the love between them.

Colt looked at Tim and grinned. "You'd better not waste any time, man. You're not getting any younger and you two should have three or four kids at....least."

Tim's eyes flashed to Christina and he knew she'd heard the remark. There was an awkward silence; then Christina put Leanne down and held her hand. She looked around the crowd and took a deep breath. "You are all our friends and I know you're going to be waiting and watching for the baby bump." She swallowed hard. "I think I need to tell you now, I..." Tears flooded her eyes and Tim stepped to her side.

"You don't want to do this, hon," he said softly.

She shook her head. "Yes, I need to," she whispered. "I've hidden this all my life and let it set me apart. I don't have to be ashamed. I never should have been."

Tim took her hand and squeezed it. Everyone was looking at them. Julie held a clenched hand against her lips and tears filled her eyes. Hazel walked over and stood by Christina's side, reaching for her free hand.

"We won't be having any children. I was born with MRKH syndrome." Hazel squeezed her hand. She looked at her mom and then across at Julie. "Most of you will have no idea what that is, but I was born without a properly formed womb, so I can never carry a child."

Silence fell on the group.

"I love kids and I've had a hard time dealing with this," she continued. "For years, I've let it define me and affect my life in too many ways. I don't want to do that anymore. Tim has helped me realize that it doesn't make me less of a woman; it doesn't make me less loveable." She squeezed Tim's hand and he put his arm around her, pulling her to rest her head against his shoulder.

Tim smiled shakily. "So, now it's out in the open, folks. There'll be no babies, but we have each other and that's enough for us. It's so much more than either of us ever dreamed of having at this stage in our lives."

Awkwardness hung in the air briefly, then everyone gradually started to circulate and the rhythm of the celebration returned. No one spoke to each other about Christina's announcement, but throughout the afternoon, every woman went to her and silently hugged her. No words were spoken, but Christina felt the love and compassion they offered her.

Christina stirred. Tim's arm was draped over her, pinning her against him. She smiled as she looked at her hand. A plain platinum band nestled next to her engagement ring. *Mrs. Timothy Bates*, she thought. Her hand reached for Tim's and she stroked her fingers around his ring. *I want to pinch myself to see if it's real.*

"What are you thinking, wife?"

"Did I wake you?"

"I felt you groping around. I was waiting with anticipation, but you just went to check my ring finger."

She chuckled and elbowed him lightly. "You've got a one-track mind. I thought I exhausted you last night."

"I've had six hours sleep. I'm up and raring to go." He grabbed her hand and pushed it against his erection.

"Someone might hear us."

"We'll just have to be quiet," he whispered as he stroked her hip. She turned into his arms and kissed him. Then they quietly pleasured each other.

Two hours later, Christina turned in Tim's arms. "What time is it?" she whispered.

"Eight o'clock."

She listened. "I don't hear any activity. Are they moving cattle today? They're probably gone already."

Tim shook his head. "Colt said he canceled the trucks and postponed the move until next weekend. I should be finished seeding by then. We'll come out and I'll give him a hand. Brad and Shauna Lee are coming out too."

"I can't believe he canceled the trucks for us to have our wedding."

"We have good friends."

"When are you planning to go home?"

"We have to go back today. Ben and Norm worked yesterday and they're out there again today. I told them to work their regular shifts and forget about the night one, so I need to get back and help them finish up. Things have been going well and if the weather holds, we'll be done in record time."

"We'd better get up and see what's going on around here."

Frank and Colt were sitting at the kitchen table when Tim and Christina wandered into the kitchen.

"Morning guys," Christina said with a smile.

Colt put his hands over his ears. "Damn you two are noisy!"

Christina's mouth fell open and color flooded up her neck and suffused her face.

"Colt!" Frank protested. Her eyes met Christina's. "He's pulling your leg. Don't listen to him."

Colt grinned, observing Christina's red face. "Well, somebody was sure pulling somebody's leg."

Tim chuckled. "You know I heard something last night too. I thought it came from down the hall. I wasn't going to say anything, but now that you bring it up…"

Frank flushed. "Coffee's ready, Christina. Pour yourself a cup and we'll sit outside in the sun and leave these two morons in here."

Before they got out the door, Colt and Tim were looking at the weather forecast.

Hazel and Bert Holmes, Julie and Jack Barnes, Joylin and Robert stayed for breakfast, before heading home to Swan River. When they were saying their goodbyes, Julie waited until last. She hugged Christina, then said softly, "I have something I need to tell you, sis."

Christina looked at her, sensing her hesitation. She frowned. "What is it, Julie?"

"I…I'm pregnant," she whispered. "I wasn't sure I should tell you, but you have to know. I hope…."

Christina's eyes shimmered with unshed moisture. "That's wonderful news, Julie! I'm so happy for you."

Julie took both Christina's hands in hers. "I…I didn't want to hurt you…but I thought it might be worse if you realized later on that I hadn't told you. We are so happy for you. Tim is a great guy and we hope we see more of you two."

"I'm glad you like him. He's the best thing that's ever happened to me." She brushed the tear from her eye and smiled. "I'd be lying if I said it doesn't hurt a bit every time I hear that someone else is having a baby, and I'm reminded that I'll never be able to do. I've come to terms with it and I don't fall to pieces and crawl in a hole anymore."

Julie hugged her closer. "Good for you…and thank you, sis."

Tim came to stand beside Christina as they waved good-bye and watched the van drive down the road. Shauna Lee stepped to her other side. "You have a nice family, Christina."

Christina nodded. "We haven't been close. I think most of that was my fault. I…when I found out what was wrong with me, I was devastated…I just…well, I withdrew into myself. When I look back on it now, I realize I was pretty impossible. I don't want to make excuses, but it was devastating to be "different". To know I'd never be like other girls. I was humiliated, angry and defensive and ashamed."

Shauna Lee looked quickly at Tim, and then focused back on Christina. "I'm glad you were up front about it yesterday. Everyone who was here are your friends and we all care about you. There are lots of couples who have different kinds of fertility issues, even Frank. She's miscarried several times and her mother had the same problem. They both wanted more children, but it just couldn't happen. Personally I'd never heard or thought of anyone not having a womb, but Christina you cannot be the only person this has happened to."

Christina shook her head. "No."

"I'm proud of you for speaking up. You put to rest all the

wondering and guessing about whether you are pregnant or not, and you know that would have happened because everyone knows how much you love kids. It also makes people aware of what can happen. Would you have felt so isolated if you'd known about someone else who had experienced the same thing?"

Christina looked at the ground. "It still would have been devastating, but I probably wouldn't have felt like such a total freak." Tears glistened in her eyes again. "Wanting to be a mom, to hold your own child, is a desperate, painful ache when you're faced with not being able to. It's a very hard thing to let go of, but I have Tim now." She looked up at him and smiled as she squeezed his hand. "His love is such a gift to me, I intend to just focus on what we have together and be grateful."

Tim pulled her against him and spoke to Shauna Lee. "Neither one of us expected to find this kind of happiness. People have a dozen babies, and never experience this kind of love." He looked into Christina's eyes. "I think we should say our goodbyes and hit the road. Tonight I need to be ready to work the midnight shift, which sounds awful...."

"No, Tim. We understand what it's like. Seeding is a crucial time. The weather has been good; you must be almost done, aren't you?"

"If the men didn't have any trouble while we've been gone, we'll be done this week. It's been a good spring."

Tim finished the seeding half way into his shift on Wednesday night. Even though Monday was the statutory holiday, Christina had gone to the office to catch up on her work. She talked to Carl on Wednesday morning and told him she was going to take Thursday and Friday off, because she and Tim were going out to the ranch to help Colt and Frank move cattle over the weekend.

Tim looked at his watch when they pulled into the ranch driveway Thursday morning. "It's twelve-thirty. There are cow tracks on the road, so they're moving cattle already."

The truck crossed the bridge over Belanger Creek, and as they drew closer to the ranch yard, they could see cattle milling around in one of the large pens in the corral. Tim looked toward the barn. "There are horses saddled and tied at the tie-rail." He slowed, counting them. "Five of them. Brad must be here already."

Christina grinned. "You enjoy this, don't you?"

"I like to come out and help when they move the cattle. I ride good enough to stay in the saddle, but I'm not a die-hard horseman like the rest of them. I don't pretend to know a lot about cattle. Colt and Frank and Ollie and Grayson understand them; they know where they'll probably try to break away, or if they're sick or hurt." He shook his head. "Frank is damned good with a lariat. She used to team rope when she was in high school."

"I heard something about that. I think she's been teaching the twins. Sam is better at it than Selena if I remember right and that bugs her. Of course, Sam loves it. It isn't often that he beats Selena at anything. It's really good for his ego."

They drove up the hill to the big house. When they opened the truck doors, a barrage of noises greeted them: the sound of disturbed cattle, the loud bawls of cows looking for their calves, calves calling for mothers, the deep testosterone-fueled roars of the bulls in the adjacent pens, excited by the smell and proximity of the cows nearby. Fresh odors from the corrals drifted on the air.

Christina wrinkled her nose. "I guess I'm sissified. I don't think I would ever get used to the barnyard smell. And the noise! To me, cows are just stupid, ugly things." She grinned at Tim and shook her head. "Don't tell these guys I said that. To them, that would heresy, but I have to tell you, I'm so glad you're a farmer!"

Tim took her hand as they walked to the house. "When you work with it all the time, you get used to the smell and the noise. And in truth, cows really have an incredible relationship with their calves. You find the odd one that is useless as a mother, but people are like that too. For the most part, even though they all look the same, a cow, and her calf know each other. The mother licks it and moos to it, and when the calves are young, she'll take a run at anything that she thinks might be intruding into their space; even another calf that is looking for its mother. Yet when they get older, the cows seem to take turns babysitting groups of calves. I have no idea how they decide who looks after which calves, but you'll see a couple of cows grazing or resting in the field with twelve to fifteen calves."

"I'm still glad you're a farmer," Christina said, before they entered the house.

That morning, Ellie had come to help Sarah cook and Colt, Frank, Shauna Lee, Brad, Ollie, Grayson, Taylor, Sam, Selena, and Patch were sitting at the table with them.

Leanne was playing on the floor. When she saw Christina, she uttered a shriek and got up, toddling toward her, arms extended. Christina bent down and picked her up. "How's my girl," Christina said softly, as Leanne leaned her cheek against hers. Leanne was babbling happily, touching Christina's face, peering at her earrings and then exploring the buttons on her blouse.

Shauna Lee watched Christina slip into a moment of bliss and her heartstrings tugged. *What a shame it is that she can't have kids.*

Everyone chatted for a few minutes, before getting up to go riding again. Tim kissed Christina and told her he'd see her later. Shauna Lee looked at them pulling their boots on and getting ready to leave.

Christina sidled up to her. "You'd better hurry up or you're going to be too late."

Shauna Lee looked at her, startled. "But…."

Christina laughed. "I don't ride, but I know you do, so take advantage of my offer. I'm happy to look after the kids."

"There's a Sippy cup full of milk in the fridge for her." She gave Christina a quick hug. "Thanks! I appreciate having the chance to go."

"The weekend is yours. Get out of here and go with the rest of them."

Shauna Lee ran to the door. "Brad!" she yelled. "Brad!" He was almost at the bottom of the hill, but he heard her and turned. "Will you saddle a horse for me? Christina is going to look after the kids so I can ride too."

He gave her a fist pump and turned to trot down to the barn.

Christina helped Ellie and Sarah clear the table and do the dishes. Then the three of them discussed what to make for supper. "I brought lasagna," Christina said. "It's still in the truck. I'll bring it in."

Ellie nodded with approval when she saw the big pan. "That's perfect. We'll make a salad and I'll make a couple dozen buns and supper will be ready."

"Ellie, why don't you take a rest?" Christina asked. "You don't want to get overtired."

"Christina's right, Ellie," Sarah interjected. "I'll make the buns and a quick dessert if Christina will keep an eye on the kids."

"Nothing could make me happier. Where are the twins and

Taylor? Did they go riding?"

"No. They wanted to go, but Colt said all the horses were needed for the adults. They're probably at the barn. Frank stuck a cow head with horns on a bale and they've been practicing with a lariat. That's what Frank's dad did for her and that's how she got started team roping."

"Tim said something about that. He said Sam was pretty good at it."

"He is. Selena is determined to get better at it than him. The three of them spend hours out there."

"It's still early days, but does Taylor like it here?"

Sarah nodded. "He loves it. The three of them get along unbelievably well. And Taylor has really become infatuated with Grayson."

Christina put light jackets on Patch and Leanne, and they walked down the hill with Ellie. Ellie went home and Christina walked over to check on the ropers. *That smell is gross. I don't know if I'd ever get used to it. At least the cows have quit making so much noise.*

Suddenly, there was a loud thump and the twins dropped the lariat and ran toward a pen. Sam was yelling, "Whoopee! Hey, Taylor and Selena…those two big guys are really going at it. Look at that!"

Christina could hear the sound of hooves pounding in the muddy corral, and a smash as the two animals slammed into the boards again. Christina yelled. "Get away from there. If they break those boards, you'll get hurt."

Sam grinned, excitement charging through him. The two huge animals did a silent dance around the corral, pushing their way through the animals that they shared the pen with. Head pushed against head, their necks bowed, their hooves slipped and dug.

Christina held her breath, fear rising in her breast. *They'll break their necks or their back, or a leg.* She winced. *How can their bodies take that pressure?* Snot slithered out of their noses and their eyes rolled in their heads.

Sam leaned in to look through the heavy boards. Selena held back a bit, but Taylor snuck right up beside him and they leaned their heads against the space between the planks, fixated by the fight. Suddenly Sam started to squeal. "Watch!! The dark one is going to take the other guy."

Christina held Leanne tight. "What makes you think that?"

"Because their heads are sliding to the side. That other one is leaning more and…See, I told you!"

The head of the lighter-coloured animal slid off the side of the darker one and his balance faltered. The darker one shoved its head into his shoulder and started pushing. With a few short pushes, the disadvantaged bull struggled to gain purchase and fought to get out of the way.

Sam made a fist pump as he turned toward Christina. "It's okay. It used to scare me, too. I was afraid they'd break the corral, but they never have. A couple of them get into a fight every day. They really beller and paw the dirt at first. They bristle up and walk sideways, but once they get at it, they don't make much noise. It's fun to watch."

"Do your mom and dad know you do this?"

"Heck yeah. Dad does it, too. You can't stop them once they get started."

"Well, don't get too close. As far as I'm concerned, you're too close right now."

Selena smiled. "Christina, he moves away when they get close enough to run into the boards next to him."

Christina took Patch and Leanne to the house. "It's time to have a nap, kids." Leanne was already rubbing her eyes and wanting to snuggle, so as soon as they got inside, Christina put her on the bed. Patch was tired too and he willingly lay down.

The next day, everyone followed the same routine. They were up at five o'clock for breakfast and saddled up and on the trail by seven. According to their head count, the riders had brought all the cows and calves into the corrals by Friday night.

At six o'clock Saturday morning, three cattle liners were lined up at the chutes, ready to start loading cattle to take to the lease. It was late Sunday night when they finished hauling all the cows and calves, as well as the bulls to the lease. Colt, Frank, Grayson and Ollie would spend the next few days riding the lease to integrate the bulls evenly among the cows, and distribute the herd into different areas.

Everyone came in tired and worn out. Christina looked at her watch after supper. "Tim, we need to go. I have to go to work tomorrow."

Shauna Lee looked at her in dismay. "Get a good sleep and

leave early in the morning. It's too late now, and Tim is exhausted."

"I've missed so many days this month; the staff won't think I work there anymore. When I took Thursday and Friday off, I promised Carl, I would be in on Monday morning."

Shauna Lee shook her head. "I'll call him and tell him you'll be in on Tuesday. You've been babysitting for me, and I own the place."

"I don't want to tick him off, Shauna Lee. He's been really good."

"He'll understand." Shauna Lee called Carl's cell and filled him in on what was happening. She hung up and smiled at Christina. "It's all taken care of. He said they'll see you on Tuesday. That will give you a chance to recover from looking after my kids."

"Recover?" Christina scoffed. "I loved it. I'll miss them, but I appreciate not having to rush home tonight."

They lounged around the table and discussed the massive job they had accomplished over the past four days. Then stifling yawns and groaning when their sore muscles protested as they stood up, they all headed for bed.

As Christina and Tim snuggled under the covers, Christina's mind swirled with the news she wanted to share with him. *He's exhausted, but if I tell him what I found now, he'll never sleep. I'll wait until we get home tomorrow...or at least until we are on the road, then we can talk it through and think about what it means.*

CHAPTER FIFTEEN

Ellie enjoyed the morning sun while she walked up the hill to the new house. She was puffing when she got there, and that was something that always surprised her because she walked it often. She didn't dwell on her recent heart attack, but awareness lingered in the back of her mind and she was grateful for Colt and Frank's consideration when they hired Sarah.

Sarah was sitting on the deck, enjoying the morning sounds and a fresh cup of coffee. She had seen Ellie coming up the hill and gone inside to get a cup and a carafe of coffee. As Ellie neared the house, she called out to her and lifted the second cup. "Come and join me for coffee before we start making breakfast."

Ellie smiled. "You are such a sweetheart. Thank you," she said as she sank into a chair. "Is anyone else up yet?"

Sarah glanced at her watch. "It's only twenty-five minutes to six. Last night Frank said breakfast would be at seven." She gave Ellie a quizzical look. "What time did you get up?"

Ellie smiled. "I couldn't shut my mind off, so I didn't sleep very well. I was awake at four-thirty. I laid there for fifteen minutes or so, but it just seemed pointless, so I decided to get out of bed and come up here. Old habits die hard, you know."

Sarah smiled as she reached out and touched her hand. "You need to take care of yourself. I noticed you were out of breath when you got here."

Ellie sighed. "It frustrates me. I need the exercise and I walk a lot, but this hill does get me. I used to walk it with no problem, but over the past couple of years it's gotten harder."

"Colt and Frank told me what happened. Maybe you should walk on level ground and ride the quad up the hill. It's pretty steep and that probably taxes your heart more than you should let happen. I haven't had a heart attack and I find I have to push myself to make it up here."

Ellie nodded. "I hate to give in, but I have to admit, once I realized how serious it was, I was scared. I'd just never thought of me having a heart attack. I was active, I'm not overweight and most of what we eat is homegrown. We get our meat from the ranch and we get our vegetables out of the garden. Still, in spite of that...."

Sarah nodded sympathetically. "I know. You see people who are grossly overweight, couch potatoes and you'd swear they're walking heart attacks; then someone like you takes a hit and you have to wonder. I think there have to be a lot of underlying factors that we don't necessarily understand, but who wants to take a chance. So take your medication, keep eating healthy and exercise down there on the flatter ground, Ellie." She glanced at her watch. "Oh, oh...it's time to go inside and start cooking. I made pancake batter when I got up. We can cook them on the big grill. We'll broil the bacon in the oven and make scrambled eggs in the electric frying pan. Breakfast will be ready by seven."

Sarah was cooking pancakes and Ellie was laying out bacon strips on broiler pans, when Frank and Colt came into the kitchen. Colt walked up behind Ellie and put his arms around her. "How are you doing this morning? This has been a busy four days, and we don't want you to get overtired."

Warmth from the love of this family flooded through her. "I'm fine, Colt. I've been taking a nap every afternoon. Sarah and Christina made sure of that." She turned to look at him. "I'd hate it if you shut me out. I love being involved. I can't just sit back and do nothing; that's not living for me."

Colt smiled and rested his hand on her shoulder. "Well, we want you to live life to the fullest, but we know you tend to overdo it. I'm just checking."

"The pancakes smell wonderful, Sarah," Frank said as she handed Colt a cup of coffee and lead him to the table. They sat down and looked out over the corrals below. "It's another fabulous day."

Colt leaned back in his chair. "It is. I'm feeling lazy, but we need to get out there and finish the job. By the end of the week, we'll have the cattle more evenly distributed over the lease and we'll be able to relax for a few days. Maybe we can do some fishing at the river." He sat up and leaned his elbows on the table. "I think there is a rodeo in Brooks in a couple of weeks. It might be fun to take the kids to it."

"I like your ideas."

Tim and Christina joined them in the kitchen and Brad and Shauna Lee arrived minutes later. Everyone sat down with a cup of coffee. Christina took a few sips and then lifted her cup in a toast; "To the energizing properties of a morning jolt of caffeine. My day doesn't really start until I have it." She turned to look in Ellie and Sarah's direction. "Thanks, to the cooks. It's nice to be spoiled like this!"

Tim and Christina left shortly after they finished breakfast. He pulled her against him when they got into the truck. They waved happily, as they pulled away from the yard, enjoying the comfortable silence that encompassed them.

Christina wanted to blurt out her news but decided it might be best to wait until they were home, when Tim wouldn't need to be distracted by driving and they could give it their full attention. Instead, they shared casual conversation about the weekend. Tim told her how much he'd enjoyed riding with the rest of the crew and she told him how much she'd enjoyed looking after Patch and Leanne. She also told him how excited Sam was about the bulls fighting in the pen.

When they arrived home, Christina ran up the steps to the veranda and sat on the wicker lounge. She motioned for Tim to sit beside her. "I have something to tell you, Tim; actually I have something to show you." She held up her cell phone.

"What have you been up to?" he asked curiously.

"I was at Ellie and Ollie's place. I walked down with her when she went back for her nap yesterday afternoon."

"And that made you this excited?"

Christina turned on her phone and brought up her pictures. She gave it to Tim. "See this?"

Tim tensed. "It's the picture of my mom that I saw in Ollie's office. Did you go snooping?"

"Not really. Well…maybe just a bit. I went to check on Ellie after I'd put the kids down for their nap. She was still sleeping, so I decided to let her rest. I passed Ollie's office when I was leaving and I thought about the picture you'd seen, so I stepped in to have a look. It wasn't on the desk this time, but it was in plain sight on that low shelf by the side of his desk. So I picked it up and looked at it. When I looked at the back, I noticed the name of the legal firm stamped on the back. When I went to put it back, I saw an envelope with the same return address on it, so I picked it up. There was a sheet of paper inside." A guilty look slid across her face. "I took it out and read it. I decided to take a picture because I thought you might want to see it." She moved to the next photo and enlarged the picture.

Tim began to read it, and then said "Let's go to the office and download these on the computer. This is too hard to see."

She followed him inside and watched while he hooked up the cable between the phone and the computer USB port. "There are seven pictures, Tim. After I read the letter, I looked at what was under the envelope. Ollie had corresponded with the lawyers. There were copies of his letters, notes he'd made about phone calls and another letter he'd received from the legal firm."

"Did you say anything to Ellie?"

"No. I just put everything back the way I found it and got out of there. I wanted to tell you last night, but I thought you'd never get to sleep if I did, so I waited until we got home."

Tim selected the pictures and downloaded them. He enlarged them on his computer screen and read the letters. "I don't get it. I know that is a picture of my mom, but this letter refers to her as Wanda Ethridge. Her name was Maddy—actually, it was Madeline, but everyone called her Maddy. And Mom and Dad's marriage certificate listed her as Madeline Webber. Wanda Etheridge doesn't fit anywhere."

"Did you read the stipulations in the will?"

"Where Ollie wasn't supposed to be notified until the adoptive father of her son was dead?"

"Yeah. Can you imagine how shocked Ollie had to have been? Click ahead and read his letter to them."

Tim read the letter Ollie had written. "He really doesn't have a

Gloria Antypowich

clue about any of this, does he?"

Christina's voice was thoughtful. "I don't think so. If you read his notes, it seems that he made several phone calls in an attempt to figure it out."

Tim picked up the picture on his desk and looked at his mother. Then he moved his fingers back to the computer and clicked a few keys. The printer activated and he waited as it printed off the picture he'd seen on Ollie's desk. He laid it next to the one that sat on his. He studied them, then, pushed it over to Christina. "Look at these. She's a little older in the picture with Dad, but these are pictures of the same woman."

Christina studied the images. "Look, they both have that dark spot or mole on the left cheek. It has to be the same person."

"Mom always said she didn't have any family." Tim frowned. "She never talked about it, but I always assumed they'd died. This Ethridge thing really throws me."

"How do you want to go about checking this out?"

"I'm not certain. Do you think it would it do any good to write the lawyers?"

"They weren't much help to Ollie. Do you think they would be able to do more for you?"

"I wonder if they'd tell me who the adoptive father was. If it was Harry Bates, then that's a strong lead. Maybe that's where we should start."

Christina was preoccupied, playing with a pen, rolling it on the desk and twirling it around. She frowned. "Tim, if that is your mom, do you see where all this leads?"

Tim looked baffled. "What are you getting at?"

"Why would they have notified Ollie and sent him that birth certificate? It seems to me that Ollie could be your dad."

Tim stared at her, his jaw dropping slightly. He clicked back until he found the picture she had taken of the birth certificate. He stared at it in disbelief, then ran his hands back through his hair, and back to rest his cheeks in his palms, his fingers cupping over his eyes. "Holy hell," he whispered as he pushed out a deep breath. "Can that be true?"

"The implication is clear." She walked around behind him and put her arms around him. "Tim, it could be worse. Ollie's a nice guy. From his letter and his notes, he badly wanted to find his son."

"It's just too weird. I've known the man for four years."

156

"Do you think you should talk to him about the possibility?"

Tim shook his head. "I don't want anyone to know about this until we do some more checking." He looked at her sharply. "Not anyone! That means Shauna Lee too."

Christina sobered immediately. "Tim, I'd never tell anyone unless you agreed. I didn't tell them when they asked why we left so early that day at the ranch."

He looked guilty. "I'm sorry Chris. I didn't mean it the way it came out. I'm just stunned."

"Do you want to write a letter now?"

Tim shook his head. "Not now. I need time to think about this. Let's just relax. Can we sit and watch TV or something?"

Chris reached for his hand. "Let's see what's on."

Tim found a baseball game and they sat down to watch. By the third inning, Tim was sound asleep. Chris sat for a few minutes longer, then got up and went into the office. She sat down at the computer and opened the internet browser. She typed in one word; Ethridge. She hit enter and watched as the various search selections came up. The name Ethridge came up several times. Some were businesses, others individual people. Some were listed on internet media sites; others on genealogy websites where most of them were American and a few were from the UK.

She changed the search to Ethridge in Canada. She found a few in Ontario. She tried to search farther and was directed to Ancestry.ca. She hesitated, then signed up for one month and began to search through family trees, census reports such as marriage, death, and birth records.

"Cripes," she groaned. "There's so much information here, it's like searching for a needle in a haystack." She entered "Wanda Ethridge" in the search bar, hoping to find a birth record or something in the census reports. Several people named Wanda Etheridge popped up, but none seemed to fit what she was looking for. "What am I looking for?" she mumbled. "I'll have to ask Tim what her birth date was. He probably knows and that will narrow down the field."

She walked out to check on Tim, but he was still sleeping soundly. She went back and studied the Certificate of Birth that Ollie received. Studying it, she didn't see anything that would help her.

She chewed on her pen, deep in thought. Then, she began scribbling on a sheet of paper; adoption papers, Tim's detailed birth record, Maddy and Harry's marriage license, could Tim's mom have been married before she married Harry Bates? If so, she must have gotten divorced, so where would I find this information? Vancouver? How can we get access to these records?

She went online again and searched for how an adult adoptee could access their adoption papers and the birth records in British Columbia. She discovered a site that directed people to the Vital Statistics Agency in B.C. *Well, that's a place to start.*

She created a new file on the desktop, then copied the information from the website and pasted it into the new folder for quick reference. She thought that if they could find the first link to Tim's past, the mystery would unravel.

She walked back to check on Tim. The baseball game was over and he had slept through it all. She bent over and shook him gently. He started to wake up, and his expression was confused. Then, he smiled. "Was I snoring?"

She laughed. "No. I just need to talk to you. I've been on the computer trying to find some information. What was your mom's birth date?"

He rubbed his eyes and yawned. "Just let me think for a minute."

"Sorry...I shouldn't have woken you, but I couldn't wait any longer." She grinned. "I'm impatient. I feel like I'm wasting time and if I have the information, I can see what I can find online."

"Let me think. Her birthday was in March." He gave his head a quick shake and blinked his eyes as if to clear away the mental cobwebs. "March twenty-fifth. Nineteen-forty-seven.... I'm pretty sure that's right. I was born in November, nineteen-sixty-five and she was eighteen years old when I was born. Does the math for that work?"

Christina did a quick mental calculation and nodded. "That sounds right. Go back to sleep if you want. I'm going to start checking."

"I'm awake now. I'll join you. Do you want coffee or something? I'll make it."

"Sure."

Christina was working on the ancestry website when Tim pulled up a chair beside her. She was scrolling through a long list of records. "What are you doing now?" he asked.

"It's amazing how much information is on here. In fact, it's mind boggling. I decided to check the Canadian census records, but I'm not finding anything online for nineteen-forty-seven. I don't think that information is available yet. I read somewhere that there's a time frame before they can be released, to protect privacy. I think we might have to get in touch with Vital Statistics in B.C. I saw a site for adopted adults to get information in B.C. too."

"That's probably the place to start. But I'm going to get in touch with this legal firm too and see if they can help me follow through."

Christina touched Tim's hand gently. "The more I think about it, I wonder if she got married and divorced before she met your dad. She may have used her maiden name on your birth certificate. It's logical that she'd have used her married name when she married your dad, because it would have been her legal name."

"I'm surprised she didn't tell me any of this before she died."

"Hon, maybe she wanted to bury that part of her life. Things happen when people are young. Then they get older and grow up. Sometimes they're ashamed of what they did, so they just want to bury it in the past."

"But if she wanted to bury the past, why did she have that legal firm track down Ollie? She obviously remembered his name; I'm sure she didn't pick it out of the hat. Even though she died first, she made sure Ollie didn't know until dad was gone."

Christina nodded. "It took them a while to track Ollie down after that, so she didn't know where he was. I'm not sure we will ever understand why she did what she did."

"It's hard for me to get my head around all this. It doesn't fit the woman I knew. She was so fair and honest and loving." He shook his head. "I knew she was a single mother; that's all I ever knew. It was just Mom and me until she married Dad." He leaned back and sighed as he looked at the ceiling. "It's hard to believe she would have kept a secret like this."

"I have to believe she was doing it for you. Ollie must have touched a spot deep in her heart. She knew you and Harry had a strong bond, but she had to see the way your siblings related to you. Maybe she knew that once your dad was gone they would turn against you.

"She may have hoped that once Ollie knew he had a son, he would find you. If she'd told you about him and he wasn't interested in a child he'd never known, she may have been afraid it would hurt you even more. So she left it in his court, and he tried to figure out the riddle, but he didn't remember her." She thought for a moment. "I wonder if he knew her as Maddy because he didn't have a clue about anyone named Wanda."

"But, he didn't recognize her picture."

"Tim, your mom would have been between seventeen and eighteen when they met. You don't know what her circumstances were at that time. She's a bit older in the picture he has, and older still in the one with you and your dad. Years and years have passed. If Ollie's remembering her differently, there's a good chance he wouldn't recognize her, the way she looks there."

"What time is it?"

Christina looked at her watch. "It's three-thirty. You slept for quite a while."

"I'm going to phone the lawyer and see what I can find out."

"Think about what you're going to say before you call, Tim. I don't think you want him contacting Ollie about this until you know for sure what it's all about. You need to learn more about your mom first. They can help you find out a bit about her background, and find out if there is an explanation for the difference in her name as Madeline Webber and Wanda Ethridge. Can he help get your adoption papers and your mom and Harry's wedding certificate? It might help if you can get a copy of your record of birth. It'll give more information than your plasticised birth certificate. Can they help get your mother's birth certificate? She had parents, at least a mother who gave birth. All those things will help fill in the picture."

Tim nodded. "You're right. First of all, I don't want to involve Ollie in any of this, until I'm sure he is my biological dad."

"How would you feel about it if he is?"

Tim scratched his head. "I guess it depends on what happened. If he used her and dumped her, I'd be pissed off, but who knows what happened. I like him as a man. He obviously had no idea he had a son. What would he have done if he had known? Would he have stepped up to the plate and shouldered his responsibility to Mom and me, or would he have taken a hike?"

"He doesn't strike me as that kind of person."

"Well, as you said, people change. Why didn't he ever marry when he was young? Did he shun responsibility, or did he just never find the right one until he met Ellie? It seems a bit unusual, but that does happen." He pulled a sheet of paper out of the printer and started to write on it. "Okay, I need to ask them about birth records for Mom and…what else did you say?"

Christina helped him with the list of questions and then Tim called the legal firm on the letterhead of the letters Ollie had received and asked for Arthur Knout. It took a few minutes before he answered. His voice was gruff, his manner impatient.

Tim was flustered at first, but as they talked, Arthur Knout's attitude softened and his interest grew. He told Tim the first thing he had to do was confirm who he was. He wanted Tim to email a copy of his birth certificate, his social insurance number, and his driver's license.

Tim hesitated; "I don't give that information out over the phone or send it over the internet. This is important to me. I'll fly to Vancouver and meet with you instead. I don't imagine you work on Saturdays, but my wife works during the week and I'd like her to come with me. Could we figure something out?"

Arthur hesitated, then said "I don't make a habit of doing this, but this file has been sitting on the pile for so long, I've begun to think I'll never get rid of it. I could meet you first thing next Saturday morning if you want to fly in Friday night."

Tim smiled. "We'll be there. How's nine o'clock at your office?"

"I'll see you then."

Tim laid the phone down and pulled Christina onto his lap. "That was easier than I thought it would be."

"Once you get interested, you're a fast mover, Tim Bates. I like that about you!"

"I'm interested right now Mrs. Bates. Can you beat me up the stairs to the bedroom or should I carry you?"

She stood up. "I want you to have some energy left after we get there. I'll beat you there."

CHAPTER SIXTEEN

Shauna Lee smiled as she tucked Patch in and kissed him on the cheek. *I am the luckiest woman in the world* she thought, as she whispered good night. She went to the living room to take a sleeping Leanne from Brad's arms. Her heart melted as she looked into her baby's angelic face. She carried her to her room and laid her in the crib, drawing a light quilt over her delicate form. Shauna Lee watched her small chest rise and fall gently with each breath. She ran her hand lightly over Leanne's soft curls and let her fingers trail down over her cheeks.

Her mind flew to Christina and she couldn't ignore the tightness that gathered in her chest. Her eyes misted as she thought of her best friend. *I can't imagine loving children the way she does and never being able to have one. Life just isn't fair.*

Brad sensed her melancholy mood when she joined him. "What's wrong, Tweety Bird?"

"It's nothing to do with us." She stood beside him, kneading a stuffed toy with her hands. "I just was thinking about Christina and how unfair it is that she can't have children."

"Well, there's always the option of adoption."

"That's true. But, she should have her own baby. Every woman with the mothering instincts of Christina has that need."

"Thousands of people adopt children, and they love them as much as they would if they had given birth to them."

"I know that, but I hear the grief in Christina's voice."

"I'm not being callous, but it isn't something that can be fixed is it? So what other choice does she have?"

"I wish there was another choice. I'd do anything to help her if I could. It just isn't fair. So many people have children and don't take care of them, and there's Christina, aching to have one and she can't. Where is the justice in that?"

Brad pulled her down onto his lap. He kissed her gently, looked into her eyes. "I love you, Tweety Bird. Sometimes it's hard to remember you the way you were when we first met. You were so defensive and distant and now you are so warm and open. It's a beautiful thing to see."

She snuggled against him, thankful for the life she was blessed to live. When they went to bed, Brad fell asleep immediately, but Shauna Lee lay wide-awake. Two hours later, she got up and went to the office. She turned on the computer and opened the browser.

She typed *born without a uterus*. She was surprised at how many sites came up. She checked out some of the forums and found posts from several women who had that condition. The same thread appeared in each one; the shock of learning their situation and the profound regret that they couldn't carry a child.

Shauna Lee went back to the list of sites: *MRKH Support*. The phrase caught her eye. *MRKH...that sounds familiar. I think that is what Christina said she has.* She clicked on the site. It opened to reveal a surprising amount of information and Shauna Lee read eagerly. An hour later, she went back to bed. Her mind was teaming with the information she had discovered, but she slipped into the peace of sleep within half an hour.

Even though she had a pile of work to do because she'd missed work on Monday, time went by slowly for Christina. *I have to get with it; I just can't get excited about work anymore, but I can't sit at home on my tush.* She swallowed hard. *Since I can't produce babies, I guess I'll have to produce here.*

Shauna Lee phoned before noon and asked her if she wanted to come for lunch. Christina jumped at the chance and left the office right at twelve. When she arrived, the twins flew to meet her when Shauna Lee opened the door. Christina crouched down and hugged them both, inhaling their scent, reveling in their touch.

Shauna Lee put two bowls of steamed vegetables and a fresh bun for each of them on the table. She placed Leanne in her highchair and told Patch to get up on his chair. Then she turned to Christina. "Grab a stool at the counter and I'll dish out our lunch." She spooned out two servings of steamed vegetables and topped them with cooked shrimp. She placed them on the counter and reached for a couple of fresh buns. "What would you like? Water or tea?"

"Water," Christina responded. "This looks and smells wonderful. It's just what I need." She looked at Shauna Lee. "I'm in a quandary. I am so distracted right now. I don't want to be at work; I want to be home at the farm, puttering in the garden, going out with Tim. Were you like that when you got married?"

"If you remember, I missed a lot of work before the wedding. Brad and I both admitted that we'd never have been able to do the things we did if we hadn't owned our own businesses. Any other boss would have fired us."

"How long did it last?"

"Well, right after the wedding we jumped into the heavy tax season, so I had to dig in. But I can understand you being distracted right now. You guys have just finished the tax nightmare, so everyone is kind of burnt out. Being engaged and moving to the farm and getting married all in one month is pretty overwhelming. Maybe you should take a few months off, Chris, and wallow in the wonder of it all."

"Are you serious? Am I that redundant?"

"Of course you're not redundant. I'd hire a temp and your job would always be waiting for you when you decided to come back, but you've worked steady for fourteen years and tell me honestly, how many times have you actually taken holidays?"

Christina shrugged.

"Hardly ever, maybe it would be good for you to take a six-month leave; even a year if you want, so you can settle into being married and enjoy it. Possibly you need to figure out what independence really means to you."

Christina considered the possibility. "I don't know what to say. Could this set a precedent that will create a problem for you? You can't let everyone take a year off when they get married."

"I wouldn't offer this to just anyone. You're my best friend and I'm thrilled to see you so happy. I know your life hasn't always been easy. I want you to enjoy it."

"I…I want to jump at the chance, but I should talk it over with Tim. I've never believed two can live as cheaply as one. Maybe we need my wage."

Shauna Lee chuckled. "Christina, I cannot see Tim turning down the opportunity to have you at home with him for a while."

"A while ago you mentioned selling the business. Were you serious?"

"I've given it some thought, but I'm not sure about it yet. There are times I think I should just relax and enjoy my kids, but what about when they are both in school? Will I wish I had a business then? It's hard to know."

"Brad's business is doing well, isn't it?"

"Oh yeah and he'd love it if I came to work with him, but I've been independent for a long time." She shrugged. "At this time, I haven't decided what I want or need to do."

"Giving up your independence is a big thing when you've worked so hard to achieve it."

Shauna Lee smiled at Christina. "It's a double-edged sword. When you own a business, you may feel you're independent, but in truth, you are dependent on your employees and your customers. You have to figure out what independence really is for you." She picked up her fork and stabbed a shrimp. "I promise I won't sell it to someone else while you're away. You'll have first chance at it if you want it. Maybe when you take time off, you'll decide to do something else. Maybe the two of you will decide to adopt a couple of kids or something life-changing like that."

"I've given thought to adoption, but honestly, I've always wanted the impossible; I've wanted to look into the face of my own flesh and blood. That doesn't diminish the value of an adopted child or the love I'd have for one. I know I'd love it totally, but it hurts to know that we'll never have even one child that we can look at and see traits of Tim in it or me, or its grandparents.

"It's probably because I know that it isn't possible that it is such a driving need, but it is. To be honest, I have to fight the longing all the time. It's stupid; maybe it's guilt or a desire to punish myself. I can't tell you."

"Do you produce eggs, Christina?"

"I think so. I haven't checked, but the doctors said my ovaries were normal. Why?"

"Have you considered having a surrogate carry a child for you?"

"Not really. Let's be honest, how many people want to commit to nine months of deliberately turning their world on end? And, do we want a stranger to carry our baby? They say babies learn a lot in the womb and they bond with the person who is carrying them. That's scary."

"It was just a thought."

Christina looked at her watch. "I have to get back to work."

As she hugged Shauna Lee, she asked, "How could I be so lucky to end up with a friend like you?" She hesitated. "I feel like I'm pushing my luck, but we are going to fly to Vancouver this weekend. It would be nice if we didn't have to hurry back. Do you think I could take time off until the middle of the week?"

Shauna Lee smiled. "Vancouver? How romantic is that!" She thought for a moment. "Take it, Christina. This will be your first trip away from home together, won't it?"

Christina nodded. "I feel guilty for asking for more time off, but it is special."

"Don't worry about it." She took Christina by the shoulder and looked into her eyes. "I'm serious about you taking time off. Take up to a year if you want. By then you'll be able to make some real decisions and you'll either be happy to come back or you'll be content with domesticity. I'm going to start looking for someone to fill in for you."

"I need to discuss it with Tim first."

"Pfttt. He'll be dancing with joy."

When she got back to the office, Christina phoned Tim. He answered immediately. "Have you booked our flights yet?" she asked.

"No, I just realized that we'll have to fly out of Regina. I'll look into it later today."

"Guess what! I asked Shauna Lee if I could take Monday, Tuesday, and Wednesday off next week so we don't have to hurry back."

"And?"

"She said yes! I'll talk to you about it when I get home this evening. I'd better settle down and get to work now."

That night when she arrived at the farm, Tim had supper ready. She sniffed appreciatively as she stepped into the house. "On top of everything else, he cooks! How did I find such a wonderful man?"

Tim came out of the office to meet her. "How did your day go?"

"I don't want to be there. I'm so distracted that I'm ashamed. It didn't matter how busy we were, the day just dragged by and all I could think about was getting home to be with you. How did your day go?"

"I was pretty focused today. I've made a lot of phone calls. I called the number I found on a website for adults who have been adopted, and then I called the B.C. Vital Statistics Agency. I have a lot of ideas. I kept wishing you were here so I could talk to you and bounce ideas off you. I'm really pumped about going to Vancouver this weekend. I'm glad you asked for the extra days off; now we can go to some of these places in the city and see if we can get more information."

"Did you book our flights?"

"I did. I'll have to pick you up after work and we'll drive to Regina from there. We fly out at eight twenty and arrive in Vancouver at nine-thirty-five their time. Right now, there's only an hour difference, because they move ahead an hour for Daylight Savings at the beginning of March and we don't."

"So we'll arrive there at ten-thirty-five Saskatchewan time."

Tim nodded. "I rented a car and booked a room close to the airport for Friday night, too. We'll take the GPS so we can find our way around. I haven't got a clue where anything is, but I thought we'd find a hotel after we decide what we're doing."

Christina looked at him for a minute. "Tim, do we need my wages? I know it costs more for two of us to live, but if I could take some time off, would it make things difficult?"

He looked surprised. "Of course not. The farm brings in enough to support us. Could you take some time off?"

Christina nodded. "I had lunch with Shauna Lee today. I was telling her how distracted I am and asked her if she'd felt the same way when she got married. Anyway, she suggested I take from six months to a year off and then I could come back to my old job. I told her I wanted to talk to you about it. I want to pull my share of the load. I didn't intend to marry you and drop the ball."

"Honey, I want you to call her right now and tell her that I love her for suggesting it and I definitely vote yes." He stepped back into the office and grabbed the phone. His blue eyes were dancing with happiness as he handed it to her.

Shauna Lee answered the phone. "Shauna Lee," Christina said, her voice filled with excitement. "Tim wants to know how soon I can stay home, and he says he loves you for making the suggestion."

"I knew he'd love the idea. Consider yourself 'on leave' as of Monday. After you get back, I'd like you to come in for a few days and show your replacement how the office works."

Christina couldn't stop smiling. "I'll be happy to do that."

"I'll give Carl and the staff the heads up and you can gather up your things and take them home on Friday. I'm glad you're doing this, Christina. It'll be good for both of you."

Christina giggled. "Shauna Lee, you know I've loved working at the office. It's been the touchstone in my life and the rest of the staff is like my family, but now…it's just different. Thank you for suggesting I take a leave, because I wouldn't have thought to ask for one. I'm really looking forward to being at home and spending my days with Tim. I don't know how to say this, without sounding ungrateful for all the years I've worked for you, but I suddenly feel *free*."

"It thrills me to see you so happy. But remember, I'll still need you to babysit once in a while."

"I'll hold you to it. I'll still need my kid fix."

Christina put down the phone and high-fived Tim. "Tomorrow is my last day. We can stay in Vancouver as long as we want. Shauna Lee asked me to come in and work with the new receptionist for a few days after we get back; just to help her figure out the office routine and the other things I've been doing as part of the job."

He grabbed her by the waist and twirled her around. "Whoopee! That is fantastic. Imagine all the things we'll be able to do together now; if I need to go to Regina for parts or out to the ranch you can come with me. We can have lazy days once in a while and maybe even sleep in."

"I can put a garden in and plant flowers and refurbish some of the landscaping. I know I'll never be bored. I just felt like I should be working to contribute to the finances."

"I can support my wife, sweetheart. I know you've always been independent and I thought you wanted to work, or I would've suggested you stay at home from the beginning."

The next morning, Carl stopped by her desk when he came in. "I hear you're leaving us for a while."

Christina nodded. "I'm so excited! I'm going to stay home and be a *housewife*. I'll put in a garden and plant flowers and cook meals for my husband. I'll do all those simple things that raging feminists have scorned for years and love it!"

Carl put his hands on her desk and leaned toward her. "I'm happy for you. We've all come to depend on you and we're really going to miss you around here, but I'm glad you're doing this. People tend to forget life's priorities once they get on the treadmill. They don't take time to enjoy the simple things and it's really a shame. Shauna Lee said you're taking a year off, so make the most of your time away. That's long enough to get a true perspective of things and you may find yourself making totally different decisions than you'd imagine now."

Shauna Lee stopped by the office Friday afternoon, bringing a cake and the children. She also brought a contract that stated the terms of Christina's leave and they both signed it. With hugs and misty eyes, the staff ate the cake and toasted Christina with coffee, wishing her well. Christina collected her personal things from her desk and took her pictures down. When Tim came for her, she left the office with a light heart.

She slid into the truck beside Tim, and they drove to Regina. Later that evening they were in Vancouver, British Columbia.

Saturday morning, Tim and Cristina followed the directions from their GPS and found Arthur Knout's address on East Hastings. The building was old and Tim started thinking about the stories he'd heard about Hastings Street.

He took in his surroundings as he parked on a side street. The area had seen better days, but the stores were free of graffiti. He looked at Christina. "Well, it's not the Ritz, but I don't see collections of homeless people loitering on the street. It's pretty quiet right now."

She nodded, but her apprehension showed in her expression.

He touched her hand. "We'll be alright," he reassured her. "I'm going to phone Arthur and make sure he's there."

Arthur answered on the first ring and told them he'd meet them at the door. They locked the car, ran around the corner and down the street.

"Where did you park?"

"Just around the corner. I hope it's safe there."

Arthur nodded. "Things are quiet at this time of the day on Saturday morning. This won't take too long to wrap up, so your tires should be there when you get back."

He led them into an unpretentious office and told them to take a seat. A file lay open on his desk. He moved it slightly and then looked at Tim. "So, how did you happen to learn about the file I sent Ollie Crampton?"

Christina shifted uneasily, shooting a glance at Tim. Tim looked Arthur in the eye. "One weekend when I was visiting at the ranch, Ollie had heartburn after we ate, so I went to his house to get medication for him. While I was there, I saw my mom's picture on his desk. I was shocked that he'd never mentioned that he knew her. It really upset me and I overreacted. I left right away, without asking him why. After I got home and had time to think about it, I decided to go back and confront him the next weekend, but his wife had a heart attack and Ollie was really shook up. I couldn't talk to him then, and I haven't had a chance to since.

"Last weekend we were helping move cattle at the ranch. Christina went to Ellie and Ollie's place to check on Ellie. She was sleeping, so Christina decided to let her rest. When she was leaving, she saw the picture on a low shelf by Ollie's desk. She looked at it and decided to use her cell phone to take a picture so we could compare it to the one I have of Mom. When she was putting the picture back, she saw the envelope with your return address on it, so she picked it up. She was going to photograph the address, but she saw there was a letter in it."

Christina interrupted. "I read it. I knew it was wrong, but my husband was so upset, I thought it might explain why Ollie had his mom's picture. It did throw fresh light on the subject, so I took a picture of it too. Then I took pictures of everything else that related to this puzzle, carefully put it back and left."

Arthur Knout drummed his fingers on the desk and let out a deep breath. "You realize that what you did is illegal, an invasion of privacy?"

"Yes, but Tim has no idea who his biological father is and it's pretty clear that Ollie had no idea that he had a son. This affects both of them."

Arthur pushed back in his chair and ran his hand through his hair. He swore softly under his breath and then leafed through the file. "Tell me about yourself, Tim: what these papers mean to you, about your childhood, your life with your adopted dad, how you know Ollie Crampton. Every thought you've had about this," he said as he waved his hand at the file. "Any ideas the two of you have come up with."

Tim put everything on the table, hiding nothing. He told him that he didn't recognize the name Wanda Ethridge; he had always thought his mother's name was Madeline Webber, but the pictures were of the same person, with the same mole in the same spot.

Christina took photocopies of the pictures out of her purse and laid them on the desk side by side, in front of him. "Tim's mom is a bit older in the picture of her with Tim and Harry, but look at them. Can you honestly doubt that they are the same person?"

Arthur studied at them closely, then picked them up and looked at them in full light. "The younger woman...she has a scar over her right eye. It's a fine one, but it's definitely there." He studied the other picture. "I don't see it on this one."

Tim and Christina looked at the pictures again. Christina traced the light scar with her fingertip. "He's right, Tim."

Tim cleared his throat. "Is it possible that two people could look so identical and not be related?"

Arthur shook his head. "You need someone with better credentials than me to answer that. You say your mom said she didn't have any family?"

Tim nodded. "She never talked about family and I never met anyone who she said was family before she married Dad...Harry that is."

Christina looked at Arthur. "If we could find out where Tim's mom was born, it might help. She had parents; she didn't hatch from an egg."

Arthur chuckled. "When this file came to me, I hired a private investigator to track down Ollie. It took almost three years to find him. We could go that route for your mom."

Tim nodded in agreement. "I hope it doesn't take three years to find out if Ollie's my dad. If he is, we've wasted too much time already. I want to know."

Christina smiled. "I went online and looked through some Canadian genealogy sites for birth records, divorce records, and census reports. So much of that information is not available online yet because of privacy issues. It's very frustrating."

"When you hire people who do that kind of work, they will

uncover things you would never expect."

"Should Tim go to vital statistics and see what he can find? There's a site for adopted adults that has an office here in Vancouver."

"Let me call the private investigator that I use and see how much access he has to these places. I need your driver's license, your social insurance number, and your birth certificate. I'll make copies of them and witness them. Then, we need to fill out some paperwork to start the process. I'm going to need a five thousand dollar retainer, too." Christina looked at Tim to see if he showed any concern, but he didn't, so she relaxed.

When they left his office, Arthur assured Tim that he would give the private detective the file immediately and promised to keep him updated regularly. When they got in the car, Christina reached out and took his hand. "How do you feel about all this?"

He shrugged. "Time will tell. At least we're doing something."

"I wondered how you felt when he asked you for the retainer. Was that much money hard to come up with? I have savings to contribute, Tim."

He smiled as he lifted her hand to his lips. "We'll be fine, hon. I guess we need to talk about our finances so you know where we stand. I'd have to suck it up a bit if I had to take that kind of a hit too often, but we're good for a few rounds without a hiccup."

"I want to contribute too. I'll need to think about selling my house, and I've got savings and RRSP's."

"Relax hon. We'll deal with all that in time, but right now we're going to enjoy the sites of the Vancouver. This will be a mini-honeymoon."

Christina placed her hand on his thigh. "I hate these cars with consoles," she said with frustration. "I can't sit close to you."

"It'll be fun. We'll just have to work harder at the foreplay." He winked at her. "I miss not feeling your thigh against mine, too. How are we going to remedy that?"

"Well, maybe we should get a hotel room and lie down and relax. We could check out a guide book and decide what we want to do while we're here."

Tim touched her thigh and gave her a wicked grin. "My guide book suggests one important destination."

Christina squeezed his hand. "I'm not going to follow up on that. Where do you want to look for a room?"

"Shall we go back to the place where we stayed last night?"

Christina shook her head. "The place was beautiful, but we don't need to pay that much for a room. That's all right if you're rolling in bucks, but we aren't. So let's find something more realistic."

"The keeper of the purse." He smirked. "I guess that's what happens when you marry someone who works in an accounting firm."

"What are you talking about? I don't work there anymore."

He shook his head. "Alright, how do we decide where we want to stay? Have you ever been to Vancouver before?"

She shook her head. "No. I've only read about it and seen pictures on TV. It's beautiful, but I'm really not a big city girl."

He tapped his fingers on the steering wheel as he thought, and then he looked at his watch and took out his phone. She watched him make a few clicks with his fingers, then smile.

"I have an idea. Would you like to go to Harrison Hot Springs for the rest of the weekend? We can come back to the city on Monday to check in with Arthur and find out what he wants us to do to help with the search. Then, if we have time, we will do some of the touristy stuff around the city."

"The hot springs? We didn't bring bathing suits."

"We'll buy some. Are you game for it?"

"It sounds wonderful!"

Tim phoned the resort and secured a room. "We're on our way. Let's set up the GPS and head down the road." They traveled out of the city to connect with the freeway on Highway One East. Traffic was heavy and Christina noted that Tim handled it with ease. She looked around eagerly, noticing the mountains in the distance on either side.

"You're pretty quiet. What are you thinking, Mrs. Bates."

"I'm feeling like a kid. It is so beautiful, I'm just blown away. Everything is so vibrant and green. The trees, all the flowers and everywhere I look I see those incredible snow-capped mountains in the distance. I'm wondering why I'm seeing all this for the first time when I'm thirty-eight years old. I haven't traveled very much. I've been to Hawaii a couple of times and Mexico, but here in Canada, I haven't been any farther west than Calgary, and no farther east than Swan River."

"I haven't traveled much either. When I was up north,

everything I did was business related. After I left there, I was dealing with my anger and frustration. I didn't even think of doing something like this for the pleasure of it. I was at Harrison once with Mom and Dad, but I was so young then that it's just a blur in my memory. I remember people canoeing on a big lake. We didn't stay overnight; we just spent a few hours and had lunch." He squeezed her knee. "I'm really excited about us doing this together."

They traveled east on the TransCanada Highway, past Surrey and Abbotsford. The mountains and the scenery captivated Christina. "This is so gorgeous. I love it."

Tim leaned forward pointed toward the sky. "See the air balloons up there?"

"Oh look, how many are there? Two, five....WOW! There are nine of them. Isn't that spectacular?"

The miles sped past and they admired the flat, fertile farm fields, the dairy farms, and raspberry fields. Suddenly Christina pinched her nose and gasped. The acrid smell of manure hung in the air. "That is so gross. How do people live with that smell?"

Tim smiled as he wrinkled his nose. "It's pretty strong, isn't it? The farmers spread liquefied manure on the fields for fertilizer."

"Yuck...That almost takes my breath away."

They continued until they came to the turn off for BC- 9 and then turned onto the Agassiz-Rosedale Highway, and followed the signs to Harrison Hot Springs.

Christina sat up and stared in wonder as they drove along Hot Springs Road and turned onto Harrison Public Road. "Tim, this is absolutely fabulous. Look there's a Thai place, and that has to be another restaurant over there. She pointed toward The Copper Room.

While he drove, Tim motioned toward a restaurant across the road. "The Black Forest Steak and Schnitzel House; now that's my kind of place, right there."

"Look at all the places along here; there's a couple of spas. Oh, look down there; that must be the resort." She whistled softly as they drove up to the entrance. "Tim, look at this place! Look at the mountains all around here and the lake."

Tim was grinning from ear to ear when he parked the car. "So, I take it you're glad that we decided to take our mini-honeymoon here?"

"Mini-honeymoon? I wouldn't trade this for a trip to Hawaii." She opened the car door and stepped out. The day was warm, but a fresh breeze wafted in off the lake. She took a deep breath. "Smell it! The air is so light and fresh."

He walked around the front of the car and put his arm around her. "I booked the Romance Package, so let's go in and see what romance at Harrison Hot Springs Resort is like."

Their room was in the East Tower. Once inside, they shut the door and looked at each other. Tim reached out and clasped her hand in his. He led her to the 'ceiling to floor' windows that looked out over Harrison Lake.

He shook his head. "There is beauty and then, there is *beauty*! No matter how beautiful it is at home, this is superlative. Look at the color of the lake and the mountains. I'm glad we decided to come here."

"Me too, Mr. Bates." Christina threaded her arms around his neck and pressed against him. She looked at the king-sized bed. "That's a whole lot of bed over there. Do you think we can do it justice?"

"Is that a challenge?" Tim asked, sweeping her up in his arms.

Later in the afternoon, they relaxed on the bed and browsed through the brochures they'd found in the room. Christina chuckled. "We get breakfast at The Lakeside Café, and dinner and dancing one night at The Copper Room—I'm too tired to go dancing tonight. I think we should leave that for tomorrow night, don't you?

"And a couple's massage, eh?"

"That sounds heavenly. Tim, tell me honestly; have you ever had a relaxing massage?"

He grinned and shook his head. "Never."

"You'll love it. Some people say it's better than sex."

"I'd be willing to bet against that," he said with a gleam in his eye."

"It leaves you so relaxed you're like a cooked noodle."

He nodded his head. "Yeah, sex does that to me." He rolled over and pinned her on the bed. "And it doesn't take me an hour to feel that way." He kissed her soundly as he pushed his body against hers. "I can get double the bang for my buck. Within the hour, I can be primed and ready again."

She giggled against his chest. "You're insatiable." He smothered her words with a kiss, and they did justice to the king-sized bed again.

They ordered room service and enjoyed eating out on their

balcony in the moonlight. Tim looked at her before he finished his glass of wine. "We should've gotten bathing suits. We could have gone in the pool."

Christina yawned. "I am too tired to think about putting on a bathing suit and going down there."

Tim poured them each another glass of wine and they watched the moon bathe the snow topped mountains. They went to bed shortly thereafter.

Tim phoned Arthur Knout at nine o'clock Monday morning.

"Good morning, Tim. I've already talked to my PI. He's working on your case as we speak. You need to stop in and sign some forms to give us authority to act on your behalf."

"We'll be there in two or three hours."

After they did what they needed to with the lawyer, they spent their free time exploring a few of Vancouver's tourist attractions: Stanley Park, Granville Island, the Vancouver Aquarium, the Capilano Suspension Bridge and they walked the seawall. When they caught their flight home on Wednesday evening, they both were relaxed, yet tired. They arrived in Regina at ten-thirty and decided to stay overnight.

The next morning it was raining lightly. Tim looked at the gray skies and smiled. "This is a gift from heaven. It's perfect timing for the crops and I hope it lasts for at least three days."

CHAPTER SEVENTEEN

June and July went by quickly and Tim heard nothing from Arthur Knout. At first, it was a constant aggravation, but gradually it slipped into the background as he settled into his busy routine on the farm. Before he started haying, Christina and he slipped away once to experience life outside their intimate bubble, and they spent the occasional weekend with Brad and Shauna Lee, but for the most part they were happy in their own world.

The first weekend in August, Colt and Frank invited them to the ranch for the Saskatchewan Day weekend. The whole 'family' would be there and Christina looked forward to the visit. Tim was hampered by thoughts of seeing Ollie again, and wondering about him.

Tim phoned Arthur's office the Thursday before they left. His receptionist answered the phone and informed him that Arthur was away for two weeks. Frustration gnawed at Tim's gut. *How can it take so long to get results? You'd think they'd have found something by now.* He sighed. *It took four years to find Ollie, so why should this be any different?*

Tim and Christina followed Brad and Shauna Lee on the drive to *Belanger Creek Ranch* and they arrived shortly after lunch. As

Gloria Antypowich

usual, each family brought their favorite potluck meal, as well as snacks and alcoholic beverages to contribute to the weekend fare. After the food was put in the large cooler at the ranch house, and they were settled in their rooms, everyone gathered on the front deck to enjoy the sunny day. They cracked a few beers, laughing, chatting, and enjoying each other's company.

Patch and Leanne vied for Christina's attention and she luxuriated in their adoration. After she finished her beer, she took them for a walk.

Tim watched her go down the road, holding the younger children's hands as the twins skipped along beside her. He smiled and looked at Colt. "Sometimes life isn't fair; she'd have been such a wonderful mother."

"There's no chance of you having kids?"

Tim shook his head. "We knew that when we got married." His gaze followed the happy group wandering down the road. He watched them stop and wave to someone he couldn't see. He tensed momentarily when Ollie and Ellie came into view. Christina stepped forward and hugged both of them. They chatted for a few moments and then Christina gathered her young entourage and shepherded them forward. Ollie and Ellie continued their walk up the hill.

Tim watched them as they walked up the driveway. He studied the older man, seeing him in a different light. *Could he be my father,* he wondered? He nodded to Ollie as he stepped onto the deck, then pushed up out of the chair and gave Ellie a hug.

Colt offered Ollie a shot of Jack Daniels and poured a rum and coke for Ellie. Tim watched surreptitiously, as Ollie smiled warmly at Ellie, placed his hand against the small of her back and guided her over to a couple of empty chairs.

I've never seen him act like anything less than a gentleman, he thought. He absently let the conversation flow over him. *Who is Wanda Ethridge? Why does she look so much like Mom?* He wandered around to the back of the house and leaned against the wall.

As he thought, he compared himself and Ollie. *I'm six feet two inches tall and muscular; Ollie is barely five feet eight inches tall and slight and wiry. Mom was a small woman too, so where did I get my height?* He ran his fingers through his sandy-coloured hair. *His eyes aren't the same color as mine. He's been gray since I met him, so I don't know what color his hair was when he was young.*

He pushed himself away from the wall and walked around to the front of the house. *He can't be my biological father; we aren't alike in any way.* He shoved his hands in his pockets and started to walk down the driveway, his eyes searching for Christina and the kids. When he saw them at the barn, he started to run, enjoying the physical motion, releasing the tension that had collected in his muscles. When he reached them, he hugged Christina close, thankful that she was his anchor, his love.

The next morning, Ollie, Grayson, Brad and Tim jumped into Colt's truck and went to the lease to check on the cattle. They planned to do some hunting too. Frank, Shauna Lee, and Christina got up later and lounged in the sun as they nursed their coffees.

"Do you miss work, Christina?" Frank asked.

"No. Tim and I are enjoying life. I never think about work."

Shauna Lee chuckled. "You wouldn't believe how domesticated she is. She planted a garden in the beds in the back yard, and there are flowers blooming everywhere."

"The place always had potential. I'm pretty sure Serena did a lot of gardening when she was younger, but I didn't have time when I lived there." Frank stretched. "Truthfully, I don't have much of a green thumb. That's Sam's forte. I'm better suited to working with animals."

Christina smiled. "That's what makes life interesting. It would be pretty boring if we were all the same." She stood up and walked to the edge of the deck. "I think I'll go for a walk."

Shauna Lee jumped up. "I'll come with you."

Frank closed her eyes and relaxed into her chair. "I'll stay here. When the kids wake up, I'll give them breakfast."

Christina and Shauna Lee walked down the driveway and turned toward the main road. They walked in comfortable silence until they reached the culvert over Belanger Creek. Christina looked down into the trickle of water that was the creek now. "I feel like dipping my feet."

Shauna Lee moved to the slope by the edge of the culvert. "We can go down here and sit on the rocks."

They made their way and sat quietly, enjoying the murmur of the water as it trickled by.

"Christina?" Shauna Lee asked, breaking the silence between them.

"Yeah?" Christina replied, staring absently at the sky.

"I've been thinking…."

Christina turned and looked at her friend. "About what?"

"Would you and Tim let me be a gestational surrogate for you?"

Christina went still, her face showing her shock. "D..Di..Did I hear you…?"

Shauna Lee nodded. "Yes. Will you let me carry your baby for you? Brad and I have talked about this." She grinned. "At first, he thought I was nuts, but now he's game for it. He knows what it would mean to you, and I love being pregnant. I always feel great and I've never had any problems with the delivery. Feeling a new life growing inside of me and finally seeing it arrive is incredible." She reached out and took Christina's hand. "I love you like the sister I never had, Chris; I would be so honored to do it."

Tears flooded Christina's eyes. She tried to swallow the lump that lodged in her throat as she reached out to her friend. "I…I …oh god. What can I say? How can I thank you?" She sobbed loudly, as Shauna Lee rubbed her back and reassured her soothingly.

"We…I…" She hugged herself in an attempt to control her trembling. "I have to talk to Tim first and make sure he's in agreement with this."

Shauna Lee put her arms around her and smiled lovingly. "Of course you do."

Christina moved away and used the hem of her shirt to wipe her face and nose. "Yuck…that's disgusting." She looked apologetic. "I mean me doing that; wiping my runny nose on my shirt."

Shauna Lee reached out and touched her again. "Don't worry, I knew what you meant."

Christina grabbed her best friend's hand and squeezed it. "I'm having trouble comprehending all this. After I talk to Tim, the four of us will have to sit down and talk this through." She shook her head. "Are you really sure about this? It would be different than getting pregnant with your own baby. And there'd be legal stuff and shot's and you'd be turning your life upside down for a minimum of ten months."

Shauna Lee squeezed her hands. "I've gone online and researched this in depth. Brad has sat with me and gone over it all, too. We understand that it'll change our lives for a while." She chuckled. "Once we start the process, we won't be allowed to have sex until we are several weeks pregnant or we'd probably end up with another little Johnson instead of a Bates. That'll be one of the hardest parts, but really, other than that, it's just being pregnant and I enjoy that. We have decided that our family is complete and this will be our gift of love to you."

Christina buried her head in her hands and took several deep breaths. Then she looked at her friend in wonder. "What can I say? I'm totally derailed. How do I go back to the house and act normal? Did you say anything about this to Frank?"

"No. It's too soon to do that, and I wouldn't do that anyway." She winked and smiled. "I think once we are pregnant we should tell the 'family' because it would hurt Colt and Frank and Ollie and Ellie if we didn't share the excitement with them."

Christina nodded, chewing her lip and looking distracted. "Could this really happen? Could Tim and I actually have a baby of our own? Could we possibly have a child with Tim's eye's and his walk, or my nose and hair? I gave up dreaming about this so long ago, it's hard to imagine it being possible now. I...we will be indebted to you forever."

Shauna Lee stood up and pulled her to her feet. "Christina, love is a gift; it has no debt. Our reward will be seeing you two with a child of your own. You're meant to be a mother and Tim will be an awesome dad." The two women held hands as they walked down the road. Christina's heart was pounding; her mind unsettled, flashing from one point to another. Shauna Lee noticed her distraction. "Are you okay?"

Christina nodded, trying to hide her emotions. Suddenly her face crumpled and tears overflowed, rushing down her cheeks. Shauna Lee put an arm around her. "What's going on, Chris?"

"I'm...I don't know. I feel like I'm falling apart. This is so wonderful, and yet I'm scared to death. I feel sort of dizzy and disoriented." She sobbed. "I just want...I need to be with Tim. I need to tell him about this."

Shauna Lee watched her friend sympathetically. "I was so excited, I didn't think about how this might affect you."

Christina's head shot up. "Oh no, Shauna Lee," she said guiltily. "Don't get me wrong. I'm totally thrilled, but it's still a shock. I'm overwhelmed; I never imagined anything like this." She shook her head. "I'm almost afraid to dream again."

"Chris, there are still no guarantees, but it's worth trying."

Christina nodded. "I know...and as long as Tim's agreeable, I'll do anything to make this happen." She hiccupped and managed a smile. "I'll break his arm if I have to, but I'm sure he won't hesitate. I'm more concerned about how this is going to affect you and Brad."

"Look at it from this point of view. You babysit for me all the time. Over the past four years you've looked after Patch and Leanne for at least five months; that's an accumulative guess. Then, we can throw in a few extra days to cover sanity leave…my sanity, that is. You've kept them over weekends so Brad and I could get away on our own, so that's marriage therapy, too. And, I know you'll still babysit my kids; they love you almost as much as they do me."

Christina laughed. "Not nearly!"

"Well, they love you a lot, so we'll just consider it a trade; I'll babysit for you for nine or ten months and you'll help me when I need you to, while I'm pregnant. When your baby comes, we'll call it square."

"But I love babysitting them."

"As I told you, I love being pregnant and this is our gift to you and Tim."

Christina and Shauna Lee turned around and walked back toward the house. When they reached the bottom of the hill, Christina stopped and looked at her friend. "I'm not going to tell Tim until we get home. This is too much to deal with when we are around everyone else. We need to go home and be close in heart and mind when we discuss this. Then the four of us will get together and talk it all out."

"I feel bad, Chris. Maybe I shouldn't have dumped this on you here."

"No!" Christina replied emphatically. "Do *not* feel bad. I'm glad you asked me now. It gives me time to get used to the idea, before the shock of it hits Tim."

That night Christina and Tim cuddled when they went to bed, each consumed with their own thoughts. Tim had sat next to Ollie in the back of the pickup all day. He'd studied the man, comparing their ears, their noses and the shape of their hands and fingers. There were similarities, yet, there were differences. Did it mean anything, or was it just part of being human? He didn't know.

Christina's mind swirled around Shauna Lee's proposal. She longed to tell Tim, but it was just too big to deal with while they were at the ranch. She stayed with her decision to wait until they were home. She turned restlessly, lying with her back against his chest.

"I don't see anything that makes me think he could be my dad; we're nothing alike," Tim whispered in the darkness.

She patted the arm he had slid around her waist. "We'll know more when we hear from Arthur," she whispered, reassuringly.

Shauna Lee and Brad and the children stayed at the ranch on Sunday. Tim was getting ready to start harvesting in a few days and he had lots to do, so he and Christina left mid-morning. They were both pre-occupied on the drive to Maple Creek. Christina sat shoulder to shoulder with him and when they turned onto the highway, she squeezed his thigh. "What are you thinking?"

"This damned thing about Ollie and Mom is driving me crazy."

Christina straightened. "I didn't really think about it, but that must have been a constant frustration this weekend."

"Damn it, I've known the man for four years and I like him." His hand tightened on the wheel. "But, now I find myself checking him out, looking for ways that we might be alike. I'm not finding them; I'd write the whole idea off, but there's the picture of the woman." He shrugged with frustration. "How do I explain it?"

"When will Arthur be back?"

"His receptionist said he was gone for two weeks. Two weeks from when I don't know."

Christina smiled as they turned onto their driveway. She loved the picturesque view; tall maple trees ran down both sides of it. It was welcoming. Tim let the truck move at a leisurely pace, as if he was enjoying the ride too. When he pulled up in front of the house, he turned the key and they sat for a few seconds in the silence.

"We're home, Mrs. Bates." He looked at the house. "Would you like a new house, like the one at the ranch?"

"Not really. I love this place. It has character."

"And it is home; our home."

"Our home," she echoed. "Let's go inside. I have something I'm dying to tell you."

He perked up. "Have you been holding out on me?"

She smiled and nodded.

"What else did you find out? Were you snooping around in Ollie's office again?"

"Ollie's office....?" She stared at him in surprise. "Oh! No...this is totally different. You'll really flip when you hear *this* news."

"Tell me, now."

"No, we need to go inside. Once we get into this, things are going to get very intense."

He opened the door and stepped down from the truck. She bailed out past him and ran to the house, laughing as she looked back over her shoulder.

Tim smiled as he watched her, and then followed her slowly. When he stepped through the door, she was already opening two bottles of beer. She was grinning from ear to ear, and lifted one, then the other and clicked them together in a toast.

Tim raised an eyebrow. "A toast? Are you going to let me in on the big news?"

She held a bottle out and walked toward him, moving her hips seductively. "Shauna Lee and I had a mind-blowing conversation." She indicated the loveseat. "Sit down and I'll tell you what she proposed."

He took the bottles of beer and set them on the end table, then placed his hands on either side of her hips and pulled her against him. "Mrs. Bates, when you wiggle your hips that way, it doesn't make me think about sitting; I'm more into getting horizontal."

She chuckled. "You've got a one-track mind, Mr. Bates. We'll get horizontal later, but right now we need to sit down and *talk.*" She picked up the bottles of beer and handed him one. She sat on the loveseat and patted the spot beside her. When he settled his weight beside her, she took a long pull from her drink. Then she rested a hand on his thigh and looked into his eyes.

"Shauna Lee and I went for a walk Saturday morning when you guys were gone to the lease. We sat on some rocks down by Belanger Creek and out of the blue, she asked me a question."

Tim looked at her expectantly. Her eyes were sparkling, her cheeks flushed. "What did she ask you?"

Her eyes glistened with tears. "She asked if we'd let her be a surrogate for us."

"A surrogate...?"

"Yes! She wants to carry our baby for us so we can have our own child."

Tim looked blank.

"Do you understand what she offered, Tim?"

He shook his head. "What are you saying? We can't take a baby of theirs."

"No, hon. That's not what she's suggesting. I have ovaries and, as far as I know, they're producing eggs, but because I have no womb my body just absorbs them. We'd have to go to a fertility clinic and do in-vitro fertilization. In simple terms, they'd take an egg from my ovaries, use your sperm to fertilise it and then put it into Shauna Lee's womb and she'd incubate it until it was time for the baby to be born."

"But the baby would be yours and mine?"

Christina nodded. "It's a huge commitment for all of us, especially Brad and Shauna Lee. She'll be pregnant all that time just so we can have a baby of our own."

"Does Brad know about this?"

Christina nodded. "Yes. They've discussed it at length and they've been researching online." She slid onto his lap and grinned. "You'll appreciate this, Tim. Shauna Lee said the hardest part would be not having sex for the first couple of months. As far as they're concerned, their family is complete and they wouldn't want to mistakenly create another Johnson, instead of a Bates."

Tim chuckled at the thought and then sobered. "Why would they do this for us?"

"Because they know how much we love kids and they want us to have one. She said it would be a gift of love from them to us."

Tim took a long drink. "I'm stunned. I don't know what to say."

Christina threaded her arms around his neck and leaned back to look into his eyes. "I felt the same way. I cried, I shook, I felt faint, I was totally off track. I couldn't take it all in. Shauna Lee and I talked and walked, and by the time we got back to the house, I knew I couldn't tell you about this at the ranch. It would have been too much to deal with. I told Shauna Lee we'd talk about it at home and then we'd get together with them."

"Do you have any idea what is involved with this?"

"No...I've heard of surrogacy, but I've never considered it. But now... it could mean the fulfillment of my deepest, most heartfelt desire, Tim. Even if I can't carry our baby under my heart, we can carry it in our arms. It won't be a stranger who nurtures it for us; it will be my best friend...our best friends, who made it possible."

"You said they researched it online?"

Christina nodded.

Tim pushed her off his lap and stood up, pulling her with him. "Let's go and see what we can find."

They spent the afternoon researching surrogacy sites online.

Many were American, others from different countries around the world, but the ones they focused on were Canadian.

Tim shook his head and reached for her hand. "Chris, this is complicated stuff. Do you understand how it all works?"

She leaned her head against his shoulder. "Not exactly, but I want to give it a shot." She sat back and looked into his eyes. "Are you with me?"

His face was solemn. "Nothing would make me happier than to have a baby with you. You'd make the most wonderful mother in the whole world." He turned her toward him. "But this is a big undertaking, and you're going to have to do a lot of the heavy lifting; you and Shauna Lee."

"From what I understand, I'll have to take a lot of shots and medications at first, but for me, that is nothing in the end game. Shauna Lee is going to be the one who has to put up with the most disruption in her life. She'll have to take a lot of shots too, and she's the one who will feel big and awkward and uncomfortable. We can't forget that she already has two young kids." Christina's eyes shone. "I'll need to help her as much as I can, Tim. I can take the kids and do housework. I can cook meals, shop if she needs me to."

Tim grinned. "Well, I've batched before and I can handle that for a year, but I wouldn't be happy sleeping alone, so make sure you make it back here every night."

Christina punched him in the arm. "You goof," she said softly.

She turned back to the computer and searched for IVF centers in Saskatchewan. "Look at this!" she exclaimed. "There's an IVF clinic in Saskatoon." She looked up, excitement sparkling in her eyes. "That's only a two and a half hour drive; we can easily do the round trip in one day."

They jumped up and hugged each other, doing a happy dance from behind the desk and out into the hallway. Tim's enthusiasm was as real as hers. "I want to call Brad and Shauna Lee right now, but I doubt if they're home yet." His voice was rough with emotion. He ran his hands through his hair. "And if they are, they'll probably be tired and so will the kids."

Christina's eyes were sparkling. "Can this be real? Or is it just too good to be true?"

"Shauna Lee wouldn't have offered to be a surrogate if she wasn't sincere. She knows how much it would mean to you." He shook his head. "I've heard rumors, but whatever Shauna Lee used to be, loving Brand and having those kids, has made her a different person than she must have been back then."

Christina sobered. "Meeting Brad totally changed her." She looked out the window, deep in thought. "He worked damned hard to convince her that she was worthy of his love. She didn't give in easily, Tim. Most guys wouldn't have hung in there as long as he did. It was amazing to watch the transformation." Tears shimmered in her eyes. "The interesting thing is, we both were living behind a lonely façade. She was hiding from her past and so was I. Both of us were smiling and brittle on the outside and lonely and hurt on the inside."

Tim reached for her. "Love has brought out the softness in both of you," he whispered, softly. He shook his head. "What am I saying? It's changed me too."

Tim and Christina went to Shauna Lee and Brad's place Tuesday night. The two women had talked that morning, and they both had made appointments with their family doctors for the following day. Shauna Lee had phoned the IVF center in Saskatoon and made an appointment. The earliest date available was the following Monday. From the day of their appointment in Saskatchewan, the surrogacy project went into overdrive.

Two weeks later Christina knocked on Shauna Lee's door and smiled when she opened it. "Hi. I've missed seeing you, so I decided to stop by. We've been together almost every other day these past two weeks, but we haven't had time to just visit."

Shauna Lee laughed as she hugged her friend. "I know what you mean. Who would've imagined there could be so much fuss and red tape involved in making a baby!"

Christina drew back. "Shauna Lee, if you want to change your mind, now is the time to do it. I'll understand."

Shauna Lee looked up at her friend. "Are you kidding? I can't change my mind now. You guys just paid thousands of dollars for legal work. And the questions! What would we do with the baby if both of you died before it was born? If we both died before it was born and it survived, who would be responsible for the baby? Whose baby is it going to be when it's born? I couldn't believe some of them!"

Christina laughed. "I know; some of them seemed ridiculous. You know it's all 'cover your butt' stuff. Between the four of us, there is no question because we're friends and we know each other, but these contracts are drawn up for all kinds of different situations. You just never know what people will do.

"Truthfully, it was probably good for us to look at some of the things we wouldn't have actually pinpointed beforehand: like how many cycles will we do, how many embryos we will transfer at one time, and if we end up with too many fetuses do we make selective reduction? I mean twins would be risky for you, but triples or quads would be impossible. We'd have to do something."

She squeezed her eyes shut as if to block out the thought. "And heaven forbid, what would we do if there was some obvious abnormality with the fetus, or if you were at risk because of the pregnancy. In either case, we'd have to make serious decisions. If your safety were threatened, there would be no question; we'd terminate the pregnancy. If something was wrong with the fetus….those are tough things to face, but they can come up."

Shauna Lee hugged her again and pulled her inside. "As you said, all that stuff is just 'cover your butt' stuff. This time next year, you're going to be a mommy! I'm so excited."

"I know. It's just kind of mind blowing."

"So, has Tim started harvesting yet?"

"Norman Walters and Ben Norland serviced the combines last week and they took the two machines out to the canola fields yesterday. They're all working sixteen-hour shifts, so we get to sleep together at night. I've been working in the garden and freezing vegetables, but to be honest I'm so distracted, it's crazy.

"I'm still trying to get my head around this whole thing. I'd resigned myself to never having a baby. Now the possibility of it happening is there and I find myself daydreaming and imagining what it'll be like. One minute I am so excited I can hardly contain myself, the next I'm afraid to dream too much, in case it doesn't work out. I don't want to be disappointed."

Shauna Lee nodded. "I understand what you're saying. I'm a bit off track, too. I took birth control pills for years, but I've been off them since Leanne was born. I'm noticing some side effects this time, but I'm so excited about doing this. I just want to put all this preparation stuff; the needles, ultrasounds, and medication, behind us and get pregnant!"

Christina hugged her friend. "Me too! I read my schedule and re-read it again every day. I can hardly wait until I can start getting those injections in my belly every night to kick my ovaries into gear."

Shauna Lee winced. "Twenty-four needles in ten days. You're going to look like a pin cushion. When I think about your protocol, I think I'm getting off really easy."

"Don't give me that! My part is over in a few weeks, you've got nine months ahead of you!"

They sat in the shade in the back yard and chatted, but the conversation always came back to the pregnancy. Christina refilled her glass and took a long drink. "I haven't talked to Tim about it yet, but I think I'll put my house up for sale. This baby-making project is expensive and I can't think of any better way to use the money than to make this dream come true."

Shauna Lee nodded. "You won't have any trouble selling it. The economy is doing really well right now and it's a nice place. It would be a perfect first home or a place to retire."

Harvest went smoothly, and by the end of September the combines were parked in front of the shop, and the grain bins were full. Three days later, Tim and Christina were on their way to Saskatoon. The weeks of tests, ultrasounds and medications were complete, and the next day Christina was scheduled for egg retrieval.

They stayed in a motel near the clinic and had a quiet evening. The next morning they were up early and waited anxiously until it was time to go. Tim reached for her hand and pulled her against his chest as they walked to the car. "How are you feeling, Chris?"

Tears welled in her eyes. "Cripes," she groaned with disgust, dashing away the moisture. "I don't know what's happening. Maybe it's the hormones. This should be the happiest day of my life, but I'm feeling weepy and bloated and just off base."

"Are you worried about something?"

"No...well, yeah...maybe a bit. What if my eggs aren't any good?"

Tim cradled her against him. "Everything will be fine, hon. You told me that your numbers are good. These guys know what they're doing. In a couple of hours, this will be all over and you'll be smiling." He kissed her softly. "You know, I'm a bit worried, too."

She leaned back and looked at him. "You are? Why?"

"Well, what if I can't perform? You won't be with me. What if I can't provide the juice to fertilize those eggs of yours? It would be all for nothing because I'm not letting anyone else do it for me."

Christina laughed and hugged him. "You'll do just fine. Let's go and get this job done."

At the clinic, they gave Christina a mix of pills to ease her nerves and help her relax. Then they took her to the operating room and an IV was hooked up to provide conscious sedation. The doctor gave her a local anesthetic, and made a small incision below her belly button and inserted a fine fiber optic nerve with a tiny video camera into her abdomen. He used a needle to inject carbon dioxide into her abdominal cavity to expand the area and create a working space. Tim was allowed to sit with her, and they watched the egg retrieval process on the ultrasound monitor.

He kept squeezing her hand reassuringly, telling her she was doing fine; both of their hands were damp with perspiration. The doctor smiled as he finished the procedure, withdrew the fiber optic tube, and put a couple of dissolving stitches into the tiny incision. "There; it's done and you two should be very pleased."

Christina rested for half an hour in the recovery room. She felt like she'd been punched in the gut because her ovaries were bruised from the retrieval. The doctor recommended Tylenol for the discomfort.

Tim was taken into a separate room, where he was given instructions and handed a sterile plastic container.

The same day Shauna Lee went for blood tests and an ultrasound to check on the thickness of the lining of her uterus.

Before they left the clinic, they were told that ten matured eggs had been retrieved. They would be mixed with Tim's contribution and then they'd have to wait and see how many would be fertilized and become embryos.

The next morning the IVF unit called and told them that eight of the eggs had fertilized and were dividing. The embryologist would let the doctor and the nurses know which day to transfer: day three or day five. Two days later, they got a call saying the transfer would take place in three days.

Three days later, the four of them drove to Saskatoon. Shauna Lee barely slept; she was excited, anxious, nervous and so ready to get the show on the road.

After they admitted her, the doctor and the ultrasonographer got Shauna Lee ready for the transfer. The embryologist came into the room and the four of them watched one embryo be deposited into Shauna Lee's uterus. The rest of the eggs would be frozen "just in case."

After the transfer, emotions ran high with everyone hugging each other, tears of expectation, relief and intense emotion rolling down their cheeks. Now, they had to wait for two weeks to get the final results...the longest two weeks of their lives.

CHAPTER EIGHTEEN

Christina snuggled against Tim as they pulled out onto the highway and headed home. Tim leaned his headed against hers. "How are you feeling hon?"

"If you want to know the truth, I'm all over the place right now. I'm excited, elated, scared, anxious, and quite honestly, exhausted. I know these past few months have been stressful for all of us, but now we have to wait another two weeks to see what happens."

She sat up and looked at him. "How are you, Tim? You've been so busy. Harvest, just sort of, went right over my head. I'm afraid I wasn't much help to you. My whole world revolved around this baby."

Tim reached out and squeezed her knee. "Just having you there was enough. Fortunately, everything went smoothly this fall; no major breakdowns, the weather held steady and the yield was good. Norman and Ben have worked here for so long they could do it without me if they had to. That's one of the great things about having a crew that understands the operation. But, I'm happy to see those combines parked in front of the shop and know that we're finished for another year."

"What's next?"

"I'll keep Ben and Norman on the payroll for another month and they'll handle most of the general work. The machines need to be cleaned and serviced before we put them away. The grain trucks need to be serviced so they're ready to go to work when we start to haul. It's time to clean the yard and make sure everything is put away for the winter." He smiled at her. "And now I can spend time with my wife."

Christina smiled with a sigh. "I'm looking forward to that."

The next morning, Tim and Christina sat on the wicker lounge on the deck, enjoying a morning cup of coffee. The colors of fall covered the countryside and crispness floated on the air.

"This is my favorite time of the year," Christina said softly.

Tim leaned back and stretched his legs out in front of him. "The ranch will be beautiful now. We'll have to take a drive out there one day."

"Speaking of the ranch, have you heard anything from Arthur?"

"No. I've been too busy to even think about it. I'll have to give him a call. Actually, I'll do that today. I can't believe he hasn't found out something by now." They finished their coffee and went inside. Christina tidied up while Tim made his call.

The conversation was brief and he came out of the office, pushing his hand through his hair in an act of frustration. "Damn, I wonder if that man is ever in the office. The last time I called he was on holidays, and he isn't in now."

Three hours later, Tim and Christina were sitting around the kitchen table discussing the decision to sell her house in Swift Current when his phone rang. Tim pulled it out of his pocket and glanced at the call display. "About time," he grumbled as he tapped it to turn it on. He looked at Christina and silently mouthed *Arthur*, to answer her questioning look.

Christina knew his impatience had been smothered by the consuming demands of harvest, but beneath the surface, it was still gnawing a hole in his gut. He'd been waiting for this call for over two months.

"Good morning, Arthur. I was beginning to think you'd forgotten me. What have you got?"

"Well, nothing about this file has been uncomplicated. Getting your birth certificate was simple--we actually had that already. And we got your adoption papers, but something unexpected came up."

Tim frowned. "What was that?"

Gloria Antypowich

Arthur cleared his throat. "I don't know how to tell you this, but Maddy Webber was not your biological mother. She was your legal guardian until she married Harry Bates, and then they both adopted you."

Shock washed over Tim. "That's bullshit! She raised me. I've seen pictures of us when I was a newborn."

"Calm down. I didn't say she didn't raise you. In fact, it appears that she took you home from the hospital. She was your mother in every way except biologically."

Tim sputtered. "I...I...." Tim swallowed hard, closing his eyes as he placed his free hand over them. "So, who was my biological mother?"

"Your birth certificate and Statistics Canada records show Wanda Ethridge as your biological mother. She was nineteen and she didn't indicate that she was married. Ten days after the birth, she gave legal guardianship to Webber. It was legal and binding. The PI is trying to track down information about Etheridge and Webber now, but they're both pretty elusive. Once we figure out where they come from we should be able to nail down their connection."

"Shit! Why is nothing simple?" Tim groused with exasperation. "Well, it is what it is, I guess. Please let me know as soon as you know anything more.

Christina laid her hand on his arm, her eyes searching his face. "What is it, Tim?"

He shook his head in disbelief. "He says my mother, Maddy, wasn't my biological mother. She was my legal guardian until she married Harry, and then they both adopted me. All those years and no one told me. I know they both loved me. But all those years? Harry knew the truth too. Why didn't they just tell me?"

"You know your mother must have believed there was a good reason to keep the secret."

"All of this seems so cloak and dagger. Why would she have kept the truth from me? Why would she have instructed the lawyers to notify Ollie that he had a son and not tell him who I was? We could have made contact right away." He rubbed his face. "It's just not like the woman I knew, to do this." He looked out across the fields, into the distance. "Mom was so honest, so genuine. This doesn't fit."

"Maybe she resented Ollie; maybe she felt he'd been irresponsible in his dealings with Wanda."

"But when you read his letters and his notes, it's pretty clear that he didn't know she was pregnant. He didn't even seem to know who she was, so they couldn't have had much of a relationship. More than likely it was a one-night stand. Clearly neither one of them anticipated making a kid. Clearly, she didn't want to be saddled with one. Welcome to the world, you little bastard. Maybe Gerard actually knew the truth."

"Don't go there, Tim. No matter what circumstances you were conceived under, you are still you. You are still the man I love, you are the person that Harry and Maddy loved, you, are the same person all your friends, neighbors, and business associates admire and respect. Don't second guess yourself. I believe Ollie is your biological father, and he'll be absolutely beside himself when he finds out."

"And how is he going to find out?"

"Tim, you don't want Ollie to hear it from Arthur."

"I told Arthur not to tell him anything."

"Look, we need to go to the ranch and lay all our cards on the table with Ollie. You need to tell him how you saw his picture and show him the one of you and your mom. I'll tell him what I did...."

"I'm not sure that will go over very big, Chris."

"Tim, if everyone gets all upset about what I did, I'll take the fallout; but to be really honest, under the same circumstances, I think a lot of people would have done the same thing."

Tim hugged her. "That's my feisty, loyal wife." He kissed her cheek. "So we go and talk to Ollie, but we still won't know anything more than we do now."

"We'll have to be totally honest and tell Ollie everything--about seeing Arthur, and what he told you about Wanda and your mom, the adoption, everything."

"I'm nervous. To be honest, I'm sort of afraid. What if he isn't my dad: and bigger still, what if he is. My whole life is upside down. I don't know who the hell I am."

"You are Tim Bates! That's who you are, no matter what else happens." She cradled his face in her hands and looked into his eyes. "I am honored to have you as my husband and I will love you no matter what we find out."

He looked at her, drinking in her sincerity, her honesty, her love. "How could it have taken me so long to realize how special you are and how much you mean to me?"

Gloria Antypowich

Christina chuckled. "Touché," she whispered before she kissed him.

Tim didn't call Ollie that day or the next. Christina didn't prompt him to, even though it was grating on her nerves. She knew that he was mulling over his thoughts, sorting out his feelings, and when he was comfortable with it, he would make the call.

On the third day, he looked at her across the breakfast table. "I guess I should phone Ollie and see if we can go out there tomorrow. That'll be Sunday, so he'll probably be around home."

Christina nodded. "Have you thought about what you're going to say when you call?"

"I don't know. What do I say? That I want to talk to him?"

"Maybe you should give him a bit of a heads-up. You know this is going to be a big shock to him too. Can you imagine? He's known you for four years and never imagined that you could be his son."

Tim nodded. "Have you got any ideas? I can't phone him and say, *Hey, I think I might be your kid.*"

She reached out and squeezed his hand. "No, you can't do that." She shrugged. "Maybe you could mention that you saw a woman's picture on his desk and you want to talk to him about it or something like that."

"What if he wants to keep talking about it on the phone?"

"You'll handle it. Tell him you have something you want to show him."

Tim sighed deeply. "Well, I've put this off long enough..."

Christina raised her eyebrow and smiled. "You think?"

"I know the waiting's been killing you, but thanks for letting me take the time I needed. I just had to sort through everything in my head. I'm no clearer about it now than I was then, but I'm ready now.

Tim went into the office and made the call. Christina wanted to follow him, but she wasn't sure if he'd gone there out of habit, or if he'd wanted privacy. She stacked the breakfast dishes and put them in the dishwasher. Then she sat down at the table with her hands clasped, looking aimlessly out the window.

Tim came into the kitchen moments later. "Why didn't you come with me?"

Christina shrugged. "I wasn't sure...when you went to the office; I thought maybe you needed to do it alone."

Tim looked surprised. "No. It was just habit. I thought you were coming."

"So, how did it go?"

"Of course he's curious. He wants us to come to the ranch today."

"And...?"

"I told him we'll be there after lunch. Now that we've got the ball rolling, I want to get this out in the open and find out where it takes us."

Christina nodded. "I agree. Let's get ready and go. I think we should plan to spend the night."

Tim nodded. "Will you throw in an extra shirt and my shaving kit for me, and I'll put together everything we have from Arthur, plus my picture and the notes we've made."

Christina ran upstairs and changed into a pair of red jeans and a black t-shirt. She put her personal things in a small makeup bag and tossed an extra top and a change of underwear in an overnight bag, along with Tim's things. Then she joined him downstairs.

They made the three-hour trip to Belanger Creek Ranch in relative silence. They sat close to each other, hands touching, even intertwining occasionally, but each was lost in their own thoughts. They had gone over the facts so often, explored every possible scenario until there seemed to be nothing left to say. Now they were like an army marching into action, eager to accomplish something and yet unnerved by what they might find.

When they reached the ranch, they drove directly to Ollie and Ellie's house. Ollie met them at the gate and Tim and Christina held hands when they followed him inside. Ellie was bustling around putting cups and small plates around the table and setting out plates of cookies and squares. Ollie gestured for them to sit down and Tim and Christina looked at each other when they noticed the two extra plates. Before Ellie brought the coffee pot to the table, the back door opened and Colt and Frank joined them.

Tim swallowed nervously and squeezed Christina's hand under the table.

Colt nodded at Tim and Christina and grabbed a chair. He turned it around and straddled the seat, resting his arms on the back. Frank smiled and said "Hi," then sat down next to him. Awkwardness hung heavily in the air.

After Ellie poured coffee and made sure everyone had cream and sugar, the only sound to be heard was the click of teaspoons stirring in the cups. Finally, Ollie cleared his throat.

Tim's gaze met his, as he laid an envelope on the table. "I want you to look at this, Ollie."

Ollie opened it and slid out the picture frame inside. Surprise flooded his face as he studied the picture. "Where did you get this?"

"That's my mom and dad and me. Her name was Madeline Webber before she married Harry Bates."

Ellie looked at the picture, and then handed it to Colt.

Colt studied it briefly and said, "That looks like the same woman in the picture you have, Ollie."

Frank leaned over and looked at the picture. "Oh," she gasped. "That's why she looked so familiar. I saw the picture on your desk, Tim."

Tim toyed with his spoon. "At Easter, when I came down here to get your medication…I found the pills in your office and I saw the picture lying on your desk."

He glanced at Ollie, and then quickly looked away. "It really threw me for a loop. All I could think was that you must have been checking up on me and I couldn't understand why. Furthermore, I couldn't understand why you were involving my mother." His gaze returned to Ollie. "I should have just come up to the ranch house and asked you then, but I didn't know what to think. I felt like you were double-dealing me somehow. I was shocked. I didn't know if I could trust anyone and I got mad."

Understanding washed over Frank's face. "That's why you left so abruptly that night."

Tim nodded. "Chris tried to talk some sense into me, but my life has been so full of crap, I automatically thought it was happening again and I wouldn't listen."

Christina covered his hand on the table and spoke. "When you guys were moving cattle, I came to the house to check on Ellie one afternoon. She was still sleeping, so I decided to leave her. When I walked passed Ollie's office, I glanced in and saw the picture sitting on the shelf by his desk, so I stepped in and looked at it. I had my cell phone in my pocket, so I took a picture of it. When I went to put it back, I saw an envelope with the address of a law firm on it, and I realized it was the same as the one stamped on the back of the picture."

She looked around the table defiantly. "What I did was wrong, but I took the letter out and read it, because I knew Tim thought the picture was one of his mom. Then I looked through everything there: your letters back to the lawyer, Ollie, and the notes you'd made. I took pictures of each page. I put everything back and when we got home I told Tim what I'd done, and showed him the pictures."

She looked down. "I'll understand if you guys don't like me much or feel like you can't trust me anymore, but I knew how much this might mean to Tim...even you, Ollie." She swallowed hard and looked up at Ollie, then Colt and Frank. "I apologize for betraying your trust, but I am not sorry I did it."

Tim shifted uncomfortably. "When I downloaded the pictures to my computer, I was dumbfounded. I had no idea who Wanda Ethridge was, but if she wasn't my mother, she certainly could have been her twin. My mother was a single mom, but her name was Maddy Webber, and I was Tim Webber until she married Harry Bates and he adopted me.

"I called the law firm and talked to Arthur Knout. We decided to go to Vancouver and meet him. I took the picture with us and after we talked, I asked him to look into my past: my birth certificate, my adoption papers, Mom and Harry Bates' marriage certificate. Mom always said she didn't have any family and she never talked about her parents or her childhood. I wanted to know about it. It just seemed too coincidental that she and Wanda Ethridge could look so much alike, yet not be the same person, or at least, related.

"I got a call from Arthur this week. His private investigator unearthed some basic stuff: my birth certificate and the hospital records of my birth, and my adoption papers. I almost wish I hadn't delved into this mess. Now I'm not sure of anything, except that I'm not who I thought I was.

"At this time, it looks like Wanda Ethridge was my birth mother. She wasn't married and obviously didn't want a kid. Madeline Webber took me home from the hospital. Ten days later Wanda Etheridge made her my guardian; signed, sealed and delivered and totally legal. Madeline raised me and when she married Harry Bates, they both legally adopted me. They never told me that Madeline wasn't my birth mother." He drummed his fingers on the table. "All those damned years and they never told me the truth. I don't understand why."

The silence in the room was deafening. Colt looked at Ollie, then at Tim.

"So, do you think Ollie is your dad?"

"How the hell would I know?" He looked at Ollie. "From your letters, it's clear you don't remember Wanda Ethridge."

Ollie shook his head. "I don't, and I've thought about it a lot. The name just doesn't mean anything to me. It's on my mind every day, and by now I'm sure I'd remember if I'd slept with her; unless I was too drunk to know."

Tim winced. "Arthur's PI hasn't been able to find anything on her, other than the record of birth and the legal guardianship papers. There was nothing before and nothing after."

Frank looked at Ollie. "We discussed this before, Ollie. She had to have known you from somewhere. She couldn't have gone through the Vancouver telephone book and picked out your name."

Ollie tilted his chair onto the two back legs, clasped his hands and raised his arms over his head. He looked up at the ceiling. "You know, Tim, I'd be proud to have you as a son, but there are just too many holes in this to pull out the cigars just yet."

"You're right. I have to admit, I've looked at you in a whole new way since I saw that birth certificate and I've tried to find something about us that could indicate we were father and son, but I don't find any resemblance. I think we need to know a lot more about this whole mystery before we use a sharp knife to draw blood, mix it and claim to be related."

Ollie chuckled. "You've got my sense of humor. That's one thing we have in common." He sat up and searched Tim's face. "Where do we go from here, *son?*"

Tim looked at him sharply. "I'm floundering in the wind now. It would be easy to grasp at straws and claim you as my dad, but I need to know the truth. I've lived with a lie for forty-eight years."

Ollie looked at him soberly. "You haven't lived a lie, Tim. The people you knew as your parents were your mom and dad in every way that counted. They legally adopted you, they loved you, and they raised you with values. That's what real parents do. Any couple of fools can make a kid, but it's what happens afterward that counts. I can tell you, if I'd known that I was a father, I'd have been there. I would never have abandoned my child or the mother.

"My old man ditched my mom before I was born, and after a few months she handed me over to an older uncle and aunt who didn't really want another kid, but wouldn't let social services take one of their kin. My mother never came to see me after she left me with them. They raised me, but as I got older, it was clear that I was an obligation and they resented me. They should have been retired by then, and here they had another kid to look after. I left when I was fourteen and I grew up on my own.

"If you're my son, I can't tell you how much it hurts to know that I wasn't there for you; how much I regret the wasted years. But I'm glad you had someone who loved you and gave you a proper home." Moisture glistened in Ollie's eyes.

Christina reached out and touched his hand. "I'm sorry your life was like that, Ollie. I hope we can prove you are Tim's dad and you'll have the family you missed when you were young."

Frank put her hand over Christina and Ollie's. "He already is part of a family. Not just our family, but also this whole 'family' that has grown around us; you and Tim and Shauna Lee and Brad. We are closer than many families with blood ties. And Ellie and Ollie are grandma and grandpa to all the kids."

Christina smiled. Her eyes met Tim's knowingly, but as much as she wanted to shout out that they were planning to be parents, too, she didn't. It was too soon.

Tim and Ollie and the rest of the 'family' acknowledged that there was little they could do, except wait for Arthur and his PI to do some more digging and see what they could find out about Wanda Ethridge. Colt suggested they find a more aggressive private investigator, but Tim and Ollie both were inclined to stay with Arthur for a while longer since they had already invested money in his search.

Shauna Lee lay on the bed and rested her hands on her belly. "Okay, little one...are you growing in there? I'm going nuts wondering?"

Brad came into the room. Concern creased his face. "Is everything all right?"

Shauna Lee nodded. "I hope so. I'm feeling fine; the waiting is just driving me crazy. I don't think I was this anxious when we tried for our own kids."

He sat on the bed beside her and took her hand. "Well, this is slightly different, hon. Then we could just have the fun of trying again."

She nodded. "I know. I guess part of it is because this whole process has taken a lot of time and energy, and I know it is costing Tim and Christina big bucks. I don't want them to be disappointed. I want them to have their baby. I've never worried about getting pregnant before. Sometimes it was a bigger concern to not get caught, but now I feel responsible."

"You're doing everything you can to make it happen. It'll be okay."

Christina and Shauna Lee drove to Saskatoon the day of the official pregnancy test. They both were anxious but hopeful. They went early and Shauna Lee had her blood work done before they went shopping.

As they sat over coffee, Christina looked across at Shauna Lee and saw tears shimmering in her eyes. She reached across the table and covered her hand. "What are you thinking?"

"It's so stupid, but I'm scared. I want to believe that there's a baby in here." She touched her tummy. "But I confess, I got a couple of home pregnancy tests and neither one of them were positive."

"When did you do the last one?"

"Last night. I want to believe it was wrong. Sometimes those home pregnancy things might not be accurate. But...."

Christina squeezed her hand. "Well, we'll know in a few hours. You've done everything you could, Shauna Lee. It's out of our hands now, so let's not worry."

Shauna Lee's fears were justified. When the results came back, she was not pregnant. The two women sat in the car, each lost in their own thoughts. For Christina, the news was a deep disappointment, but for Shauna Lee it was devastating. She sobbed as she said, "I'm so sorry. I feel like I've failed you and Tim."

Christina consoled her, assuring her that they did not feel she had failed them.

Shauna Lee looked at her through her tears. "We'll try again, as soon as we can. We're not giving up."

Christina looked at her. "Are you sure you want to go through all this again?"

"Absolutely! This was our trial run. Next time, it will work. We'll do it again as soon as the doctor says we can.

That night, Christina lay in Tim's arms and released her tears of disappointment over the loss of a dream.

A week later, Shauna Lee and Brad, and Tim and Christina got together and decided to wait until after Christmas before they tried again. When Christina and Shauna Lee went back to the clinic in Saskatoon, the doctor agreed it was a good plan. After the transfer, three of the remaining embryos had deteriorated in quality before they were frozen, but there were still four healthy ones so Christina wouldn't have to do another retrieval. The doctor would start Shauna Lee on her program during the first week of January.

***

A burst of icy cold weather and snow brought in the Christmas season. Tim suggested they visit Christina's family in Swan River. She was hesitant, but with Tim's encouragement and support, they made the trip and enjoyed the visit. Hazel and Burt Holmes welcomed them with open arms. Julie was very pregnant and feeling tired. Jack, Joylin, and Robert were excited about the prospect of having a new baby.

The day after Christmas, Christina and Tim went for a walk and she showed Tim around her old hometown. Their cheeks were rosy and their noses cold when they stopped at Tim Horton's for a cup of hot chocolate.

There weren't many patrons, and Christina was relieved that she didn't recognize anyone. Most of them were teenagers showing off the loot they'd gotten for Christmas.

She looked across the table at Tim. "Thank you for suggesting we spend Christmas with my family. It's been fun, and thanks to you, I've been able to relax and enjoy myself. It's felt good to walk around town and I haven't run into anyone who I wanted to hide from."

"You're not hiding from anyone anymore, remember? You are a strong, wonderful woman and I'm very proud to be married to you. I walk with my head held high and so should you."

"Old habits die hard Tim. At home, I never think of hanging my head, but here…I felt inferior for so many years. It's hard to get above it."

As Tim reached over and rubbed his thumb across the back of her hand, the door opened and a good-looking man came in. He felt Christina stiffen when the newcomer laughed, her head snapped up and she looked in his direction. Her eyes met his, and then slid away. Christina picked up her gloves and stood up. "Let's get out of here."

Tim followed as she hurried toward the door. The man sneered as he stepped toward her, but Tim moved between them, putting his hand on Christina's arm, steering her away. He could hear laughter as the door closed behind them.

Tim took her hand and pulled her against him, stopping in the middle of the sidewalk. "Was it him?" She nodded. "Christina, he has no power over you now. I want you to turn around and go back in there with me."

She shook her head.

"He's a loser. You have no reason to run from him. Do you trust me, Chris?"

She nodded.

"You need to prove to yourself, and him, that he can't hurt you anymore. You're the one who holds the cards now. I'm right here beside you."

"Tim," she protested.

"Come on. Hold your head up and put a smile on those beautiful lips. I'll handle the ex if it needs to be done. You are no longer Christina Holmes Isanov. You are now Mrs. Christina Holmes Bates. Let's go back inside."

She hesitated, and then gave in. As he opened the door, he stopped and kissed her cheek. "Remember, head up and smile as if you love me."

Her eyes widened. "I do love you."

"Then show the whole of Swan River how happy you are, Mrs. Bates."

She gave him a gentle nudge and smiled. They walked in and ordered two more large hot chocolates, and carried them to the booth. Tim waited until she sat down and then walked across the room and faced Christina's ex-husband. "Dave Isanov?"

"What the fuck do you want?"

"I want to introduce you to someone very special."

"If you're talking about Christina Holmes, I knew her long before you did," he sneered.

"I understand she had the misfortune of marrying you once, and I know how you treated her. The Christina Holmes you knew doesn't exist anymore." Tim twisted the front of his coat and propelled him toward the booth. "Meet Christina Bates."

Christina took one look at the expression on Dave Isanov's face and her anxiety disappeared. His bullying bravado had slipped away when he realized that Tim was seriously confronting him. She smiled. "Hello, Dave. I see my husband introduced himself to you."

Tim tightened his hold on Isanov's coat and gave him a hard look. "Remember this; I am very protective of what's mine. We'll be around town whenever we come to visit the Holmes family and you'd better treat Christina with respect or you will answer to me."

Tim released his coat and gave him a light shove. "Now, get out of my face. My wife and I are going to sit here and enjoy our hot chocolate."

Christina stared at Tim in amazement, and then she burst out laughing. "You are full of surprises. I've never seen this side of you before."

"I wish I'd met him in a dark alley. I've wanted to punch that guy out since I first heard what he did to you. He's not worth getting in trouble with the law over, but I just couldn't sit back and let him sneer at you." Tim glared at the man as he slithered out the door and beat a hasty retreat down the street.

Christina and Shauna Lee drove to Saskatoon, the first Monday after the New Year. The day was cold and crisp, ice crystals glimmered in the sun on the snow covered fields.

Shauna Lee looked at Christina. "Well, this is a perfect way to start the year. I have a good feeling about this. It's going to work this time, mommy," she said as she reached out to touch Christina's hand.

Christina smiled as she clasped Shauna Lees. "I hope so. I'd rather have seen you pregnant before Christmas so you didn't have to carry the baby through the summer heat, but I guess the universe had other plans for us."

"It'll be worth it and its only one summer out of my life, Chris. Not the end of the world!"

"I'm still holding my breath. After all these years, I'm afraid to get my hopes up too much, in case it doesn't work. At times, it's hard for me to believe that you are really doing this for us."

The doctor ordered blood work and did another ultrasound of Shauna Lee's uterus to make certain nothing had changed. Then he set up the schedule for hormone meds to ready her body for the second embryo transplant.

Christina hugged Shauna Lee when they left the fertility clinic. "I feel guilty. I get to sit back and wait this time, and you have to do all the work."

"It'll only be three weeks until we'll be putting the little one in its new home. You'll have your baby before Thanksgiving this year. How exciting is that?"

The next three weeks seemed to drag by. Finally, the day came to make the embryo transfer. Everything went smoothly, and after Shauna Lee rested at the clinic for a couple of hours, Christina got behind the wheel to drive home.

She sighed. "The waiting is the killer in all of this, isn't it? Now, we wait for another two weeks. There are lots of things that I could be doing, but all I can do is wonder if it will happen this time."

"It will. I feel really good about this time and I know it's going to work."

Christina dropped Shauna Lee off at her place and headed home. Tim met her at the door when she arrived. "How are you doing, Hon?"

Christina tried to smile, then laid her head on his chest and let her tears spill over. "Not having the pregnancy take last time was really hard for me. I want this to happen so badly, but now I'm afraid to get my hopes up. Shauna Lee is so optimistic, but what if it doesn't work this time. Can we expect her to be willing to try again? There is nothing we can do, but wait…wait…wait. Now we are going to wait for another two weeks, and then what? If it doesn't work…."

Tim held her close and stroked her hair. "Hon, try not to lose yourself in the fear of the unknown. There is as good a chance that it will happen, as there is that it won't. Remember that.

"If by some chance it doesn't work, we still have each other. We didn't think there was a possibility of having a child when we got together. If it wasn't for Shauna Lee and Brad's generosity, we wouldn't be considering it now."

"I know."

Two weeks later, Shauna Lee and Christina drove to the fertility clinic again. Shauna Lee was bubbling with excitement. "I'm sure I'm pregnant! I feel like I am this time."

Christina smiled. "Did you do a pregnancy test?"

"No. I'm just so sure I am pregnant, I didn't want to jinx it by checking it out."

They stopped at the fertility clinic and Shauna Lee had blood drawn for the pregnancy test. Shauna Lee gave the clinic her cell number and they went shopping. Four hours later, she eagerly grabbed the phone out of her purse when it rang.

Christina held her breath as she watched Shauna Lee's happy expression turn to disappointment. Her voice was a whisper as she put down the phone. Tears flooded her eyes and ran down her cheeks as she turned to look at Christina. "I…I'm so sorry, Christina." Her words were choked. "I can't believe this has happened again. I was so certain I was pregnant. I felt like I was. I *knew* I was."

Disappointment overwhelmed Christina. She brushed at the tears that ran freely down her cheeks as she fought to stifle her sobs. She felt like she'd been gut-punched, her breath driven out of her, the urge to vomit rising in her throat.

Shauna Lee was inconsolable. "I'm so sorry. I've let you and Tim down. All your dreams, all the time we've spent, all the effort, all the money. I feel so guilty."

Christina shook off her grief and reached out to her friend, grasping her hand. "Shauna Lee, you did *not* let us down. This isn't your fault. It's nobody's fault. I'm simply not supposed to have a child."

Shauna Lee looked shocked. "NO! You're going to be a wonderful mother. We are not giving up on this. I've never had any problem getting pregnant before. We'll talk to the fertility specialist. Maybe we can approach this from a different angle. You are going to have your baby."

Christina looked at her with tear-washed eyes. "How many times can you go through all of this, Shauna Lee, and what about Brad? This has to be hard on him, too. The waiting, the uncertainty; your mood swings from the hormones, the lack of sex while we're waiting for it to happen. We want to stay friends after all this."

Shauna Lee smiled weakly. "I'm always moody…aren't all women supposed to be? And the waiting and uncertainty; isn't that part of life? As for the sex, there are a lot of ways of making love, Chris. We're not really missing out, it's just different and we have to be more creative."

Christina blushed lightly. "I just feel guilty, turning your life upside down."

"Well, I'm not ready to throw in the towel yet. I'll call the clinic tomorrow and make another appointment."

Tim was out when Christina got home. She was almost glad that she didn't have to face him with the disappointing news. She went directly upstairs and crawled into bed, where she gave way to her anguish and cried herself to sleep.

An hour later, Tim came in and sat on the edge of the bed, waking her up. He looked into her reddened, puffy eyes and groaned as he lay down beside her. "It didn't work?" he asked gently.

"No. Maybe it never will. Maybe I'm not supposed to have a baby."

"Honey, if you weren't supposed to have a baby, Shauna Lee would never have offered to do this. This is hard, but we have to be strong. No one said it would be easy. If Shauna Lee is still game to go, we'll try again. We are going to give it every chance that we can."

She sighed. "I'm just so disappointed. Sometimes I wish we'd never done this; that I'd never dared to dream of having a baby again. It's like tearing open an old wound." She rubbed her eyes. "God, that sounds so ungrateful. I am ashamed of myself." She looked at him. "How are you doing with all this? I'm acting like it's all about me, but this would be your child, too."

"I'm alright. I want to have a baby with you, and it is disheartening right now. But, as much as being disappointed about not getting a baby, I hate seeing you hurt this much. I can't protect you from this, although I can be here for you, and be strong for you."

"I am so lucky to have you. Maybe I should have been satisfied with that, instead of wanting more."

"No, hon. This is a wonderful gift for us. It isn't over yet."

"Where were you when I came home?"

He hugged her and said, "We had some good news today. Someone wanted to look at your house. Brad told one of his employees about it. The guy's parents are looking for a retirement home in Swift Current. I went into town and showed the place to them. They seemed to really like it and I think they'll buy it. They'll let us know in a couple of days."

"At least something went right today. I hope they do take it. Making a baby this way is expensive. We're going to need the money."

The next morning, Christina and Tim were enjoying a relaxing breakfast when Shauna Lee called.

"How are you this morning, girlfriend?"

"I'm being lazy. Tim and I are just having breakfast."

"I just phoned the clinic and made an appointment to see Dr. Finn tomorrow morning. Are you ready to go?"

"Are you serious?"

"Without a doubt, we're not giving up. I talked with Dr. Finn this morning and he's going to use a different hormone program this time. He's optimistic and so am I. So we'll see you tomorrow at around seven am? My appointment is at eleven-thirty."

Christina assured her she would be there.

Four weeks later, Tim and Christina drove to Saskatoon with Brad and Shauna Lee, for the third embryo transfer. Dr. Finn suggested they implant two of the best of the remaining embryos. That would give them the best chance of the transfer resulting in pregnancy.

Shauna Lee was excited and enthusiastic, certain that the third time would be the lucky one. Her mood was catching and Christine dared to hope again.

The next two weeks were a long and excruciating time of waiting for Christina. Anxiety was a constant companion, gradually smothering her sense of hope. Many nights, she cried herself to sleep while Tim listened helplessly. Repeatedly she wished they could turn time back to when they gotten married and were contented and happy.

Shauna Lee insisted that she knew she was pregnant. She felt like she was. Yes, she had thought that last time, but this was different. She used two home pregnancy tests. The first one was negative, but she reasoned that it was too soon to tell. The second one was positive and she was ecstatic.

Christina wanted to believe it was true, but she didn't know how she could face the crushing disappointment if it wasn't. She was quiet and withdrawn when they drove to Saskatoon for the pregnancy test.

Tim and Brad accompanied them on the trip. After Shauna Lee had her blood taken, they went shopping and then stopped for coffee. When Shauna Lee's phone rang, her eyes locked with Christina's. She took it out of her purse and looked at the call display. She stared at it as it rang, then handed it to Brad and squeezed her eyes shut.

Brad's expression relaxed as he listened. Then he smiled. "I think I'll let you tell Shauna Lee the news."

He handed the phone to Shauna Lee and nodded as she looked at him beseechingly. Tears sprang into her eyes and she handed the phone to Christina. "This is your call, Christina."

Christina's words were choked when she spoke into the phone. She began to tremble as she listened to the caller. "Thank you," she whispered. "I think you should speak to Shauna Lee now." She turned to Tim. "The baby…the embryo…Shauna Lee is pregnant."

Shauna Lee finished the call, stood up and walked around the table to hug Christina. "I know how hard this has been for you. Sometimes I wondered if I'd been wrong to suggest this surrogacy thing, but now…we're not completely safe yet, but the HCG numbers are great and I've never had any trouble carrying my babies, so I think we can be optimistic. "

Christina was still crying, but there was a smile behind the tears now. "I've been so afraid…sometimes I've actually wished we hadn't started this. But now, all I can do is thank you. I promise I will do everything I can to help you through the next months. I…we…owe you both so much."

Tim reached for Shauna Lee and gave her a warm hug, then turned and gave Brad a man hug. Everyone had glistening eyes. Curious people in the restaurant watched the emotional moments and finally Shauna Lee stood up and declared, "We are pregnant." There was a warm round of applause.

CHAPTER NINETEEN

The next day, Christina arrived at Shauna Lee's door with her arms full. "I made a casserole for supper and there's a batch of cookies for the kids."

Shauna Lee shook her head. "Christina! Quit fussing. It's not like I have a rare disease. I'm pregnant. It's a perfectly normal condition that I've experienced twice before."

"But you're not just pregnant. You're pregnant with our baby. There aren't words to express what that really means to me. I…I need to do something; I need to help you, take care of you." Tears filled her eyes. "You are doing the one thing I can't do for Tim and me. You're giving us the baby I'd given up all hope of having."

Shauna Lee reached for her hand. "I know that, Chris. That's why I wanted to do this, but I don't want you to wear sackcloth and ashes for the rest of your life. I want to share this journey with you. I want you to enjoy the magic and the joy of it."

"I know, but I can help with the kids and help clean house."

"Christina! I don't even think about being pregnant yet. I feel great. I'll gladly take your help later on if I need it, but right now you're in danger of becoming a pain in the ass. Go help Tim haul seed grain or plan your flowerbeds. Look around the place and imagine your baby running around in the back yard."

"But…"

"I'm serious. There's nothing for you to do right now, except enjoy the fact that you are going to be parents."

Christina looked confused.

Shauna Lee reached out and hugged her. "Come in for coffee and we'll sample those cookies. Thank you for bringing supper for tonight, but for the next few months, I don't want you showing up to help me unless I ask for it. I want you to come as my dear friend, not my handmaiden."

Seven weeks after the embryo transfer, the four of them drove to the fertility clinic in Saskatoon. The scheduled ultrasound would show how the baby was developing and verify if the pregnancy was progressing according to schedule.

They watched the nurse put jelly on Shauna Lee's stomach and move the transceiver over it. Immediately, she smiled as she shot a glance at them.

Tim and Christina held hands as they watched the ultrasound monitor. Christina leaned forward, staring at the screen. The rapid sound of the heartbeat beat a quick tattoo. Tim frowned as he listened, picking up a rhythmic change.

He felt Christina tense, then gasp in awe. "Oh my God! Are there two of them?" Everyone stared at the image, watching tiny pulses in two distinct places. "Tim…there are two little blips there." She stared at the nurse, amazement registering on her face. "Are there twins?"

The technician nodded.

Christina turned to Tim. "Can it be true?" Then she sobered and looked at Shauna Lee. "Can you do this? We never thought of more than one."

Shauna Lee stared at the monitor. *Twins?* She was temporarily apprehensive. Her eyes darted to Brad's, then to Christina and Tim's. Their looks of amazement and awe erased her doubt. She grinned. "I think we can handle this, Christina."

"Are you sure? You're so tiny. We never considered this."

"Of course, I'm sure. We should have transferred two embryos the first time. You weren't supposed to have *a* baby, you were meant to have two of them."

Dr. Fin met with them after the ultrasound. He congratulated them and asked them if they had concerns.

Christina's question was full of worry. "Shauna Lee is so small, is it safe for her to carry twins."

Dr. Fin chuckled as he looked at Shauna Lee. "Twins are always considered a higher risk pregnancy, but smaller women than Shauna Lee give birth to perfectly healthy twins all the time." He looked through his notes and then directed his next question to Shauna Lee. "From the records here, I see you've had two children already, right?"

Shauna Lee smiled. "I have and I've loved being pregnant."

"You've never had any problems? No incompetent cervix issues or signs of gestational diabetes?"

Shauna Lee shook her head.

"And you carried to full term?"

"Everything went perfectly," she assured him.

He looked around at the four of them. "The majority of twin pregnancies result in healthy babies. However, there are complications that are slightly more common in twin pregnancies than single births. There can be a higher risk of miscarriage, especially with identical twins, but there is always a higher risk of miscarriage in the first trimester of any pregnancy. And your babies are not identical, they are fraternal twins."

Tim interjected, "How do you know that?"

"Both eggs took hold in this pregnancy; they have individual sacks and are in separate places in the uterus."

Brad nodded. "What other issues can arise with twins?"

"Premature labor is one we hope to avoid. Many women expecting twins give birth before thirty-seven weeks, which can lead to low birth rates and prematurity problems. We'll keep an eye out for gestational hypertension. Also, pre-eclampsia is more likely with multiple births and tends to develop earlier and be more severe."

He looked at Brad and smiled. "We'll keep a close eye on her and her precious cargo. We know exactly when she conceived and we know from the start that it's twins. We'll be doing regular ultrasounds to make sure everything stays on track, and if anything looks problematic, we will deal with it immediately."

He looked at Shauna Lee. "You've given birth already, so I'm sure you are familiar with the warning signs of pre-eclampsia and premature labor, but we'll be checking to make sure that you are aware of them as the pregnancy develops. Also, you are going to gain more weight with twins. You'll need to, particularly during the first half of the pregnancy because it helps reduce the risk of premature labor and low birth rates.

"Make sure your diet is nourishing and stay well hydrated. Keeping fit and healthy can help you cope better with carrying twins. The uterus will expand as much as it can, but I can guarantee that by the end, you're going to feel unbearably uncomfortable and they are going to be pushing and poking constantly, looking for room to be comfortable." He closed the file and looked around the room. "Does anyone else have questions or concerns?"

Christina cleared her throat and looked at Shauna Lee and Brad. "I'll be there to help with Leanne and Patch, and I'll do the housework and cleaning."

Dr. Fin laughed. "She'll probably appreciate the help later on, but initially she'll be fine."

"I want to do everything I can to make sure Shauna Lee and the babies are safe."

Dr. Fin looked at her with compassion. "Christina, I understand your concern, but at this point there is nothing you can do to help keep her and those wonderful babies safe. Shauna Lee will take care of the important things: nutrition, hydration, and rest. Nature will take its course. At this point, the fetuses appear to be strong and healthy. That's all we can ask for now."

Shauna Lee looked at Christina and smiled. "See, the doctor agrees with me."

***

Tim, Norman Walters, and Ben Norland had been readying the equipment since the middle of April and they started seeding canola during the first week of May. Once again, the three men worked rotating shifts, spending eight hours on the tractor, also spending four more hours delivering seed, fertilizer, fuel, helping with repairs and running for parts when needed. It was a constant flow of activity and the weather held for them.

The fields that had grown Durham wheat the year before were planted with lentils, and the acreage that had grown lentils the previous year, was planted with barley. Zero-tillage equipment and the rotation of crops in an orderly fashion helped to maintain the quality and structure of the soil, and that was vital in their modern day program. Farming wasn't just a way of life anymore; it had become a finely tuned business that required scientifically-based planning.

Christina drove to Saskatoon with Shauna Lee for both the eight-week and the ten-week ultrasounds. The pregnancy was progressing as it should have, which helped to ease Christina's apprehension. Shauna Lee glowed with health and happiness. She hadn't experienced morning sickness with her first two pregnancies and in spite of the possibility that the hormones created by having an extra fetus on board, she wasn't suffering from it this time.

Christina was having a hard time focusing on anything. Several times, she had gone out to the back yard, planning to work up the soil and pull weeds in the beds that had been so beautiful the season before, but her restlessness drove her back into the house.

When Tim came in from his shift in the field, she had to stifle the desire to pour out her frustrations, but she knew he was tired and needed to rest. When he slept, she would lay cuddled in his arms, her mind refusing to calm down. Tim's preoccupation with the heavy workload filled his mind and his time, and he wasn't aware of the toll Christina's emotions were taking on her.

She teetered on the edge of depression, driven by the extreme anxiety that she couldn't shake. One day, he came in unexpectedly and found her curled up on the couch crying. Fear rippled through him. He rushed to her side and kneeled on the floor beside her. "Chris, what happened? Is something wrong with the babies?"

She sat up, shaking her head as she wiped away her tears with her shirt. "N..no."

"Then, what's wrong?"

"I don't know. I should be so happy right now, but I'm just in a funk. I...I'm filled with anxiety." She hiccupped on a sob. "I'm almost sick with fear. I'm afraid something will go wrong."

He sat down and pulled her into his arms. "Chris, I feel like such a jerk. I've been so busy that I haven't noticed what's been happening to you. You've been here and you've come to bed and cuddled with me, and I've just zonked out. I haven't realized what you've been going through."

Christina shook her head. "I'm being irrational. Everything seems to be going perfectly according to schedule with the babies. Why can't I just relax and be happy?" She snuffled against his shirt. "I just have this overwhelming fear and I feel so damn useless. I can't do anything to justify my part in this pregnancy. Shauna Lee has told me she doesn't need my help right now. I'm not getting anything done around here." She tried to laugh but failed. "Cripes, I can't even be happy. I'm just a mess."

Tim sighed and held her close. "Can you hang in there for a couple more days? We're almost done seeding the barley. When we get to the last day, I'll let the guys finish up and we'll go see Doctor Wilfred and see if he can give you something to help you get on top of things." He kissed her hair. "I feel guilty, like I should be taking you right now, but if I just get this finished before it rains, I'll be done until the haying starts. Then we can spend all the time we want together."

Christina sat up and looked into his eyes. "I know you have to get the seeding done. I'm just so mad at myself for being like this." She stifled a sob. "It scares me; I think I'd die if anything happened to those babies."

"Nothing's going to happen to them. You're going to be the most wonderful mother in the world." He kissed her. "Chris, I have to go to Swift Current for a part for the grain truck. Why don't you come with me?"

Christina shook her head. "I look like such a mess. I can't go to town."

He stood up and pulled her to her feet. "Go wash your face and run a brush through your hair. You look beautiful to me, and you can wait in the pickup while I run in to get the parts. We haven't spent any real time together for over a month. Come on."

He went to his office and got his wallet, and then met her in the bathroom. As he watched her brush her hair, he reached for a tube of lipstick on the counter and handed it to her. "Put on a bit of color and you'll feel wonderful."

She smiled and took the top off the tube, applying the color to her lips. She rubbed them together and looked at him. "Better?"

"You always look terrific to me. Let's go."

He pulled her against him as they drove to town. They talked about how green the landscape looked, and Tim told her tidbits about what had been going on with Ben and Norman. He leaned over and kissed her ear. "I've missed this…just being together and talking."

She sighed. "So have I; everything has been so mixed up since Christmas. We were both so intense about getting pregnant and having it fall apart. Then when it finally happened, you had to go right into seeding and I couldn't distract myself. I'm glad you made me come with you this afternoon. I feel better. I just have to work at getting a healthier attitude and I'll be alright."

The first week in June, Shauna Lee, Christina, and Tim drove to Saskatoon for the twelve-week checkup and ultrasound. Dr. Fin was pleased with the development of the twins, proclaiming they were doing incredibly well. They had reached their first trimester and the chances of a miscarriage, were greatly reduced. Shauna Lee's only complaint, other than being tired, was her weight gain, but Dr. Fin was happy about that.

On the way home, Shauna Lee squeezed Christina's hand. "Is it time to share the good news yet? Frank, Colt, Ollie, and Ellie will feel like we left them out."

Christina looked at Tim. "Is it time, hon?"

Tim was grinning from ear to ear. He reached out and squeezed Christina's knee. "I think it finally is. We can all give a sigh of relief now and spread the word. When shall we go?"

Christina smiled. "It's Father's Day next weekend. Maybe we should run out to the ranch and let you celebrate with the rest of the daddies."

Shauna Lee giggled. "I can hardly wait for them to know. They'll be so happy for you guys. It's been hard for me to keep my mouth shut, but it's your news to tell and after all the ups and downs we've had since we started this project, I'm glad we didn't say anything before. From here on out, it'll be smooth sailing guys, so shout it to the world."

They dropped Shauna Lee off at her place and headed home, stopping to pick-up the mail on the way. When Tim came back to the truck, he was studying a large envelope that had come.

"What have you got there?"

His look was puzzled. "The return address is from my oldest sister. I didn't think she even knew where I was, let alone my address.

"Actually, it wouldn't be hard to find out where you live. All she had to do was go on the internet and search with Canada411.ca and she could find out exactly where you lived, your phone number and address."

He turned the envelope. "That may be what she did. She didn't have our box number, she just put a question mark in its place, but she had our full physical address at the farm. It looks like it's been shuffled around a bit through the postal system. Someone has written

'Try Box 3412,' and there's a form attached letting me know it was addressed incorrectly."

He felt the package, searching for a clue to its contents. He frowned. "There's paperwork in here, but it feels like there's a thin book too, like a scribbler or something. Maybe she found some of my old school stuff and decided to send it, but after all this time, that doesn't make much sense." He shrugged his shoulders and put it on the dash. "Shall we go out for supper? Then we won't have to cook when we get home?"

"That sounds like a great idea, and we can check out the mystery envelope while we wait for our meal."

Tim made a phone call, then, headed, out of town.

"Where are we going?"

"You'll remember soon."

Christina looked puzzled and then said, "Crawford House? You are a romantic man!"

Tim nodded as he pulled up in front of the old manor and parked. Christina reached for the envelope, but Tim shook his head and stopped her. "That can wait. Tonight we're going to celebrate. We've been so busy with everything else these past few months, that we haven't taken time to enjoy being us. We even missed our first anniversary."

Christina looked shocked. "You're right. We did."

"And how long has it been since we really made passionate love, instead of grabbing a quickie?"

Christina blushed as she trailed her finger down his sleeve. "Far too long, Loverboy" she whispered.

He grabbed her hand and nibbled on her fingers. "Far, far, too long. We've got some catching up to do tonight."

He helped Christina out of the truck and they went inside. He asked for a table in a quiet corner, smiling at the hostess as he told her they were celebrating. When she asked what the occasion was, he laughed as he pulled Christina against him, "Our first anniversary, learning we are going to be the parents of twins, wonderful friends and I think we missed mother's day, too. We have a lot to celebrate."

They drank wine, savored the scrumptious food, shared precious memories of the past year and dreamed about the future. Two hours later when they went to the truck, they looked at each other and Christina giggled. "Loverboy, we're tipsy. I don't think we should drive to the farm now. The deal isn't closed on the house yet. Can we go there?"

Tim shook his head. "Let's get a room."

"Where? We have to be sure we don't get caught driving under the influence!"

Tim thought for a moment. "You're right. Putting ourselves in the position of being able to get a DUI wouldn't be smart. I'll go inside and call a taxi, and we'll pick up the truck in the morning." When he returned, he was smiling. "They got a laugh out of us celebrating until we were tipsy. They called a taxi for us and there's no problem with us leaving the truck overnight."

The taxi took them to the Super 8 Hotel. People smiled as they entered the lobby, their happiness obvious to everyone who saw them. They kissed and groped each other as they rode the elevator. When they got to their floor, they were still kissing when they stumbled out and found their way to their room.

Tim opened the door and turned, lifting Christina in his arms and carrying her inside, kicking the door shut behind them. He lowered her feet to the floor beside the bed. Their hands moved frantically, removing clothing, touching skin, firing their arousal. Hungrily, they stripped away their confining garments and fell onto the bed. They took each other fast and hard. In minutes, they lay sated and exhausted.

After their heartbeats settled and their breathing slowed, Tim looked at her apologetically. "So much for making, slow, deliriously sensual, love to you!"

Christina giggled and hooked her leg over his hip, pulling herself up onto his chest. "That was fast and furious, but we were due for a firestorm. It was perfect." She kissed him softly.

He rolled on top of her and ran his hands along her face, threading them back through her hair. "You are my life's treasure, Chris. I can't imagine living without you. And now we are going to have a family; not one, but two babies." He kissed her gently. "I never imagined I could be so blessed. You have brought me my life's greatest gifts."

Eventually, they got up and showered, helped each other towel off and walked hand in hand back to the bed. They snuggled and talked about the things they hadn't had time to do through the anxiety and busyness of the past six months. They agreed they'd need a van to transport their new family, and they'd have to prepare the nursery. They dreamed about the future, wondering what the twins would be like. They talked about the prospect of selling Christina's house and what they'd do with the money from the sale. They discussed going out to the ranch to share their news with the rest of 'the family.' They wondered what was happening with Arthur Knout's investigation. And, they vowed to keep in touch with their feelings, no matter how busy they might get. They drifted drowsily, then, resurfaced to make slow, sensuous, passionate love.

In the morning, they awoke late and took their time, enjoying their togetherness. They had breakfast, nursed their morning coffee and then called a taxi to take them to Crawford House. When they got into the truck, Tim took the large envelope off the dash and tossed it onto the seat next to the passenger door. They drove home slowly, savoring the closeness of being inside the truck cab, secluded from the stresses of the world.

When they arrived home, Christina collected the mail off the seat and slid out of the cab behind Tim. When her feet touched the ground, he dropped his arm around her shoulder and guided her into the house. They stopped at the door and looked into each other's eyes.

Tim touched her face. "I'm glad we did this."

"So am I. It's so easy to lose touch when things get complicated and crazy busy over a long period of time."

Once in the house, Tim went straight to the office and phoned the ranch. His excitement colored his voice when he talked to Frank and asked if they could come out to the ranch for the weekend.

Christina made coffee while he was talking. She sat down at the table to look at the flyers that came with the local paper. When Tim came back to the kitchen, he poured them each a cup of coffee, brought the two cups to the table, and then sat down with her. He thumbed through the mail, avoiding the envelope.

CHAPTER TWENTY

Christina watched him as she sipped from her cup. When she put it down, she said, "You're avoiding that letter, Tim. Please open the damned thing and find out what's in it. I'm dying of curiosity."

He sighed. "Yeah, I guess I am avoiding it."

"Why?"

"I can't imagine what she wants after all this time. Both Mom and Dad have been gone for years, and since all their kids made it clear that I wasn't considered part of the Bates family; it's hard to imagine what they're up to now. I left that mess behind me and I'm not getting sucked into it again."

Christina reached out and touched his hand. "No matter what it is, you can't just turn away and act like you didn't get the letter. You have to protect yourself by knowing what could be in the wind."

"You're right. I'm just reluctant to punch a hole in this happy bubble we're in before I have to."

She brushed her thumb over his. "Do you want me to look?"

"No. I have to do it myself." He reached for the envelope and opened it. He frowned as he peered into it. He tipped the contents onto the table. There were two white envelopes addressed to him. There was also a sealed Kraft envelope, and an old lined scribbler.

Tim let his finger fan the edges of the pages of the scribbler. He could tell it was filled with his mother's handwriting. He looked at the front cover and noted that she had written his name on in.

His stomach clenched and a knot of anxiety rose in his chest. He didn't want to look at it yet. He looked at the two white envelopes addressed to him. He recognized one as his mother's handwriting, the other was his sisters and was marked *READ THIS FIRST*.

He fingered the letter and considered the message to read it first. He looked across at Christina. "I'm being a chicken-shit, but I'm afraid to find out what's inside. I already know that the woman who was my mom was not my birthmother. The family wanted no part of me. Do I really want to find out anything else?"

"Tim, maybe she'll fill in the blanks; the things Arthur hasn't been able to find."

Tim sighed. "You're right. There's no way I can ignore it, no matter what." He tore open the letter with the message and drew out the folded sheets of paper. As he started to read the letter, he blinked away the moisture that crept into his eyes and swallowed hard. When he finished it, he handed the letter to Christina, then got up and walked to the door to stare outside.

Christina absorbed the contents, tears filling her eyes. Janelle's letter was filled with guilt and pain, apologizing for the way the family had allowed their brother, Gerard, to persuade all of them to denounce Tim and push him out of their lives.

She stated that the girls had found the adoption papers after their mother had died. When they had realized that he was not their half-brother as they had always believed, Gerard's anger and resentment had escalated and boiled over. He had always been jealous of the close relationship between Tim and their dad, feeling he could never compete for his father's love and affection. He'd refused to recognize the legitimacy of the adoption and aggressively promoted the idea that Tim was not a Bates in any way and was fraudulently claiming to be one.

She further stated that their mother had stipulated that Tim was not be given the included information, until after their father had died. By then there had been so much animosity between Tim and the rest of the family that she had deliberately withheld it. Now with some distance in time and location, she had come to realize that not honoring her mother's wishes had been wrong. She asked him to accept her apologies and forgive her.

Christina wiped away the tears and stood up. Tim turned to face her. She walked over and wrapped her arms around him. "I'm so sorry, hon."

"It isn't so much what she said," Tim said, his voice filled with pain and anger. "It's what she didn't say. Nothing about caring about me, nothing about wishing me well, no mention of the others or what they're doing. Her guilty conscience got the best of her because she hadn't honored Mom's wishes...well, at least she has a remnant of conscience. I guess I can be thankful for that."

"Would you like a drink, Tim? Would it help to numb the pain and help you deal with the rest of the package?"

He shook his head. "It won't change anything. I still have to face it." He walked to the table and sat down again, reaching for the envelope his mother had addressed to him. Christina pulled her chair next to his and sat down, resting her hand comfortingly on his thigh.

He opened it and shared the pages with Christina, so they could both read it together. In her letter, his mother told Tim many times, how much she and his dad had loved him. She explained that his birth mother was actually her half-sister. They had both been born near Kitchener, Ontario. Fredrick Webber had fathered both of them, but they had different mothers. Fredrick was a wealthy, influential man with several business holdings.

He was married to Belinda Tucker, who gave birth to Madeline (Maddie). He had been having an affair with his secretary, Sonja Mercator, who became pregnant and gave birth to Melissa Wanda Mercator. The two children had been born within six months of each other.

When Melissa was three years old, her mother committed suicide. On her birth certificate, Fredrick Webber was listed as Melissa's father. It was a locally known fact, and he claimed the child and took her into the home he shared with his wife. They raised her, but he never gave her his name.

The two girls grew up in an extremely dysfunctional home. Love had fled the relationship when Belinda discovered that Sonja was having Fredrick's child. When Sonja committed suicide, it was also public knowledge that he had ended the relationship with her, and moved on to someone new. Belinda lived with the humiliation and the helpless anger of knowing that everyone in town knew about her husband's philandering. It was doubly devastating to have him bring his mistress's child home for her to look after.

Madeline and Melissa clung to each other, becoming best friends. They looked so much alike that people, who did not know their history, thought they were twins. Belinda died of cancer when the girls were almost seventeen. They both finished high school that year. Fredrick was rigid and controlling, trying to keep them under his thumb. After graduation, they took the small inheritance that Belinda had secreted away for Madeline and caught a ride to Toronto with a friend. From there, they took the Greyhound bus to Calgary, Alberta. They stayed there for a couple of weeks, before moving on to Vancouver, B.C.

Madeline had gotten a job in a grocery store and Melissa found work in a bar. The two girls shared a room and started a new life, far away from their painful childhood. Although they looked alike, the two girls were different in character and personality. Madeline was inclined to be more serious and cautious while Melissa was carefree, outgoing and very popular. Men were attracted to her and she enjoyed their company. She met many of them at the bar where she worked and often went partying with the man of the moment.

Madeline had tried to caution her, but Melissa brushed her concerns aside. When she met Ollie Crampton, she took a special liking to him. She knew he was a man on the move, looking for work as a ranch hand. He had stayed in Vancouver for a few weeks, which was much longer than he'd intended. When he left, Melissa had no idea where he'd gone.

Another man caught her attention and the party went on...until she realized that she was pregnant. Then, she'd panicked. The thought of having a child on her own terrified her. She remembered the things she'd heard about her own mother and what had happened to her.

When she went to a doctor, he determined that she was about three months pregnant. Melissa realized that Ollie Crampton had to be the father. Instinctively she knew Ollie would have taken on his responsibility and made a good husband and father, but she had no idea how to find him. Madeline had tried to offer comfort, reassuring her that she would help raise the baby.

Melissa quit working in bars and found work in a restaurant. She changed her appearance, abandoned the party girl persona and projected a respectable image. She started using her middle name and became known as Wanda Mercator.

She quickly met Brian Ethridge. He had a good job and was

stable. She worked the relationship hard and encouraged intimacy. After two months, she told him she was pregnant. He offered to marry her and she'd been happy to accept.

They were married in a quiet ceremony and everything went well for them until he began to realize that her pregnancy was much further along than it could possibly be if he was the father. Justifiably outraged, he'd left her. She moved in with Madeline again. During the last months of the pregnancy, it became very clear that she did not want the responsibility of a child. Fearing for the child's future, Madeline agreed to become its guardian and look after it.

When her son was born, Melissa wanted nothing to do with him. Madeline took them both home with her. As soon as possible, Melissa signed legal guardianship of the baby over to Madeline and disappeared. Madeline never saw her again. She raised the baby, loving it as if it were her own. When she married Harry Bates, they jointly adopted Tim, legally making him their son.

Tim lay the pages down, put his elbows on the table, and interlaced his fingers. He rested his head on them and sighed. Christina stood up and massaged his shoulders. After a few moments, he reached up and clasped her hands. "Thanks, hon," he said softly.

He turned his chair and pulled her into the circle of his arms, resting his head against her breast. She ran her finger through his hair and he sighed again. "Well, now we know the whole story. It's not surprising that Arthur has had so much trouble trying to put the pieces together."

"Are you going to phone him?"

"Yes. I'll fill in the missing pieces. There is nothing for him to look into now, so we might as well close the file. I'll tell him that I'll talk to Ollie."

Shauna Lee smiled when she answered the phone. "Christina! You sound great this morning...like the woman I used to know, before I turned your world upside down with this surrogacy thing. Sometimes I've almost felt guilty about it, but in the end, I know it will be worth every moment of anxiety and fear, and doubt."

Christina laughed softly. "I must seem like such an ungrateful hag. Here you are doing all the heavy lifting, and I'm freaking out and falling apart. It's just...I had learned to live with knowing I'd never have a baby, and then once I opened the door to that possibility…I don't know how I could handle it if something went wrong."

"I understand, Chris. You are afraid of getting hurt again. I didn't realize how deep you'd buried your pain until we got into this. I was disappointed when we didn't conceive the first time and shocked when it didn't happen the second time, but I could see that you weren't only disappointed. It devastated you. But now, we are past the most dangerous time and those little guys are just doing exactly what they need to do in there." Shauna Lee chuckled. "And I'm so thrilled that you are having twins. It's the most incredible thing that could have happened."

"You are such a wonderful friend, Shauna Lee. I hope carrying two isn't more than you bargained for. I can't imagine how you'll stretch to accommodate them."

"Pffft…you heard the doctor. Small women have twins with no problems all the time. I feel great, other than being tired, but they say that's natural. It takes a lot of energy for the body to grow two munchkins."

"I wish I could help you. I feel so useless."

"Look mommy, you did your share already. Thank God I didn't have to take all those injections like you did and I didn't have to go through the egg retrieval. I'm just the incubator. I'm sure I'll need your help later on when all three of us are trying to find a comfortable position to be in; so enjoy your freedom for now. Believe me, you are going to be the one needing help once you take these two home. It's a good thing Tim will be around home for the first few months. It would've been a disaster if they'd made their appearance at one of the busiest times on the farm; like seeding time, haying or harvest."

Christina smiled. "He'll be a great dad and I know he'll pitch right in. Speaking of dads, he phoned the ranch and Frank and Colt are expecting all of us on the weekend. This is going to be wild; telling them about the babies and Tim has something else to share…."

"What's that?"

"It's his secret to tell, not mine. I can guarantee that it will stun you."

"Christina, you're not being fair."

"The weekend is only two days away. We'll share our secrets

with everybody then."

"Shall Brad and I meet you guys at the highway and travel to the ranch together?"

"That sounds like a plan. What time do think you'll be there?"

"Well, you know what Leanne is like in the morning. If she's not too miserable, we should be able to leave by seven o'clock. Patch will just stay asleep when we put him in his car seat, but with Leanne it can be like stirring up a hornets' nest. I'll pack everything and we'll put it in the truck Friday night so we can just get up and leave."

"So, we should be waiting at the highway at around seven forty-five Saturday morning? You can give us a call if you're going to be later."

Frank and Colt were sitting on the deck with Ellie and Ollie when the two vehicles arrived at the ranch Saturday morning. Frank was waiting on the sidewalk when the pickups parked in the yard. Colt stood up and stretched lazily while the doors flew open and everyone started getting out. He walked over and shook hands with Tim and Brad, then gave Christina a hug. He took Leanne out of Shauna Lee's arms and reached down to ruffle Patch's hair.

"Are you feeling okay, Colt?" Shauna Lee asked.

"Yeah." He frowned. "Why would you ask that?"

She looked at her watch. "It's eleven o'clock and you're sitting here on the deck, instead of chasing cows or fixing fence like the workaholic we all know would usually be doing."

"It's Father's Day. I'm celebrating my manhood."

Shauna Lee laughed. "Is that what they call it now? Manhood? Not fatherhood?"

"Are you feeling okay, Shauna Lee?" Colt countered.

"I've never been better. Why would you ask?"

"I don't know…you've lost that Twiggy look."

Frank studied her. "He's right. You've gained some weight, but it's more than that." She studied her friend and then gasped. "Oh my God! Are you pregnant?"

Christina giggled. Shauna Lee shook her head. "Jeeze, you guys don't even let me get settled in and you start ragging on me."

Frank smiled knowingly. "You *are* pregnant! Congratulations, guys."

Shauna Lee shook her head. "Don't congratulate us."

Frank frowned. "What do you mean?"

Tim and Christina reached for each other, coupling their hands. Tim was beaming. "We didn't plan to tell you this way, but this whole scenario is moving much faster than we'd intended. I thought we'd at least get to sit down and talk for a while before we sprang the good news, but here we go.

"We came out here today to tell the rest of the family that Shauna Lee offered to be a surrogate for us last fall. It's taken a bit of doing, but she is carrying our twins. They used Christina's eggs and my...uh...manhood...." He grinned at Colt. "They mixed them together in the lab and put them in a to Petrie dish to grow. Then they transferred them into Shauna Lee. We didn't say anything before because we wanted to make sure that we got through the most critical period, to lessen the possibilities of losing them."

"No way!" Frank squealed with delight. "That is fabulous! Shauna Lee, you're amazing."

"Brad's the amazing one. I think he thought I was nuts when I first suggested it to him. But when he thought about it and realized that I really wanted to do this, he agreed to put up with my bitchiness and the big belly one more time. It's no hardship for me. I like being pregnant and I know how much these guys love kids. Christina has motherhood written all over her...I realized that I could incubate their embryos and help them have the babies they deserved.

Frank chuckled. "You love being pregnant, but you haven't carried twins yet!"

"I'm not worried. I'm glad it's twins. This is a one-time offer. It's perfect that Christina and Tim are getting two in one."

Frank hugged Christina. "I'm so happy for you! This is so exciting! It's almost hard to comprehend." She shook her head. "You must be beside yourself!"

"I'm overwhelmed." Tears filled Christina's eyes. "I've been anxious and sick with fear, afraid something will go wrong. It's like reaching for the golden ring and being afraid you will miss it and fall into a deep, dark hole."

Frank nodded. "I understand that. I have miscarried and we did try several times after, but it didn't happen. Every month I hoped and hoped. When I was late by a day, I was so happy and certain that I was pregnant again. I finally went back on the pill, because I couldn't stand being on the roller coaster every month." She squeezed Christina's hands. "Things will be fine for you now. When are the babies due?"

Christina's eye sparkled. "Full term would make them due on New Year's day. With twins, that isn't very likely, but if we make it to thirty-six weeks...better if it was thirty-eight...everything should be fine. They're keeping tabs on what's happening. Shauna Lee has an ultrasound every two weeks, so if anything slightly iffy shows up, they'll be on it. Right now, the babies are text-book perfect."

"Reach out and grab the golden ring, Christina. Don't fear the fall. Send those babies positive, joyful energy. They'll thrive on it."

"Thanks." Christina looked around for Tim. He wasn't with the others. She glanced toward the truck and realized that he and Ollie were sitting in it. She could see that they were looking at papers, so she knew that Tim was sharing his news with Ollie. The weekend had started with the speed of a runaway train.

Leanne found Christina and tugged on her slacks, demanding attention. "Up, up," she called. Christina smiled and her heart melted when she picked her up and cuddled her. The child put a hand on each of her cheeks and planted sloppy kisses on Christina's face, then inspected her earrings, toggling them with her fingers. "Pretty, pretty," she babbled, tugging at them.

Christina gently took her hand and redirected her attention, then sat down in a chair and talked with the toddler. Shauna Lee's heart filled with warmth as she watched. She was filled with joy, knowing that she had made the decision to carry her friend's babies.

Colt came over and crouched down by Christina. "What's going on with Ollie and Tim? I see they're having a serious conversation in the truck."

Christina looked at them and spoke softly. "Tim got a package in the mail this week. It contained a letter that his mother had written to him before she died. He'll tell everyone about it, but I guess he wanted to talk to Ollie first. She cleared up most of the unanswered questions."

She looked across the deck at Shauna Lee, then back at Colt. "We've never talked to Shauna Lee and Brad about it. Everything was swallowed up in the surrogacy project. That started six months ago and it's been stressful for all of us. On top of that, Tim's been totally focused on seeding for the last month. After the package came, he decided to talk to Ollie and then share it with all the 'family'."

"So, I guess this is going to be a pretty special Father's Day for

Ollie too."

"Well, there is no more actual proof, but there's lots of food for thought," she answered, soberly.

Minutes later, Ollie and Tim joined them on the deck. Tim held up the envelope he'd received. "Hey, everyone, let's go inside and sit around the table. Ollie and I have some things to tell you."

Shauna Lee's questioning eyes met Christina's as she stood up. *Is this it?* She mouthed silently.

Christina nodded.

The adult members of the 'family' sat around the table and Ollie told them about the letter he had received four years earlier. Tim filled them in about seeing what he'd assumed was his mother's picture in Ollie's office, how he'd felt about it and later the role Christina had played. Gradually, he and Ollie revealed the entire story.

Tim turned to Christina when they were finished. "The other day, when we read Mom's letter, I was so stunned that I didn't open the other envelope." He picked up the Kraft envelope and showed it to her. "These are pictures Mom took from the time I was born until she married Harry. There's a picture of Ollie and Mellissa in here. He remembers her now. He never knew her as Wanda Ethridge, so it's no wonder he didn't have a clue as to who she was. We agree Ollie is probably my dad, but there is still no absolute proof of it."

Frank rested her elbows on the table and put her chin in the palms of her hands. She stared at the table, lost in thought. "There is a way you can find out."

Ollie's chair scraped the floor. "Yeah?"

"Have a paternity test."

Ollie looked at Tim. "Are you okay with that?"

Tim nodded. "Absolutely." The two men looked at each other. A shimmer of moisture glistened in Ollie's eye before he looked away. Christina saw it and looked at Tim.

Ollie looked at Ellie. Their eyes held as Ellie gave him an imperceptible nod. Ollie sighed and turned back to Tim. "Let's do it. Where can we get DNA testing done?"

Frank stood up. "I'll check on the internet, but I think it can be done in Swift Current."

Tim reached across the table to Ollie. "I'm convinced that you are my dad, from what Mom wrote. I hope you are: but it sounds like Mellissa was pretty active, so I think it's a wise idea to find out for certain."

Ollie squeezed his hand. "I think it's pretty safe to say it's true, and if we aren't a match, we'll adopt you and make it legal. I like the idea of having a son, even if I'm finding out close to fifty years late."

Christina drove to Saskatoon with Shauna Lee for the sixteen-week ultrasound. The embryos were strong and developing normally.

They were sitting at a table after lunch when Shauna Lee looked at Christina, sensing the underlying anxiety that still lingered in her. "Christina, what's wrong? Everything is perfect; you should be so happy."

Tears shimmered in Christina's eyes. "I know I should be. I just always have this niggling remnant of doubt. Don't misunderstand me...I am so grateful for what you're doing for us." She reached out and clasped her friend's hand. "I want these babies so much I can hardly breathe sometimes, but deep down I'm still afraid something will go wrong. There are times when I feel like I don't deserve them. I know that's silly, but I just can't shake it. I even find myself thinking that I'm not supposed to have babies, or I wouldn't have been born so flawed."

Shauna Lee's heart ached. "Christina, you are not flawed. You were born with a challenge, but you also have the most important thing necessary to produce your own children. You have healthy ovaries and they produce fertile eggs. Without you, these embryos could not have been created."

Christina brushed away the tears that trickled down her face. "I know that. But I feel so useless."

Shauna Lee shook her head. "That is not true. You really have to find a way to accept that you deserve these babies."

A week later, they both went to Saskatoon for the eighteen-week ultrasound. The babies were strong and growing. Christina declined knowing their gender. She wanted Tim to be there when they found out.

Shauna Lee expressed surprise at how big she was. When they measured her, her womb was as big she normally would have been at around twenty-nine weeks. Dr. Fin was unfazed by it. "Your body is making room for two in there," he said matter-of-factly. "Are you feeling movement yet?"

"I think I did the other day. It was just a flutter. I could have mistaken it for gas, but it brought back memories of when I was pregnant before."

He nodded. "A first-time mother can miss that, but since you've been pregnant before, you probably did feel them." He touched her shoulder, giving it a slight squeeze. "You're doing a great job, girl."

He looked at Christina with a smile. "In a few weeks you'll be able to feel them kick when Shauna Lee lets you put your hand on her belly. Right now, you have to be feeling left out, but pretty soon you should start spending time with Shauna Lee and talk to them so they know your voice. You and your husband could make an audio tape or save your messages on an iPod so Shauna Lee can play it when she's resting. You should both talk to them so they get used to the patterns of your speech, the cadence of your voices. It's important that you interact with them while they are growing in her womb."

Tim went with Shauna Lee and Christina for the twenty-week ultrasound. He and Christina watched in awe, as they watched the babies moving their arms and legs, stretching and yawning in the safe, comfortable environment of Shauna Lee's womb.

Tim was moved to tears. "Look at them. They're so real, such perfect little people." He turned and pulled Christina in his arms. "Those tiny people are unique extensions of you and me, Chris. There are no other people in this world like them." He looked over her head at Shauna Lee. "Thank you for making this possible."

Shauna Lee brushed away the moisture in her eyes and nodded.

The nurse cleared her throat. "Would you like to know what you're having?"

Tim and Christina quickly looked up at her, both nodding in unison. The nurse ran the transceiver over the child on the right. "This spunky one is a boy. We'll call him baby A." She moved to the other baby. "We'll call this one baby B, and I made note earlier that it is a...a girl. You've got one of each here; a complete family. Congratulations."

Christina started to tremble. Her eyes were fixed on the monitor, watching the two tiny, moving creatures. Her mouth was open in a silent "OH". She clamped her hand over it as tears streamed down her cheeks. Suddenly her body was shaking and Tim felt her start to waver. "Christina!" he exclaimed. "Honey, what's wrong?"

Christina shook her head and collapsed. Tim caught her in his arms. She was only out momentarily; she was struggling to stand up and didn't even realize everyone was looking at her with concern. She pushed away from Tim and reached for Shauna Lee. "They are real…and as Tim said, they are uniquely ours."

She clasped her friend's hand. "I…we will be the best, the most deserving parents in the world. Thank you for this wonderful gift." She stared at the monitor and started to smile. "Now, I realize that I do deserve these children. They are still as much mine as they would have been if I'd have been able to carry them here under my heart." She lifted Shauna Lee's hand and kissed it. "You have shown me that I am worthy of love because you have done this out of love."

Tim stepped to Christina's side and ran his arm around her waist. She looked up him and smiled tremulously. "I've never truly accepted how special and blessed my life is, until now."

In early August, Shauna Lee was beginning to feel the discomfort of carrying twins. At twenty-two weeks, she started to have small twinges a few times a day. They weren't dramatic, but she did notice them. When she and Christina went for the twenty-four week ultrasound, she mentioned them to Dr. Fin. He assured her that it was normal to have them. Her body was stretching, making room for the growing babies.

Shauna Lee was bigger than she'd imagined she could be at twenty-four weeks. Her uterus had stretched to a size that would have been normal at thirty-five weeks. She could feel the babies moving frequently, and she was getting mild Braxton Hicks contractions regularly. Dr. Fin told her to lie down and rest often.

Christina began to spend more time at Shauna Lee and Brad's place, helping with the children and housework.

One day, Patch swung his gaze from Shauna Lee to Christina. He went to his mother who was sitting on a chair in the shade. "Mommy, what happened to your tummy?"

Shauna Lee smiled. "What's wrong with my tummy?"

"It used to be flat like Christina's. Now it's big." He poked his finger against it. "It's hard, too. Like a big ball."

"Well honey, do you remember when mommy told you that you came from my tummy?"

Patch nodded. "But I'm not in your tummy now. I'm right here."

She ruffled his hair. "You're right. But see, Tim and Christina are going to have two babies. Christina's tummy doesn't have room for a baby, so we went to the hospital and the doctor put Tim and Christina's babies in mommy's tummy, because she has lots of room in there for them to grow big. When they are ready to come out, they'll let us know, and Tim and Christina will take them home. Then mommy's tummy will get small again."

He looked at Christina thoughtfully. "You put two babies in Mommy's tummy?" He held two fingers.

Christina smiled. "Two babies, Patch. And your mommy was so nice; she gave them a warm, comfortable place to stay, because I didn't have room for them in my tummy."

He looked up at Shauna Lee. "How long will they stay there, Mommy?"

"It'll be a while yet, and they'll get a lot bigger. You and Leanne are going to have to be careful about mommy's tummy. We don't want to hurt the babies."

Patch laid his head against his mother's tummy. He listened for a few minutes, then placed his mouth against it and said "Hey babies. Are you awake in there?" Shauna Lee and Christina stifled their laughter. He listened for a moment. "I don't hear anyone in there, Mommy."

"They're probably sleeping."

"How long have they been in there?"

"Do you remember when you and Leanne started going to daycare when Mom and Christina went away for the day? A couple of times Daddy and Tim went with us and Mrs. Atchinson came and stayed overnight with you?"

Patch looked at her with big eyes. "That's a long, long, looong time ago."

Shauna Lee nodded. "They were little bitty when they came to live in Mommy's tummy. They've grown a lot, but they still need to grow some more, before they can live with their mommy and daddy, the way you and Leanne live with Daddy and me."

Patch's lips formed an 'O', and he stared at the floor. Christina and Shauna Lee smiled at each other. "It was bound to come up," Shauna Lee said softly. "Brad and I have discussed how we would tell him together, but now...well, it's out there."

Christina smiled. "It's interesting that he suddenly noticed it today. You've been getting bigger for quite a while."

"He'll have more questions. His mind is constantly working. Sometimes he comes out with the most incredible things."

The next six weeks flew by. Shauna Lee and Christina made regular trips to Saskatoon for ultrasounds. Shauna Lee was gaining weight and growing bigger by the week. Christina began to come over every day and Shauna Lee didn't complain.

Christina handed her a cup of coffee after Shauna Lee settled on a chair at the kitchen table. "You look tired this morning."

"I just couldn't get comfortable last night. My back hurt and these little guys were on a different schedule than mine. It felt like they were wrestling. I played your tapes to them, but they didn't seem to listen." She shrugged. "Maybe they were too busy looking for a comfortable place to settle, too."

"Can I do anything to help?"

Shauna Lee smiled crookedly and shook her head. "You're doing what you can. Making room for two is a little different than doing it for one. Ten more weeks at the most...even eight. Then we'll all be happy."

"Are you sorry you got into this?"

Shauna Lee looked shocked. "No, hon. I'm feeling whiney today, but I'd do it again in a heartbeat. I can't wait to see you and Tim holding these little ones."

She lifted her cup to take a sip, then gasped and smiled. "Quick, come here and feel. Someone is kicking like a quarterback in there." She took Christina's hand and held it against her belly.

Christina felt the push beneath it. "Oh," she breathed, gently working the spot with her hand. She felt it push back again. "Hello, sweetheart," Christina said softly.

By mid-October, Tim had finished harvesting the crops. The DNA results had come back weeks earlier, but life had been busy for both Ollie and Tim. Tim had started haying and then he had moved into harvest. Ollie had been busy on the ranch. Now life had quieted down in both quarters and Tim invited Ollie and Ellie to spend a night at the farm so they could celebrate. When they arrived, Tim drove them to Brad and Shauna Lee's place to pick up Christina.

Brad met them at the door. "Hello old-timer," he greeted Ollie. "I hear you are officially Tim's dad, and now you are going to be a grandfather. Congratulations!" He nodded at Tim and gave Ellie a hug. "Come on in. Christina is getting the kids ready for bed and then she'll be ready to leave." He squeezed Tim's shoulder. "Her help's a godsend these days. Shauna Lee would have a tough time without her right now."

He led them into the living room, where Shauna Lee was reclining in a big chair.

She smiled and looked up at them. She started to sit up, but Tim insisted she stay where she was comfortable. They had just sat down when Patch and Leanne came running into the room, followed by Christina. Patch ran to Ollie to give him a hug, he ran over to Shauna Lee and pointed at her bulging belly. "Ollie! Mommy's got two babies in her tummy."

Shauna Lee protested, trying to silence him. "Shhh…Patch."

But Patch's wonder and excitement overrode her protests. He brushed away her hand. "They are Tim and Christina's babies. The doctor put them inside mommy a long, looong time ago." He giggled, his eyes sparkling. "Sometimes you can see them fighting in there."

"Patch!"

"They do Mommy. You can see them make a big bump on your tummy. I hope they come out pretty soon. I want to see them." He turned to Ollie. "Sometimes I talk to them in there. Christina and Tim talk to them on Mommy's iPod and mom plays it to them, too. It's fun!" Patch clapped his hands and laughed. "Mommy got after them the other day when they were kicking her. She told them she didn't appreciate them trying to break her ribs."

Ollie chuckled. "Come here, Patch."

Patch ran across the room to Ollie, who took him up onto his lap. "You know Patch, I want to see those babies too. I'm their grandpa. Isn't it exciting?"

Patch smiled. "You're my grandpa, too, and Leanne's. You're Selena and Sam's grandpa, too. You're *everybody's* grandpa."

Ollie hugged the young boy and looked at Tim. "I am a lucky man, aren't I?"

Tim rested his hand on Ollie's shoulder. "That's right, Dad. We're all one big happy family."

That night after supper, Ellie asked Christina what they needed for the nursery. Christina looked startled, then embarrassed. "We…I haven't even started the nursery."

Ellie and Ollie both looked shocked.

Tim put his hand over Christina's. "Christina was afraid to hope or plan at first. When the invitro didn't work the first two times, it devastated her. She was a wreck. Even after Shauna Lee was finally pregnant, Christina had a lot of issues. She was still afraid something would go wrong."

Tears glistened in Christina's eyes. "I could have gotten the nursery ready and then have to look at it when something went wrong again." She snuffled. "I felt I didn't deserve my own children; I wasn't supposed to have them or I wouldn't have been born the way I was."

Tim looked across the table at Ollie. "It took a long time for her to be able to accept that we would have these babies. By then, I was busy with haying and harvesting, and she has been totally involved with helping Shauna Lee. As you could see tonight, carrying twins hasn't been easy on her.

"But we'll have to get on the babies' room right away. The pregnancy is at thirty-one weeks now. Everything is going well, but we know things could change. Twins don't usually make full term, so if they reach thirty-six or thirty-seven weeks we'll be doing well."

Ellie smiled at Christina. "We understand how you felt. Would you let us help with the nursery? I'm sure you will need to spend more and more time with Shauna Lee as the pregnancy continues. You could tell us what you want to be done and we'll help Tim do it. I could even help Shauna Lee for a few days so you could shop for things you need: cribs, bedding, curtains, pictures, paint."

Christina brushed her eyes. "I really appreciate the offer, Ellie. I'd love it if you'd help get the nursery ready."

Ellie reached across and touched her hand. "Have you told your mom and dad yet?"

Shauna Lee shook her head. "Not yet. Again, I didn't want to say anything until I was certain, and then I just got too busy."

"Your mom and dad will be thrilled for you, Christina. They hurt for you too, you know. Phone them. Let them share your happiness. Let them heal, too."

Tim put his arm around Christina's shoulders. "I didn't think about that, but Ellie's right. I bet they'll be here right away. In fact, they'll probably want to help, too."

When Shauna Lee went for the thirty-four-week ultrasound, Dr. Fin had made arrangements for the twins to be delivered in Swift Current, rather than necessitate the trip to Saskatoon for the birth. She and Christina made an appointment to see Dr. Cochran, who was going to be her OBGYN when the babies arrived. He went over the latest ultrasound and all the notes that Dr. Finn had sent to him.

At the end of the consultation, both she and Christina felt completely at ease.

Shauna Lee's water broke at about nine o'clock on the evening of December the fourth. Brad called Tim and Christina and they rushed to the hospital to meet them. On the way, Christina phoned her mom and dad and then she called Ollie and Ellie and asked them to let Colt and Frank know.

The medical team did an ultrasound to see how the babies were presenting for birth. Both were head down, with Baby "A" in the birth canal. They wheeled Shauna Lee into the operating room, explaining that it was regular procedure with twins, in case they had to perform an emergency C-section.

Tim and Christina waited with Brad and Shauna Lee. Christina became lost in her empathy for Shauna Lee's plight. Her arms crossed over her belly, she found her stomach muscles tightening and pushing in unison with her friend. Tears filled her eyes as she mirrored her pain. Eventually, Shauna Lee asked for an epidural to ease the pain and Christina's demeanor relaxed with her.

Tim and Christina's son heralded his arrival with a lusty cry. There was a flurry of activity as a pediatric team took the infant and laid him on a special table in the room. Tim watched as they inspected him from top to bottom. He weighed five pounds and fourteen ounces and measured nineteen inches long. After the medical team had recorded all the stats, they put a soft cap on his tiny head, wrapped him in a cotton blanket and handed him to Tim.

Tim cradled Shay Oliver in his arms, an expression of awe on his face. He moved to Christina's side and held the baby up for her to see. Christina was numb; she wanted to hold her son and touch him, but in another dimension, her heart was still connected to Shauna Lee's pain, and the impending arrival of their daughter.

She reached out and touched the baby, but her attention was divided as she watched the doctor work with Shauna Lee. Tim was puzzled by her lack of response. "Do you want to hold him?" he asked softly. She tore her eyes away from the birthing chair where Shauna Lee reclined, her legs still in the stirrups, her body wet with perspiration and her expression exhausted. Her gut twisted, knowing that there was still one more demanding performance to be played out, and she could only watch as Shauna Lee delivered their baby girl.

She nodded and lifted her hands to take the child and cuddle him against her chest. Her eyes filled as she looked down into his tiny wrinkled face. For a few moments, she was caught in the wonder of his being. She caressed his tiny hands, ran her finger gently along his chin and around his face.

Tim wrapped an arm around her shoulders and placed his other hand under her forearm, helping her support the precious bundle that she held. She brushed her finger lightly over the baby's lips and they automatically responded with a sucking motion. Mother and fathers eyes met with delight. Tim squeezed her shoulders and kissed her cheek.

Suddenly, Christina became aware of Shauna Lee's muffled cry. She looked up to see Brad squeezing her hand and talking with the doctor who had seated himself in front of the birthing chair. Panic flashed across Christina's face. She quickly, but carefully, handed Shay back to Tim and resumed the position where she had stood before.

Tim watched her as she mirrored Shauna Lee. He could feel her emulating the contractions as she pushed, trying to help the second baby out, the agony she felt stamped on her face. Minutes later, when their baby girl made her way into the world, Christina gasped when the doctor guided her into his hands and lifted her free.

He looked at Christina. "Would you like to cut the cord?"

Shauna Lee tried to smile, encouraging her. Like a sleepwalker, Christina moved toward the doctor and the baby. A pediatric nurse took her hand, guiding it to cut the pulsing, life-giving rope. Christina sobbed when it was done, then turned toward Tim.

He took in her white face and glazed eyes. *She's going to faint.* "Steady her," he warned. Brad's head shot up. He reached out and caught her. She slumped against him and he supported her until the faintness passed.

The pediatric team quickly whisked the newly delivered baby to the stats table and began their assessment of her. The doctor continued to work with Shauna Lee and Tim cradled their son as he watched Christina and Shauna Lee clasp hands. The love that flowed between them transcended the ties of friendship or familial bonding. It was deeply spiritual.

Christina turned to look at Tim and moved toward him. He put his free arm around her and pulled her close against him, snuggling her face against his chest and the tiny bundle in his arms. "We've witnessed a miracle."

"In so many ways!"

A nurse finally handed Christina their little girl. She weighed five pounds and seven ounces and was eighteen inches long. She was feisty and active, protesting loudly about her transition into the big, strange world. Zaira Lee had made her debut.

Later that night, they moved Shauna Lee to the maternity ward to recover from the effects of the epidural. She was exhausted, but exalted. Brad sat by her side and held her hand. "Are you going to miss them?" he asked softly.

She chuckled and shook her head. "No. I've completed my mission. Tim and Christina have their babies, and in a few months, I'll have my body back. All I have left to do now is pump my breasts for the next month and freeze the milk so they get breast milk to start with. Gradually Christina will put them on formula and I will be completely finished with this project."

"Would you do it again?"

She squeezed his hand. "You have been so patient and wonderful. You can't begin to know what it's meant to me." She touched his face gently. "I've missed our life together. Let's face it, me being as big as a house, crabby and feeling so miserable, was not an easy thing to deal with for any of us." She touched her belly, which was still distended and paunchy. "I hadn't thought about having twins, but when it happened this way, I couldn't be anything but happy for Tim and Christina.

"Will I do it again? No. Now it's time for us and our family. Knowing what I do know now, would I still do what I did? Yes, without hesitation. Just seeing Christina and Tim with those babies was worth everything we went through."

Brad chuckled. "You probably weren't aware of Christina when you were in labor, but she was so in tune with you, she was pushing as hard as you were to deliver those babies."

Shauna Lee smiled tiredly. "She needed to help so much."

The newborns were taken to the nursery and Tim and Christina were given a room to stay in overnight, where they could hold the infants and comfort them, letting them bond with their touch and smell and acquaint themselves with their sounds. By morning, they were changing diapers and assuming their role as parents.

Christina slipped down to check on Shauna Lee. Her milk was coming in and the nurses were helping her pump for the babies. She winced as the pump pulled, but smiled at Christina. "So, how is

Mommy this morning?" she asked cheerfully.

"I'm totally in awe! They're so beautiful. As soon as we feed them we can take them home."

"I'm working on it. You should have a few ounces in a few minutes. I bet you'll have a house full waiting for you at the farm."

Christina shook her head. "I hope not. We've asked everyone to give us a few days to settle in and try to establish a routine of sorts. Of course, they all want to come right away, but we can send pictures with our cell phones and satisfy some of the curiosity."

Shauna Lee chuckled. "By Christmas, you'll be hoping each family will be willing to come and spend a week at a time to give you a break."

Christina rolled her eyes. "Thanks, I really needed to hear that. I can't imagine spending a whole week with my Mom and Dad."

Christmas day the farmhouse was filled with family. After the gifts were opened, Hazel and Ellie took over in the kitchen. Ollie and Burt played cards with Sam and Selina. Patch and Leanne played with their new toys in the living room, while Frank and Shauna Lee took turns looking after Zaira and Shay. Christina was thankful to be able to catch a nap. Tim, Brad, and Colt relaxed in Tim's office.

Brad smiled as he looked at his old friend. "The past two years have been life changing for you. You found a good woman and got married again."

Tim grinned. "Who would have thought that would happen? I have to thank you guys for showing me what a real marriage could be like or I probably wouldn't have had the courage to do it again."

"You would have. You and Christina are meant to be."

"She's the best thing that's ever happened to me."

Colt smiled. "She says the same about you."

"We're good together."

Brad nodded. "And you and Ollie found each other. That was another biggie for you guys."

Colt's look was serious. "You can't imagine what that has meant to him."

Tim nodded. "I'll always love and appreciate Maddy and Harry. They were wonderful parents, even though they didn't tell me the truth about my birth. But I'm glad I finally connected with Ollie. He is such a great guy. It's hard to accept that we've known each other for so long and had no idea that we were father and son."

Colt nodded.

Tim looked at Brad. "Having Shauna Lee offer to be a surrogate for Christina and me was unbelievably life changing for both of us. It was such an unselfish gift from both of you... it fulfilled Christina's deepest need. It gave us a family of our own. There will never be words to express what it means for us to have Zaira and Shay. They are true gifts of love."

Colt quirked an eyebrow. "How is the daily routine with them working out?"

Tim chuckled. "We're getting there. Christina is fantastic with them, and I've learned to do a lot of things I hadn't thought about five years ago: laundry, changing diapers, getting up at all hours of the night, walking the floor with a screaming baby who only wants its mother. It's amazing how two little creatures can take over the whole household."

Colt chuckled. "I remember those days with our twins; two howling, squirming, bundles, demanding attention at the same time."

Brad smiled. "I'm glad this part of the journey is yours."

"So am I! It's amazing how everything fell into place to make this picture complete. It's as if someone orchestrated every move to bring us all together."

Colt nodded. *"The Hand of Fate,"* he said thoughtfully and lifted his glass in a toast.

***

Watch for *A Second Chance, Book Four of the Belanger Creek Ranch Series.* You can check out a sneak peak of it at the end of this book!

***

Thank you for taking time to read *The Hand of Fate, Book Three of the Belanger Creek Ranch Series.*

Few people realize how gratifying reviews are to an author and how important they are to the success of a book. Reviews are read by potential readers, who will value your opinion of a book and may decide to buy it (or not) based how on your experience with it.

Writing a review can seem intimidating, but *please do not feel that you can't do it*. Think about *how you felt* about the characters, *what you liked* (or disliked) about the book, and *how you connected with the story* when you were reading it. *Then write it down in simple words*. That is what really counts. Fancy words do not replace simple *honesty* and *enthusiasm*, which are the most compelling ingredients in a review.

Connecting with readers is a heartwarming experience, for an author. It reaffirms the value of what we spend hours doing in solitude. I would love to hear from you and learn a bit about your life.

If you enjoyed this book, I would be delighted if you could leave a review at any one of the following sites: Goodreads.com, ePrintedbooks.com, Amazon.com, Facebook, Twitter, or my website at **http://www.gloriaantypowich.com**

If you could post your review on several sites, I would be absolutely thrilled!

Facebook: Gloria Antypowich Author, (Please stop by and like my page!)

Twitter: @gantypowich

Website/Blog: Gloria Antypowich-Romance and Love Stories at **http://www.gloriaantypowich.com**

Email: gloria@heartsatrisk.com

I look forward to hearing from you!

AUTHORS NOTES

I did extensive research online for this book. I read everything I could find about Mayer-Rokitansky-Küster-Hauser syndrome (MRKH) and the Laparoscopic creation of a vagina or Neovagina (Davydov procedure). It was fascinating.

I also researched Surrogacy in Canada and the US. I followed two blogs: One was *A Tale of Two Mothers* (**http://journeythroughcanadiansurrogacy.blogspot.ca/**) and the other *was A Belly for Me, A Baby for You.* (**https://www.facebook.com/ABellyForMeABabyForYou?fref=nf**) At the time the latter one was a blog—now it has become a documentary and a very wide movement that supports surrogacy.

I read books about surrogacy—*Bringing in Finn by Sara Connell* was one. I read books about having twins, *Twins? Are You Kidding Me?* His and Her Perspectives by Kelliann Bateman and *When You're Expecting Twins, Triplets, or Quads* by Barbara Luke

I looked up IVF sites that showed step by step *In vitro* procedures. One site was the baby center at **http://www.babycenter.ca/a4094/fertility-treatment-in-vitro-fertilization-ivf**, but there were others that described in detail the medications and showed pictures.

It has been an interesting journey, filled with learning.

I also did a lot of online research about heart attacks and I talked to people who had experienced them. It was very informative, and I learned things I didn't expect to find.

Here is a sneak peek of *A Second Chance,*
Book Four of the Belanger Creek Ranch Series.
ISBN: Softcover: 978-0-9939166-6-3
E-book: 978-0-9939166-7-0

BOOK FOUR CHAPTER ONE

Sarah Brite stood at the living room window and looked down over the buildings and corrals that were the heart of Belanger Creek Ranch. Coming here was the best thing that had happened for her and her son, Taylor, in recent years. The ranch 'family' was close-knit, and they looked out for their own. The area was rural, not a place where the father of her son would be apt to find her. Of course, she would never let her guard down. She'd always remain aware and alert, ready to move at the slightest hint of danger. Duncan Talbot had resources and he'd tracked her down before. If that happened, and if they managed to get away again, she and Taylor would immediately disappear, slipping under the radar, just as they had done before.

It was Christmas day. They had been invited to the farm at Cantaur for Christmas dinner. The rest of the 'family' would be there. Frank and Colt Thompson and the twins, as well as Ellie and Ollie Crampton, went there on the twenty-fourth. Brad and Shauna Lee Johnson and their two children would be there, as well. Everyone was excited about Christina and Tim Bates new twins, but Taylor didn't care much for babies. He said they just cried and puked and messed their diapers. He had wanted to hang out at the ranch and help Grayson McNaughton do chores. Sarah appreciated the invitation, but she was reluctant to allow herself to get very close to anyone, so making the decision to stay home hadn't been difficult.

She smiled when she saw her son go flying down the steep driveway on his plastic snow saucer. She watched him swerve around the ranch hand. The man jumped aside as Taylor narrowly missed him.

Her gaze settled on Grayson. He was a nice man; attractive, unassuming, gentle, soft-spoken, and kind hearted. But.... She frowned as she acknowledged that he was the biggest threat to her peace of mind at Belanger Creek Ranch.

***

Taylor Brite loved the feel of the wind on his face as he flew down the steep driveway. He swerved the well-worn plastic snow-saucer around Grayson McNaughton, spraying him with the dry, crystalline snow. Grayson jumped aside, and Taylor laughed with glee.

Grayson was really cool. In Taylor's mind, he was the best friend he had; even better than Sam and Selena, the Thompson twins, who were a year younger than him.

Sam was OK. He was laid back and fun; but Selena was bossy and very competitive. She always wanted to win, and she pouted when she didn't. Sometimes he was tempted to push her down and wash her face with snow, but he knew he couldn't do that. He'd be in big trouble all around if he did.

When Grayson reached the bottom of the hill, he tipped Taylor off the saucer and rubbed his ears against his head. "You little devil you. You tried to run me over, didn't you?"

Taylor was laughing when he protested. "No. I was just trying to see how close I could get. "

Grayson rolled him around in the snow and then reached out to take his hand and pull him to his feet. "I'm going start the snow machine and I'll pull you behind on your saucer if you want me to. Do you think your mom would like to come along?"

Taylor was jumping up and down. "That'll be fun. I'll go get her." He turned. "Where are we going?" he asked, as he started to run up the hill to the house.

"We'll go across the road."

Sarah Brite was still watching from the big window in the living room at the main ranch house. Taylor had blossomed during the year and a half since they'd come to the ranch. A day didn't go by when she wasn't thankful that Colt Thompson had hired her. Although she remained alert and ready to act for Taylor's safety, she felt safer on the ranch, than she had since she'd worked for the Harahan's in Toronto. The only thing that shadowed her peace was Taylor's attachment to Grayson; for her son's sake, she knew it was a relationship that she shouldn't have allowed to develop.

She smiled as she watched Grayson roughhousing with her son. She saw them exchange friendly banter, then watched Taylor start running up the hill. He was out of breath, but grinning from ear to ear, when he came in.

"Hey Mom! Grayson asked if you'd like to go for a ride on the snow machine. He's going to go across the road, into the pasture, and he's going to pull me behind on the saucer."

She frowned. In recent months, she had grown very aware of Grayson as a man, and he hadn't hidden the fact that he liked her. She hadn't encouraged his tentative advances because she didn't want to get involved with anyone. She knew how uncertain the future could be.

"Aww mom, come on. Have some fun for a change. All you do is work."

"Taylor... you know why I do what I do."

He looked crestfallen. "We're safe mom. Nobody will find us away out here."

"Taylor! Not another word about that! We can't get too comfortable."

His smile disappeared. "I know. But it's Christmas. Won't you come out for a ride? For me?" he added pathetically."

She sighed. He knew how to push her buttons. "Oh...alright, I'll pull on a warm pair of pants and my winter coat. Just give me a minute."

The smile reappeared and his eyes twinkled again. It took so little to make him happy.

He fidgeted while he waited impatiently. When Sarah followed him outside, he persuaded her to sit on the snow saucer with him and they sped down the hill.

Grayson was surprised when he saw the sparkle in her eyes and the color in her cheeks. Most of the time, Sarah looked like she was carrying the weight of the world on her shoulders. He often wondered what her story was. Why was she on her own with ten-year-old Taylor?"

He watched Taylor lean back and shove her off the saucer.

"You rascal," she gasped. "I'll get you for doing that."

Taylor landed on top of her and pushed her down in the snow. It feathered into her dark hair and snuck over her collar.

"Taylor," she squealed. "You're getting snow down my neck."

"If I let you get up, will you promise not to come after me?"

She shook her head and struggled to push him off.

"No? Then I guess I can't let you up."

"Taylor. I'm your mom. You have to listen to me."

"Sorry; I've got to look after myself."

Grayson started to laugh. "Do you want some help, Sarah?"

Taylor lifted his head and looked at him in disbelief. "You trait...."

"Got you," Sarah crowed as she threw him down and pushed him into the snow, burying him as he had her.

Grayson grinned as he listened to Taylor giggle while he thrashed around in the softness, struggling to get out from underneath his mother.

When Sarah finally let him up, he turned onto his hands and knees and crawled away from her. Then, he stood up. He pulled off his gloves and began to shake the snow out of his hair. He ran his hands along his collar, under his coat and up his back, around the waistband of his snow pants and finally digging tiny balls of it out of the fabric around his wrists. "You're mean."

"Hey! You started this, remember?"

He grinned good-naturedly and grabbed the saucer, giving his mother a hip check when he walked by her.

Grayson smiled as he walked to the back of the snow machine. He knotted a light nylon rope to the hitch and tied it to Taylor's snow saucer. "Have you ever done this before?"

Taylor shook his head.

"What? Where did you grow up?"

Taylor laughed nervously and looked at his mom.

"We didn't have snow machines," she said flatly.

Ouch, that hit a nerve, he thought. He turned to the boy. "Okay, first of all, you have to wear this helmet." He tossed one that he had hung on the snowmobile handle to him. "When I start to pull, let the rope tighten. Then you'll have to hold on and try to steer the saucer, but if it starts to tip or flip, let go. You don't want to get dragged. I'll keep an eye out for you." He looked at Sarah. "Your mom will too."

Grayson handed Sarah the second helmet that was on the seat behind him. While Taylor settled on the saucer, Grayson sat on the snow machine seat. He motioned for her to get on behind him. She tried to sit back, ramrod stiff. He turned to look over his shoulder. "Have you ever done this before?"

She shook her head.

"Put your arms around my waist and hang on. You'll need to move with me as we ride or you'll throw the machine off balance."

She felt conflicted, and it showed.

He winked. "Come on Sarah. It's just a ride. I'm not going to get any crazy ideas."

She blushed. "I wasn't thinking that."

He smirked, even though he almost felt sorry for her. "No? What were you thinking?"

"Just…"

"Aww mom, just put your arms around him so we can get moving. You'll fall off if you don't, and I'll run right over you."

"You would, too," she muttered as she slid her arms around Grayson's waist.

He didn't go too fast, keeping an eye on Taylor. Sarah gradually relaxed and rested against his back. Her mind spun off, remembering another life, when she had ridden with her arms wrapped around another man.

BOOK FOUR CHAPTER TWO

Fourteen years earlier, she had eyed Duncan Talbot with distaste when he'd swaggered into the corner store where she worked. *A bad ass biker*. He was everything she'd been warned about when he came through the door; leathers, chains, tattoos, a scarf tied backward over his head, eyes hidden behind sunglasses. *Degenerate*. Her dad's summation of him rang in her ears.

He'd shopped for smokes and beer, further confirming that opinion of men like him.

Duncan Talbot was in many ways a degenerate, just as her dad had declared him to be. He was twenty-five years older than she was, but he was a charming degenerate, and he came back repeatedly throughout the next year. In the end, he wore down Sarah's resistance. She had fallen for him, and despite her mother's tears and her father's outrage, she had hopped on behind him on his bike and sped away. She had threaded her arms around his waist and rested herself against his back, moving in unison with him as they rode through the curves and passed in the traffic.

Sarah was jolted from her memories when Taylor yelped. Grayson uttered a curse and turned the machine around. She became alert immediately and turned to see what had happened. The saucer had flipped and was bouncing crazily behind the snow machine. Taylor had rolled off. As she watched, he rose up on his knees and shook off the snow. He was wearing a happy grin.

A wave of love flooded through her. His father may have been a useless, violent, degenerate, but their folly had produced the most precious thing in her life. While she feared and detested everything about his biological father, Taylor was the one thing she cherished more than anything.

She watched as Grayson helped him straighten out and settled on the snow saucer again. *He's good with Taylor. Duncan would never have been like that. He didn't want a child and he had no patience with the inconvenience of having one.*

She stood up to let Grayson ease himself onto the seat in front of her and then settled down behind him. She slid her arms around his waist, conscious of their position and more acutely aware of him as a man than she wanted to be.

He eased the machine forward until the rope tightened and then he accelerated. As he became more confident, Taylor wove crisscross paths behind the machine, whooping with glee as the snow saucer briefly became airborne on occasion, then dipped down to catch the snow and whipped across the other way. Sarah's heart filled with happiness when she turned her head and saw her son's exuberant, smiling face. *Coming here has been the best thing that could have happened. I don't know when I've ever seen him so uninhibited. He's always been so serious and careful.* She swallowed hard.

Grayson slowed the machine and stopped. He looked up at the sky, noting the position of the sun. "I think it's time to head back to the ranch. It's about two-thirty."

"How do you know that?" Taylor asked.

"See where the sun is?"

Taylor looked toward the hills in the west. "Yeah, it's just above the trees.

"In a couple of hours it will be dusk, so we'd better head in and do the chores for the night."

When they got back to the ranch, Grayson drove up to the house. He let Sarah get off and she walked to her apartment. He helped Taylor unhook the snow saucer and then they both got back on the machine and rode down to the barnyard. Taylor wrapped his arms around Grayson's chest and hugged him. Grayson's heart lifted with happiness. It felt good to be hugged so freely.

Later, the three of them sat around the table, chatting as they enjoyed the Christmas feast that Sarah had made. Minutes before Taylor had come to ask her to go with them on the snow machine ride; she had put the turkey in the oven. She had prepared the vegetables earlier too, so she'd only had to cook them when she'd come back. Taylor heaped his plate with turkey and mashed potatoes and gravy and corn casserole. He wolfed it down and went back for seconds. Grayson looked at Sarah and chuckled. "This guy's got a hollow leg."

She nodded. "It must be from the day out on the snow saucer. He's not always like this."

Taylor was grinning from ear to ear. "Come on you guys. I had a great day; I don't know when I've ever had so much fun." He pushed away his plate. "What's for dessert, mom?"

Sarah looked at him with disbelief. "Dessert, are you serious?"

He rubbed his stomach and then felt down his leg. "I'm pretty sure I have room...right here in my hollow leg." He looked at Grayson and smiled.

Sarah shook her head. "Why don't we have dessert later? Maybe we could play a game, or watch a movie and give all that food time to settle. Would that be alright with you, Grayson?"

Taylor was up in a shot and pulling on Grayson's arm. "Please stay. We could watch a movie. The Thompsons lent us some good ones."

Grayson messed his hair and looked at Sarah. "That sounds like a nice way to spend the evening." Sarah nodded and asked him if he'd like a drink. He thought for a moment and said, "I'll make my own after I help you clean up the kitchen."

Taylor hurried into the living room and picked out three movies while Grayson helped Sarah clear the table and made his own drink. Sarah poured herself a glass of red wine. Taylor was leaning against the doorway, waiting impatiently for them. "Which movie do you want to watch, Grayson?"

Grayson studied the three Taylor had lain out. He winked at Sarah as he rubbed his chin thoughtfully. "They all look interesting, son. You pick one and we'll watch it."

A flush stole over the boy's face. "You called me son."

Grayson shot a look at Sarah. She bit her lip and looked away. He didn't miss the glisten of tears in her eyes.

"Hey Taylor, if you'd been my son I'd be proud of you." He hugged him. "Now let's watch a movie. He knelt by the DVD player and let the boy slide the disc into the empty slot. Then he handed the remote to the youngster and taking his other hand, lead him back to the couch. Taylor sat in the middle, with the two adults on either side. Sarah noticed that he rested his head against Grayson's shoulder and eventually the man lifted his arm to drape it around her son's shoulders, letting the child's dark head, rest against his chest.

A knot of anxiety rose in Sarah's chest. Grayson was a great guy and he'd make a wonderful father, but he wasn't Taylors. She squeezed her eyes shut. *Why couldn't he have felt that way about Colt? She sighed with resignation. Colt is Sam and Sarah's dad. Taylor wants one of his own, so it's easy to see why he's drawn to Grayson.*

She felt Grayson's hand touch her shoulder. Her eyes flew open and she met his questioning look. Their gaze held for a moment, and then she looked away. Taylor reached out, took each of their hands in his, and leaned against the back of the couch. "Sitting here like this is nice isn't it? It's just like we're a family."

Sarah squeezed his hand. "Taylor, Grayson is a wonderful friend, but you are going to embarrass him if you keep saying things like that."

Taylor leaned over and looked into Grayson's face. "Am I embarrassing you, Grayson?"

"I'm not embarrassed, Taylor. But, you have to realize that for us to be a family, your mom and I would have to have a different relationship than we have. When you say things like that, you are putting us in an uncomfortable spot. We're friends and I like your mom a lot, but we're not...well, we're not like a mother and father."

"But you could be. Then we'd be a family, wouldn't we?"

Sarah placed her hand over his mouth. "Enough! I'm embarrassed now."

Taylor pushed her hand away. "But mom, Grayson's said he likes you a lot, and he's nothing like Duncan. We aren't afraid of him. He isn't mean and he wouldn't hurt us." He looked at her earnestly. "He'd be like Mr. Thompson. He'd take care of us...."

"Taylor Brite! That's enough." She jumped up. "I'm sorry you had to listen to all that Grayson."

Grayson stood to face her. "Sarah." He reached out and touched her arm. "Please don't apologize. Taylor is a great kid; as I said

Gloria Antypowich

before, under different circumstances I'd be honored to be his dad."
Sarah looked at Taylor. "I think it's time for you to go to bed."
"Aww, Mom. It's Christmas. And we haven't had dessert yet."
"Taylor…I mean now! Grayson and I are going to have a talk."
"About him becoming my dad?"
"No, about why he cannot become your dad."

BOOK FOUR CHAPTER THREE

Taylor's disappointment was obvious when he ejected the disc and stood up. He threaded his arms around Grayson's waist. "Thanks for the best Christmas ever! Don't listen to mom when she tells you that you can't be my dad. I'd love it if we were a family."

Grayson rubbed his head. "This was the most special Christmas I've had in ten years, Taylor, and people are what make my Christmas special. I'll see you tomorrow."

Taylor hugged his mom and gave her a peck on the cheek. "I love you, Mom." He gave her a cheeky grin. "And I know everything is going to be okay."

After he had gone to his room and shut the door, she turned toward Grayson. She felt awkward because of her embarrassment, and she couldn't quite look into his eyes. " Uhmm…would you like another drink?"

"Are you having one?"

"Yes. I think I will. I need to help you understand Taylor and me…where we come from, what our life has been like and what it will be in the future."

"Okay. I'll make my own drink. Can I pour you a glass of wine?"

She nodded, walked over to sit at the table. She watched him as he mixed his drink, and then poured her glass of wine. He carried them to the table and she sighed deeply as he put the glass in front of her. He walked back to the island, collected the bottle of rye, a can of coke and the wine and brought them to the table with him. "I think we might need these."

Sarah laugh was strangled. "You must be clairvoyant."

He touched his glass to hers, his expression serious. "Alright, Sarah Brite; tell me why you are carrying the weight of the world on your shoulders."

Her head snapped up, her expression one of quick denial.

Grayson held up his hand. "You initiated this talk, Sarah. I recognized that you were hiding something when you first came here."

Sarah's mouth dropped. "Wh..a..t do y..ou mean?" she sputtered

He reached out and touched her arm gently. "Even after a year and a half, you're still always on guard. You're careful about how much you tell about your past, and so is Taylor. You've schooled him well. If he lets anything slip, one look from you and he covers it up and changes the topic.

"You're constantly checking to see where he is. I'd bet the two of you could find each other and disappear in a shot if the right situation came up. I'd say you've rehearsed it, practiced it, and possibly even done it. Today is the first time I've seen you relax and lose that haunted look for a while."

Sarah rested her elbows on the table and entwined her fingers, resting her forehead against them, her thumbs pressing against her temples. Tears slipped down her cheeks.

Grayson moved to the chair beside her, putting his arm around her shoulders. "Sarah, tell me what's going on. If you are in danger, if someone is looking for you and Taylor, we need to know so we can protect you. In the city, you can slip away and get lost in the crowd. Here in the country, you might be harder to find, but it could be harder to get away too."

Sarah began to sob. "I'm so tired of looking over my shoulder, and it's not fair to Taylor."

Grayson pulled her head against his shoulder and let her relieve her tension. Finally, she snuffled and heaved a big sigh, then pushed away and sat up. "I'm sorry about that."

"Don't be. I think you needed to let all that go."

"I can't say I feel better right now, but it was a release. If I ever really let go, I couldn't stop."

He pushed her glass of wine in front of her again. "Have a drink and then we'll talk."

Sarah sipped at first, and then took a long drink. When she sat the glass on the table, Grayson refilled it and then moved back to the chair at the end of the table, so they were facing each other.

Sarah reached out and twirled the stem of her glass with her fingers. "When I finished high school, I was a typical teenager. My dad was old fashioned in his thinking and his attitude really grated on me. To him everyone, who didn't see life through the same prism as he did, was just a useless, degenerate. That was his favorite word. In his mind, every teenager's brain was fried by drugs; they drank themselves into oblivion and partied endlessly. They were just bone lazy and didn't want to work and they would steal the good folk blind.

"His plan was for me to remain at home and help mom. I would look after my younger brothers and sisters, do housework, work in the garden and help in the office where she did the books for his logging operation, just like I had all through my adolescent and teenage years.

"But I was ready to get out and spread my wings. I wanted to live a normal life, outside the four walls that had confined me through all of my growing up years. So, against his will, I got a job at the corner store in town. It was a minimum wage, dead-ender, but I felt so free, I felt like I could fly." She looked into his eyes with appeal. "Can you understand that?"

He nodded.

"I went home once in a while, but dad was so critical and disapproving, it spoiled the visit. Mom and the younger kids were happy to see me. My older brothers kidded and joked with me, but dad just heaped guilt on me every chance he got, pointing out how heavy mom's workload was. He mocked my minimum wage and asked me what park bench I was sleeping on, or how comfortable the local YWCA digs were. Then he'd remind me that my room was still there." She shook her head sadly. "He never did get it...he never understood how controlling he was and how he drove me away from him and the home where everyone else that I loved lived. I needed freedom to breathe and grow.

"I worked at the corner store for a year. I wanted to be a teacher, but on my wage, I couldn't save any money to go to university, so I just went to work day after day like a rat on a treadmill. Shortly after I started working there, Duncan Talbot came into the store. He pulled up next to the sidewalk on a big Gold Wing. He had a black silk scarf tied backwards around his head, wore sunglasses and was covered with tattoos and leather; when he came swaggering through the door I could hear my dad's derisive description ringing in my ears. *Degenerate!* I have to admit, he didn't fit my idea of a stand-up guy either. The average logger or millworker around town didn't look anything like him.

"He had stopped to buy a package of cigarettes, but he was scoping out the territory too, though I was too innocent to know it then. He was a lot older than I was, but he flirted a bit and I flirted back. I thought he was just passing through.

"He wanted to know where the parties were around town or where everyone hung out. It was a Monday night and as far as I knew, there wouldn't be much happening again until the weekend when all the bush monkeys came back to town. The weekend would be a blur of activity and then they'd all head back out to work. The guys that worked at the mill just carried on with their shifts. If they happened to have the weekend off, they'd join in. If not they'd just get together in small groups, often at someone's home.

"He left and I never expected to see him again, but he came back on the weekend. Then he started coming in during the week occasionally. I got to know him better and he seemed like he might not be such a bad guy, so when he asked me out for dinner I went. On my day off, we started traveling on his bike to other small towns.

"I introduced him to my older brothers. Brian is easy-going and willing to accept anyone. Al is more like dad and he picked up on the age difference right away. I didn't take Duncan to meet Mom and Dad until he asked me to move to Montreal with him. Of course, mom was shell-shocked. Brian and Al had mentioned him, but she couldn't believe I was moving to Montreal with him...for God's sake *Montreal?* That was so far away and they didn't even speak English there!

"Of course, Dad blew his stack and he ranted on and on. What was I thinking? Well, as usual I wasn't thinking! What did I know about this degenerate? He was old enough to be my dad. Look at all those tattoos, and... Jesus Christ, did he have pierced ears? Didn't I remember anything that he'd tried to teach me? What did Duncan do to make a living? He'd bet his bottom dollar he was a drug dealer.

"Mom was crying and dad was steaming when we left. His parting shot was to let me know that if I left with that degenerate, I was making my own bed and I had to sleep in it. The door would be slammed in my face if I ever dared to come back. In defiance, I yelled back, telling him I would never darken his doorstep again ... and I haven't."

Grayson finished his drink, shaking his head as he placed the glass on the table. "Sarah, people say things they don't really mean when they feel they're losing their grip on the situation. If you'd gone back ..."

"I couldn't eat that much crow." She looked away. "Especially, when it turned out that he was right for the most part, but at the time I was desperate to get out of The Pas, and all I could see was a wonderful future ahead. Duncan had recently settled in Montreal. Two months before he asked me to move in with him, he'd bought a fancy condo in a well-respected part of the city. He showed me pictures. The condo was beautifully furnished, a dream home for a country bumpkin like me. When he wasn't a biker, he cleaned up nicely and wore expensive clothes. Now I realize that I was his trophy "wife", dressed to kill and dripping with expensive jewelry. He drove an expensive car; we went to expensive restaurants and parties and mingled with high profile people."

"Are you...were you...did you actually get married to him?"

She shook her head. "No, I just assumed he'd marry me in time. Other than the few people I met on a superficial basis when we went out, I had no idea about his life. And I knew nothing about his work, or where he went when he was out of town. When I said I wanted to become a teacher, he was agreeable and paid my tuition. When he was home, we were like a husband and wife. I was getting my education and when he was away I had time for myself. It seemed ideal.

"I found out I was pregnant early in my second year at university. I was thrilled. It was hard to tell how Duncan felt. He wasn't as excited as I thought he'd be. When Taylor was born, he wouldn't let me record him as the father."

Grayson shook his head. "I can't imagine a man not wanting to claim his child."

"He insisted on a paternity test. I was shocked because I knew he was the only one who could be Taylor's dad. He said he didn't believe he could father a child because he had a very low sperm count."

Grayson reached out and covered her hand. "That had to be hard for you."

"It hurt that he'd doubted my fidelity. Taylor was born the first week in June and our life totally changed. Duncan stayed out overnight more often. When he was home, he lashed out at me. At first, he'd say scathing things. Then he started to slap me around. I was constantly off balance because I never knew what to expect. Would he be civil, would he simply ignore me or would he hit me?

"One Friday night he beat me and in the scuffle he dislocated my shoulder. The pain was excruciating. He wouldn't take me to the hospital because the bruises would have raised too many questions. He brought in a 'private' doctor who put my shoulder back in after he gave me a sedative.

"I think I woke up before they thought I would, and I heard them talking in the hallway. The doctor warned Duncan to be more careful. He said that he was tired of me anyway. He should have dumped me months before.

"The doctor laughed and said there was a good market for women like me in South America. Duncan said he wished it was that easy; having the kid was an additional problem. I heard them talking about a shipment that was coming in. The doctor asked him if I had any idea about what he was doing. Duncan snorted and said I was just a country hick and I didn't question anything. The doctor warned him to be careful because if I ever found out, he'd have to make sure I couldn't talk. That scared me half to death."

"Jesus, Sarah..."

She nodded. "My world had been ripped to pieces. Duncan Talbot wanted to get rid of me and I had no doubt that he was involved in the drug trade. It was hard not to react, but I didn't dare."

"You had to be sick at heart and absolutely terrified."

She squeezed her eyes shut and hung her head. "If I hadn't been so naïve, I would have wondered about that possibility earlier. I never really understood what his job was. He usually dressed in a suit, so I thought he was going to 'work,' I just didn't know what kind of work. When I look back, I have to admit that I didn't want to see it. I didn't want to acknowledge that my dad had been right about him from the beginning.

"I knew I had to make a move soon. Every day, I could only

hope he wouldn't come home and tell me we were going to South America...or anywhere else for that matter. Every day I considered my options and thought about what I could do. Duncan had been very generous during our first months together, and true to my roots, I had saved a few thousand dollars. It was a start. It would help us travel and find a place to rent somewhere, but I knew we'd be desolate in no time and that frightened me.

"One night, about a week after he'd dislocated my shoulder, Duncan hadn't come home by midnight. It had become a regular occurrence and usually meant that he'd be out all night. I wrapped Taylor in his blankets and put him in the stroller. I put the bag that I'd packed for him in it, as well as the one I had put together for myself. I filled my pockets with all the good jewelry he had given me. Then I put on my raincoat and zipped it closed, pulled the hood up over my head and slipped out the door of the condo. I knew the surveillance cameras would record my movements and the time I left, but it couldn't be helped. The opportunity had presented itself and I had to take it."

Grayson realized he was holding his breath. He exhaled and turned his empty glass. "So, did you get away without any problem?"

Sarah looked exhausted. "Have you any idea how frightening it was to be in a big city like that and not know where I was going or what I was doing?"

"I can only imagine. It must have been terrifying."

"I had no idea who I could trust. He undoubtedly would try to track me down. He'd check the taxi companies and find out where I went. If I took a bus or the train, even if I flew, he could trace me. If I walked down the street, I could be noticed, especially if I was pushing a stroller. If I walked down a back alley, I could get mugged. Taylor and I could both be killed."

"What did you do?"

"I walked down the street. There were trees along the sidewalk and I stayed in the shadows. Fortunately, it was quiet and I didn't meet anyone. I went two blocks. Then I turned the corner and went two more blocks. Thank god, Taylor was sleeping. I looked around and there wasn't any traffic moving, so I crossed the street and walked for another few blocks. I could tell by the lights in the distance that I was moving closer to a commercial area. I crossed the street again and just kept walking toward it. I'd turned off the GPS tracking on my cell phone before I'd left the condo, so he couldn't easily find out where we were. I was tempted to use it to call a taxi, but I knew he could check the records right away, so I hoped I'd find a pay phone. It was three in the morning by then, and I was emotionally and physically exhausted.

"By three-thirty, I had reached a main thoroughfare. I didn't want to walk down the brightly lit street, so I decided to go down the back alley and peek between the buildings. My heart was pounding in my throat. I saw a bus stop about a block away. There was a bench there and nearby there was a payphone, so I decided to chance it. When I'd almost reached the phone, a bus pulled in. My heart almost stopped. Then, I realized it might be the answer to my problem.

"There was only one passenger and he was sleeping, so I fished in my purse for the fare and we got on. I rode it until we got into an area that I'd never seen before. I decided to get off in front of an old hotel right next to a stop. I stood on the street and watched the bus pull away. It was almost five o'clock. I went into the hotel. It was old, but it looked clean. The man at the desk was half-asleep, but he took my money and didn't ask any questions. I took Taylor up the stairs to the room and prayed he would sleep for a few more hours. I needed to figure out where I was and decide what my next plan of action would be. If I was really lucky, I might have until noon, or even that evening before Duncan realized I was gone. Then I suspected all hell would break loose and I'd be hiding in earnest."

She took a sip from her glass of wine.

"I found an information package in the room. It included the bus and train schedules. I decided to take the Megabus to Toronto. I put Taylor back in his stroller and left. The guy at the desk was asleep, so he didn't even see us. I called for a taxi from the payphone outside and asked the driver to take us to the station at Rue St. Antoine. After he let us out on the street, I put Taylor back in the stroller. Then I took the battery out of my phone and dropped them both through the grid covered water drain along the curb. There was no way for Duncan to contact me then. When I bought the tickets, I paid cash and held my breath while I gave them phony names for both of us. No one asked any questions, so I tagged the stroller to be stored underneath and carried Taylor onto the bus. The bus left at eight thirty that morning and we were in Toronto by midafternoon.

"I found a motel in the suburbs and we stayed there for a while.

It was older and quiet, a bit out of the way. I needed to rest. I had to rethink my life and come up with some idea about how I was going to protect Taylor and myself. I was scared to death, because I was certain that Duncan would use his contacts to track us down. I knew that if he ever found us, we'd never get away.

"Living in the city offered anonymity, but I needed to make money, and I couldn't consider leaving Taylor with anyone. I watched the classifieds for a few weeks and one day I saw an ad for a companion that looked promising. I called the number and arranged to meet the people. They lived in a beautiful home in an older area of the city. Julie Hanrahan, was the name of the woman who needed help, and she was in a wheelchair. She'd been injured in an accident years before. Although she managed very well, she needed a companion; a housekeeper, cook and someone to help her with the things she couldn't do herself.

"Ryan was an engineer who worked in a mine in northern Russia. He was gone for three months at a time, and then came home for a month and left again. The three of us made an immediate connection and Julie fell in love with Taylor. They had no children of their own, and the idea of having a happy, smiling baby in the house sealed the deal. The fact that I didn't have a driver's license surprised them, but Julie had a handicap converted van and she drove wherever she needed to go, so it wasn't a major obstacle.

"The job was an answer to my prayers. The pay was reasonable and it provided board and room for Taylor and me. I was able to relax for the first time since the night I'd heard Duncan and the doctor talking.

"I realized that I could attract trouble for them by being there, and it bothered me. After I'd worked there for six months, I decided to tell them everything when Ryan came home the next time." She smiled weakly. "And I did. I even admitted to being a stubborn, pig-headed teenager who wouldn't listen to my parents."

Grayson grinned. "You were stubborn, you still are. But in fairness to you, it sounds like your dad was out of touch with things, Sarah."

"It was his reality, and unfortunately it bit me in the ass."

Grayson chuckled. "So how did the Hanrahan's take it when you told them what had happened?"

"I was afraid they might ask me to leave, but instead they were protective. They both thought we were pretty safe there. The neighborhood was made up of older people, so it wasn't likely that Duncan's kind would be cruising around and come into contact with me. Ryan had installed alarms on the house and garage and perimeters of the yard when they'd bought the place several years earlier.

"I never went out by myself anyway; not that I couldn't have, I was just too afraid. Ryan also set up a joint bank account, for himself and me. He used his grandmother's name to give me signing authority."

"What?"

"I know. Crazy...but he brought the paperwork home and we filled everything out using his grandma's name. He took me to the bank and introduced me as his sister and I signed everything as if I was her. He also got a credit card and an Interact card. Most of my wages went into the account and gradually he took all of the pieces of jewelry that Duncan had given me and pawned them in different places when he traveled. He'd put the money into the account, and it added up. Later it gave me a safety net when I needed it."

Her eyes met his and he saw the fear and tiredness in them. "I worked at their place for four years. Then one morning, when I went out to get the morning paper, there was a package sitting on the step, addressed to me. I took it inside; it wasn't until I had the brown paper wrapping half torn away, that I realized there were no stamps or postal markings so it hadn't come in the mail. Furthermore, I never got mail, as I'd completely dropped off the grid."

Tears filled her eyes. "I knew that he'd found me. I started to shake and my heart pounded so hard, I thought I was going to faint. I was crying when Julie came into the room. She finished opening the package. Julie is a real lady, but she swore like a logger when she got that package open. It contained a sharp knife and a note for me. It's engraved in my mind.

Did you really think you could give me the slip? You made a big mistake when you ran out on me. No one gets away with that. So now, we'll play the game of cat and mouse, babe. Keep looking over your shoulder, cause you'll never know when it's going to happen, but know this—IT WILL and it'll happen when you least expect it— like now. I never wanted the kid, but he is mine. I'll probably let you raise him until he's old enough to be of use to me. But then again, I might get tired of toying with you and decide to put an end to this. If I do, rest assured, I'll do away with him first and make sure that you watch.

Sarah was sobbing. Grayson stood up and moved over to the chair beside her. He slid his arm around her and pulled against him so that her head rested against his chest. He stroked her hair gently, letting her cry. "What did you do, Sarah?"

"I wanted to take Taylor and run, but Julie convinced me not to. She begged me to wait until Ryan came home, so we could all decide what to do. When I calmed down and thought about it, I realized she was right. The note was a taunt, meant to terrify me and send me running. I'd be much more vulnerable if I left, than I was there behind the Hanrahan's alarmed doors. I'd be leaving Julie there alone and I knew that I couldn't do that. I loved her as much as she loved Taylor and me. Ryan was going to be home in six weeks, so I stayed.

"Julie put the knife and the note in the safe, and we carried on with life. A month later, there was an envelope on the step for me. Inside, there was a picture of Taylor and me in the backyard and another note. *"I'm getting tired of this game. Keep looking over your shoulder. The time is near. .*

"Julie was afraid too. There was no doubt that he was there, watching us. Once again, I wanted to just disappear, taking Taylor with me, but I couldn't. I wondered if we could survive two more weeks until Ryan came home; but then what? Julie put the envelope and its contents in the safe with the first package.

"We counted down the days. It wasn't much of a homecoming for Ryan. The entire evening was focused on the threats, and how we should handle everything. Ryan decided to involve the police. He had a couple of close friends in the department and one of them worked undercover. He phoned them the next day and told them what had happened.

"Sergeant Maxham came over the same day. We showed him the packages that had shown up on the doorstep and I told him about my past with Duncan; including what I'd heard Duncan and the doctor say.

"After they talked a while, it was decided that the police would make a presence in the area by going house to house and asking if anyone had noticed any unusual vehicles or different people walking around on the sidewalk or in the back alley. Besides that, they would randomly patrol the streets in a ten block radius so no one would know for sure when they would be there.

"Charlie Adcock came by a day later. He was an undercover member of the Drug Squad. He logged in on Ryan's laptop and showed me a bunch of mug shots of guys they were interested in. Half way through, I spotted Duncan Talbot. When I pointed him out, Charlie nodded and told me that I needed to be careful. They suspected he was involved in violent crimes; that he would have people killed at will and wouldn't be above doing it himself. Charlie thought that I would be a personal score that Duncan would want to settle himself. He wasn't used to being thwarted.

"That day he and Ryan spent most of the day in the back yard, drinking beer and hunkering down like old buddies. They were very visible the next day too. They drove off in Charlie's Hummer. They went to Ryan's bank and then to a department store where Ryan bought a set of luggage. When they came back to the house, Ryan made a big deal about putting the Hummer in the garage.

"When they came into the house, Charlie and Ryan explained what they had been doing while they were out. Charlie had contacted another undercover agent that he'd worked with in the past. He'd asked him to him to meet Suzanne Cunningham and her four-year-old son, at the Halifax airport early the next morning. He explained that he was asking as a favor for a special friend of his, and we were coming in on a private jet. He gave him all the specs, assuring him he'd have clearance to meet us at the plane on the runway.

"When asked to do it, Bert Chambers also agreed to drive us to a small resort near Peggy's Cove about thirty miles away. He said he'd help us get settled in a cabin that had been reserved for Suzanne there. Charlie and Ryan impressed upon me how important it was to maintain my identity as Suzanne Cunningham and Ryan gave me a cell phone registered in her name. He'd made arrangements for the monthly payments to automatically come out of our joint account and he assured me that, even though, the Interact card was under Suzanne Hanrahan's name, it would work anywhere, so I would be alright. He advised me to withdraw money from a bank machine or ATM as I needed it, and pay cash for everything."

Grayson nodded. "No paper trail with cash."

"That evening, Ryan barbecued steak in the backyard and we ate out there. Ryan surprised Julie with the luggage and announced that they were going to fly to Vancouver for a week. When she protested and asked about Taylor and me, Ryan said we would look after the house while they were gone. They put on a convincing show for the small camera the guys had scoped out in the back yard. When they studied the picture of Taylor and me, they'd realized that it had been taken by a surveillance camera mounted near the perimeter of the yard.

"Later that evening, we put all of Taylor's things in one of Julie's old suitcases, along with most of his toys. I packed everything I had in another one. We went into the garage. There were a lot of tears as we hugged and said goodbye. Then Taylor and I curled up in the very back of the Hummer and covered up with blankets. Our luggage was put on the floor in the back seat. When we were settled, Charlie backed the vehicle out of the garage and pulled up in front of the house to wait.

When Ryan stepped out of the back door, he pulled it shut, and then, as if it was an afterthought, he opened it and called me by name, reminding me to set the alarm, adding that they wouldn't be long."

Grayson picked up the bottle of wine and topped up her glass. "They paid meticulous attention to every detail," he said as he set it back down.

"They did. Charlie drove us to a small airport out of town where Taylor and I were put on a private jet that belonged to a business associate of Ryan. Everything went smoothly and by mid-morning, we were settled in our new home. It was small but cozy, and the McNeils, who owned the resort, were really friendly. They knew Charlie well, but I'm very sure he never had told them anything about Taylor and me. They loved Taylor and the two other members of the staff doted on him too. Eventually, I worked at the resort for minimum wage. We were there for three years."

"Did he find you there?"

"I didn't see him, but one morning the owner knocked on our cabin door. It was about four thirty, and I was shocked when I opened it and found him there. He stepped inside without waiting for me to invite him in and shut the door quickly. Then he apologized, but said he had to talk to me.

"A man on a Harley had come cruising into the resort the evening before and asked a lot of questions. Mr. McNeil didn't like the guy, so he brushed him off: afterward, the more he'd thought about it, he wondered if the biker had been fishing for information about the baby and me. Following his gut instinct, he'd phoned Charlie in the middle of the night and told him what had happened.

Charlie was alarmed. He told him to take us to his cabin near the lighthouse and hide us there until he could talk to Ryan and make other arrangements.

"One look at my face was all it took to convince him that I was terrified. I quickly packed a light bag for us. He took it, and I carried Taylor to the pickup. He told me to crouch down, so no one could see us when he drove through town. He turned toward Halifax. After he had traveled a several kilometers, he took a side road and backtracked, snaking through back trails until we came to a broken down cabin nestled in the trees. I looked at it curiously until he shut off the motor and calmly said, "This is it.

"I was confused. I asked what it was.

"He said we were at Charlie's cabin. When I asked if he was serious, he grinned and told me that was the old cabin. The new place was back through the trees behind it by a lake. It had running water, solar power for the lights and propane for cooking and a fridge. He assured me I'd be safe there until other arrangements were made for us. He carried our suitcases through the trees to the cabin. His wife had boxed up some food for us so we wouldn't go hungry. Then he left, cautioning me not to let anyone see me if they came around. He said he'd be back as soon as he heard from Charlie."

She was crying again. "I felt so helpless and vulnerable."

He held her against his chest, feeling every bit as helpless as she must have felt then. He couldn't imagine the anxiety she had experienced.

She sat up and looked at him, shaking her head. "Charlie called Ryan's friend and reminded him of the trip he'd made to Halifax three years earlier, when he'd used his jet to fly Taylor and me there. The guy had remembered, because even though he was Ryan's friend and he trusted him, he said the whole thing felt off. Charlie gave him a very brief explanation and told him we were in trouble again. He asked if he would fly him to Halifax. The guy welcomed the chance to get out, so they were in the air in a couple of hours.

"Charlie rented a truck and arrived at the cabin mid-afternoon. When I heard the vehicle, I freaked out and we ran deep into the bush. He put two and two together and realized what had happened. He stood on the deck and called me, telling me who he was and that he owned the cabin. I was so relieved to see him; I threw myself into his arms and hugged him."

"How could Duncan have found you?"

"Charlie and I went over and over that. The only thing we could come up with was that when I registered Taylor in the home schooling program I had to provide his birth information. I'd stayed off the grid until then, but I ordered the DVD courses so he'd have the lessons even if we found ourselves in a place where we didn't have the internet."

She shook her head in frustration and looked at him imploringly. "But Grayson, he has to have an education. I want him to graduate in a program that has recognition so he can go on and have a decent future. That poor child has lived his whole life under such deplorable circumstances. We live in a free country, but because of his father, I have taught him to live in fear. We never make any deep friendships, I'm forever looking over my shoulder, alert and suspicious of almost everyone and ready to pack up and move at a moment's notice. It's not right to do that to a child, but I don't know how else to protect him.

"If it weren't for Julie and Ryan, I'm certain I'd have collapsed years ago. Their love and support have kept me going. I never get to talk to them, but every once in a while I find an unexpected extra amount in my account. It's their way of assuring me that they still are watching out for us. I appreciate it so much, but God, there are times when I get so tired being afraid, of running. Sometimes I just need a hug, and I need to be able to talk about how I feel."

He pulled her against him as they sat side by side. "Sarah, I'm here anytime."

She nodded. "I can't believe I'm telling you all this. I'm putting you in danger too, just by being here, by letting you know all this. He will find us again, and he won't care who he hurts as long as he punishes me and eventually gets rid of me."

"He is not God, Sarah. He'll make a mistake one day and get caught. Where did you go after you left the resort?"

"Charlie took us back to Ryan and Julie's place. We flew back on Air Canada. He booked the flights; when I insisted that I'd pay for them, he told me he traveled a lot and he had air miles to burn. He used them. Julie was excited to see us. Of course, she had another companion by then, and it felt strange for me to just visit."

"I tried to keep Taylor on track with his lessons, but that was really difficult. He was distracted by the sudden move from the resort, and the weirdness of the two of us staying in Charlie's cabin. Children sense things we often don't realize; things they don't know how to express. He was seven by then and he started voicing his concerns and asking questions. While we were at Charlie's cabin, I gave him a sanitized version of what was happening.

"How did he react?"

She frowned. "He didn't really know how to act. He wanted to protect me. But that's one of the things that is so wrong about the way I've raised him."

"Sarah; you've done the best you could. How could you fight something like that, all by yourself?"

"I've kept the two of us in a protective bubble. Truthfully, until we came here to the ranch, Taylor had no idea about what a family was; a mother, a father, other children or friendships. I don't know if you remember, but the first weekend after we arrived, it was Christina and Tim's wedding. Do you realize he'd never been in such a big group of people before, and certainly not without being glued to my side? They were all strangers. I asked him later how he felt about it."

"I remember he was pretty quiet and kept to himself most of the time. What did he say to you?"

"He didn't know how to act. He felt out of place, almost afraid. I was busy helping and while I was constantly checking on him mentally, I wasn't afraid so I wasn't seeking him out. He must have felt like he was drowning."

"How did you end up coming here?"

"When Ryan came home, he and Charlie met with Charlie's boss. After I'd first identified Duncan's mug shot, Charlie had told Ryan that the drug squad had been watching him. They knew he was involved with the trade, but he was careful. He'd built a wide network among the respectable elite in major cities across Canada. He's a chameleon and when he was a high roller he associated with the top end of society, but he also was known to get on his Harley and explore the rural areas, looking for any small niche to get a hold in. That was what he was doing when he met me at the corner store.

"Truthfully, no matter how strong the friendship between Ryan and him was, Charlie probably wouldn't have gotten involved otherwise. Anyway, while we're not in the witness protection program, they gave us new identities; that included a new SIN and birth certificate. We became Sara and Taylor Brite. Ryan closed our joint account and put the money in a new account that they'd set up under my new identity in Regina. I was given a new Interact card and a credit card. Ryan, bless his heart, provided me with a new cell phone and this time he paid the contract in full.

"Julie and Ryan had friends in Swan River, Manitoba. It's a smaller, out of the way town and I felt it could be a good place for Taylor and me to start over. We brought Taylor into the conversation, and later he and I talked when we were alone. Taylor would like to have stayed at Julie and Ryan's; he liked them and he felt safe there. But, when I explained that we had to start over and it would be different this time, he just shrugged and said OK.

"We rented an apartment and lived there for almost a year. I met Julie Regeer and we became friends. Taylor hung out with her kids, but he was never really free with them. The economy was tight and I could only find part-time work at the restaurant. When Christina phoned Julie and told her about the job with Colt and Frank, I felt good about it.

"And when we drove out here, Taylor was more excited than I'd ever seen him about anything. Things clicked between all of us, and suddenly my son found himself living in a healthy family environment. He's home schooled and I know enough about what Ellie is doing to be confident that she does a great job. It's the best thing that's ever happened to us, but..."

"But?"

"Grayson, you're not blind or insensitive. You have to know that Taylor is bonding with you. He sees you as a father figure. And god only knows he deserves one; he needs one. But it will kill him if..."

"Sarah, don't do this."

"I can't just sit back and let him get hurt again. When Duncan finds us, we're going to have to run again."

He stood up and pulled her to her feet. He placed a hand on each shoulder and looked deep into her eyes. "Sarah, Taylor is ten years old. I hate to tell you this, but he's going to start resenting you if you keep trying to push him back into that protective bubble you've created. Every year his personal feelings are going to get stronger and just as you resented your dad, he will come to resent you."

Tears started to run down her cheeks. "I know that, but what do I do?"

Grayson's arms enfolded her as he pulled her against him and rested his chin on her head. "Sarah, let's talk to Colt and Frank when they come home. This scumbag has controlled you with fear for far too long. He's not invincible. It's time somebody stood up to him." He led her to the couch in the living room. "You're as wound up as a ten-day clock. Let's sit down. Maybe if we watch something mindless, you'll relax a bit."

He turned on the TV. Sarah rested her head against his shoulder and stared aimlessly at the old western movie he'd selected.

In the early morning hours, Taylor came to the living room to see why the TV was on. His eyes widened in surprise when he saw his mom snuggled into the curve of his best friends arm, with her head nestled against his chest while they slept on the couch. He giggled as he headed back to bed. *He's going to be my dad.*

ABOUT THE AUTHOR

Photograph by Suzanne Englund

Gloria Antypowich grew up on a farm and most of her married life has been lived on a ranch. Human relationships fascinate her. Ideas for stories can be found everywhere; overheard conversations in a public place, a couple fighting in a restaurant, a story in the news, even a chance remark in a conversation with a friend. She is enamored with the power of words and she loves to use them to paint images of characters that become so real, they feel like they could be your next door neighbor.

Gloria is an avid reader of several different genres and listens to a wide selection of music. A good game of cards, sharing a laugh with a friend over a glass of wine and spending time with her family are a few of her favorite things to do. She loves to write and says her husband was her inspiration for the heroes in this series of books. He was a cowboy, a rancher—and a lover. Gloria lives with her husband, in the central interior of British Columbia, Canada. They are retired now, but they still have "chemistry".

Made in the USA
Charleston, SC
09 October 2015